THE RULES of DATING
My One-Night Stand

PENELOPE WARD
VI KEELAND

THE RULES OF DATING MY ONE-NIGHT STAND
Cover Designer: Sommer Stein, Perfect Pear Creative
Editing: Jessica Royer Ocken
Formatting and Proofreading: Elaine York, Allusion Publishing
www.allusionpublishing.com
Proofreading: Julia Griffis
Cover Photographer: Marq Mendez
Cover Model: Karl Kugelmann

THE RULES of DATING

DATING

My One-Night Stand

❤CHAPTER 1

Owen

"Earth to Owen."

Billie, my buddy's wife, waved her hand in front of my face.

I blinked a few times. "Sorry, what did you say?"

"I didn't say anything." She motioned to my phone. "But you've been on that damn thing for the last half hour. We're at a bar for happy hour, and you didn't even notice the woman who sidled up next to you and was trying to get your attention."

I looked to my left. The seat was empty.

Billie shook her head. "She's long gone, buddy. But what is so important on that phone?"

"Nothing really. Just catching up on work emails."

"You know what you need?"

"What?"

"A tattoo, a nipple piercing, and a few shots of tequila."

I chuckled. "First off, that list sounds like it's in the wrong order. I'd need the tequila in order to even consider the other two, and it would have to be a hell of a lot more than *a few* shots for me to get a nipple pierced. I've never understood the fascination."

Billie shrugged. "It's sexy."

"What's sexy?" My buddy Colby returned from the bathroom. He slung his arm around his wife's neck. "It better be me you're talking about."

"I'm talking about nipple piercing."

Colby grimaced. "It freaking hurt, man."

My eyes bulged. "You, tight-ass Colby Lennon, got your nipple pierced?"

"The wife likes it. So why not?"

I shook my head. "Never thought I'd see the day, dude."

Colby knocked back the rest of the beer in his glass. "Why are you two talking about nipple piercings, anyway?"

"Owen needs to get his nose out of his cell." Billie motioned to the packed bar. "This place is filled with hot women, and he's sitting here answering emails."

While Billie was right, I just wasn't in the mood to talk to women tonight. In fact, I hadn't been in the mood a lot lately. No one sparked my interest. So I'd thrown myself into my work even more than usual the last few months.

"You know what you need to do?" Colby asked.

"Let me guess…a tattoo, a nipple piercing, and a few shots of tequila?"

Colby grinned. "Nah. You need to pay our bar tab. Because the little wifey and I only have the sitter for another half hour, and I'm going to ditch you to suck this beautiful woman's face in the alley next door before we have to head home."

I smiled. "You got it, man. Go enjoy. I'll talk to you later."

After we said goodbye, I tried to get the bartender's attention to close out our tab, but he was busy. So I headed to the men's room to get rid of some of the tequila and soda I'd drunk. The hallway that led to the restrooms had a long line of women waiting, but the men's was practically empty. As I relieved myself, my phone rang. I dug it out of my pocket to answer, only to realize it hadn't been

2

my phone making noise after all. The one other guy in here had just left, so I zipped up and walked around the empty men's room, looking for where the sound was coming from. I found the culprit in the second stall, on top of the toilet-paper holder.

Phones were a grand or more these days, so I figured it would be safer to give the cell to the bartender. Otherwise, some drunk guy might stick it in his pocket. But before I made it back to the bar, it started buzzing again. I thought maybe the owner was calling his phone to find out where he'd left it, so I swiped to answer.

"Hello?"

"Uh…who's this?" a woman asked.

"This is Owen."

"Owen, why do you have Devyn's phone?"

"I just found this cell in the men's room."

"The men's room where?"

"At the bar—Polo Place on Twenty-first."

"Shoot. That's what I was worried about. My friend had a bad day—a bad week, actually."

"Can he not hold his liquor or something?"

"He is a she, and no, she's pretty much a lightweight. It takes her three sips to finish a shot, and a frozen margarita is liquid by the time she's gotten through half of it."

"Devyn is a she? I found her phone in the men's room."

"Was there a long line for the ladies'?"

"Actually, there was."

"Then she would have used the men's room. Devyn *hates* public restrooms. So she waits until the last second, thinking she can hold it until she gets home. Then it turns into an urgent situation, and she has to go wherever she can. That's often the men's room in bars."

"Why does she hate public restrooms? Is she a germaphobe or something?"

"No, she's had two bad experiences. The first time, she was a teenager in an Applebee's. The stall wouldn't lock, so she closed it as best she could. But a drunk lady barged in and puked all over her lap while she was hovering over the toilet bowl peeing."

"You're kidding?"

"Nope. I wish I was. She jumped up, but it was too late—covered in puke and also wound up peeing on her clothes when she stood."

"I'm almost afraid to ask, but what was the other bad experience?"

"Oh, another time she was on a blind date in a quiet restaurant when she had to use the ladies' room. The woman next to her apparently brought her son into the stall with her. The little boy stuck his head under and watched her pee, and then when he saw her in the restaurant, he started yelling at the top of his lungs while pointing and demanding to know why she had no hair on her pee-pee."

I chuckled. "That's pretty funny."

"For us, yes. For her…not so much. But that pretty much sums up the kind of luck my friend has. Lately, it's been even worse."

I had no idea why, but I was curious. "What happened recently?"

"She's got a shitty mom who dumps her problems on her. And then there's the guy she's been in love with for years who strings her along. Don't even get me started on the siblings from hell she believes are angels. I'm pretty sure they're the spawn of Satan."

"I'm sorry to hear that."

"Are you really?" the woman asked.

I thought about it. "Yeah, I am. It sucks to have shitty parents and be strung along."

"You sound like a nice guy. What was your name again?"

"Owen. What's yours?"

"Mia." She paused. "Listen, now that we're buddies, would you mind looking around the bar for my friend? That way you can return her phone to her, and I can also make sure she's okay."

4

"Yeah, I can do that. But this place is pretty packed. Can you give me an idea what she looks like?"

"Long, wavy auburn hair. Fair skin with bright green eyes. She's short, but curvy. She kind of looks like she stepped out of the seventies—she has a boho-chic vibe about her, like Stevie Nicks back in the day, but even hotter."

I scanned the room, but no one came close to that description. "Sorry, I don't see her."

The woman sighed. "Let me send a picture. If it's dark in there, you might not realize her hair is auburn. Hang on. I'll shoot it to her phone. I'm always yelling at her for not having a password, but this time it's working for us."

A few seconds later, the cell in my hand chimed. I opened the message, and a photo popped up. At the risk of sounding like a complete puss, my heart skipped a beat. The woman was gorgeous, but it was more than that. Her head was thrown back in laughter, and...I had the craziest urge to find out what it sounded like.

"Wow," I said. But I was still staring at the picture on the phone, not holding it up to my ear. I'd completely forgotten I was on the phone with anyone. Until I heard Mia's voice in the distance.

"Hello? Owen, are you still there?"

"Shit." I raised the phone to my ear. "Sorry. It took a minute for the photo to open."

"Oh, okay. I figured you were busy drooling. That's what men tend to do when they see Devyn."

I frowned. *Great.*

I shook the ridiculous jealous thoughts from my head and scanned the room again. "I'm going to take a lap around the bar, see if I can get a better look."

Squeezing through the leftover happy hour crowd that was now feeling *really* freaking happy, I circled the bar. I was just about to give up and tell Mia I'd leave her friend's phone with the bartender, when I spotted the woman in the photo.

And it happened again. *A second skip of the heart.* Though, this time I realized it was probably just because I'd had too much coffee today. Caffeine can cause palpitations. My heart was *not* going pitter-patter over a glimpse of some random woman. Lately that didn't even happen when one invited me home with her.

I wedged my way through a group of hipsters drinking Moscow mules out of copper mugs to get a better look at the guy she was talking to.

Shit. Evan Cooper—otherwise known in my circle of friends as *McLoser*. The guy was a complete jerk-off.

"Anything?" Mia asked through the phone.

"Yeah, I think I found her."

"Oh, that's great!"

"But…she's kind of getting cozy with this guy I'm not a fan of."

"Ugh. Let me guess. He's good-looking, but a womanizer. Probably looks like a movie star or rocker or something?"

"How did you know that?"

"Because my friend is amazing, but she has crap taste in men."

"This dude is good-looking, even I can admit that. He could pass for Jared Leto's brother. But he's completely full of shit. Tells women he owns a string of fast-food restaurants when he really works at McDonald's."

Mia sighed through the phone. "Yep, that sounds about right."

"You want to stay on the phone while I walk over and hand it to her?"

"That would be great. Thanks a lot, Owen."

"Alright, hang on."

I made my way toward the corner where McLoser and Devyn were huddled, but stopped short when Devyn threw a drink in his face. McLoser put his hands on her shoulders and gave her a little nudge, and I pushed my way through the rest of the people to get to them.

"What the fuck is going on here?" I yelled.

McLoser raised his hands into the air. "This bitch just threw a drink at me."

"Yeah, and I saw you push her. You don't fucking touch a woman. I don't care if she spits in your face."

"What business is it of yours, Dawson?"

I took a step toward him, broadened my shoulders, and looked down my nose. McLoser was six inches shorter than my six foot two and lanky; I'd snap this twig in half. "I'm making it my business. Now apologize and get the hell out of here."

"I'm not apologizing."

I took another step, crowding his personal space. "Then you got even less time to get the hell out of here, Cooper."

McLoser grumbled, but he also turned and walked away. I couldn't help myself, though. "And don't come back without a ten-piece chicken nugget for me!" I added.

I watched as he slinked through the crowd, amused with myself. But when I turned back, the woman was *not* so amused.

"You think this is funny? Some guy puts his hands on me and you're smiling?"

"*Whoa.* I don't think what he did was funny. You got the wrong idea."

"Just get out of here. I don't need any more *assholes* hitting on me tonight."

My neck pulled back. "Assholes?"

"That's right. You're all the same. You only want one thing."

I shook my head. Here I was helping, and this woman is calling me names. "Don't worry, sweetheart. I don't want anything from you. You're not my type."

I turned to walk away and then realized I still had her phone in my hand. I wasn't sure if her friend had hung up or not, but I tossed the cell on the bar. "Oh, and you're welcome for saving your ass *and* returning your phone. You have a great night."

There was definitely no pitter-patter in my chest as I returned to the other side of the bar. I was *pissed*. I would've walked straight out, but I still had to close my tab. So I returned to where I'd been hanging out with my friends and stewed while I waited for the bartender to come by. At least I didn't have to wait long.

"Hey, could I close out my tab, please?" I asked as he approached.

"Sure thing."

"Actually…can I get a shot of tequila before you close it? I just got bawled out for trying to help someone."

The bartender smiled. He grabbed a bottle of tequila and a shot glass. "No problem." He poured and slid the glass to my side of the bar. "This one's on me. I'll be back in a minute with your receipt."

I lifted the shot to my lips and looked over at the other side of the bar. The woman was now on her phone and looking in my direction. I shook my head and knocked back the shot. A few minutes later, I was signing the bar receipt when I felt someone walk up next to me.

"So *what is* your type?" a woman asked. Her voice was playful and friendly.

Looking up, I found the last person I expected to be speaking to me sweetly—Devyn, the woman who'd just told me off. I picked up my credit card and tucked it back into my wallet, not bothering to give her the courtesy of looking at her when I spoke.

"My type? Women who don't call me an asshole for trying to help, for starters."

"I came over to say I'm really sorry about what happened. My adrenaline was pumping, and I've been so angry at the world this week. I shouldn't have taken it out on you."

She sounded sincere, so I chanced a glance over at her and…
th-thump.

Fuck. What the hell?

Even though it had happened earlier, it still caught me off guard. I stared at her, trying to figure out what the hell was going on. But she must've taken my silence to mean I wasn't accepting her apology.

"Can I at least buy you a drink?" she asked. "I feel terrible. My friend Mia told me how you went out of your way to find me and bring me my phone. She said you seemed like a nice guy. I totally screwed up."

I was hesitant. Drama was *not* my thing. But this woman's eyes were mesmerizing, and I hadn't felt a pull toward anyone in ages. Still, a red flag was a red flag...

But then she smiled. And it was damn near blinding. Resplendent. Radiant. Magnificent.

And suddenly I'm the king of freaking adjectives.

She batted her eyelashes. "Just one drink?"

I nodded. "Sure. Just one."

Famous last words...

CHAPTER 2

Owen

My head was up my ass this week.

For the first time in my career, I'd brought someone to the wrong damn property. I'd also lost an account to a competitor. And I'd been late to meet clients numerous times. I had not gotten to be one of the top luxury realtors in the City operating this way; that was for damn sure.

But I knew exactly what was wrong. For the past few days, I'd been fixated on one of the best and worst nights of my life—the night I'd met the mesmerizing, bohemian woman with the auburn hair. Also, the night she…ghosted me. There's a first time for everything, right?

How could I have let her go like that? But what was I supposed to do, run after her? That's not who I am. Owen Dawson doesn't chase women. Women chase me, and most of the time, I have no interest in them. But it'd been three days since my encounter in that hotel room with Devyn, and I hadn't been able to stop thinking about her. It was ironic that after months—scratch that, years—of not being able to feel a damn thing for anyone, the first person to ignite anything inside of me had decided to take off like a bat out of hell immediately after.

None of it made sense. Devyn and I had engaged in stimulating conversation, had shared many laughs, and by the time we left the bar together, I was certain it was the beginning of something potentially epic. We'd gone to the nearest hotel, just a couple of doors down, because it hadn't seemed like we could wait long enough to pick a place any farther away. That's how damn combustible our chemistry had been. And what happened once we got behind those closed doors could only be described as euphoria.

Yet now all I had was her first name and the memory of her taste, smell, and how good it had felt to be buried deep inside her.

I'd had one-night stands before, but never one where I'd wished I could slow time to make sure I didn't miss a single moment. That's exactly how I'd felt with her—even before we'd had sex. That's the thing: it wasn't *just* the sex. It was *everything*. And I'd wanted more than just one night. Not once had I considered that she'd run off without giving me her number. Devyn was like Cinderella, except she didn't leave behind a damn shoe—or a clue. Not a single thing besides her first name.

"I'm sorry."

That's all she said before she left me in that hotel room—speechless, with my dick still hard.

Sorry for what? It was the best damn sex of my life, and even if I never saw her again, I was still glad it happened. I wouldn't have traded it. So there was certainly nothing to be sorry about. That night had gotten me out of a very long funk. I'd thought I was broken because nothing, certainly not any woman, had stimulated me in what felt like forever.

Maybe someday I would share the story with the guys, but I needed to get over it first. Although, I was certain at least one of them would know by looking at me that something was off.

My three best friends and I owned the forty-unit apartment building we all inhabited in New York City. Colby was the oldest of the bunch. And he'd been the biggest playboy of all of us for several years, until he finally met the love of his life, Billie. Holden was a drummer in a band and had been quite the womanizer himself, until he settled down with our friend Ryan's sister, Lala. Brayden was the one in our crew I was probably closest to, and he and I were the only single ones left. All of us were constantly up in each other's business. We were more like brothers and typically told each other everything. Seriously, if one of us farted, the others would know about it from across the building.

But if they knew about *this*, they'd surely bust my balls. Not sure if they could berate me any worse than I was berating myself right now, though.

A knock at my apartment door interrupted my thoughts.

I opened.

Brayden strolled in, smelling like his favorite Polo cologne. "We're all heading over to the hospital to see the new baby. You comin'?"

Holden and Lala had just had their first child. The fifth member of our posse, Ryan—Lala's older brother—had passed away from leukemia when we were in our early twenties. We'd used the inheritance he left us to purchase this building. He wasn't here physically anymore, but his spirit had never left us.

I'd been so lost in my head that I'd nearly forgotten about the plan to visit baby Hope.

"I'm going," I told him. "But I'll meet you guys there. I have some stuff to take care of first."

Brayden looked skeptical. "Like what?"

"Holden gave me a list of shit to do in his absence, and there's one thing I've been putting off. I want to be able to tell him everything is under control and that I've knocked everything off the to-do list. So I'm gonna get that done before I head over there."

"What is it?"

"It's that family in four-ten. That woman, Vera, with the two rowdy teenagers—the ones we call Frick and Frack. There have been more noise complaints about that apartment lately. We have to issue a warning that if it doesn't stop, they're going to be evicted."

"Ouch. Sounds like fun."

"Yeah." I lifted my brow. "That's why I've been avoiding it. Feel like doing the honors for me?"

"Nah. You're better at that shit. You're the mean one out of all of us."

That was probably true. "Thanks."

"No problem." He snickered, then looked closer at me, tilting his head. "You okay?"

My lip twitched. "Yeah. Why?"

"I don't know. You seem…preoccupied, maybe?"

"Nope," I lied. "I'm good."

He squinted. "Okay. Whatever you say."

After Brayden left, I headed up to 410, unsure how to approach this. All I knew about the woman who lived there was that she was a single mom. I sympathized with her in that respect; it couldn't be easy dealing with those kids. But she never responded or did shit about all the other warnings we'd issued over the past several months. I knew it wasn't always possible to control teenagers, but there was only so much the other tenants could tolerate.

I took a deep breath before knocking on her door.

The door opened. "Finally. It's about ti—" She paused.

Huh?

It felt like all of the air had rushed from my body. In fact, I might have been hallucinating, because the woman in front of me was *not* the middle-aged lady who lived in this apartment with her kids.

Not her at all.

But I knew this person.

I knew this bohemian beauty intimately. I just never thought I'd see her again.

What the hell is she doing here?

Practically speechless, I uttered, "Devyn?"

She shook her head. "No. I'm sorry."

The door slammed closed.

"I'm sorry."

That was the last thing she'd said to me before she left me in the hotel, and now it was the last thing she'd said before she shut the damn door in my face.

Think.

Think.

What do I do?

My pride got the best of me. I decided not to knock again. *Fuck that.* I was not one to grovel or push things. I didn't know whether to be pissed or confused right now.

She clearly didn't want to see me. But I had a job to do at this place, and she wasn't even the person I needed to speak to. *Is she the nanny?* That had to be it.

I was going to need some time to think about how to approach things.

Did that really just happen, or was I in the middle of one fucked-up dream?

After leaving the hospital, I opted to walk the several blocks back to the building in order to clear my head.

I hadn't been planning to say anything to Holden about what had happened before I came to visit. But when he pointed out the look on my face, I sloppily confessed everything. Brayden overheard part of that conversation—only about a mystery woman in the building, not that I'd had a one-night stand with her.

Brayden admitted that he'd seen this woman around the building over the past few days, but he had no idea who she was or that she was living in 410. How the hell could *I* have not noticed her? But more than that, who was Devyn? Why was she living in that problematic apartment? Was she, in fact, the nanny? Those two tyrants were too old for a babysitter, weren't they? Though it would've helped to have someone watching over them with the havoc they wreaked.

When I got back to my apartment, I grabbed a beer from the fridge to take the edge off. I downed about half of it before I left it on the counter, grabbed myself by the virtual ball sac, and headed back to 410.

Adrenaline pumped through me as I traveled down the hallway and up in the elevator. For all I knew, Devyn wasn't even there anymore. Maybe her shift had ended, and she'd gone back home. But I still hadn't issued the warning I was supposed to, and that needed to happen whether she was there or not.

At least that's the excuse I'd told myself about why I was going back.

When I made it to 410, I hesitated for a few seconds and psyched myself up to knock. Finally, I forced myself to rap my knuckles against the door.

Knock.

Knock.

Knock.

A couple of minutes passed with no answer. Maybe no one was home? But my gut told me a certain auburn-haired woman might be intentionally ignoring me from behind the door. I was just about to turn around when the door finally opened.

Devyn's beautiful eyes looked tired, the carefree glow from the night I'd met her nowhere to be found. I imagined running into each other earlier had rattled her just as much as it had me. And now she seemed just as speechless as I was.

We stood there for probably ten seconds, just looking at each other. But with each moment that passed without her slamming the door in my face again, I felt a little less tense.

That was a win.

"What are you doing here?" she finally asked.

As stressed as she apparently was, Devyn looked so damn beautiful. I wanted to cup her face with my hands, bring her mouth to mine, and taste her again. Instead, I reminded myself that she apparently wanted nothing to do with me anymore.

I crossed my arms. "First, tell me why you slammed the door in my face earlier."

"How did you even find me?"

"*Find* you?"

Oh fuck.

Maybe because my head had been stuck in my damn ass for the past few days, but it had never dawned on me that she might think I was *stalking* her. It kind of offended me a bit, actually.

"I wasn't looking for you, Devyn. After the way you left the hotel the other night, I got your message loud and clear. Believe me, I'm no stalker."

"Then what are you doing here?"

"This is my building."

Her eyes widened. "You're the owner?"

"Yes. I was coming to issue a noise complaint to the woman who lives here."

Devyn's expression softened. "You didn't know I was here?"

I looked deeply into her beautiful green eyes. "No, I didn't."

"I'm..." She shook her head, looking down at her feet. "God, I'm sorry."

"You know, you say that a lot."

Devyn looked up. "Say what?"

"That you're sorry."

"I'm..." She hesitated. "Jesus, I almost just said it again." She swallowed. "I'm nervous."

She's nervous?

"Don't be," I told her, attempting to sound confident. "There's nothing to be nervous about. I'm figuring this situation out by the second—just like you are. When you came to the door earlier, I was shocked. You seemed upset before you slammed the door in my face, so I didn't knock again. But I knew I needed to come back. I have official business here, so I couldn't just leave things like that." I sighed. "Can I come in for a moment?"

She nodded and moved aside. I entered to find the apartment cluttered, with loads of unfolded laundry on the couch and piles of books stacked up on the floor.

As we stood across from each other in the living room, our chemistry still felt tangible. It hadn't waned a single bit—for me at least—since the other night, despite the difference in circumstances. I wanted to tell her how amazing our time together was, and how happy I was to see her again. But nothing came out. And I continued to hold it all in because her body language told me she wasn't going to be open to hearing any of that. Her stance was rigid, her breathing labored. This woman was guarded—layers upon layers of virtual armor.

"As I was saying..." I cleared my throat. "I came here because we've been receiving noise complaints about this apartment from other tenants. The two teenagers who live here have been problematic around the building for a while. But as of late, it's gotten to the point where we need to do something about it. Where is the woman who lives here...Vera Marks?"

"She's not here."

"Where is she?"

"I actually don't know," Devyn muttered. "She took off."

"You're looking after those kids? How much is she paying you? It better be a shitload."

"She's not paying me."

"Nothing?" My brows furrowed. "How is that possible?"

Devyn stared off for a moment. "Heath and Hannah are my brother and sister."

I felt my eyes widen. "Vera Marks is your mother?"

"If you want to call her that…" She rolled her eyes. "She gave birth to me, yeah. That's about it."

I remembered Devyn's friend, Mia, telling me Devyn's mom was a piece of shit. So understandably, there was some bad blood there—probably a long story I wouldn't be hearing today, or maybe ever. I didn't want to bombard her with questions while she was still getting over the shock of me showing up out of the blue. My curiosity was endless, though.

What had brought her to the bar the other night?

Why did she run off from the hotel?

What did her mother do to her?

Did she live here in New York?

How long had she been here in this apartment?

Before I could contemplate what to say next, the door burst open and in walked Frick and Frack. The brother and sister were in their early teens, and the boy looked a bit older than the girl. Maybe fifteen. I couldn't believe these infamous kids, whom I now knew as Heath and Hannah, were Devyn's siblings.

"There's a strange woman in the elevator who was bothering us just now," the boy said. He had long, shaggy brown hair that practically covered his eyes, and he wore a vintage Def Leppard T-shirt.

"She was scary and asking us for money," his sister added. "We don't think she lives in the building. We've never seen her before."

Heath pointed out to the hallway. "You'd better go check it out."

I ran down the hall to the elevator. When the doors opened, I panicked at the sight of a woman with long blond hair, lying lifeless on the ground.

My heart raced. *Fuck!*

When I bent to touch her, I realized the body was plastic, and her hair had shifted off her head.

It's a mannequin.

A fucking mannequin.

I gritted my teeth and dragged it out of the elevator, leaning it against the wall in the hallway.

Turning around, I was ready to race back to the apartment, but the two kids were right there behind me with their phones in my face. It seemed they'd recorded the entire prank. And now that their secret was out, they were openly laughing at me.

I was about to rip them both new assholes, but then I saw Devyn standing behind them, not a hint of a smile on her face. She clearly had her hands full and very little control of these kids. I didn't want to look like a jerk, so instead of screaming at Frick and Frack, I forced a laugh—even though there wasn't anything amusing about this.

Devyn scolded them. "Where the hell did you get that mannequin?"

"We stole it from Macy's," the girl said. "Walked right out with it."

Devyn pointed behind her. "Get the hell inside the apartment and wash up. Both of you!"

They disappeared, leaving Devyn and me standing across from each other in the hallway.

My chest heaved as I stood there, torn between anger and feeling like a dog in heat because of this beautiful woman. More than anything, I wanted to wrap her in my arms and assure her that whatever she was going through right now would get better.

"I have to go," she finally said, turning toward the apartment.

I followed her. "Devyn, wait. We should talk."

She turned and shook her head, regret in her eyes. "I really can't."

"I understand you have your hands full. I don't mean tonight."

"I don't think so, Owen." She walked backwards. "I'm sorry."

If I had a nickel for every time this woman apologized to me...

Devyn returned to the apartment—and closed the door on me.

Again.

❤️CHAPTER 3

Owen

"**W**hat's going on? Did something happen?" Two days later, I walked through the front door of the apartment building after work to find a lobby full of cops.

"Do you live here?" the tallest of the bunch asked.

I nodded. "Up on the second floor. I'm also one of the owners."

"I'm Officer Wells." He motioned to another cop, who stepped over to join us. "This is my partner, Officer Tambour. One of the residents in the building came home and interrupted a robbery in her apartment—her name is Mrs. Unger."

"Shit. Is she okay?"

The cop nodded. "She's fine. The perpetrator was a kid. We found him up on the roof. The only thing he had was one of her cats. An expensive Persian type, apparently. The thing's been vandalized."

My brows pulled together. "The *cat's* been vandalized?"

"Yep. It was white. Now it's dyed orange and black with stripes. Sort of looks like a tiger."

I closed my eyes. A teenager who stole a cat to dye it? I had a pretty good idea who the perpetrator was.

"Do you know the kid's name who did it?"

The cop shook his head. "Won't talk. Other than to call my partner a pig."

Jesus Christ. "Is he still in the building?"

"Already on the way down to the station for booking."

Shit. "Alright. Can I go up to my apartment?"

"Sure. We'll be out of here in just a few minutes."

Rather than hit two on the elevator panel, I pressed the button for the fourth floor. I wasn't sure if Devyn was home, but I was guessing Heath wasn't—since he was likely on his way to *jail.*

I knocked on the door of unit 410 and waited, but no one answered. I was just about to leave when I heard a sneeze from inside. So I knocked again, this time louder. "Devyn? Are you home? It's important."

It wasn't Devyn who opened the door; it was Hannah—the younger of the teenage Bonnie-and-Clyde duo.

I planted my hands on my hips. "Did you not hear me knock the first time?"

"I thought you were someone else."

"Like who? The *cops*, maybe?"

Hannah leaned forward and stuck her head out of the door, looking left then right. "Are they here?"

"Not on this floor, but they are downstairs."

"Did they get Heath?"

I sighed. "What the hell was he doing breaking into Mrs. Unger's apartment?"

"We didn't *break in*. She left the door open. She *always* leaves her door open."

"*We?* So you were part of this, too?"

Hannah pursed her lips.

I shook my head. "Is your sister home?"

"No."

"Where is she?"

"How should I know?"

Jesus, these kids were not easy. "You need to call her and tell her what's going on."

Hannah folded her arms across her chest. "I'm no rat."

"They took your brother to *jail*, Hannah. He needs help."

Her eyes bulged. "To jail? Just for spray painting a cat? It isn't even permanent. The temporary stuff was cheaper."

I pointed to the cell in her hand. "Call your sister."

"I already did. She didn't answer."

I shook my head. Why the hell did she give me a hard time if she'd already called? "Did you leave her a message?"

"Yeah, but she hasn't called back."

I sighed. "Alright. Tell me exactly what happened, and I'll see what I can do."

"We went down to the third floor to ring and run, but when we got off the elevator, that old lady who lives in the apartment on the end had her door open. Her prissy-looking cat walked out. So we borrowed it."

Borrowed. "Okay, and then what?"

"I said the cat walked like a tiger. And Heath said let's make him into one. So we locked the cat in our apartment while we went to Duane Reade and got orange and black hair dye. When we were done, the old lady's door was still open. She didn't even notice her precious cat was gone. Heath wanted to video her reaction when she saw the paintjob, so he snuck in with the cat. He wasn't supposed to get caught."

"Pretty sure prisons are filled with people who *weren't supposed to get caught*."

"Can you help Heath? It was just a prank."

Mrs. Unger did have a habit of leaving her door open so her cats could come in and out and roam the hall, so the story sounded plausible. I didn't know if there was anything I could do, but I supposed I could try.

I pointed my finger at Hannah. "Stay here. Do not go out and cause more trouble."

The girl rolled her eyes. "Whatever."

"Yeah, you're welcome."

I took the stairs down to the third floor, to Mrs. Unger's apartment. I had no idea why the hell I was getting involved in this shitshow, but I knocked anyway.

She opened, cradling her *vandalized* cat in her arms. I wasn't about to say it, but they'd done a pretty good job on the stripes. It really looked like a tiger.

"Hi, Mrs. Unger. How are you doing?"

"I've been better." She frowned. "Some hoodlums tortured my little Snowball here."

"I heard. That's what I came to talk to you about."

"We could use better locks on our doors."

I bit my tongue rather than say, "*You'd have to shut your door to get the benefit of locks.*"

"That's a good idea. I'll look into it. But I was hoping we could talk about the kid who dyed Snowball's fur."

"What about him?"

"Well, is there any chance I could talk you out of pressing charges? I know the family. He's not a bad kid, just sort of acting out."

Mrs. Unger didn't look too sympathetic, so I laid it on thicker.

"His mom took off. She left him and his little sister on their own. They've been doing some stupid things and making videos, trying to get attention from someone because they've been missing it at home."

Her face softened.

Who knows, maybe what I was pulling out of my ass had some truth to it. Mrs. Unger looked like she was buying it, so I kept going.

"The kid's actually a cat lover. He used the temporary hair dye because it's gentler. He didn't mean any harm. Just a dumb way to get some attention."

"I don't know…"

It took another fifteen minutes, and me committing to wash the dye out of Snowball's fur later, but Mrs. Unger finally agreed to not press charges. I knew the police could move forward with the case without her if they really wanted to, but they usually dropped it if they didn't have cooperation from the complaining witness—unless of course, they wanted to make an example out of someone. *Shit.* Like maybe a disrespectful brat who called a cop a *pig* and needed to be taught a lesson.

There was a good chance Heath was digging his own grave at this very moment, so I figured I'd better go down to the police station. On the way, I called my dad. He was retired now, but he'd been a Philadelphia cop for thirty years, the last fifteen as a detective. I reached out to him for advice, but he offered something better—to make a call to the precinct and see what he could do. He had a bunch of friends in the NYPD from years on joint task forces.

I walked into the local precinct and went straight to the front desk. "Hi, I'm looking for Heath…" *Shit. Is the kid's last name the same as Vera's?* "Umm… He's about fifteen and was brought in maybe an hour ago."

The guy lifted his chin. "Are you Frank Dawson's kid?"

I smiled. "I am."

"Smart move calling your dad. That boy is a real pain in the ass. You're lucky I like to collect favors." He shook his head. "I called the complainant. She doesn't want to pursue it. So we'll let him go…for now. But trust me, that kid is going to be back here if something doesn't change."

"Thanks a lot, Officer. I appreciate it."

"I'll call back and get him brought up for you. Might take a few minutes."

"Great. Thanks so much."

A few minutes turned into almost an hour. I guess they didn't tell Heath who had come to bail his ass out, because he looked pretty shocked to see me.

"What are you—"

I raised my hand and stopped him. "We'll talk outside. And by *we'll talk*, I mean *I'll talk* and you'll listen."

Heath frowned but nodded.

The cop at the desk lifted his chin again. "Good luck with that one."

Once we were out on the street, I walked a few buildings down from the police station and turned to face Heath. "What the hell were you thinking?"

"I thought it would get a lot of views."

"First off…" I held out my hand. "Give me your phone."

"What for?"

"I'm deleting the video you took. And if you give me a hard time, I will walk your ass back into that police station. I had to convince Mrs. Unger to not press charges. And I used my dad who's a retired cop to call in a favor."

Heath handed over his phone, and I deleted the video and gave it back.

"Are you going to tell my sister?" he asked.

"Of course I'm going to tell Devyn. She's responsible for you."

The kid frowned but said nothing.

I nodded toward the subway station. "Come on. Let's go."

"That's a downtown station."

"We're making a little stop."

"Where?"

"You'll see."

It wasn't Angelo's in Philly, but it was damn good. I'd taken Heath down to Joe's Pizza in Greenwich Village for a slice, something my father always did with me when he wanted to have a talk. Usually it meant I was in trouble, but over the years I'd come to appreciate that my father didn't just yell and punish me for a month like most dads did. He talked to me man-to-man while sharing pizza, which sort of made it impossible for me to zone out and not listen. Don't get me wrong, I still got punished for a month—but Dad made it so I listened first.

I waited until Heath picked up his second slice before I started in on him.

"So, let's talk. Why are you and your sister always being little shits?"

Heath shrugged. "It's boring here. There's nothing to do."

"You live in *New York City*. This place is a lot of things, but boring is definitely not one of them."

He shrugged again. "What is there to do?"

"Homework, studying, helping your big sister around the house."

"Like I said, boring."

"What would not be boring?"

"I don't know."

"Do you have any hobbies? Play any sports?"

"Not really."

I scratched my chin. "You take a lot of videos. Do you like doing that?"

"Yeah."

"Is there a film club or a photography club at school you can join?"

"I don't know."

"Well, why don't you find out?"

"Yeah, maybe."

"Here's the deal—you can't be doing the shit you've been doing the last few months anymore. No more throwing crap off the roof, stealing mannequins from department stores, or dyeing tenant's cats. If you're bored, you're going to have to find something to do that won't get you into trouble. But I think maybe the reason you're getting in trouble is about more than being bored. You want to know what I think?"

Heath frowned. "Not really."

I grinned. "I'm glad you asked. I think you're looking for attention. Your mom isn't here, and even when she is, she's not watching you guys. It's not uncommon for teens, and sometimes adults too, to seek negative attention—after all, at least someone gives a shit if they're yelling at you, right?"

"I'm not trying to get attention."

"Oh yeah? Then why post the videos on social media?"

Of course he had no answer for that.

I sighed. "Look, it's not my place to lecture you. In fact, I have no damn idea if anything I'm saying is even right. But for some insane reason, I decided to get involved. And I don't do shit halfway. So I would like to try to help."

Heath shoveled his slice of pizza into his mouth and stayed quiet for the next few minutes. I was surprised when he eventually spoke.

"I used to have a video camera. I did like making movies and stuff."

"Oh yeah? What happened to it?"

"We sold it at a pawn shop."

"Why'd you do that if you liked making movies?"

"Because there was no more of my mom's cheap jewelry to sell after she left, and we were out of canned food."

My heart squeezed. "Sorry, man."

He shrugged again. But since he'd opened the door, I decided to pry a little.

"How often does that happen? Your mom leaving, I mean."

"A lot."

"Do you know where she goes when she leaves?"

"She says she needs her space." Heath rolled his eyes. "Usually that means she met some guy, and he doesn't want to hang around kids. So they take off for a while."

"I'm sorry."

"Don't be," he said. "I don't need your pity."

Damn, this kid had a lot of emotional baggage for his age. "Does your sister always come when your mom leaves?"

Heath shook his head. "We don't usually call her, because if we do, she shows up. But we had no money for food. We don't want to be a pain in her ass."

I didn't know what to say, so I just nodded, and we both finished our pizza in silence. Heath wiped his mouth. "Can we go now?"

"Sure."

We hopped on the subway, and fifteen minutes later we were outside of our apartment building. I thought I'd probably regret it, but this kid really needed someone. So when we got into the elevator, I didn't immediately press the button for the fourth floor.

"Listen, if you ever want to go for pizza, come down to my apartment. We can talk, or we can just eat in silence. I don't care."

Heath shrugged yet again. "Thanks."

I figured I should have a conversation about everything that had transpired with his sister, so I went up to the apartment with him. He didn't have his key, so he knocked.

Devyn opened the door, and her brows drew together. "Owen? Why are you with Heath?"

"Didn't Hannah tell you?"

"Tell me what?"

Crap. Now I got to be the bearer of bad news. Meanwhile, Heath tried to walk into the apartment and escape the conversation. I grabbed him by the back of the shirt as he crossed the threshold.

"Not so fast, kiddo."

Devyn squinted. "What's going on? Did something happen on your date, Heath?"

"Date?" I said.

Devyn thumbed over her shoulder. "Hannah said Heath went on a date."

"Unless the date was with Officer Wells, I think she was feeding you a load of crap."

"The police? What happened, Heath?"

"We borrowed the old lady on the third floor's cat and made it look cooler. She got bent out of shape."

Devyn looked to me. "Can you possibly interpret that for me?"

I nodded. "They took Mrs. Unger's Persian cat and dyed its fur black and orange. Then Heath snuck into her apartment so he could video her reaction when they brought the cat back. She called the police, and they found Heath up on the roof and brought him in for attempted burglary and vandalism."

Devyn's eyes bulged. She looked to her brother. "Are you out of your mind?"

"It was just a joke."

"So you were, what, arrested this whole time and not really on a date?"

"They let me go after Mrs. Unger said she didn't want to press charges."

Devyn shifted her glare to me. "And what do you have to do with all of this?"

"I spoke to Mrs. Unger and went down to the police station to get him."

Her voice rose. "Without calling me?"

"Hannah had said she'd already called and left you a message. So I figured she'd fill you in."

Devyn pointed to Heath. "*You*, go inside. Take a shower and then plant your butt on the couch. We're going to talk."

The kid was smart enough to keep quiet and do as told. When it was just Devyn and me, she stepped out into the hallway and closed the door behind her. I figured she probably wanted to lament how difficult it was managing the kids, or maybe even thank me for helping out today. But boy was I wrong...

She gripped her hips. "Why did you do all that?"

"Do all what?"

"Get involved. Go down to the police station?"

Was she being serious right now? "I thought it was pretty obvious. I was trying to help."

"Why?"

"What do you mean, why?"

"I'm not sleeping with you again as payment, if that's what you think."

I shook my head, feeling my cheeks heat. "You know, sometimes people help just because they're good people."

"Not in my experience. When someone wants to *help* me, they usually expect something in return."

"You know what? I'm not listening to this shit. You don't know me well enough to think the worst of me." I leaned down so we were eye to eye. "*You're welcome.*" Then I turned and stormed away.

A few hours later, I was still fuming. I had a giant knot in the back of my neck, not to mention a throbbing headache just above my eyebrows. And now my hundred-dollar dress shirt was covered in orange and black dye. I'd been too angry to think straight and take it off before washing Mrs. Unger's damn cat. I was just about to pour myself a glass of whiskey to calm down when there was a knock at my door.

Devyn was the last person I expected to find standing here. She held out a glass filled with clear liquid. "I can't bake for shit.

But I wanted to apologize for the attitude I gave you earlier. Plus, I figured you could use a drink after the evening you had with my little brother. It's a tequila soda. You drank one the night we met."

I hated that I softened so easily. I'd been pissed for hours. "I didn't help because I wanted something in return," I told her.

"I know you didn't. It was just my knee-jerk reaction, and it was totally inappropriate." She smiled. "I have a bad habit of being overly defensive. I'm not used to nice guys, I guess. Can you forgive me?"

I opened the door wider. "You want to come in? We could share that drink. I'm sure you could use it too, right about now."

"Thank you for the offer, but I really shouldn't."

I looked back and forth between her eyes. "You *shouldn't*, or you don't want to?"

She bit down on her bottom lip. "Shouldn't."

I held out my hand, and she passed me the drink. "Apology accepted."

"Thank you. And thank you for everything you did for Heath."

I nodded. "No problem."

"Have a good night."

"You too."

I stayed at my door, watching Devyn walk to the elevator. Just as the door slid open, I yelled after her. "Hey!"

Devyn turned back.

"You shouldn't come in because the dynamic duo are upstairs unsupervised, or you shouldn't come in because you don't trust yourself alone with me inside my apartment sharing a drink?"

Her lip twitched with a hint of a smile as she stepped onto the elevator. "The kids are asleep. I don't think they'd get into trouble."

Well, well, well…maybe there's hope after all.

❤CHAPTER 4

Devyn

C*runch.*
Crunch.
Crunch.

The sound of Heath chomping on his Cap'n Crunch cereal grated my nerves. I'd thought I couldn't stand the sound of chewing in general, but this crunching was far worse. Maybe I was just on edge lately, with everything that normally bugged me amplified.

He slurped some milk.

Slurp.
Slurp.
Slurp.

That was worse than the crunching.

Heath wiped his mouth with his sleeve. "That Owen guy is alright."

Just the mention of his name made my pulse speed up. A fleeting memory of my nails digging into Owen's back flashed through my mind. I willed it away, suddenly wishing we could go back to the crunching and slurping.

I leaned my arms against the table. "What made you think of him just now?"

"We talked the other day when we got pizza."

"What did you talk about?"

Heath drank the last of his milk straight from the bowl. "Just stuff."

"Stuff like what?"

He hesitated. "I told him about Mom."

Ugh. One more reason for Owen to feel sorry for us.

"You shouldn't be talking about Mom to anyone."

"Why not?"

"They won't understand, and it's no one's business."

"It's not like I can avoid it. People are gonna start to wonder where she is if she doesn't come back."

I sighed. "Exactly how much did you tell him?"

"Just like…how this isn't the first time she's disappeared and stuff."

I had to stop myself from scolding him again. The truth was, my feelings on the matter had to do with *my* trauma, the shame I felt about having been abandoned by my own mother. I should've been asking myself what kind of mother takes off and leaves her child? Instead, my mind often twisted it to *what kind of child makes her mother want to leave?*

Heath should be able to talk about his shitty family situation with whomever he wanted, I reminded myself. That was good for him. I needed to respect that.

"Okay. I understand why you felt you needed to explain things," I told him.

"He said I could stop by his place if I ever needed to talk."

That made me uneasy, but how could I be mad that Owen had offered my brother a shoulder to lean on?

"Well, that was nice of him."

There were seemingly many *nice* things about Owen. I wished I could get to know him better, but I couldn't afford to get emotionally involved with anyone while I was here.

That afternoon, I dropped Heath and Hannah off at the local YMCA. They'd walk back home themselves later, but I had to accompany them to pay for the membership. Heath was going to play basketball, and I'd signed up Hannah for an art class. It was tough figuring out things for them to do with their time so they stayed out of trouble. The Y, where they would be somewhat supervised for a couple of hours, seemed like a good alternative to them walking around the building wreaking havoc.

That also meant I had a little time to myself, so I took a walk to clear my head.

As I returned to the building, a beautiful woman with wild, curly blond hair stood outside the front entrance, holding a tiny baby in an infant carrier. The mom or nanny was all dressed up. It seemed almost illegal not to pause and dote on the adorable little peanut.

So before entering the building, I stopped. "Boy or girl?"

"Girl." She smiled, looking down at the infant. "This is Hope."

Aw. She couldn't have been more than a week old. "Is she yours?"

"Yes. I'm her mom." She laughed. "Gosh, it's so weird to say that. It's hard to believe sometimes."

"I would imagine it's surreal." I grinned.

"Do you live in the building?" she asked.

"Temporarily. I'm looking after my siblings while our mother…is on a trip."

"Oh, that's nice of you." She offered her hand. "I'm Lala. Well, my name is Laney, but everyone calls me Lala. I live here with my fiancé and our daughter."

"Very nice to meet you. I'm Devyn."

"Which apartment are you in?" she asked.

"Four-ten."

She paused and then realization seemed to hit. "Oh…those teenagers are your siblings."

I straightened. "I know Heath and Hannah have a bit of a reputation around here—"

"They do. But I mean, they're young. I get it. We all did crazy stuff when we were younger, right?"

"I suppose."

"Well, my brother and his friends did." She sighed. "Are you working while you're here?"

"I'm a casting agent out in L.A. I'm able to work remotely, though it's easier to be on the West Coast, of course."

"That sounds like an exciting job." Lala rocked her daughter. "I'm on maternity leave now, but I'm a scientist. I conduct research studies. I'll be going back to work in some capacity, just haven't figured it out yet."

"Wow. A scientist. That's very cool."

Lala looked up at the building. "Have you met anyone here yet?"

"A few people." I bit my lip, debating. "Let me ask you, what do you know about the owner of this building?"

Lala chuckled.

I cocked my head. "What's so funny?"

"Well, the owner of the building is the father of my baby. So…I know him pretty well."

A rush of adrenaline coursed through me.

Oh my God.

What?

This is Owen's baby?

This can't be happening.

I swallowed. "Owen is the father of your baby?"

"Owen?" Lala's eyes widened. "Oh gosh. No, no, no. *Holden* is my fiancé. Owen is one of Holden's best friends. They own the building together, along with Colby and Brayden. The four of them formed a company that technically owns the property."

Relief washed over me. I'd thought I was gonna have a heart attack for a second there.

Lala explained that the four guys had grown up together in Pennsylvania. Lala's brother, Ryan, had been the fifth member of their crew until he died of leukemia. His friends had been the beneficiaries of his insurance policy, which they'd used to purchase the building in his honor. They were thick as thieves.

I nodded slowly, taking it all in. "That's a fascinating story. I had no idea."

"Was there a reason you were curious about Owen?" She winked. "He *is* one of the two single ones."

I felt my cheeks burn. "I've met him. That's all. He…came to issue a noise warning one night, expecting to find my mother. I just assumed he was the sole owner."

"Oh, I see." She covered baby Hope's head with a little hat. "Do you know how long you'll be here in New York?"

"No. It could be weeks or maybe months…"

"Well, you should really meet Billie. She owns the tattoo shop on the ground level and is an awesome person. She's married to Colby, one of the guys." She snapped her fingers. "Actually, why don't you come upstairs and say hello? She's waiting on me right now because she's helping me put together Hope's first photoshoot. Her friend is the photographer. We're having a little photo-shoot party today."

I shook my head. "Oh, I don't want to impose…"

"That's nonsense! There aren't that many women our age in the building. She's a good person to know. And it's rare she's not working in the shop, so it's the perfect time for me to introduce you. I don't know what I would've done without her when I first moved here." She seemed to notice my hesitation. "You don't have to stay long. Just come say hi."

I didn't want to, but I didn't know how to say no either. So I shrugged. "Sure. Why not?"

I followed Lala upstairs to this woman Billie's apartment.

When Billie opened the door, I was immediately taken by her beauty. She had long black hair, and her arms were covered in colorful tattoos. She was like a human piece of art.

"Hey, Lala." She turned to me. "Who's this?"

"This is Devyn. She's living temporarily in four-ten."

Billie's mouth opened then closed, and she held out her hand, a hint of a smirk on her face. "Great to meet you."

Why is she smirking? I could only assume it had to do with my siblings. It seemed everyone knew about the ruckus they'd caused around here.

A photographer was setting up in the corner of the room against a giant black backdrop. There was also a table with appetizers and drinks laid out.

"How's the setup going?" Lala asked.

"Good." Billie arranged a few things on the table. "We're all ready to go whenever you are."

Billie then introduced us to her friend Cash, the photographer.

Lala looked around. "Where's Colby?"

"He took Saylor and Mav out while we set up. They should be on their way back soon." Billie turned to me. "Okay, so I have to confess, Devyn. Your reputation precedes you…"

"What do you mean?"

"Well, for a while, inquiring minds have been wondering who you were. You've been spotted around the building, but you were a mystery."

I arched a brow. "There are a lot of inquiring minds around here?"

"You have no idea." Billie laughed. "Anyway, I'm sorry if I seemed a little weird when you first walked in. I'd just put two and two together. It's really great to meet you."

The door opened, and a handsome tatted guy wearing a beanie over his longish hair entered. I assumed that was Lala's baby daddy since he wrapped his arm around her and kissed her cheek. He immediately took baby Hope from her.

Lala brought him over to me. "Babe, this is the mystery woman in four-ten. She has a name! Devyn."

"Ah." Holden's eyes sparkled. "Very nice to meet you, Devyn." He held out a hand, and we shook.

"You, too."

A few moments later, another guy who looked to be in his late twenties strolled in. He clasped hands with Holden, and I wondered if he was one of the other friends who owned this place. He was super good-looking, too. Was there something in the air around here? Every single guy was hot.

His mouth spread into a smile as he made a beeline for me. "Who do we have here?"

Lala smiled. "This is Devyn. The woman in four-ten."

"I know. I recognize her." He grinned. "I'm Brayden. It's amazing to finally meet you."

"I hadn't realized people were waiting to meet me," I said with a laugh. "But it's wonderful to meet you, too." All the attention made me feel a little warm. Maybe I needed to get out of here before it was totally overwhelming.

"Well, it's just that no one knew who you were for a while there," Brayden explained. "And I mean, we typically know everything around here, so it threw us for a loop." He chuckled. "What brings you to New York?"

"Just here temporarily, looking after my brother and sister while my mother is away."

"Is she on vacation?" he asked.

"Something like that." I gritted my teeth.

"Cool." He nodded. "Well, welcome."

"Thank you." I exhaled.

A few minutes later, yet *another* handsome dude walked in, this one flanked by two kids: a little girl and an infant in a car seat.

The girl ran up to me—even faster than Brayden had. "Who are you?"

I smiled down at her. "My name is Devyn. And you are?"

"Saylor Lennon." She pointed over to the baby. "And that's my baby brother, Maverick Ryan Lennon."

These must be Billie's kids.

I looked over at the baby. "He's got so much black hair."

"I know. It looks like a teepee!"

"A toupee," Colby corrected, holding out his hand. "I'm Colby, Billie's husband. Nice to meet you."

"Colby, Devyn is currently living in four-ten," Billie added. "She's the mystery woman."

"Ah…the famous mystery woman." He snickered.

I felt myself blush. "That's me, apparently."

The next thing I knew, Saylor had brought out a guinea pig to show me. "This is Guinevere," she announced.

I petted the chubby animal. "He's so cute."

"It's a she…"

Duh. Guinevere would be a girl's name.

Brayden slipped into the spot next to me. "Who's cute? Me?" He winked.

This one was *such* a flirt.

"I'm kidding, of course," he said. "So, how do you like living here, Devyn?"

I spent the next few minutes chatting with him—told him all about my job and briefly alluded to the challenge of keeping up with my siblings. Brayden was certainly a charmer, attentive to every word that came out of my mouth and seemingly *very* interested in me. This was a problem for multiple reasons.

Then Holden had grabbed him by the shoulder and dragged him away.

"I'll be back." Brayden lifted a finger as he walked backwards, looking confused.

Odd.

I was left standing there, feeling awkward among this group of close friends. It felt like the right time to leave as everyone started noshing on the food, and Holden and Lala prepared to take a family photo.

I debated sneaking out but decided to say a quick goodbye to Billie, who wasn't in the middle of anything at the moment.

"I have to head back to my apartment. It was great meeting you."

"Why don't you stay? We have plenty of food!"

I placed my hand on my stomach. "Oh, thank you so much. But I have to be home when my brother and sister return from the Y."

"Okay, well…we should do lunch sometime. You, me, and Lala."

"That would be great." I smiled.

Agreeing to that seemed harmless enough. They were nice women, and it wouldn't kill me to get to know them. That was certainly safer than getting to know say, *Owen* better. Billie and I exchanged phone numbers.

As I went to the door, Brayden came after me.

"You're leaving so soon?"

"I am, yeah."

"You can't leave yet." He practically pouted, batting his lashes—sinfully long for a man. "Just stay for one drink. You don't have to drive to get to four-ten, right?" Before I could say anything, Brayden grabbed a glass. "What's your poison? Wine? Tequila?"

I didn't want to seem like an antisocial bitch, so I caved. I had a little while before the kids would be back. "Okay, just *one* quick drink. Tequila and seltzer with lime would be great."

"Comin' right up."

The moment Brayden handed me the glass, I turned to find that someone else had entered the apartment.

My body quivered as I gulped. *Owen.*

I should've known he might show up. He was dressed to the nines, looking like he'd just come from work, even though it was Saturday.

He flashed Brayden a dirty look and turned to me. "What are you doing here? You stalking me or something?"

I probably deserved that. "I'm not staying for the photoshoot," I told him. "I met Lala outside, and she invited me to come over to meet Billie. I didn't realize it was going to be a party."

Owen looked down at my glass. "Looks like you're partaking, though."

"Brayden convinced me to stay for one drink before I have to leave."

His eyes moved to Brayden. "He did, did he?"

"What's up, dude? You come from work?" Brayden asked.

Owen fidgeted with his expensive watch. "Well, my showing got canceled, so I came back. I wasn't originally going to be here."

"I thought you were just late as usual," Brayden teased.

"Looks like *you're* getting a nice *early start* on things as usual," Owen snapped.

There was tension between these two. It hit me that Brayden likely knew nothing about my history with Owen, as he was making a play for me right in his friend's face. I respected the fact that it seemed Owen wasn't someone to kiss and tell.

"Just getting to know our new neighbor—being neighborly," Brayden said, looking between Owen and me. "I didn't realize you two had met, though."

"Yeah, actually, we've spoken a couple times," Owen answered. "Right, Devyn?"

I cleared my throat. "Owen helped me with a situation concerning my brother and sister," I finally said. "They'd gotten into trouble. Owen got his dad to pull some strings."

Brayden chuckled. "Well, that was really nice of you, Owen. I'm sure your intentions were pure as could be."

Owen looked like he wanted to kill him. The testosterone in the air was noxious, and Owen looked particularly jealous. All the more reason I needed to create a boundary between him and me. Although a bigger reason was perhaps the way my body reacted to Owen every time he was near.

I took a long swallow of my drink until it was nearly empty. I set the glass on an end table.

"I really do have to get back. My brother and sister will be home soon, and I need to get dinner started. It was wonderful meeting you, Brayden." I turned to Owen. "And it's always good seeing you. I hope you guys have an amazing rest of the day."

I turned and practically ran out of the place—once again running away from Owen. He didn't try to stop me, and for that I was grateful.

Back inside the apartment, I busied myself with some dinner prep. But as I stirred tomato sauce on the stove, I couldn't stop thinking about the party at Billie's. They were such a tight-knit crew. I'd never been part of a group of friends like that—never had a sense of family, either, because of my mother's decisions and being separated from Heath and Hannah for so many years. I'd always had to fend for myself, so I knew having people to lean on was an amazing gift. Mia was probably my one true friend. And of course, she was back in Cali. I was overdue in catching up with her after the night I'd met Owen... The sooner I could get back to my life in L.A., the better. But with my mother nowhere to be found, I wondered if anything would ever be the same again. It seemed more and more like I'd need to take my siblings back to California with me.

The door opened, interrupting my thoughts, and Heath and Hannah blew in like a storm.

"How was the Y?" I asked them.

"Lame," Heath answered as he kicked off his sneakers. "I was the oldest kid there."

"Lame is better than getting into trouble again." I turned to Hannah. "How was the art class?"

"I painted a giraffe, and it looked like a big, hairy penis."

"Where is it?" I chuckled.

"I dropped it off in front of Owen's door—as a thank you for him helping Heath."

Great. I didn't have a response for that one. "Go get washed up for dinner. It's almost ready."

As we sat down to eat a few minutes later, Heath kept checking his phone.

"Put that away while we're eating," I scolded.

"I can't."

"Excuse me?"

"I have to watch. It keeps going up and up."

"What keeps going up and up?"

"The number of views and comments on that video I posted of Owen finding the mannequin in the elevator and thinking it was a dead body."

I grabbed the phone and looked at his social media account.

Four-million views.

♥CHAPTER 5

Owen

"**H**ey! Hold the elevator!" I jogged toward the closing doors. Holden was already inside. He reached for the button panel, and the doors bounced open just as I made it across the lobby. "Thanks."

"No problem." Holden nodded. "You just getting home from work now?"

"Yeah. Long day. And it's only freaking Wednesday."

I pushed the button for the second floor, but noticed that the fourth floor was illuminated, not the third, where Holden's apartment was. "You going up to four or didn't press three yet?"

Holden held up his toolbox. "Gotta change a showerhead before I can call it a day. Told Devyn I'd get to it tonight so the kids can shower before school in the morning."

My pulse quickened at the mention of her name. "Devyn, huh?"

Holden raised a brow. "There was a little tension between you and Brayden the other day at Billie's photoshoot."

I raked a hand through my hair. "That fucker hits on anything with legs."

"Don't worry. I got the feeling he took the hint when you growled at him."

"I didn't growl."

Holden smiled. "You definitely marked your territory, dude."

I sighed. "I should probably talk to him—tell him Devyn and I had a thing."

"That's a good idea. I'd want to know if I was him. He'd never hit on her if he knew you were interested."

"Yeah." I shook my head. "Though, being *interested* isn't getting me anywhere. Devyn wants nothing to do with me."

"That sucks. Sorry, man."

"I don't know what it is about that woman. But I can't stop thinking about her."

"*Whoa.* That's a strong statement coming from you. It's been a while since anyone has caught your attention."

"I know. And of course, I have to pick someone even more closed off than me."

"What's her deal? Does she have a boyfriend back home or something?"

I shrugged. "You probably know as much as I do. We had that one great night together. Then she disappeared on me before I could get her number, and every time I go anywhere near her now, she either slams a door in my face or hightails it out before I can get in more than a sentence or two. The only reason I know anything at all about her situation is because the kid, Heath, filled me in the other day."

The doors slid open at my floor. I'd worked thirteen hours today and couldn't wait to get out of this suit, but...

I looked at Holden. "You mind if I change that showerhead?"

A smile spread across his face. "By all means."

He handed me the toolbox and pressed the button for his floor.

"Good luck, buddy. Sounds like you're gonna need it." He waved as he stepped off the elevator. When the doors slid open again, I walked down the hall on the fourth floor. It had seemed like a good idea, but once I stood in front of Devyn's door with the toolbox and showerhead, I started to doubt myself.

This is a bad idea.

How many times do you need to be blown off before you take the hint, Dawson?

After a few minutes of standing there, I started to turn around. But I stopped when the door abruptly swung open.

"Owen? What are you doing out here?" Devyn asked.

"Uh…" I held up the toolbox and showerhead. "I'm here to fix your bathroom."

"I thought Holden was going to do that?"

"He's, umm…on baby duty tonight. We all chip in to give him a break when we can since he didn't get any official paternity leave."

"Why were you standing out here for so long? Why didn't you knock?"

Shit. "I was trying to remember if I had the right wrench in the toolbox or not."

Her eyes narrowed. "Uh-huh…"

"How did you know I was out here?"

"I heard a noise and looked through the peephole. Thought it might be my brother and sister. You've been staring at my door for almost five minutes."

"If you saw me standing here, why didn't you open the door?"

She shrugged. "I was curious how long it was going to take you to knock."

"Well, are you going to invite me in to fix your showerhead or leave me standing out here for your amusement a little longer?"

The corner of her lip twitched, but she took a few steps back and opened the door wide for me to enter.

"Thank you," I said as I passed.

Her apartment was quiet. I set my supplies on the kitchen counter and looked around. "Where are Frick and Frack?"

"They stayed after school."

"*Voluntarily?*"

Devyn shut the door and chuckled. "That's how I reacted, too. I figured they had detention, but Hannah wanted to try out for something, and apparently Heath has a crush on some girl who's also trying out. They promised they'd walk home together after."

I nodded. "Heath seems like a good kid when he lets his guard down."

"Ummm... You might rethink that statement after I tell you he posted the video he took of you running to save a mannequin in the elevator. Apparently it's gone viral."

I shook my head. "I should make him tag my real estate company so I get something out of it, other than looking like an idiot."

Devyn smiled. "Speaking of your job, are you going to change the showerhead in that suit?"

I tilted my head. "Are you suggesting I take my clothes off, Devyn?"

Her cheeks turned pink. "No. I just wouldn't want you to get it dirty."

"Uh-huh."

She rolled her eyes. "Come on. Let me show you what's going on."

Devyn and I went into the bathroom. It was a tight squeeze for two people, which I appreciated. I slipped off my suit jacket and held it out to her. "Would you put that on the towel hook on the back of the door for me, please?"

"Sure."

I stepped into the bathtub and rolled up my shirtsleeves. "So what happens when you turn it on?"

"It sprays in five different directions, everywhere but down, and the entire bathroom floor gets soaked."

I leaned over to the toolbox on the vanity. As I opened it, a big whiff of Devyn's perfume wafted by. "Are you wearing Baccarat Rouge?"

She blinked a few times. "Yes, but how did you know that?"

The day after she ditched me, I'd spent two hours at a perfume counter trying to find the damn scent she'd worn. I probably would have bought it too, if it hadn't turned out to be three-hundred-and-fifty bucks.

I shrugged. "A woman at work wears it."

"Oh."

I eyed her as I took a wrench from the toolbox. "It's pretty expensive."

"Is it? It was a gift."

I couldn't help but wonder who was buying her perfume. But rather than push my luck and ask, I kept my mouth shut and focused on taking off the showerhead. It wasn't that tight, so it only took a few turns of the wrench. But the moment I slipped it off, water spewed all over.

"*Fuck.* What the hell?"

"What should I do?" Devyn yelled.

"Nothing, just scoot over so I can get underneath the sink."

I hopped out of the bathtub, pulled open the cabinet, and reached inside to twist the main shut-off valve. The water stopped, but I'd already had a free shower. A damn cold one. I shook droplets from my hands. "There shouldn't be any water going to the showerhead when the water isn't turned on. The shower body must be broken, too."

"Which part is the shower body?"

I pointed to the wall. "All of this."

"Oh." Devyn bit her bottom lip. "I guess I should've mentioned that the cold-water knob just spins. We have to use pliers to turn it off and on. I hadn't told Holden because the kids broke it. Heath was making some video."

I frowned. "Well, I can replace the showerhead and see what happens when I turn the water back on. But the plumbing-supply store closes at six, so I won't be able to get a new body until at least tomorrow."

"Whatever you can do." Devyn looked me up and down. "Your shirt is soaked. Let me see if I have something for you to change into."

"Pretty sure nothing of yours is going to fit me."

"Be right back."

While Devyn went to check her room, I peeled off my dress shirt. The T-shirt underneath wasn't as wet, but had been starting to absorb the water from the first layer.

Devyn returned with a folded gray shirt. "This should fit you."

I took it and shook it open. It was a Nike dry-fit running shirt and had to be an extra-large. "This can't be yours."

"It's not."

"Whose is it?"

She pursed her lips. "Umm... A friend's."

I frowned. "And you just *happen* to have it here with you in New York?"

"I like to sleep in it sometimes."

No way in hell was I putting on some other dude's T-shirt—*a guy whose clothes she likes to sleep in.* That was worse than when a woman stole your hoodie. I shook my head. "No thanks."

"Why? I think it'll fit."

"I'm sure it will. But I'm not wearing the T-shirt of a man you like so much that you wear his crap to bed."

Devyn shook her head. "You'd rather stay in a wet shirt?"

"Absolutely."

She rolled her eyes. "Fine. I'll put your shirt in the dryer."

It took me less than a half hour to change the showerhead. When I was done, it worked, though it didn't solve the problem of the spinning cold-water knob. "You're going to have to use the pliers again tomorrow, but I'll grab a new shower body on my way to the office."

"Alright. Thank you."

I packed up my tools and tossed the garbage into the wastebasket.

"Do you want a water or something to drink?" Devyn asked.

Even though I was still stewing over the stupid T-shirt she'd tried to give me, I didn't want to leave yet. "Sure. Thanks."

But out in the kitchen, the damn shirt was folded on the counter. I kept looking over at it as I chugged from the water bottle. Devyn followed my line of sight. When our eyes met again, I couldn't help myself. "What's the deal, Devyn? Are you married or something?"

She looked offended. "God, no. I wouldn't have slept with you if I were."

"Then whose T-shirt is it? A boyfriend or something?"

"Not really."

"An ex?"

She sighed. "I don't know how to label things with Robert."

"Robert?"

"He's a man I've been involved with for a few years. I guess you could say it's casual, an on-and-off type of thing."

"Is that how you want it? Casual, I mean?"

Devyn shrugged. "I don't know. Robert's an actor. I'm a casting agent. That's how we met. But that was before he made it big. He's busy a lot now, traveling for movies and stuff."

"What movies has he done?"

Devyn looked away. "I probably shouldn't say. He likes to keep his private life private, including our relationship."

Robert sounded like a dumbfuck, if you asked me. I'd want every guy in the world to know this woman was mine. Yet I kept my mouth shut again and finished the rest of my water.

"So a casting agent, huh? Does that mean you pick which actors get movie roles?"

"Not exactly, but I have a hand in it. I collaborate with producers and directors to find the best talent for each role. But the final say is theirs."

I nodded. "Sounds like a cool job. How did you get into that?"

"I've been obsessed with movies since I was a little kid. I always knew I wanted to work in the business somehow. I'm not comfortable in front of the camera, so I went to college to be a screenwriter. I did an internship for a producer who does a lot of book-to-screen stuff. He was in the middle of filming one movie and adapting two others. One of the supporting actresses had to drop out of the production he was shooting, and I mentioned that I thought a little-known actress would be a great replacement. The producer had never heard of her before, but he wound up watching her work and hiring her. After that, he asked me who I thought would be good for the roles in another screenplay he'd just acquired. He liked all of my recommendations and suggested I do an internship for a casting agency to see if I might be interested in that as a career. I never looked back after that. Five years later, I opened my own company, and that producer was my first big client."

"Wow. That's a cool story. You must be really good at your job."

Devyn smiled. "I like to think I am. I love what I do anyway."

"So you're working remotely while you're here?"

She nodded. "I am, but it's not ideal. I really need to be accessible for my clients. People in L.A. like to do lunch and take meetings to make things happen, not Zoom."

"How long are you planning on staying in New York?"

She blew out a breath. "I have no idea. The kids really need to finish the school year, which is another two months. I don't want to pull them out mid-semester. Lord knows I had to do that enough times growing up, and I hated it. But if Vera isn't back by the time school lets out, I guess I'll have to relocate them to California with me. I don't want to displace them again. They've been in New York for four years now, and that's the longest they've ever lived in any state. It's hard moving and changing schools at any age, but it's really tough when you're a teenager in high school. Kids form their cliques, and it's not as easy to make new friends as it was when you were little."

I'd had the same friend crew since kindergarten, but she was probably right. "Do you have any idea where your mom is?"

"No clue."

"Heath mentioned that he was the one who called you. So she took off without even knowing who was going to take care of them?"

Devyn nodded. "Sadly, that's normal for her. In Vera's book, once you hit double digits, you can fend for yourself."

The front door blasted open. Hannah rolled in first, and Heath was right behind her carrying a pizza.

"I got a job!" he announced.

"A job?" Devyn's brows pulled together. "Where? You're only fifteen."

"At the pizza place down the block."

"Doing what?"

"Cleaning tables and making boxes and stuff." Heath lifted his chin to me. "What's up, Rubber Ranger?"

I tilted my head. "Rubber Ranger?"

Heath smirked. "That's your new superhero name, since you saved Judy and all."

I assumed Judy was the mannequin he'd stolen. "It's cute that you name your dolls before you make them your girlfriend."

Heath chuckled as he tossed the pizza box on the table. "Come on, let's eat. The owner gave me a free pie when he hired me."

"I made chicken and broccoli," Devyn said.

Hannah wrinkled her nose. "Again?"

"I'm sorry if my menu isn't as diverse as you'd like."

Hannah pouted. "Can we just eat the pizza? It smells so good. We can eat your boring chicken tomorrow."

Devyn shook her head, looking frustrated. "Fine. But you're eating the chicken tomorrow."

Heath flipped open the top to the pizza box. "Want a slice, Rubber Ranger?"

I glanced over at Devyn, who seemed hesitant. But fuck it. I hadn't eaten, and I'd already overstayed my welcome prying. So why not?

I shrugged. "Sure. It smells good."

The three siblings' dynamic was interesting to observe over dinner. Devyn seemed more like a mother than a sister to Frick and Frack.

"How did tryouts go, Hannah?" she asked.

Hannah shrugged. "Okay, I guess."

"She was the best one there," Heath countered. "Besides Daisy, of course."

Hannah rolled her eyes. "Daisy isn't even that good of a singer. She's just pretty and has big boobs."

I wiped pizza grease from my hands with a napkin. "What did you try out for, Hannah?"

"*PS Idol*. It's my dumb school's version of *American Idol*."

"You sing?" I asked.

"Hannah is an amazing singer." Devyn smiled. "She also plays the guitar and drums. She wants to go to Juilliard someday."

"Really? That's cool. I always wished I could sing. My friend Holden is a drummer, but he has a great voice, too. He lives here in the building. Maybe you've seen him around?"

Hannah's face turned red.

"Oh, she's seen him." Heath pressed his hands into the praying position and held them to his cheek. "*Holden the hottie*," he said in a high-pitched voice.

Hannah stood and tossed her napkin on the table. "You're such a jerk, Heath."

"At least I'm not in love with a fifty-year-old."

Since Holden and I were the same age, I took offense to that comment. "Hey, calm down. Holden's only thirty."

Heath shrugged. "Same thing."

Hannah stormed off to her room.

"Do you have to pick on your sister all the time?" Devyn asked.

"What? It's the truth. She's in love with the dude. The other day she tripped over her own feet when she saw him in the lobby."

Devyn shook her head. "Just go do your homework, Heath."

After he disappeared, I collected the dirty paper plates from the table and tossed them in the garbage. "So Hannah's got a little crush, huh?"

"Apparently so."

I shook my head. "Thirteen or thirty, women can't help but love that guy. Holden's a chick magnet. Always has been."

"I can see why. He has a certain way about him."

A spike of jealousy coursed through my veins. "Oh yeah? You got a thing for Holden, too?"

"Me?" Devyn shook her head. "No, he's not my type. But that doesn't mean I can't see the appeal. He has that aloof, musician thing going on that women love, especially young ones like Hannah."

I rubbed my bottom lip with my thumb. "Not your type, huh? So what exactly *is* your type, Devyn?"

Her eyes dropped to my lips for a half second before she looked away. "I don't have a particular type. But it's getting late, so…"

"Soooo…don't let the door hit me in the ass?"

"I didn't mean—"

I held up a hand. "It's fine. I can take a hint."

I scooped up my toolbox, and Devyn followed me to the door. But I stopped after I opened it. "Can I ask you something?"

"What?"

"You said your relationship with the actor guy is casual, right?"

"Yes."

"So is it just me, then? Was our night together not good for you?"

Devyn's face fell. "Oh gosh, no. Our night together was great. It's not you at all, Owen. It's just that my life is complicated enough without getting involved with someone while I'm out here. I'm only in town for a short time."

I nodded. She had a lot going on. "Okay. I get it."

"Do you really?"

"Sure." I leaned in to kiss her cheek and winked. "But it won't stop me from trying."

♥CHAPTER 6

Devyn

A week had gone by, and I hadn't run into Owen again, nor had he reached out. That brought me mixed feelings, but mostly relief. Because every time I was around him, I second-guessed pushing him away. His eyes, his smell, the way he looked at me, and the memories of our night together were difficult to contend with when he was right in front of me.

The window by the small desk in the living room of the apartment provided a perfect view of the street in front of the building. Heath and Hannah had just left for school, and it was quiet. I couldn't help looking out occasionally to see if I might spot Owen. I wasn't sure what time he normally went to work, but I was pretty sure he'd be gone by now since it was past 9 AM. But that didn't stop me from glancing out anyway, in the hopes of shamelessly observing the guy without him knowing.

I did manage to spot Billie walking back toward the building with a coffee in hand. Her long, black hair swayed in the breeze. She hadn't reached out to me since the day we met, even though she'd mentioned us going to lunch. I suppose it hadn't been that long, but I wondered if I should make the first move. That was very unlike me. And my gut told me not to push starting a friendship that would have to be short-lived anyway. This temporary stay was about business, not pleasure—despite the *pleasure-filled* way I'd kicked it off with Owen.

My phone rang, putting a halt to my window watching. Robert's name flashed on the screen. I took a deep breath in and answered. "You're up early…"

"Hey, babe. I actually haven't gone to sleep yet."

"Ah. I should've known."

"How's it going over there?" he asked.

"It's…been busy."

"Yeah? Why?"

Why? "Well, for one, my brother and sister are a handful and—"

"You need to come back, Devyn," he interrupted. "They upped the start date for shooting in Italy. I'm leaving in less than three weeks, and I'm not gonna be back in the States for four months."

Is he serious? "Why can't you come to New York?"

"I have press here in L.A. almost every day. Let me buy your ticket. You don't have to stay long."

This was yet another example of how self-absorbed Robert was. "I can't just leave Heath and Hannah alone to go screw you for three days."

"Your mother can leave them permanently, but you can't leave them for a few days?"

My mouth dropped. "Is that supposed to be funny?"

"Okay, I'm sorry. That wasn't funny. I get it." He paused. "Why don't you just bring them with you? I'll pay for their tickets, too."

Throwing my pen, I shouted, "They're in school, Robert. And I can't even get a handle on them here, in their own environment. I certainly can't trust them out in L.A. I'd need to keep an eye on them every second, and that defeats the purpose of me coming out to see you." I shook my head. "I'm sorry. It's just not gonna work."

"What's not gonna work? You coming out here...or us?"

Both.

Maybe?

"What are we, Robert? We're not together. We're not even really friends."

He sighed. "You mean something to me, Devyn. I know I'm busy, but I want you in my life."

"You've always wanted to have your cake and eat it, too. But I have a life of my own and responsibilities you obviously can't understand."

"Yeah. I guess you're right." He exhaled. "Well, I tried. And I didn't mean to get you all worked up—at least not in *this* way. If you change your mind, let me know. I'll book the tickets."

I blew out a frustrated breath. "I'm sorry. That's not gonna happen."

He sighed. "Yeah. I'm sorry, too."

After I hung up, my mood disintegrated. I was angry at myself for wasting so much time infatuated with a man who wouldn't even try to understand my current predicament. One positive thing about being in New York was the distance and clarity it provided me about the things in my life that had been weighing me down for so long. Robert was certainly at the top of that list.

Rather than continue stewing over that phone call, a little while later I decided to take a walk to get some fresh air.

As I approached the building on my way back, a Town Car pulled up. To my surprise, Owen emerged from it. My heart pounded. He wasn't alone. A beautiful, tall blonde exited the vehicle right after him. A wave of nausea hit as she wrapped her arms around him in a hug. Then she got back inside, and the car took off.

Swallowing my jealousy, I contemplated sneaking into the building before Owen spotted me, but his eyes found mine before I had a chance.

"Hey, you." His mouth spread into a smile.

Owen looked gorgeous in a crisp, blue, collared shirt with the sleeves rolled up. It fit perfectly over his broad shoulders. His navy dress pants and shiny brown shoes finished off the look. When he removed his shades, the sun caught his eyes, which were a gorgeous aquamarine.

"How was your date?" I asked, tasting the unjustified bitterness on my tongue.

"Date?" He laughed. "It went *very well*, in fact."

Fighting the urge to flee, I nodded. "Well, that's good."

"It was a *business* date," he clarified. "I took my *client* to see a few properties. She had her driver drop me off after."

"Oh." I looked down at my feet, hiding my relief. "Well, she was very beautiful. I just assumed…"

"Carolyn is married, and her husband is a friend of mine. They're in the market for a bigger place in the City."

"Ah." My cheeks burned with embarrassment.

"I would've gone back to the office, but I left my laptop behind and was going to fetch it before returning to work." He tilted his head. "What are you up to?"

"I was just taking a quick walk between getting some work done. Trying to make the most of the time when the kids are in school."

Owen checked his phone. "It's just about lunchtime. I know you prefer not to hang out with me recreationally, but would you want to grab a quick bite to eat?"

I chewed on my lip. "I don't know, Owen…"

"Just two neighbors sharing a meal, Devyn. Nothing more." He chuckled. "How much trouble can we get into in public anyway?"

I pushed my reservations aside. "Okay, why not?"

Owen ran upstairs to grab his laptop, and I opted to wait here.

When he returned, he suggested a place he liked that was only a few blocks away but in the direction of his office.

When we arrived, however, I realized it was way too fancy for the way I was dressed—in a T-shirt dress and Chucks. "This is your idea of a simple lunch?"

"I might be a little jaded," Owen confessed. "I'm used to wining and dining clients, so I tend to frequent places like this."

"Well, it's very nice, but I'm underdressed. I would've changed if I knew."

Owen gave me a once-over, which sent a chill down my spine. "You look perfect. Plus, I know the manager, so if anyone tries to kick you out, I'll just call him. Unless you're really bothered by it? I didn't mean to make you uncomfortable."

I looked down at myself. It wasn't that bad, I guess. "No, it's fine." I sighed.

Thankfully, the hostess didn't appear to care at all how I was dressed. She lit up when she saw Owen and brought us right to a table in the corner, despite the fact that we didn't have a reservation.

Owen pulled out my chair. It seemed chivalry was alive and well in his world. I couldn't remember the last time Robert had done something like that for me.

Owen sat across from me. "So, how has your day been, other than the surprise ambush lunch with me?"

"Pretty basic. I got some work done and then needed to walk off some stress. You caught me as I was heading back to the building."

"So you're saying I'm the *best* part of your day thus far…" He winked.

"Maybe." I grinned.

His expression changed. "Seriously, what's got you stressed?"

I hesitated. "I got a phone call from a friend who pissed me off."

"Was it Mia?"

I'd nearly forgotten that he'd spoken to my best friend the night he'd found my phone.

"No, it wasn't."

Owen cocked a brow. "Was it a *guy* friend?"

I swallowed. "Yes."

"Is this the guy whose T-shirt you offered me the other night?"

I nodded.

"This is the actor you mentioned before…"

I blew some air up into my hair. "Yes."

"Does he *also* happen to be the guy Mia said you're in love with?"

My eyes widened. "She said that?" *I could kill her.*

"She did." Owen smiled guiltily before taking a sip of his water.

"Well, she's exaggerating. It's not love. Maybe infatuation that's gone on way too long." I narrowed my eyes. "What else did Mia tell you?"

"Enough for me to know that no matter how many drinks you have at lunch, you won't be going to the bathroom here." He wriggled his brows.

"Ugh. I'm gonna strangle her." I laughed. "I *am* a bit scared of public bathrooms, yeah."

"I get it." He chuckled. "No judgment."

A waitress came by to take our orders, and we hadn't even looked at the menu yet. So we stopped talking and took some time to peruse the specials. I settled on wild salmon with capers while Owen got the swordfish.

When we were alone again, he fluffed his napkin, placing it on his lap. "So what did this *friend* of yours say to piss you off?"

I guess he's not going to drop it. "He wants me to come out to California to see him before he has to leave for Italy. He'll only be here a few more weeks before he's gone to film for four months."

"How the hell would he expect you to fly out now? Doesn't he know why you're here?"

Well, that feels validating. "He does know why I'm here, but unfortunately he's a narcissist, so…"

Owen shook his head. "Why do you waste time with a guy like that?"

"Old habits can be hard to break. Sometimes we keep toxic people in our lives for no good reason. He's not a bad person. He's just caught up in his fame. He wasn't always like that, which is probably the reason I have a hard time letting go. I remember the person he used to be."

"You say he's not your boyfriend, though."

"No," I clarified. "He never was. In fact, he's been photographed many times with other women, so if he were my boyfriend, we'd have a big problem."

Owen played with his watch. "Do I know this actor?"

I'm sure. "You might."

"You don't want to tell me who he is?"

Is it getting hot in here? "Maybe someday, but not today."

"Okay. Fair enough."

Our food arrived, and thankfully the subject changed. Owen told me about some of the luxury properties he'd sold recently, and I talked about how I'd been managing my casting-agent duties remotely.

After we finished our meal, Owen wiped his mouth and looked at me like he wanted to say something. "I've always wanted to ask you something…" he began.

"Okay."

"The first night we met… If you'd come to town to take care of Heath and Hannah, what were you doing at that bar?"

"Are you judging me?"

"Hell no." He shook his head. "I'm very grateful for that night. Just curious what made you go there."

I sighed. "I'd just gotten into town, and I was stressed about how I was going to handle everything. A friend of my mother's here in the City—a really nice woman named Laurice—came by the apartment and saw how frazzled I was. She's one of those rare people who understands my mother's true colors but somehow stays friends with her anyway. She told me she'd give the kids dinner and look after them for the evening while I went out for a breather. I took advantage of her hospitality—a little too much."

"I should probably thank Laurice, then."

I blushed, and when I looked back up, Owen was staring at me intently.

"I don't get too much time alone with you, so I'm just gonna say this before we both have to go back to work." He lowered his voice and leaned in. "I think about our evening together a lot. Not just for the obvious reasons, but because… I was broken before that. That's something you don't know about me. I'd been unable to feel anything for anyone in a very long time. And you brought me out of that. It was a great night—even if that's all it was, one night. And even if we're never anything more than friends, Devyn, I want you to know you're someone I won't forget."

I said nothing. *Why had he been broken?*

"If you're definitely going back to California, it *is* probably best if we don't date," he added. "You're not the type of girl I'd want to just mess around with and walk away from. You're going through a lot. And you're right, you don't need any more complications. So, I want you to know I respect why you've been hesitant with me. I don't blame you at all."

"Why were you broken, Owen?" I asked. "Did someone hurt you?"

He ran his finger along his glass and shook his head. "It's not as dramatic as that. I don't have a clear answer as to why." He stared off for a moment. "It's been strange watching two of my best friends fall in love while I've been unable to feel anything for anyone, unable to relate to their experiences. I've always kept busy with work, and everyone thinks I just have no time for more in my life." He paused. "But the truth is, there's *always* time for the things you really want."

"So you *want* to find someone to spend your life with?"

"I do. But I'm not in any rush. I couldn't care less if I get married or have kids. But I do want a connection with someone—the right person. It can't be forced, just because you feel like you're at a certain age or need to keep up with your friends." He looked beyond me for a moment. "I think I changed a lot after our friend Ryan passed away. Part of me died with him. And that might have something to do with the funk I'd been in for so long. It made me more apathetic and closed off." Owen shut his eyes for a moment. "All this to say, no one I'd met in all that time did it for me. Until you."

My heart fluttered. Owen and I were more similar than I'd thought. "Marriage and kids are not something I need to be fulfilled, either," I said. "I have a great career that I'm very proud of and don't need all that much more. I get annoyed when people assert that you need to have those things to be happy. I think part of the reason I've hung onto whatever I had going with the actor I told you about is that I haven't wanted anything complicated."

"Have you ever been in love?" Owen asked.

"No. And I don't know if I'm capable, to be honest."

He frowned. "Really?"

"I'd prefer not to get into it right now, but basically my family life—or lack thereof—trained me not to get too attached to anyone."

Owen nodded and didn't push for more. "I've never been in love, either," he said. "All of my friends have been at one time or another. And I've felt happy for them—don't get me wrong. But I've also felt detached from their joy, because of my own hang-ups."

"Well, aren't we just a cheery pair?" I grinned.

He pressed the tips of his fingers together as he leaned his elbows on the table. "It's nice to have an honest conversation with someone. Even if you're not telling me everything, I appreciate how much you've opened up."

I stared over at his masculine hands, trying not to remember the way it had felt when they explored my body.

The waitress came by again. "Can I offer you some dessert?"

"I'm pretty full." Owen turned to me. "We still have time, though. You should get something."

I held out my palm. "I shouldn't…"

The waitress set a piece of paper on the table. "Well, here's the menu just in case."

One glance was all it took. "Actually, yes," I told her. "I would like dessert."

Owen chuckled. "That changed fast."

"Well, there's Key lime pie on the menu. I never turn down Key lime pie. *Ever.*"

"One Key lime pie coming up," the waitress said.

Owen smiled. "You like it that much, huh?"

"It's the one thing I can't say no to."

"Well, maybe I need to take some lessons from Key lime pie," he teased.

A minute later, when she placed the perfect lime-green triangle in front of me with just the right amount of whipped cream, I dug in. I sighed as the tangy concoction entered my mouth. I might also have moaned.

"Wow," Owen murmured. "I have to say, watching you eat that is quite satisfying."

I held out my fork. "Have some."

He shook his head. "There's no way I'll appreciate that bite as much as you will. Please, finish it. I'm enjoying every second."

I gestured with my fork. "Is that like a fetish or something? Watching me eat dessert?"

"I wouldn't have thought so until today…" He grinned mischievously. "But I'm down for pie porn."

I laughed and stuffed another bite into my mouth. I finished every last morsel.

After Owen paid the bill, he checked his phone. "I have a client meeting at two. But damn, I could stay here all day and talk to you. I'd definitely get you another slice of that pie, too."

I stood, wiping my mouth. "Go. You don't want to be late." *And I can't afford to fall for you a second longer.* "I can't thank you enough for lunch."

"It's my pleasure. The fact that you enjoyed it so much was the icing on the Key lime pie." He winked. "Let me call you a car."

"I'm completely capable of the three-block walk back. Plus, I *really* need to walk off the pie now. Is your office far from here?"

"Ten minutes on the subway. There's a station around the corner. Sometimes I drive to work; other days I take the train. Depends on my mood."

"Well…thanks again," I told him awkwardly once we'd stepped outside.

"My pleasure. Thanks for hanging with me." His eyes lingered on mine, and I wondered if he would hug me or something, but instead he simply turned around and walked away.

As I headed home, I realized Owen hadn't asked me out again. It seemed this had been just a casual lunch after all, and he'd officially moved on from the idea of anything happening between us. That was a little unfortunate, because spending time with Owen today had only made me like him more.

❤CHAPTER 7

Devyn

I *think I'm getting the hang of this.*

The last six days had flown by. It had been—dare I say—a good week. Hannah had been accepted into the *PS Idol* contest at school and made friends with a few of the other contestants in the process. Heath had managed to score a ninety on his English test after failing last semester, and I'd taken him to the doctor for a checkup and to get the immunization forms filled out that the school had been bugging us for. God forbid Vera pay attention to things like healthcare and school rules. Even when that woman was around, she didn't prioritize my sister and brother. And in addition to making some inroads with Heath and Hannah, I'd taken on a new client and successfully placed *three* actors in some very promising films this week. All in all, things were looking up.

Until the knock came.

I opened the door to find a woman wearing a beige pantsuit. She adjusted the bulging briefcase hanging from her shoulder and didn't smile.

"Are you Vera Marks?"

I frowned. "No."

The woman looked over my shoulder into the apartment. "Is this the home of Heath Marks?"

Uh-oh. My stomach dropped. *What did he get himself into now?* "It is. And who are you?"

The woman dug into the front of her briefcase and pulled out a business card. "I'm Melinda Rollins, a case worker with the Department of Child Protective Services. And you are?"

I took the card, wishing I hadn't answered the door. But there was no way around her questions now.

"I'm Devyn Marks, Heath's sister. Is everything okay with Heath?"

Ms. Rollins pursed her lips. "I need to speak to your mother. Do you know when she'll be back?"

"Umm... She went away for a while."

"So she left you in charge of Heath and Hannah while she's gone?"

"Yes."

"When exactly will Ms. Marks be back?"

"I'm not sure."

The woman's brows pulled together. "She left you in charge of two children, but she didn't tell you when she would be returning?"

Shit. "Oh. No, I meant I wasn't sure of the *time* she would be back. I'm not sure of the exact time. But she'll be back Sunday."

"So you're staying to mind the children until Sunday?"

I nodded. "Yes."

"I'll come back Monday to speak to Ms. Marks when she returns."

Oh crap. "Can you tell me what this is about? Is Heath in some kind of trouble?" She didn't seem very interested in sharing, so I pushed. "Since I'm keeping an eye on them, I'd like to know if there's something going on."

She nodded. "Heath was truant again last week. Twice."

My eyes bulged. Just when I'd thought I was doing so well... "He cut school *last week*?"

"It's not the first time it's happened. The school attempted to reach Ms. Marks, but apparently her phone number is no longer in service. How long has she been gone?"

"Umm… About a week," I lied.

"That means they were under your supervision when he was truant? Were you aware that Heath missed two days of school last week?"

I frowned. "Yes, they were, and no, I wasn't."

"Would it be okay if I came inside? Took a look around?"

I'd dealt with CPS enough growing up to know that I didn't legally have to let them in. But if I didn't, it would only make things worse. So I forced a smile and stepped back to open the door.

"Of course. Come on in."

Ms. Rollins spent ten minutes nosing around the apartment. Thankfully, I'd tidied up this morning and had gone food shopping yesterday. Because after she asked to see the kids' rooms, she opened the refrigerator and perused the kitchen cabinets. When she was satisfied the kids weren't living in a hovel and eating bread and water, she concluded her visit by taking a picture of my ID and handing me a piece of yellow paper with a bunch of emergency contacts on it. As if I didn't know the number for 911.

"I'll be back on Monday to speak to Ms. Marks."

"Okay. Great. Thank you."

I shut the door behind her and watched her walk down the hall through the peephole. When I could no longer see her, I banged my head against it.

Fuck my life. I have until Monday to find Vera.

I decided to walk up to the school at six o'clock that evening to meet Hannah after *PS Idol* practice. Heath had been working this afternoon, and he would probably get home from the pizza place a few minutes before his sister. I wanted a chance to talk to her alone.

Hannah took two steps out the front door of the school and stopped when she saw me. "Why are you here?"

"I had to run some errands nearby, so I thought we could walk home together."

She shrugged. "Okay."

I asked how her day and *Idol* practice had gone, and then I eased into the questions I needed to ask.

"So, how are you doing otherwise? You must be starting to miss Mom?"

Another shrug. "Not really."

"You know, when I was little and she'd take one of her trips, I used to count the days on the calendar by marking them off with an X. Do you ever do that? Count the days, I mean?"

"Nope."

"Is it because you already have an idea how long it usually takes her to come back?"

"No. I just don't care how long she's gone."

God, she reminds me so much of me at her age. I'd never have admitted that I missed my mother. But back then, I had. Aside from being scared in our apartment at night when I was alone, I always got an unsettled feeling in the pit of my stomach when she'd pull her disappearing acts.

"She's been gone almost a month already," I said. "When I was a kid, she always came back before the seventeenth day. Has she ever taken off for longer than a month?"

"I said I don't count."

"But does this time seem longer than the others to you?"

Hannah stopped walking. "You don't have to stay, if you don't want to. Heath has a job now, so we have money for food."

I shook my head. "Oh no, that's not what I meant, Hannah."

"Then what do you really want to ask? Because it sure sounds like you're itching to get the heck out of here, with so many questions about when Mom's coming back."

I sighed. "I'm sorry if I came off that way. I'm not trying to ditch you. I promise."

"Then what's with all the Vera questions?"

I supposed we were all in this together. "How about if me, you, and your brother talk when we get home? All together?"

"Fine."

I couldn't get more than a shrug or a one-word answer the rest of the walk.

As expected, Heath was already at the apartment when we arrived. I was going to have to deal with him skipping school, but that was a separate conversation. Right now, the priority was finding Vera.

Hannah tossed her backpack on a kitchen chair and spoke to her brother. "Do you make enough money for food and stuff? Devyn said she wants to leave."

"No, that's *not* what I said at all, Hannah." I shook my head. "Can you two please sit down at the table so we can talk?"

Heath pulled a chair out and flipped it around, straddling it backwards. "I make enough for food. I can ask for more hours to try to pay the rent."

I looked over at Hannah, who was still standing. "Can you please sit?"

She rolled her eyes but took a seat at the table.

I sat between them. Beating around the bush with these two only caused them to fill in the blanks with the idea that no one wanted them, so I figured I should shoot straight this time.

"CPS came to the apartment this morning. They wanted to speak to Vera. I was able to buy us some time, but they aren't going to go away. We need to find your mother—our mother. They're coming back in a few days."

"What happens if we can't find her?" Hannah asked.

I didn't want to scare the kids and mention my *four* stints in foster care. "Let's take this one step at a time. Right now we just need to focus on finding her."

"How are we supposed to do that?" Heath asked.

"I don't know. What can you tell me about the new guy she's dating? The one she left with?"

"Bo? He's got a bad accent," Heath said.

"What kind of accent?"

"He sounds like that dude in the *Ted* movies. The one with the stuffed animal that talks."

"Mark Wahlberg?"

"Yeah, I think that's his name. He doesn't say car. He says *ka*." I nodded. "Boston."

Hannah pointed to her brother. "I think he said something about moving there. He fixes trucks, like big eighteen-wheelers. His hands are all cracked, and they always look dirty, but he says they're not. Mom said she wanted to help him decorate his new apartment."

"Do you know Bo's last name?"

Both kids shrugged. "No. He only started coming around a few weeks before Mom left," Heath said.

That sounds about right for Vera. "Alright, well, anything else you can think of about Bo?"

Hannah wrinkled her nose. "He burps a lot, and he strings together the sounds to form words. He thinks it's funny. But it's not."

Sounds like a real peach. Bo the burper from Boston. I had a lot to go on now.

We talked for a little while longer, but neither of them knew much of anything about Bo or the trip Vera had taken with him.

A few hours later, after the kids were in bed, I poured myself a much-needed glass of wine. Heath wandered back into the kitchen as I sipped and took the seat across from me.

"Did CPS come because I cut school?"

"Yeah, buddy, they did. I was going to talk to you about that tomorrow. You can't cut school."

"I did it to work at the pizza place. One of the day guys took off a few days, so I lied and said I didn't have school and could help out. I wanted to pay you back for all the money you've spent since you got here—for food and stuff for me and Hannah."

My heart squeezed. "Oh, Heath. You don't have to do that. It's not your job to support yourself and your sister."

"It's not yours either," he said. "I guess I really screwed things up by not going, huh? Are they going to put us in foster care?"

"Not if I can help it. I promise to do everything in my power to keep that from happening, Heath."

He nodded, but his face was glum. I reached out and covered his hand with mine. "You said you wanted to pay me back for things I bought for you and Hannah. Do you feel like it's okay for you to pay for Hannah's food?"

"Yeah, of course. She's my sister. And she's too young to have a job."

I squeezed his hand. "I feel the same way about both of you."

He looked me in the eyes, but said nothing.

"We're a family," I explained. "We take care of each other. Besides, I promise I'm not hurting for money. I do pretty well for myself. Okay?"

Heath nodded.

"So no more cutting school. Do you promise?"

"Yeah."

I mussed his hair. "Go get some sleep, kiddo."

Once it was quiet again, I couldn't help but reflect back to my own childhood. I'd walk into our apartment each day not knowing what I would find. I'd squirrelled away canned food under my bed so there would be more to eat when Vera inevitably took off the next time. I'd felt like maybe if I was a better kid—smarter, prettier, more helpful around the house—she wouldn't want to leave as much.

I hated that Heath and Hannah were going through the same turmoil. Tears streamed down my face as I thought through the emotions they likely dealt with on a daily basis: abandonment, resentment, fear, unworthiness, disdain. No child should ever be made to feel like they were a burden and unwanted.

It took me a solid ten minutes to get my emotions under control. When I finally did, I decided to wash down the pain with a second glass of wine, but when I got up to go to the fridge, there was a knock at the door.

I looked at the time on my phone. *Nine forty-five.*

God, I really hoped it wasn't CPS again. What if they were coming to remove the kids? What would I do? Should I pretend to be sleeping and not hear it?

Taking a deep breath, I tiptoed to the door and looked through the peephole. I was relieved to find Owen and not Ms. Rollins again.

He held up a brown paper bag when I opened the door. "Key lime pie. I was at the restaurant we went to for lunch last week and thought you might like a piece."

I forced a smile. "You didn't have to do that."

He winked. "I might've hoped you'd let me watch you eat it."

I didn't laugh.

"What's wrong?" Owen scanned my face. "Why were you crying?"

"I wasn't."

He was quiet a moment. "I would imagine uprooting your entire life and being thrown into parenting two kids is tough. I'm here if you want to talk. But I won't push." He held out the brown paper bag. "You can enjoy the pie by yourself in peace."

"Thanks, Owen. It was really thoughtful of you."

"No problem. You have a good night."

He turned to leave, and I started to close the door. But I could really use someone to talk to. And he seemed like a good listener. "Owen, wait…"

He turned back.

I smiled. "Would you like to come in and share the pie?"

The light that filled his eyes was absolutely adorable. "I sure would."

I chuckled. "Come on in."

In the kitchen, I dug two forks from the drawer and pulled the bottle of wine from the refrigerator. "Want a glass?"

"I'd love one."

Owen took the pie out of the bag while I poured our wine. It wasn't until I sat down that I got a good look at what he'd actually brought.

"Oh my God. You brought an *entire* pie?"

He smiled. "I got lucky that they had a full one left to sell."

I licked my lips. "You mean *I* got lucky."

He laughed and grabbed a fork. "Dig in."

"We're not even going to cut it up?"

"Nah. Slices are for quitters."

Owen and I went to town on that Key lime pie. After eating what amounted to probably two big slices, I had to take a break. I leaned back in my chair with my hand on my stomach.

"Oh my God. That was so good."

"Feel better?" he asked.

"Yeah. I really needed that. Your timing is impeccable."

He put down his fork. "Talk to me. What's going on?"

I sighed. "I got emotional thinking about my childhood and what Hannah and Heath must be feeling."

"Tell me about it."

"About what?"

"Your childhood."

My eyes widened. I rarely talked to anyone about my years with Vera. At first I'd been ashamed. But as I got older, I realized I had nothing to be ashamed about—my mother did. But I still didn't open up to many people because I didn't want pity or to be judged. I'd never told Robert how traumatic things had been when I was little. Yet somehow, it felt okay to let Owen in, at least a little bit.

I traced the rim of my wine glass. "When I was nine, my mom started dating a biker named Q. That was all I knew about him—his one-letter name. He wore a black vest with all these patches on it, and had a long ponytail that he tied at his neck and at the bottom. My mom decided to go to bike week with him, so she dumped me at the elderly neighbor's, saying she'd be back in a few hours. But of course, she didn't come back for days."

I glanced up as I continued. "The neighbor let me sleep on her couch for the night, but the next morning, she said my mother better be back because she had things to do. I pretended to go next door and check, then returned and told her my mother was back. She didn't care enough to check whether a nine-year-old was telling the truth or not, so I decided I could manage myself for a few days. That was the first time Vera took off, at least that I can remember. I guess because I wasn't ten yet, she still thought she had an obligation to mother me, so she left me with the neighbor and not alone."

I paused and looked away, picturing our apartment back then. "We lived on the second floor of a four-story apartment building in Chicago. It was next to a parking lot that had a big tree in the corner. At night, the branches would hit the side of our building, and stray cats would fight and cry. It scared the living crap out of me. After a few days, I learned that if I rolled tissue into tight balls and stuck them in my ears, it helped drown out the sound. To this day, I sleep with earplugs."

Owen shook his head. "How long was she gone?"

"Nine days. She came home the day *after* my tenth birthday."

"Jesus. That's young to be alone that long. Did you tell anyone?"

"Nope. I was afraid I'd get in trouble. I never told anyone when she'd disappear. I hid it as best as I could and covered for her. Sometimes an adult who gave two shits figured it out and CPS would come. Then I'd be stuck in foster care for a while until my mom came back and reclaimed me."

"Why do they keep giving a child back to a mother who abandons her for weeks at a time?"

"Sometimes they'd keep me for a while, and Vera would have to come visit and stuff. But then she'd take a parenting class, or go to counseling, and eventually they'd give me back." I shrugged. "The system isn't great. And sadly, there were kids far worse-off than me—abusive parents, drug addicts who lived on the streets. Vera knew how to play the game and turn on the charm when she had to."

Owen nodded. "Did something in particular cause you to get upset tonight? Or just the circumstances in general?"

I sighed. "CPS came by today. Apparently Heath cut school a few times last week, and they couldn't get in touch with Vera, so they called social services. The case worker wants to speak to his mother. I blew her off today, saying Vera was on a planned trip. But the woman wanted the exact date she'd be back. I told her Sunday. So now I need to find my mother and drag her ass home by then, because CPS is coming back Monday."

"Shit."

"Yeah…"

"What are we going to do?"

I couldn't help but smile. "*We*? That's kind of you, but it's not your problem."

"I want to help."

"I can't ask you to do that."

"You didn't ask. I'm offering. My dad was a cop. Maybe he could help us find her. Plus, I'm good at finding a needle in a haystack. Ask my clients."

Warmth spread through my chest. Just the fact that he *wanted* to help endeared him to me. But this was my problem. "I really appreciate the offer, Owen, but I'm good."

"Do you have any idea where Vera might be?"

"The kids said her new boyfriend is a truck mechanic. They think he got a new job in Boston, and that might be where they went. But my mom's cell phone is disconnected. Sometimes she gets a prepaid for a month or two, but it always winds up getting turned off because she doesn't pay the bill."

"Why don't we road trip up to Boston?"

"I'm not even sure that's where they were going, and I have no clue what the guy's last name is. Is Bo even a real first name, or is it short for something? What would I do, just walk around yelling *Bo*?"

Owen smiled. "I have a car. I can drive, and you could hang your head out the window and yell."

I chuckled. "I'm hoping it doesn't come to that and she miraculously shows up in the next few days."

"Well, if it does come to that, you know where to find me."

"Thank you."

A little while later I yawned, and Owen took the hint. "I should get going."

"Okay."

I walked him to the door, but he stalled in the doorway.

"Thank you for the pie," I said. "And the ear."

"Anytime."

"You're a good friend, Owen."

He winked. "I could be that *and* more—doesn't have to be one or the other."

The offer was more tempting than ever. But I had to steel myself. "Goodnight, Owen."

He leaned down and kissed my cheek. "'Night, beautiful."

❤️CHAPTER 8

Owen

As usual, the following night I was the last one to show up for our monthly apartment building board meeting, which was really just an excuse for us guys to catch up over drinks. Although, there was typically some actual business on the agenda—just not as much business as general debauchery.

Colby, Holden, and Brayden were seated at a table at L-Bar when I strolled in.

"Hey." I pulled out a chair and sat down. "Sorry I'm late."

"Is you being the last to show up anything new?" Brayden chided as he perused a menu. "Happens every damn time."

"I guess not." I turned to Holden, who had bags under his eyes. "How's Hope? I ran into Lala in the hallway the other day. She told me the baby has her first cold."

"Toughest week of my life. But thank God, she's getting better. Still a little stuffy, though. It's been hard watching her struggling to breathe." Holden exhaled. "We hadn't been getting good sleep before the cold—she's been a night owl from day one—but that was even worse."

"A night owl like her daddy, right?" I smacked him on the back. "I thought your years of partying would've prepared you for staying up all night, drummer boy."

"Mav went through that no-sleep phase, too," Colby said. "But thankfully he's doing pretty well now."

"Okay, enough of the *Daddy Day Care* shit. It's boring to the single guys among us," Brayden teased.

I took advantage of a rare lull in conversation to hand Colby something.

"Hey, Devyn gave me this rent check for you. She was on the way down to your place, but I told her I'd be seeing you anyway."

"Okay." He tucked it into his pocket. "What's the deal with that situation? Where the hell did their mother go that Devyn had to fly in to stay with those kids?"

I exhaled. "It's bad, man. She's basically MIA."

"You seem to know the ins and outs of that situation in four-ten, Owen," Brayden noted. "Something you want to tell us?"

I realized my side conversation with Colby just now hadn't been so private.

Holden cracked up behind his beer bottle.

Brayden looked at Holden and me. "What the hell is so funny?"

I'd put off filling Brayden and Colby in on my history with Devyn long enough. Holden was the only one who knew the story of how I had really first met her. By some miracle he'd kept my secret all this time, but Holden was known for having a big mouth. So it was only a matter of time before he'd end up spilling the truth if I didn't.

A waitress came by and took my drink order, but when she left, the guys were still staring at me, waiting for an explanation.

I filled them in on the Vera situation first. "Here's the deal. Vera Marks took off. She left with some guy, and no one knows where the hell she is. She did the same thing to Devyn when she was younger, multiple times, and Devyn ended up in foster care. The whole thing is very messed up."

"Shit," Colby muttered.

"So, wait…" Holden said. "She may never come back?"

"In the past, she's always returned after a while. We just don't know when it will be this time."

I was using *we* again.

Brayden raised a brow. "*We*? You seem very invested, Owen." *Of course, he caught that.* I glared at him. "I'll get to that."

"Oh?" Brayden's eyes widened. "I'm intrigued."

The waitress put my beer in front of me. She also set down a plate of assorted appetizers.

I took a long sip and continued. "Anyway, Devyn had been living in L.A., and her brother called and filled her in on their situation. That's what prompted Devyn to come out here. She's not babysitting them as a favor. This was more like an emergency."

Colby shook his head. "Holy crap, that's terrible."

"Well, it actually gets worse," I said. "Heath skipped school more than once recently, so Child Protective Services showed up at their place. Devyn had to basically lie to them and say the mom is on vacation until Monday. But the truth is, we have no idea when and if she's ever coming back."

Holden frowned. "Damn, I knew those kids were trouble, but I never imagined how bad it was. That explains a lot. I really feel bad for them."

"Yeah. History is repeating itself. The woman is not capable of being responsible." I took another drink of my beer. "Devyn has a lead that she might be in Boston, though. So I offered to road trip it up there with her to see if we can locate Vera before CPS comes back."

Brayden pointed his bottle at me. "Wait a minute. Hold up. You need to back up, dude. Why would you offer to go to Boston with her if you barely know her? Something is missing here…"

Holden snorted, and I shot daggers at him.

"Can I please do the honors?" Holden asked. "I've been good for so long. Don't I deserve it?"

Rolling my eyes, I leaned back in my seat and crossed my arms. "Go ahead. Tell them. I know you're dying to."

Holden leaned in and paused for effect before blurting it out. "Owen and Devyn had a one-night stand." He sat back to enjoy the aftermath of the bomb he'd just dropped.

Brayden blinked. "What?"

"When?" Colby asked, just as stunned as Brayden.

"Before I knew she lived in the building," I said. "It was a complete coincidence. I met her at a bar. We had amazing chemistry, which then...carried over to the hotel next door."

Colby gaped, and Brayden's jaw dropped.

I relayed a bit more about that night, including how Devyn had taken off on me. I also explained how I'd told Holden the truth at the hospital after running into Devyn, when I'd gone to issue the noise complaint.

Brayden's reaction was exactly as I'd expected.

"Are you kidding me?" he raged. "When I was taking my shot with her at Colby's that day, you let me make a fool of myself, knowing you'd already slept with her?"

I gritted my teeth. "It wasn't like I was trying to set you up. This has nothing to do with you. I just didn't feel like kissing and telling about this one."

Colby narrowed his eyes. "We tell each other everything. What's different about this? What's the big secret?"

I hesitated. "I don't know exactly. I guess I feel protective of her or something. I didn't want to cheapen it by bragging. I was a little ashamed of the way she ghosted me, too." I stared down at my bottle. "It also didn't feel like *just* a one-night stand—Lord knows I've had those before. Then once I found out she lived in our building, it became about protecting her privacy more than anything else."

Colby nodded. "Okay. Fair enough."

Brayden laughed. "I wondered why you looked like you wanted to kill me that day you saw me talking to her at Colby's."

"You're right. I did want to kill you. But I understood that you didn't know what was going on. You were never in danger of getting punched."

"You're lucky I'm not interested in her anyway," he huffed.

I smacked him on the arm. "Oh yeah? You're too good for her now, asshole?"

"No." Brayden brushed some lint off his shirt. "But I'm turning over a new leaf."

Holden stopped drinking mid-sip. "What the hell are you talking about?"

"I've actually found myself attracted to…a more *mature* woman lately." He tossed a jalapeño popper into his mouth.

"Devyn is very mature," I defended.

"She's too young," he said with his mouth full.

Is he serious? "She's not that much younger than us," I pointed out.

"Yeah, but I'm finding that the women around our age, mid-to-late twenties, early thirties even, tend to be superficial and immature, in general."

"Is that so?" Colby raised a brow.

Holden chuckled. "When did this come about?"

"Let's just say I have secrets of my own." Brayden winked.

Colby slammed his bottle down. "Jesus. Both of you are shady lately."

When Brayden refused to divulge anything more, the subject returned to Devyn and me.

"So what's the deal?" Colby asked. "Why aren't you dating her now if you had such a great night together?"

"I don't have a clear answer for you. I do really like her. And you know I don't say that very often."

"You really like her. That's your reason for not dating her?" Colby asked.

"There's a *but* in there somewhere," Holden prodded. "Spill it."

"Things are complicated with her life right now, and the last thing I wanna do is complicate things for her more. That's all there is to it."

"So why are you offering to go to Boston with her?" Colby asked.

"Because I want to help her."

"I'm calling bullshit." Brayden laughed. "I think you want to *help her* right into another hotel room."

I rolled my eyes. "Maybe in the back of my mind, I wouldn't mind if that happened… But whether you believe me or not, that's *not* my motivation. Sorry if you don't think I'm a decent-enough person to just help someone who has a lot on her shoulders right now." I sighed. "Anyway, she may not take me up on my offer."

"You know what I think?" Brayden looked at me skeptically. "I think you're being cautious because of *you*, not her."

"Really?" I rested my chin on my hand. "Enlighten me, since you seem to think you know me better than I know myself."

"She's only here temporarily. You know she's leaving. So you're being overly cautious because *you* don't want to get hurt."

That was certainly Devyn's rationale, but I wasn't ready to get into this. "Think what you want," I told him. I downed some of my beer before reaching for a mozzarella stick.

Colby looked around the table. "Anyone else got skeletons to pull out of their closet tonight?"

Brayden and I looked at each other and chuckled.

Holden smacked his hand on the table. "If not, let's get this meeting over with. I have a sniffly baby girl waiting at home for kisses from Daddy."

On the way back to my apartment that evening, I debated whether I should stop by Devyn's to see if there were any updates on Vera. I decided to check in, and the moment she opened the door, I could tell from the stressed look on her face that things hadn't changed.

"Hey." She stepped aside. "Come in."

"How are you?" I asked.

"Long day." She let out an exasperated breath. "I've been trying to get some work done, and the kids were fighting at dinner, but thankfully they're in their rooms now doing homework." She looked up at me with tired eyes.

"I take it nothing's changed in terms of the situation with your mom?"

"No. Unfortunately, I'm no closer to knowing what the hell to tell CPS on Monday."

"Well, the offer still stands about Boston. I'm not gonna bug you about it, but I'm ready to go when you are."

"I appreciate you wanting to help, Owen." Then she changed the subject. "How was your board meeting?"

"Like it always is, mostly an excuse to drink together and bust each other's chops—eighty-percent bullshitting and twenty-percent going over building business." I paused. "Actually..." I cleared my throat. "I should let you know that I chose to tell the guys about the night we met. Up until tonight, only Holden knew."

She looked at me blankly. "Oh..."

Unable to read her, I continued. "Brayden clearly had his eye on you, so I thought he should know what happened between us. But mainly, it's difficult for me to hide things from these guys. They're like my brothers, and they can pretty much always tell when something's up with me. I didn't mention it to brag. I need you to know that. When I handed the check to Colby, he asked about your situation, and that led to a discussion of why you and I seemed...closer than strangers." I tried to gauge her reaction. "I didn't want to lie."

"I get it." She nodded. "I tell Mia everything, too. I wouldn't expect you to not open up to your closest friends." She shrugged. "We're both adults. There's nothing to be ashamed of."

"Well, thank you for understanding."

She nodded but didn't say anything further.

"I should probably get out of your way. I just wanted to check in and say hello."

To my surprise, her expression dampened. She tucked a piece of her hair behind her ear. "I was going to put on a movie and unwind. Would you want to watch it with me?"

Bingo. My heart rate quickened. "That sounds nice, yeah."

"I still have the rest of the pie you brought me in the fridge. You can help me finish it off?"

That made me think about how much I wanted to finish *her* off right now. Pie would have to do. I nodded. "That sounds great."

"I'll get the pie and two forks." She winked.

After a moment, I followed Devyn over to the couch in her living room. She set the pie on the coffee table and fiddled with the remote to try to find the streaming channel. She kept landing on either cable TV or another setup screen.

"I take it you don't watch TV all that much?" I teased.

"How did you ever tell?" She laughed.

"Wild guess." I reached for the remote. "Let me?" I navigated over to the right menu and pulled up Netflix before handing the remote back. "That setup is just like mine, so I know it like the back of my hand; although, I can't remember the last time I sat through a movie. Most of the time, I'm so tired after work that I end up falling asleep."

"Yeah, sadly I can't remember the last time I finished a movie either. I don't know if it's my attention span lately due to all the distractions, or just pure exhaustion." She offered me back the remote. "You pick."

"Well, I won't take it personally if you fall asleep." I chuckled, scrolling through the options. "Anything you're in the mood for?"

"Just nothing too heavy or with too much violence."

I moved the cursor along the most-popular list. There was a romantic thriller sitting at number three that looked like something we could both get into.

I stopped on it. "What about this one?"

She leaned in to get a better look. Her face reddened. "Uh, any one but that one, please."

"Okay…" I arched a brow. "You're not into romantic thrillers or…"

When she didn't say anything, I looked back at the image of the actor in the thumbnail—good-looking guy with dark blond hair and striking blue eyes.

Ahhh… "It's him, isn't it?"

She nodded.

Robert Valentino.

Now I had a face and a name for the "secret actor" I'd been detesting.

And I also had a name for the unwelcome feeling in my chest: jealousy.

❤CHAPTER 9

Devyn

"What's this?" I asked.

Heath shrugged. "I don't know. I just found it on the floor by the front door."

I took the manila envelope with my name written across the front and tossed it on the kitchen counter. If someone didn't want to hand it to me in person, it might not be good news. It could wait until the kids left for school. They didn't need anything more to worry about. Heath had asked me a dozen times if I'd heard from Vera since CPS showed up, and Hannah had been quieter than usual. Clearly, they were both worried about what might happen when social services returned.

Once I was alone, I tore into the envelope. Inside, a thick packet of papers had been stapled together with a sticky note on top.

I'll drive.
X
Owen

The first page was a map, with a highlighted yellow route and a ton of black Xs marked. Confused, I fingered through the rest of the pile. My heart squeezed when I realized it was a printout of all the truck-mechanic shops in the greater Boston area. At the bottom of one of the pages, I noticed a timestamp at the corner—*2:12 AM.* Owen must've stayed up all night putting this together. I wasn't sure if it was his kindness or my frayed nerves, but I got a little choked up.

I swallowed and grabbed my phone, checking for the millionth time to see if Vera had called or texted. Of course, she hadn't. My cell was still in my hand when it vibrated with an incoming message.

Owen: Morning, sunshine. I slipped something under your door before I left for the office.

I smiled and texted back.

Devyn: I just opened it. That was sweet of you to put together.

Owen: FYI, I looked at the websites of a few of the places. A lot of them aren't open on Saturdays and Sundays. So we'd have to go tomorrow. I figure if we leave at four AM, we could beat traffic on our way up and be back by early evening so the kids aren't alone too long after school. And I can ask Colby to stop at the apartment in the morning, to make sure they actually *go* and don't play hooky.

The man had thought of everything. When he'd first suggested going to Boston to search for Vera, it had sounded outlandish. It was a damn big city. But with the clock ticking and seeing how nicely he'd organized a plan of attack, I was starting to feel like it wasn't so crazy.

Devyn: Don't you have to work tomorrow?

He typed back almost immediately.

Owen: Came in early this morning to get shit done, just in case.

I chewed on my fingernail. I'd always hated to take favors from others. I prided myself on my independence, but deep down I suspected that was less about needing to be self-sufficient and more my inability to trust others because my mother always let me down. Yet for some reason, I wasn't nervous about Owen disappointing me, even though I didn't know him that well. My heart told me he was reliable. That thought—that I wouldn't mind relying on someone a little—scared me the most.

Devyn: Can I let you know later?

Owen: Of course. Have a good day.

After that, I forced the thoughts of Vera out of my mind because my schedule was jam-packed. I had three video calls with producers looking for fresh talent, and a script I needed to read in order to put together a pitch for roles. Before I knew it, it was almost time for the kids to come home, and I still needed to run down to the grocery store and grab a few things to make dinner. So I gathered up the papers strewn all over the kitchen table and shut down my laptop.

In the elevator, I scrolled through my cell. There were half-a-dozen text messages from actors I represented. As I went to open the top one, a new message arrived. I smiled seeing it was Owen. We were on the same wavelength.

Owen: What's your favorite junk food? I'm picking up some road-trip snacks in case we go tomorrow. I can't drive without a bag of Swedish Fish and a pound of wasabi peanuts. Are you sweet or salty?

Before I could reply, another message came in.

Owen: Oooh. They have Pop Corners—kettle corn flavored. My favorite. Though I better get two bags, because I don't share this shit.

My smile widened. I was a road-trip-snack girl, too.

Devyn: Never tried Pop Corners but I love Swedish Fish.

A few seconds later, a picture arrived. I clicked on it and a snapshot of a very full basket of crap popped up. There had to be twenty different snacks in there—chips, chocolate, candy, nuts.

I chuckled as I typed.

Devyn: Umm...how long is this trip? A month?

Owen: I might be driving to Canada and back if you decide you don't want to find Vera. I'll need an excuse to eat all this shit.

Another text popped up.

Owen: So are you in? Or do I need to pack my passport for tomorrow?

Monday was barreling down on me, and I really needed to try *something*. My wait-and-hope approach wasn't working out too well. And let's face it, my hesitancy was more about me being afraid of getting close to Owen than anything else, and I shouldn't let anything stand in the way of finding Vera. My sister and brother needed her back home. So I took a deep breath and typed.

Devyn: Think you have room in that basket for Reese's Pieces?

Another photo arrived a few minutes later. Owen smiled in a selfie with a *five-pound* bag of Reese's Pieces. His message was underneath.

Owen: Meet you in the lobby at 4 AM.

"I got one." Owen waved a Twizzler at me as he drove. We'd been playing a game I'd dubbed *Guess Which Buddy*, for the last hour. "In fifth grade, we had to do a creative writing project where we made up a story about Santa Claus. One of the guys wrote about Santa leaving Mrs. Claus for a hotter, younger woman, who was secretly a disciple of the Grinch and replaced all the toys he delivered with ugly brown turtleneck sweaters knitted by grandmothers."

"Oh my God." I laughed. "That had to be Holden. Only because there's a hot woman involved."

Owen smiled. "Nope. That was me. My grandmother knitted me a lot of itchy sweaters. I hated them, but my mother made me wear one whenever we visited. Meanwhile, Holden's grandmother bought him shit like an electric keyboard and a Nintendo 64."

I laughed. "You guys must've been some crew growing up. I bet the girls went crazy when you walked into places all together."

"Are you saying you think my friends are *hot*, Devyn?"

"I'm pretty sure you must know that already. I can't imagine that any of you struggled to get dates."

Owen glanced over at me. "I'm sure you didn't, either."

I sighed. "I actually didn't have many boyfriends growing up. My mom brought home so many random men, and they all used her for one thing or another. They'd be around for a few weeks, and then my mom was always sad when they'd disappear without warning. And half the time they left with whatever cash she had in her wallet. So I assumed that's the way all men were. Made me not very interested."

He frowned. "Do you still feel like that?"

"No, I've been lucky enough to have some good examples of stand-up men in my life. Remember the producer I told you about? The one who guided me toward casting and was my first official client when I went out on my own?"

"Yeah…"

"Well, he's like family. He's thirty years older than me and has been married to the same woman since he was nineteen. I've learned a lot from him, and not just about the movie industry."

"Would it be too intrusive if I asked about your dad? Do you have any contact with him?"

I shook my head. "His name is Rick. He took off when my mom told him she was pregnant."

"So you've never met him?"

"I did once. I was maybe seven or eight. My mom and I were in the supermarket. Some guy with a long beard walked up to us and said hello. My mom turned to me and said, very matter-of-factly, 'Devyn, this is your deadbeat father who doesn't support you.' I remember they talked for a minute or two, and then he looked at me, shrugged, and said, 'Have a good life, kid. Try not to grow up and be like your mother.' And that was that. My mother never talked about it with me, and I never mentioned it again."

"That's fucked up."

"At least he gave me good advice. I spent the next twenty years trying to be *nothing* like Vera."

Owen's navigation system interrupted, telling us to get off at the next exit for our first truck-mechanic shop. We had thirty-eight places plotted on the paper map he'd marked up. Five miles from the highway, we pulled into shop number one. It was a bit off the beaten path, but the big trucks parked all over required a lot of space, and downtown Boston was expensive.

Owen and I went in together. The guy at the front counter had a cigarette hanging between his lips, and the nearby ashtray was overflowing. He didn't look up when I said hello.

"Is there any chance you have someone working here named Bo?" I asked.

"Nope. No Bo."

"Is it possible you might know a truck mechanic with that name?"

The guy raised his head and frowned. "What do I look like? A directory? No, I don't know no Bo, and there ain't one who works here. Anything else?"

I sighed. "No. Thank you for your time."

The guy manning the desk at the second shop was a lot friendlier, but he didn't know Bo either. By lunchtime, we'd hit sixteen shops, and I was starting to feel like this trip was a big waste of time.

"Don't get discouraged," Owen said. "We'll find them."

I appreciated his positivity, but he didn't have a lifetime of experience trying to find Vera. The woman disappeared better than a magician.

We spent the next four hours following the map from stop to stop. A few places weren't in business anymore, and by three o'clock we only had one left to visit.

We went inside, but I felt defeated before we even spoke to anyone. Owen must've sensed it, because he spoke to the guy behind the desk this time, instead of me.

"Hey. How's it going? We're looking for a mechanic named Bo."

"What did he do? Did your rig break down?"

Owen shook his head. "No. Nothing like that. We just need to talk to him. It's personal, actually."

The guy nodded. "Bo's off today."

My eyes widened. "But he works here?"

"Are you looking for Bo Ridge?"

"We're not sure of his last name," I said. "Did he start recently?"

"About a week and a half ago. Maybe two?"

"Is there any chance you saw a woman with him? Her name is Vera."

"Didn't catch a name, but there's a blonde that drops him off and picks him up sometimes. Came at lunch the other day. I'm pretty sure they boinked in the car. She was sitting on his lap in the front seat, and that hunk of junk they drive was rocking away."

That sounds like Vera...

"Was she thin, with too much makeup and a ton of bracelets?"

"Not sure about the bracelets, but skinny with makeup fits the bill."

"When does Bo work next?"

"Tomorrow morning. Eight AM. We're open a half day on Saturdays."

I sighed. "Is there any chance you could call him for us, or give us his number?"

The guy pursed his lips.

"Please?" I said. "It's really important that I get in touch with them."

He gave a curt nod before rummaging through a file cabinet and pulling out a stack of papers. I peeked over as he removed one from the pile, trying to read upside-down chicken scribble while the guy scanned the one-page application with his finger. Halfway down, his pointer stopped at a telephone number. He tapped twice before dialing the number from his desk phone on speaker.

But it didn't even ring. Instead, the call went right to an automated message saying the number had been disconnected.

He frowned. "It worked the day after he came in to apply. I used it to call and tell him he could have the job on a probationary basis."

"Maybe you dialed wrong?"

The guy frowned, but he disconnected and punched in the numbers again. This time, I watched what he entered and checked the digits against the paper. He'd dialed right, but the automated message came on once again.

"Guess it was disconnected?" He shrugged.

If the description of the skinny blonde who'd boinked him in the car at lunch wasn't enough to identify Vera, the turned-off phone clinched it. This was my mother's MO.

"Do you have an address?" I asked.

He looked down at the page and shook his head. "He was staying at a motel when he filled out his application. Said he was waiting to hear if he'd gotten an apartment."

"Do you know what motel?"

"No, but it wouldn't do you any good. He's not there anymore. He moved into the new place a few days ago. Was supposed to give me the address to update my records, but he didn't yet."

I sighed. "Alright. Would it be okay if I called him here tomorrow, on your shop's phone?"

"As long as you don't make it too long. He's got a lot of work to do. We're backed up."

"Can I get your telephone number?"

The guy slipped a card from a holder and handed it to me.

"Thank you so much for your help."

Outside, Owen raised his hand for me to high five. "We did it!"

I slapped with a smile. "I cannot believe this worked. I don't know how to thank you, Owen."

"No thanks necessary. But do you think it's a good idea to leave and call in the morning? Then you're relying on your mother to make her way back to New York in less than forty-eight hours."

My exuberance waned. "You're right. I wasn't thinking. Getting in touch with her is only half the battle. She's not like a normal mom who would run home when I tell her the kids might get put in foster care. That might be a reason for her *not* to run home. In her warped mind, knowing someone else has them is license to keep flitting around. I might need to drag her back. But I also can't leave the kids alone tonight."

Owen thought for a moment. "Why don't we set you up at a hotel nearby, and I'll go back and stay with the kids?"

"I can't let you do that. Plus, I'm not sure how Hannah would feel about you staying at the apartment."

"You could go home, and I could stay and talk to Bo?"

I blew out two cheeks of air and shook my head. "I'm not exaggerating when I say she might need to be dragged home. I think it has to be me."

"I have an idea." Owen put up a finger. "Hang on a minute. Let me make a quick call." He slipped his cell out of his pocket and fiddled with the screen for a few seconds before bringing it to his ear. I listened to one side of a conversation.

"Hey. What's up, buddy?"

Pause.

"Listen, I need a big favor. Do you think Hannah and Heath can crash with you tonight? Hannah really likes Billie and the kids, so I think she'll be fine with it. If she's not, invite Holden to come hang for an hour or two—that'll seal the deal."

Another pause.

"Yeah, everything is fine. Devyn and I are in Boston. We thought it would be a day trip, but turns out we need to stay the night."

A few seconds later, Owen smiled.

"Thanks, buddy. I'll text you the plan for getting them after Devyn lets them know."

Owen swiped his phone off and looked at me.

"Problem solved. Probably better if we have four hands anyway, in case we need to tie Vera up and carry her home. Plus, I don't like the idea of leaving you alone around here."

My heart started to race. "So we're staying overnight... together?"

A smile curled the ends of Owen's lips. "Yep. You're one lucky girl."

❤CHAPTER 10

Devyn

After Owen and I stopped at a Target to pick up a change of clothes, we arrived at a hotel downtown, hoping they could accommodate us.

The girl at the desk checked the system to see their availability. She clicked on some keys. "We do have a room."

"Actually," Owen corrected. "As I said, we need *two* rooms."

Her eyes widened. "Two separate rooms?"

Owen nodded. "Yes."

"I'm sorry. I assumed you were together and must've heard you wrong." She tilted her head. "Business trip?"

"Something like that," he answered.

The girl batted her lashes at Owen and was suddenly extra enthusiastic to help us. I imagined he got hit on like this everywhere he went.

"Okay." She tapped on some keys. "We do have two separate rooms next door to each other. Will that work?"

He turned to me with a serious look on his face. "Is that far enough away from me?"

I elbowed him. "That's perfect." Turning to her, I asked, "Can you put them on two separate cards, though?"

"No." He held his palm out. "What are you doing?"

"I want to pay for mine," I said, reaching into my purse. "Actually, you're helping me, so I should pay for both of them."

He shoved my wallet away. "This whole thing was my idea, Devyn. I got it. I'm not letting you pay."

While I hated feeling like I owed him, it seemed he wasn't going to take no for an answer. "Thank you," I told him, putting my wallet back inside my bag.

"No need to thank me. I'm just glad I didn't have to leave you here."

Goose bumps peppered my skin. I couldn't imagine scouring Boston alone looking for my mother. As much as I'd resisted this trip in the beginning, I knew I'd made the right decision.

The girl handed me my key and Owen his. "If you need anything at all…" she said, looking at him. "My name is Colleen. I'm on until midnight. And more importantly, I'm *off after* midnight."

"Thank you," he replied, seeming unaffected by her proposition.

"That woman deserves to be punched," I whispered as we walked toward the elevators.

Owen laughed. "She wasn't very subtle, huh?"

"Just because we aren't sleeping in the same bed doesn't mean we're not together." I quickly corrected myself. "I mean, we're *not* together, but *she* doesn't know that."

"Yeah, that was a little brazen. Kind of reminds me of a spitfire I met one night not too long ago who told me very clearly what she wanted."

I blushed, realizing he was referring to me. "It was unlike me to let loose…to that extent."

We stepped into the elevator. "Well, I'm glad you took me along for the ride, even if it was only a fleeting moment." He pressed the number for our floor. "I'm sorry if I made you uncomfortable by bringing it up."

I tucked my hair behind my ear. "You didn't."

The elevator doors opened, and we stepped out onto our floor.

"What do you say after we drop our stuff, we find the best restaurant around here and go out for a nice dinner?" Owen suggested. "Make the best of this?"

"That's tempting, but I sort of feel like just crashing in the hotel room," I told him. "I'm so exhausted from this day. Can we do takeout instead?"

"Of course. I'll go pick something up while you relax."

"Are you disappointed we're not going out?" I asked as we walked down the hall.

"I spend my life in restaurants with clients, Devyn. A low-key dinner here with you sounds even better."

After we located our rooms, Owen went to his to drop off his stuff. After a minute I heard a knock, but not at the front door. Our rooms were not only next to each other, but there was a door that adjoined them.

He joined me to look at the spectacular Boston skyline outside the window in my room.

"Wow, this is really beautiful," I said.

"It is," he agreed, although in the reflection of the glass, I could see him looking at *me*, not the skyline.

Knowing that he was going to be right next door made me nervous, but I wouldn't have wanted it any other way.

"Anything in particular you want to eat?" he asked.

I shrugged. "Surprise me."

"Seriously? No requests? The world is your oyster, Devyn." He smiled. "The North End isn't too far from here. They have great Italian."

"No requests. I'm feeling indecisive, but I have no food allergies or anything. So anything will be great. Literally the only thing I don't like is ginger. You know, the pickled kind they put on the side of sushi? That makes me want to vomit."

He laughed. "Okay, I'll steer clear of pickled ginger."

After he left to go pick up food, I called to talk to Heath and Hannah for a minute before taking a long, hot shower. I needed it after this day. I felt spoiled having this alone time in a beautiful hotel room while an even more beautiful man went out and bought me dinner. It made me realize just how crappily men had treated me in the past. This feeling should not have been so foreign.

After my shower, I lay in bed, wearing the pajamas I'd bought at Target and feeling grateful. I turned on the TV, wondering how pathetic it would be if Owen came back to find me totally asleep—I was *that* tired.

As I started to doze off in the comfy bed, my phone rang.

Robert.

I picked up. "Hi."

"Hey, babe. What's going on? I haven't heard from you. I thought you might've changed your mind about coming out here by now."

I sat up against the headboard. "Sorry to burst your bubble, but no. Nothing has changed. I won't be able to make it out there."

"What are you up to tonight?" he asked.

"I'm in Boston, actually."

"What are you doing there? I thought you couldn't travel," he pointed out, his tone bitter.

"It's not a trip for fun. I'm here because I got a lead that my deadbeat mother might be here with her boyfriend, and I'm trying to locate her before CPS takes my brother and sister away. Heath and Hannah are staying with my neighbors."

"Oh, damn. Okay. Are you alone there?"

"No. My friend is here helping me. We think we found where her boyfriend works. But we have to wait until morning to confront him."

"What friend is this?"

"His name is Owen."

He paused. "Owen, huh?"

"Yeah."

"Does this Owen have anything to do with why you're not out here in my bed right now?"

"No." I swallowed. "We're just friends."

"Are you at a hotel?"

"Yes."

"Is he sleeping in the same room as you?"

"No, we have separate rooms."

"And this guy helping you has no ulterior motive?"

"Believe it or not, Robert, there are some men in this world who don't just want sex from me." I rolled my eyes.

"I don't just want sex from you. I can get sex anywhere."

"Classy," I muttered.

"Sorry. I didn't mean it to come out that way." He sighed. "Anyway, I don't know if I buy that this guy has pure intentions, no matter what you say."

"What if he *was* more? You and I are not exclusive anyway. Lord knows you certainly haven't been monogamous."

"You don't trust me to be, remember? I *wanted* you to be my girlfriend. You've said no every time I asked you."

"That would be a recipe for disaster. You know you wouldn't be able to be faithful with all the traveling you do. And you're right. I don't trust you. Because you've never given me a reason to."

"I can't believe I'm gonna go to Italy without seeing you first."

"Well, you claim you're too busy to fly out to see me, so it can't mean that much to you."

"I told you, I have press every single day out here."

"People can always change plans and make time for the things that matter to them."

"Exactly. Which is why I'd hoped you'd come out here—for even a day." He let out a long breath. "Look, you *do* matter to me, Devyn. I know I have a strange way of showing it sometimes. But you're one of the rare people I trust. You knew the real me before I blew up. Why do you think I haven't been able to let you go, no matter how much has changed? The one constant in my life is that I want you in it."

My body tightened as I fought against being manipulated. "You only want me on your terms, Robert. That will never work. *We* won't ever work."

"You say that, and yet you always come back to me, even if I only get you for a week of amazing sex… You *always* come back, Devyn. What does that say?"

"That I'm not very smart and perhaps need to work on myself to avoid such bad decisions." I ran a hand through my hair. "That's clearly gotten me nowhere."

He was silent for a moment. "I'll let you go. You don't sound too happy to hear from me anyway. Good luck trying to find your mother. I mean that. I hope you locate her so you come back before I have to leave. That would be amazing."

Always about him. "Thank you. Have a good night." I hung up and threw my phone aside.

As always, talking to Robert put me in a pissy mood. But that was overshadowed by the realization that Owen should have been back a long time ago. He'd been gone for well over an hour. I assumed he hadn't gone to Timbuktu for the food. Even stranger, when I texted him, he didn't respond. That was certainly not like him.

A half hour later, I heard him enter his room next door. I jumped off my bed and went over to find him looking frazzled, holding a large paper bag and…a pie?

I covered my mouth. "Oh my God. What did you do?"

"Well, unfortunately our food might be cold. When I went to pick it up, I walked by this bakery. I decided to go in to see if they had Key lime pie. They did, but when the woman took the pie from the display, it slipped out of her hands and fell on the floor. I told her not to worry about it, but she insisted that the chef could whip me up a new one. It took forty-five minutes, and my phone died in the midst of it, so I couldn't even tell you why I was late. I felt bad leaving once he'd started making it. She didn't even charge me." He sighed. "Anyway, it needs to chill for an hour in the fridge."

"I was getting so worried."

"I'm sorry," he said.

A piece of his dark hair was out of place. I lifted my hand and ran my fingers through the strands to straighten it. Owen closed his eyes momentarily.

"You have nothing to apologize for," I told him. "Thank you for going out of your way to make me happy. I'm not used to that."

"You deserve to be happy," he whispered. Then he clapped his hands together. "Let's eat this food, shall we? Before it gets even colder than it already is."

He placed the pie in his fridge and brought the paper bag of takeout over to the small table in my room. Owen had gotten two entrees for us to split: pasta primavera and chicken parmesan from an Italian place. My stomach growled as the smell of cheese and oregano filled the air. He'd also picked up a bottle of red wine—thankfully with a screw top since we had no opener here.

Owen poured the wine into two water glasses and placed one in front of each of us. He lifted his. "Cheers."

The glasses clinked together.

"Did you have a nice shower while I was gone?" he asked as we ate. "You look cozy."

"I did. It was divine."

"I can't wait to take one myself after dinner."

"You probably need one." I took a sip.

He cocked a brow. "Are you saying I stink?"

"No, actually, you smell great. But after all the running around you did tonight, you must feel like you need one."

"Nice save." He winked. "Anyway, I was so worried, wondering what the hell you were thinking the entire time I was gone."

I cut into my chicken. "Normally, I would've thought I'd been ghosted or something, but I didn't think you'd do that."

Owen put his fork down and narrowed his eyes. "Why would you ever think that, though?"

"I guess because of my childhood, having been left alone so much. I'm used to seeing people leave—walk out of my life, rather than stay." I took a bite.

Owen shook his head. "I'm sorry. I hadn't thought of it like that. I hope I didn't worry you."

"Like I said, I didn't think you'd do that. It's just something that always crosses my mind when someone is late—that they're never coming back." I shook my head. "Oh my God. It's way too late for my crazy to come out tonight."

"I love your crazy." He smiled. "But it's *not* crazy. You have every reason to feel that way based on what you've been through."

"I barely know you, Owen, and I've already unloaded so much of my baggage."

He stared into my eyes. "You feel like you barely know me. But…" He paused. "I've been inside of you. And I've loved learning about you ever since. Even if the order of events is kind of unusual, all in all, I think we know each other better than most."

His words—*"I've been inside of you"*—gave me chills. He had, hadn't he? And yet I'd always treated him like a virtual stranger.

"I have a hard time letting people in, even if I care about them." I needed to shut this down before I started to cry, so I stood to throw away some of the garbage.

"Do you want me to take out the pie?" he asked.

I felt horrible telling him no, because he'd gone to all that trouble. But I was too full. In fact, my stomach was quite upset at the moment.

"How about we have it for breakfast? I'm stuffed."

"That sounds good, actually. It'll go well with coffee."

Owen got up and finished cleaning off the table. "I'm gonna go next door and take a shower. We should probably get some sleep in case we have to hog-tie your mother and carry her to my car tomorrow."

I laughed. "That's more of a possibility than you think, you know."

"Oh, I know." He grinned. "You prepared me for that."

"Goodnight, Owen." I grabbed his hand and didn't let go. I found myself silently begging for him to kiss me. Even if I often pretended that wasn't what I wanted, I would've given anything to feel his lips against mine right now.

Instead of leaning in, though, Owen pulled his hand back. "'Night, Devyn. Sleep tight."

Then he disappeared into the adjacent room.

Well, I guess I lost that chance.

The following morning, I woke up to the worst nausea I'd ever had. Was it nerves?

It kept escalating until finally I had to run to the bathroom and hurl into the toilet.

What the hell? Was it the Italian food?

The last thing I wanted was for Owen to know I'd thrown up—because how gross. But it was loud, and my gut told me he'd probably heard.

There was a knock at the door soon after I cleaned myself up.

Shit. I straightened out my look and went to the door between our rooms.

"Hey, did I just hear you throwing up?" Owen asked, his face concerned.

I sighed. "Yeah. I woke up with an upset stomach."

"Damn. Do you think it's food poisoning?"

"It's possible. But it could also be nerves about today."

Owen pulled me into a hug. Despite feeling like crap, it was nice to be held.

"Are you okay now?" he asked.

I rubbed my stomach. "I'm a little better. Yeah."

"And I didn't even bring you pickled ginger."

"I know." I chuckled.

"Well, shit. I guess no Key lime for you this morning, huh?" He pulled back. "Come to think of it, my stomach was rumbling when I woke up, too. I thought it was the three cupcakes I ate at the bakery last night while I was waiting. But maybe it was the Italian?"

"As much as I love that pie, I definitely can't stomach it right now."

"You think I can get some ice from the machine and figure out how to take the pie home with us?" He laughed.

"It would probably last a few hours on ice, yeah."

He tugged gently at my shirt. "What can I get you right now?"

"Nothing. I'm just gonna pour some hot water and make tea."

"I'll go downstairs and get some saltines from the store in the lobby. You should have something in your stomach."

"Thank you. That'll be great."

I'd been so caught up in my vomit shame that I hadn't appreciated how hot Owen looked in the fitted black T-shirt he'd bought at Target the day before.

After he brought the crackers, I forced a few down with my tea. Owen joined me in my room with his coffee and a granola bar he'd picked up downstairs.

We didn't have much time. So once we were finished, we grabbed our stuff and checked out of the hotel. When we got to the truck repair shop, it wasn't open yet. We waited outside until we saw someone approach the door with a key.

Exchanging a look, Owen and I exited the car and walked toward him.

"Hello," Owen said. "I was hoping you could help us. We're looking for Bo."

"I'm Bo." The man narrowed his eyes. "How can I help you?"

Owen and I looked at each other.

"You can tell us where we can find Vera Marks," I told him.

"Who?"

"Vera Marks," I repeated. "Your girlfriend. Unless she gave you a fake name. She's been known to do that, too."

"There must be some misunderstanding. I don't have a girlfriend. And I don't know any Vera."

"Are you sure?" I asked.

"Pretty sure I'd know if I had a girlfriend, especially since I haven't been interested in women since kindergarten. My partner would be quite upset if I were two-timing him with a woman."

Owen raised his chin. "What about the blonde you've been supposedly hanging around with?"

The man seemed genuinely confused. "My *man* has long, blond hair. Is that what you mean? Other than that, there ain't no blonde."

Realizing we'd hit a dead end, I hung my head. "Thank you, Bo. I'm sorry for wasting your time this morning."

He nodded and disappeared into the shop, leaving Owen and me standing outside.

Five hours later, we pulled up to our building in Manhattan.

Owen parked, and we got out, staring at each other blankly on the sidewalk.

He rubbed my arm. "I'm so fucking sorry, Devyn."

"Yeah. Me, too."

He brought me into an embrace. I closed my eyes, relishing every second of being in his arms. As down as I felt, I was still eternally grateful for Owen and his support.

I looked up at him. "Thank you for everything. Even if it didn't work out, I will never forget what you did for me."

He nodded and exhaled. "What are we going to do now?"

We.

"I don't know." I rubbed my eyes. "Maybe grab that Key lime on ice and eat our worries away upstairs after I round up the kids?"

"That sounds like a plan. Though I have to go into the office for a couple of hours first." He smiled, lifting the bag he'd been holding. "But maybe they can help us finish off these road-trip snacks, too."

I smiled. "Pretty sure we can share those with the whole building and still not make a dent."

♥CHAPTER 11

Owen

Later in the afternoon, I had to go into the office for a few hours, but I couldn't seem to concentrate. I kept looking at my watch, feeling stressed about how fast the minutes were ticking down to Monday morning. I tried to remind myself it wasn't my problem—Devyn was just a friend, nothing more—but this was about more than just Devyn. In a very short time, I'd started to care about Frick and Frack, too. I couldn't stand idly by while the state did God knows what with them. So I decided to call my friend Marcus, a family law attorney. We'd gone to undergrad together and still kept in touch.

Marcus picked up on the first ring. "O-man. Are you calling me from happy hour at a bar where you're chatting up a beautiful woman and her equally hot single friend and you need a wingman—I hope?"

I chuckled. "Close. I'm sitting in my office annoyed that someone ate the yogurt I left in the fridge. I'm getting old."

"Yeah, no shit. Yesterday I threw my back out leaning to put an empty can in the garbage. But how's it going, man? How's business?"

"Pretty good. The market's on an upswing, so I can't complain."

"When are we going for happy hour? It's been a minute…"

"Soon. I promise. But listen, I have a friend who has a family issue, and I was hoping I could pick your brain for some legal advice."

"You do know this is the brain located inside the skull that holds the record at Kappa Sigma for most cans crushed against it, right?"

I laughed. "Sadly, you're the best choice I've got."

"What's going on?"

Over the next ten minutes, I filled Marcus in on the crap going on with Devyn. I told him about her mother's history of taking off, our unsuccessful trip to find Vera in Boston, and the recent CPS visit.

"Is the sister a fuck-up, too?"

I got defensive. "No, she's not *a fuck-up*. She's a good person, shit-for-brains. I wouldn't be calling you for help on a Saturday if she wasn't a good person."

"Alright, well, then the best bet would probably be for her to go to family court and file a petition for emergency custody. I'd do it bright and early Monday morning, as soon as the courthouse opens, so when CPS comes back, there's already a pending petition. It'll show CPS that she means business, and emergency orders usually get heard within twenty-four hours, maybe even that afternoon."

"Does it matter that she lives in California?"

"She's there now?"

"No, she's here in the City with the kids. But her permanent residence is out there."

"Would she want to leave the state with the kids immediately?"

"No. She thinks it's important for the kids to finish the school year. They've moved around a lot. I'm not sure about after the semester ends, but there's still another month and a half of school, so she has no plans to bolt right away."

"That's good. Then it's not really important what state she's a permanent resident of, only that she's sticking around here with the kids for a while. Does she have a criminal history or anything?"

Again, my immediate reaction was to get defensive. But I didn't actually know that much about Devyn's history, other than the things she'd shared about her relationship with her mom growing up. "I don't know for sure, but I doubt it."

"Family court likes to keep kids with people they know," Marcus explained. "They'll almost always consider a blood relative for placement, rather than pulling the kids out of their home and sticking them in foster care. But even a sibling needs to go through a background investigation to get temporary custody. Though if she files, and there are no red flags during her appearance, they'll probably keep the kids with her while they go through the process."

I blew out a deep breath, more relieved than I probably should've been. "Alright. Then can I ask you a favor? Do you think you can see her today or tomorrow, if she decides to go that route? And handle things for her Monday? I'll need to talk to her first, obviously."

"It'll cost you a bottle of Don Julio—the good shit, not the hundred-dollar stuff."

"You got it, buddy. I really appreciate it. Let me talk to Devyn, and I'll get back to you as soon as possible."

"Sounds good. By the way, is this Devyn single?"

"Yeah, she is. Does that hurt her chances?"

"No. But it helps mine. Is she hot?"

I felt my face heat. "She's off limits. Don't even think about it."

"Holy shit. That sounded almost territorial, Dawson. Are you in *a relationship*?"

I frowned. "Just give her legal help and keep your eyes and hands to yourself, okay?"

Marcus chuckled. "Sounds like someone's got it bad."

"I'll talk to you in a little while."

I was still shaking my head when I hung up. Marcus had hit a nerve. I did *have it bad.* For a woman who had zero interest in me…

Nevertheless, a few minutes later, I decided to go talk to Devyn in person. It wasn't like I was getting any work done this afternoon anyway.

Devyn smiled when she opened the door to their apartment. "Hey, Owen."

Unlike when I'd left her a few hours ago, she now wore a flowy, white dress and a full face of makeup. Maybe she was getting ready to go out?

"Sorry I didn't call first. But I wanted to talk to you about something."

"Umm…" She didn't step aside for me to enter.

When she looked over her shoulder and back at me, my stomach dropped. *Fuck.* Did she have a guy in there or something?

"If it's not a good time…" I said.

She shook her head. "No, no. Come in. I'm just on a Zoom call. I'll be off in a few minutes."

My body untensed. *It's just a work call, you jealous idiot. Relax.*

Devyn's laptop was set up in the living room. I didn't want to get in her space, so I went to the kitchen to wait. But the apartment had an open floor plan, so it wasn't like I could completely mind my own business.

"Sorry about that," Devyn said, settling onto the couch. "Where were we?"

"We were talking about you meeting me in Italy next week."

I froze. I knew that voice. *The fucking actor from the movie we almost watched last week. Her* actor.

Devyn's eyes jumped to meet mine. I suddenly felt like a damn fool. I pointed to the door and spoke quietly. "I'm going to go."

"No, don't."

She was talking to me, but the idiot had no idea.

"Don't what?" he asked. "Buy you the ticket?"

She shook her head. "No, I'm sorry. I wasn't talking to you. But I need to run. Someone just came by."

"Oh. Well, give me a call back later and let me know what day is best for you. Alright, sweetheart?"

Sweetheart.

It felt like someone stuck a pin in my swollen heart, causing it to deflate.

Devyn reached for the top of her laptop. "I'll call you when I can." She shut it without waiting for a response and stood, biting her lip. "Sorry about that."

I swallowed. "I just came by to tell you I spoke to a buddy of mine. He's a family law attorney here in the City. I told him a little about your situation, and he said he can probably get you emergency temporary custody. He thinks you should file the paperwork before CPS shows back up here on Monday."

Her eyes widened as she smiled. "Really? He thinks I can get emergency custody? It would keep them out of foster care?"

I nodded. "He had some questions, like about your criminal history and stuff. But I think you should talk to him."

"I don't have a criminal history."

"Good. Then you should definitely speak to him."

"Do you think he can see me early on Monday?"

"He'll talk to you today, if you want."

"Oh my God." She covered her heart with her hand. "That would be great. Thank you so much, Owen. I don't know what I would do without you."

I couldn't even enjoy being her hero; I was too disappointed by the conversation I'd walked in on. *He wants his sweetheart to come to Italy.*

But I managed a smile. "Let me text Marcus and tell him you want to talk."

Marcus answered my message almost immediately. We went back and forth for a few minutes, setting him and Devyn up for a Zoom call in an hour. I gave him Devyn's email so he could send her a link to join the call. After, I tucked my phone into my pocket.

"Do you want to have some dinner before I have the call?" Devyn asked. "I made a Waldorf salad—it's the only kind of salad I can get Heath to eat. He likes the walnuts and apples, so the greens seem to slip in unnoticed. But the pizza place called a little while ago and asked if he could come in, and Hannah is practicing with a friend for *PS Idol*, so now I have a giant salad all to myself."

Normally, I'd jump at the chance to spend time alone with Devyn, but I just wanted to get the heck out of here now. So I lied. "Thanks. But I still have some work to do."

"Oh. Okay. Want me to make you a doggie bag?"

"No, thanks. I'm good."

I walked to the door feeling like my feet were weighed down with concrete blocks. I didn't even bother to turn around to say goodbye. "Good luck. Hope everything goes well with Marcus."

Halfway out the door, Devyn put her hand on my arm, forcing me to look up. "Thank you, Owen. You're really an amazing friend."

Friend. One little word, yet it felt like the final nail in the coffin. I forced a smile. "Anything for my *friends.*"

I was still trying to blow off steam at eight PM. Forty-five minutes of weightlifting hadn't done the trick, so I thought I might go for a run before jumping in the shower. A remix of the Beastie Boys blared through my earbuds as I tucked the sweaty T-shirt I'd taken off into the waistband of my shorts and moved my head to the groove of the beat.

But when I opened my front door to go, I jumped back, startled. "Shit." I ripped an earbud from one ear. "I didn't expect anyone to be standing here."

Devyn smiled. "Sorry. I knocked twice. You didn't answer so I was just about to leave."

I held up the earbud. "I was exercising. Had the music cranked up."

But Devyn's eyes didn't move toward my hand. They stopped at my bare chest and took their sweet-ass time moving down. When they got to my abs—which were a glistening six-pack thanks to a hundred torturous sit ups—her little pink tongue peeked out and ran along her bottom lip. The entire thing lasted mere seconds, but it was crystal clear that she liked what she saw.

Devyn shook her head and raised a bottle of wine in one hand. "I just came down to say thank you for setting me up with Marcus. He's amazing. He's going to prepare an affidavit and petition for custody and file it with an order to show cause as soon as the courthouse opens on Monday morning."

"That's great."

She held up a brown paper bag in her other hand. "I bought you some dinner to go with the wine."

"You didn't have to do that."

"No, *you* didn't have to do any of the things you've done for me. Really, Owen, you've helped so much."

I nodded toward the inside of my apartment and stepped back so she could enter. "Come in. Share it with me."

She hesitated, and once again her eyes dropped to my chest. "Umm... Weren't you on your way out? I don't want to interrupt."

As much as I enjoyed her ogling me, I didn't want to chase her away. So I tugged my T-shirt from my waistband and slipped it over my head. "I already exercised, and I freaking hate to run, so you're doing me a favor."

She smiled and nodded. Inside, I opened the bottle of wine she'd brought and poured two glasses. Passing her one, I motioned toward the living room. "Why don't we go sit in there. It's more comfortable than the kitchen."

"The lasagna I brought you is warm. It's from that Italian place you like."

I patted my stomach. "I just finished exercising. I can't eat too soon after. But I'll have it in a little while."

"Oh, okay."

We settled on the couch, and Devyn gulped her wine.

"Talking to Marcus today has my head spinning," she said. "I really did bring the wine for you to say thank you, but I might've needed this more than I realized."

I smiled. "Yeah, I might've needed it too."

"Oh? Is something bothering you?" She shook her head. "I'm so wrapped up in my chaotic life. I haven't even asked what's going on with you lately. Is everything okay?"

"Everything's fine. Talk to me about why your head is spinning."

Devyn sighed. "Well, Marcus asked me some questions that I think I've been avoiding asking myself."

"Like what?"

"Well, for starters, he asked what I would do if Vera *never* came back. Of course I'd keep Heath and Hannah if that were to happen. But it got me thinking...why would I *allow* them to go back to Vera, even if she does show up? The more I hear about our mother's recent antics, the more I realize that even when she's home, she's not really parenting. The two of them need stability—especially Heath. I'm a little afraid that without it, he might continue down the wrong path. Right now, he's making dumb *kid* decisions—stealing a neighbor's cat and a mannequin. But how long until those decisions grow to be dumb *adult* decisions—like stealing from a store. Feels like that could be the direction he winds up going without some intervention."

"Does that mean you're considering trying for more than temporary custody?"

She gulped back her wine. "I might..."

"Wow. That's a lot to take on—two teenagers."

Devyn's face fell, and it made me realize how negative my reaction had seemed.

"Sorry, that came off as not very supportive. I think it would be amazing if you did that. It's a very noble thing to do, and I'm sure it would change the course of Heath and Hannah's lives in a positive way. I just meant, it would obviously change your life a lot, too." I paused. "What about children of your own someday?"

Devyn shrugged. "I'm not sure. My mom didn't exactly show me the joys of motherhood. I think I've mentioned it's not something I've felt like I needed to be fulfilled. Though, if the right person came along...I don't know...maybe?"

I nodded.

"How about you?" She traced her finger over the rim of her wine glass. "You've said in the past that you weren't sure about marriage and kids..."

I shook my head. "I've never seen myself as a dad. I'm not sure why. My father was a great role model, so it's not that. But I guess like you, maybe if the right person came along, and they really wanted kids..."

Devyn sighed. "I need to give it a lot more thought before I make a decision about anything permanent. Luckily, right now I only need to deal with getting temporary custody. So...baby steps."

Her wine glass was almost empty, so I refilled it. I figured she could use it.

"Anyway, let's talk about something else. I think my head is going to explode if I think about petitions and hearings anymore today." She sipped her wine. "What do you want to talk about?"

The Zoom I'd interrupted this afternoon had been bugging me all day, and she'd just given me the perfect opening to dig around. I caught her eyes. "Would it be alright if we talked about the Zoom you were on earlier this afternoon?"

She sighed. "You mean Robert."

I nodded. "I can't help it. It's been gnawing at me. What's the deal with him? Is he the reason you don't want anything more than what we had?"

"Yes and no. No, I'm not in a committed relationship with him, but yes, maybe my experience with him has factored into my not wanting to be in a relationship at all."

"Did he screw you over that bad?"

"To be fair, he didn't really screw me over. I saw from the beginning that he wasn't ready for a relationship. But I liked him. His star was on the rise, and I accepted whatever he wanted to give." She rolled her eyes. "Boy, saying that out loud, it sounds pretty pathetic."

A few months ago, I would've thought taking less than what you really wanted from a relationship was pathetic, but I wasn't so sure I wouldn't do the same thing right now—take what I could get from *her*.

I shook my head. "It doesn't sound pathetic at all."

"Thank you for saying that." She smiled. "Even if you're full of shit."

"Are you going to Italy with him? I couldn't help but overhear him mention a ticket and figuring out dates."

Devyn shook her head. "No, I'm not going anywhere. The kids are my priority right now. Robert can't comprehend anyone but him being the priority, no matter how many times I've told him I have my hands full."

"No offense, but he sounds like a douchebag."

She smiled. "He definitely can be."

An awkward silence descended. I would've liked to probe a little more, but the conversation felt over. No use beating a dead horse, anyway. Plus, she'd had a shitty day and didn't need my whining to bring her down. So I changed topics and spent the next half hour amusing her with stories about all the crazy shit I'd come across in real estate—buyers caught banging in the bedroom when they were supposed to be discussing a possible offer, owners leaving a vibrator out on the nightstand only to have the five-year-old child of a couple looking at the apartment play with it like it was a rocket… At least making her laugh made me feel good inside.

When Devyn finished her second glass of wine, she let out a deep breath and stood. "I should get back upstairs before the kids paint the apartment purple or something."

"I'd say you're exaggerating, but I saw the striped cat."

At the door, Devyn paused. "Thank you again for everything, Owen. You really are an amazing friend. If this keeps up, Mia might have some competition for the title of BFF."

For the first time since we met, I felt like Devyn friend-zoning me might be the best thing for both of us. She had so much going on in her life, and things with that Robert clown were far from settled.

"Are you going to make us matching friendship bracelets?" I asked.

Devyn pushed up on her toes and kissed my cheek. "You know I'm totally making them now."

I smiled. "Good luck Monday in court, if I don't see you before then. Let me know how it turns out."

"I will. Goodnight, bestie."

CHAPTER 12

Devyn

I woke up with my nerves shot on Sunday morning, so tense about tomorrow. This felt like the last normal day before all hell broke loose. When I got up, Heath was already working at the pizza shop, assembling boxes before they opened for the day, and Hannah was still sleeping.

Since it was still early out in L.A., I waited as long as I could before dialing Mia. Thankfully, she was an early riser, typically up and about by 5 AM. I filled her in on everything, including what had happened with Owen since the night we met when I arrived here.

"I can't believe you've been holding out on me like this!" Mia shrieked.

"I know. I'm sorry. Things have been crazy. This conversation was long overdue."

"You know the saying love at first sight?" she asked. "Well, I fell in love with Owen at first *voice*. From the moment he answered your phone at the bar, I knew he was good people."

I sighed. "You should see what he looks like."

"You'd better text me a photo after we get off the phone."

"I actually don't have a single photo with him, which is kind of sad. But if you Google Owen Dawson, realtor in Manhattan, I'm sure it will come up."

"Doing it right now." Sure enough, within a few seconds, she gasped. "Well, hot damn. He's perfection, Dev. Look at those eyes. What's wrong with you? Why aren't you marrying this dude and having his babies? Are you insane?"

"I'm trying to spare him," I told her. I truly felt that way.

"This better have nothing to do with Robert," she scolded.

Just the mention of Robert's name made my blood pressure spike. He had really gotten on my last nerve lately, the way he wouldn't let up about me paying him a visit.

"It doesn't have anything to do with Robert, although he's a whole 'nother story for a different day."

"Then what's the problem?"

"For one, I'm probably leaving soon. I need to be careful who I get attached to out here."

"Who says Owen can't follow you out to L.A.?"

That was laughable. "Believe me, Owen is *never* leaving New York. He and his friends he owns the building with are so tight— thick as thieves. They're like one big family. Or a gang."

"You'd be surprised what someone would do for love."

My cheeks burned. "He's not in love with me."

"Yet. From everything you've said, it sounds like he would head that direction eventually, if you don't sabotage things first."

Gazing out the window at the smoggy street, I smiled. "Well, he certainly has been the best thing about being in New York."

She cleared her throat. "Speaking of New York..."

"What?" My heart lurched. *Is she coming to visit?*

"I kind of have some news," Mia announced.

"Okay?"

"This is going to come out of left field, but...I'm moving there!"

I gasped. "You're moving to New York? How did this happen?"

"The gallery is opening a new location, and they want me to manage it. Isn't that crazy? It only became official yesterday. I was gonna call you today if you hadn't called me. Can you believe it?"

My pulse raced with excitement. "This is amazing! When are you coming?"

"Sometime in the next couple of months, but I'm gonna have to make a trip sooner than that to find a place. God, I hope we don't miss each other, if for some reason you're gone by then. That would be awful."

My mouth hung open. "Holy crap. This is the last thing I expected you to say."

"I knew you'd be shocked. Heck, even *I'm* shocked that I'm leaving L.A. I've never lived anywhere else."

"You're gonna love it here, Mia. I just hope I'm still here so I can enjoy it with you before I have to go back." A pang of sadness squeezed my chest.

"Well, I'm currently apartment hunting from afar. So if *cough-cough* you know of any handsome realtors who have spare apartments in their buildings, let me know."

"I'll ask Owen for sure. If there's nothing opening up here, maybe he knows of some other places. I'm sure he has connections."

"Add it to the list of favors he's done for you?"

I cringed. "Great."

She laughed. "How weird is it gonna be that our situations reverse? I'm gonna be there, and you're gonna be back here. What universe is this?"

I didn't know whether to be happy or sad. I would potentially get to see Mia soon, but I'd be losing my best friend once I got back to L.A. That felt like a sucker punch. With no family out there, it was a hard pill to swallow.

"Well, as much as it's gonna suck not having you around every day, I'm so proud of you for this promotion. And I'll definitely be coming back here to visit, especially if you're in New York. Talking to you right now made me realize how much I've missed you. I have, like, no female friends out here."

"That's 'cuz your best friend is Owen."

"Truth." I sighed.

After Mia and I hung up, I noticed my sister looking morose on the couch. I hadn't seen her come out of her bedroom. She was hunched over, staring intently at her phone. And she looked upset.

I walked over. "What's wrong, Han?"

She wiped her nose with her sleeve. "Nothing."

She's crying? "Don't give me that. You've been crying. Is it about Mom?"

I hoped not, because that woman wasn't worth anyone's tears.

"I *wish* it were about Mom."

"Talk to me."

She handed me her phone and showed me the screen. It was the social media page of some girl from her school. The little bitch had solicited other kids to list the ugliest people in their grade. Some asshole had listed Hannah's name in the comments.

Irate, I handed her back the phone and worked hard to remain calm. "You don't believe this, do you?" I asked. "These are people who just get off on being mean. Nothing else."

"I wish I didn't believe it." She sniffled.

My sister was beautiful, inside and out, and I couldn't understand how anyone could be so cruel. It brought back memories of being teased by girls in expensive clothes and shoes when I had to wear the same ratty garb over and over back in the day.

"I know it's hard for you to understand this, Hannah. But I'm gonna be straight with you. People who do this have low self-esteem. They do it to make themselves feel better. And often times, they're actually jealous of the people they're bullying."

Her lip trembled. "What do they have to be jealous of when it comes to me?"

"You're smart, funny, talented in the arts? What's not to be jealous of?" I rubbed her back. "I know it's hard to see now, but kids your age are the worst when it comes to this kind of thing. The same stuff used to happen to me."

"It did?"

I nodded. "But social media wasn't as bad back then. Now people use it as a weapon. You know what else I didn't have back then?"

"What?"

I wrapped my arms around her. "A big sister who could set me straight about what's really going on with those miserable kids. And I want you to understand that when people do this, they're being mean, and you shouldn't place any value on what terrible people have to say."

She frowned. "You're not gonna be around forever, though, Devyn."

I squeezed her tighter. "That's not true anymore, Hannah. I'm gonna make sure you guys are taken care of, and I'm gonna do my best to be around, okay? I can't guarantee I'll be living with you, but I will always be looking out for you. And if I get my way, we won't be leaving each other at all. Okay?"

She nodded hesitantly, seeming unsure about whether she could trust my assurances. This conversation confirmed that the most important place I could be right now was with my siblings. *Fuck you, Robert.*

"What do you say we get out of here and spend the rest of the day wreaking some havoc around the City? Let's forget about those stupid girls and go have some fun."

Her face perked up. "That sounds awesome!"

Hannah and I proceeded to have the best girls' day out. I took her to lunch at a hibachi restaurant—her favorite—and then to Sephora for a makeover. I didn't want to feed into the idea that physical beauty is all-important, but it did seem to make her feel more confident. I also bought her some much-needed new clothes.

As we walked home, she turned to me and smiled. "Thank you, Devyn. I feel so much better."

"You're welcome. We need to have more days like this. Believe me, I needed it, too." I elbowed her playfully. "We Marks girls need to stick together."

We passed the café around the corner from the building, and I noticed Lala and Billie having coffee together. Both had their babies next to them in their respective baby carriers.

Once they spotted me, I knew I had to go in and say hello. "Let's stop in here for a bit, Han." I opened the door to the café, and my sister followed.

Billie smiled. "Hey, Hannah. Long time no see."

"Hi, Billie." My sister grinned.

"What's with the fancy makeup? Looks pretty rad," Billie said.

"Devyn took me to Sephora." Hannah raised her chin. "They did my face."

"That's the happiest place on Earth, if you ask me." Billie winked.

"You look beautiful," Lala chimed in.

Hannah blushed. "Thank you."

I looked down at the two babies, who were both sound asleep. "How are they sleeping with all the noise in here?"

Lala adjusted the blanket over her daughter. "Well, in Hope's case, it's because she's been keeping us up all night. So, she just sleeps at random times throughout the day."

"I'm sorry," I said. "That must suck."

"It's par for the course." She moved her curly blond hair behind her ear. "Thankfully, Holden and I take turns getting up."

I looked over at my sister, whose face had turned red at the mere mention of her crush, Holden.

"Mav sleeps through the night and also sometimes during the day," Billie said. "We definitely have it easier than Lala and Holden do. Mav's also a bit older than Hope, so that probably has something to do with it." Billie turned to my sister. "Did Hannah tell you how much fun we had the other night? I'm grooming her to be our future babysitter." She winked.

I placed my hand on Hannah's shoulder. "You want to go get us something yummy from the counter?"

She nodded. "What do you want?"

"Get me a latte and a cookie, please." I handed her some cash. "Get whatever you want, too." I reached for her shopping bags and set them on a spare chair. Then I sat down next to Billie.

"She's a great kid." Billie looked over to where Hannah stood in line. "We loved having them over for the night."

"Thanks again for helping out with that."

"Of course. They're good kids. And you're totally a saint for giving up your life to be here with them." She took a sip of her coffee. "Forgive my language, but I'd love to wring your mother's neck."

I rolled my eyes. "Get in line."

Billie reached for my arm. "I'm sorry you guys took that trip for nothing."

"Well, I certainly could've had worse company. Owen made it seem like a mini-vacation." My cheeks tingled thinking about him.

Lala chuckled. "We've never seen Owen so interested in something besides his damn job. You've definitely cast a spell on him."

"We're just friends," I was quick to say.

Lala flashed me a skeptical look. "Really?"

I swallowed. "How much do you know?"

"We know about the one-night stand," Billie said matter-of-factly.

Great.

"Okay." I sighed. "He mentioned that he told the guys, so I figured maybe you knew. I'm glad I asked. I don't want to sit here and bullshit you." I exhaled. "Obviously our history makes things complicated between us, but it doesn't change the current status of our relationship. We are truly just friends, despite what happened the first night we met."

"I think the way you met is fucking awesome. The coincidence of you living in the building after he thought he'd never see you again?" Billie grinned. "What are the freaking chances?"

"It's the stuff romantic comedies are made of," Lala added.

Billie shook her head. "I thought you guys were on your way to something special. We love Owen and want the best for him."

I nodded. "Exactly. But I don't think the best for him is *me*."

Lala tilted her head. "Why do you say that?"

"We won't have enough time before Hannah gets back for me to list all of the reasons." I looked out the window for a moment. "If I'd met Owen at some other point in my life, things might've worked out. But it wouldn't be fair to drag him further into the current mess. And also, his life is here. Mine is in L.A. That's a pretty big factor, too."

Those were the last words I was able to get out before Hannah returned. We sat with them for about a half hour before the babies woke up. Then we all walked back to the building together, and before we parted ways, Billie, Lala, and I vowed to go out to dinner soon. Billie told me I could drop my siblings with Colby while we were out, which brought me a ton of comfort, because leaving them for any great length of time in the evenings was always a recipe for disaster. Laurice, who'd watched them the night I'd met Owen, was down in Florida for a month, so I had no one else to keep an eye on them right now.

That night, after both kids were in their rooms, I began ruminating again about tomorrow. I'd done a pretty good job distracting myself today, but that was wearing off now that I was home and essentially alone.

My phone chimed.

Owen: Just wanted to let you know I'll be thinking of you tomorrow.

Devyn: How did you know I needed a distraction right now? I've been pretty worried about it.

Owen: Well, I'm here to distract.

Devyn: I had coffee with Billie and Lala today.

Owen: Holden told me.

Devyn: He has a big mouth.

Owen: Understatement of the year. LOL

Devyn: They know the whole story about us. I figured they did, but they confirmed it.

Owen: Does that bother you?

Devyn: No. They're cool.

Owen: Did they try to pry?

Devyn: A little, but with the best of intentions.

Owen: You told them the truth?

Devyn: Yes.

Owen: Damn, you admitted that you're scared to go near me out of fear that our combustible chemistry would be too much for you to handle? I'm surprised you were that candid. ;-)

I smiled.

Devyn: Thank you. I needed that laugh.

Owen: Ouch! LOL

Owen: Seriously, I'm sorry tonight is rough.

Devyn: It is, but I'll get through it.

Owen: I've got just the thing to make you feel better, if you let me.

Devyn: Oh?

Where is he going with this?

Owen: I bet there's a pie shop open somewhere.

Ah.

Devyn: Believe it or not, I think I'm all pied out after the last one from Boston we demolished.

Owen: When you ghosted me, I never thought I'd get to hear you moan ever again. And then came the Key lime. Sad to see it go, though, if you're over it.

Devyn: Don't worry. I'll want it again by next weekend.

Owen: Me or the pie? ;-)

I knew he was kidding, but it made me sad.

Devyn: I'm sorry that I did that.

Owen: What are you referring to?

Devyn: Oof. Not good that you require clarification. That must mean I've screwed up more than once with you. I was referring to leaving you that first night at the hotel.

Owen: Anyone in your shoes would've done the same thing.

Devyn: How so?

Owen: You'd just had the best sex of your life and needed to rush out immediately to tell the world. You tried to come back and find me, but I'd literally fucked your brains out, and you no longer remembered which hotel you'd left me at. Happens to the best of us.

Devyn: LOL, if only that fable were true.

Owen: That's my story and I'm stickin' to it.

Devyn: Thank you for making me happy tonight. Now I'll be going to bed with a smile on my face.

Owen: That's what "friends" are for.

Devyn: Friends...emphasis on the quotation marks.

Owen: Exactly. I'm banking on those.

CHAPTER 13

Owen

I checked my cell phone for the tenth time. Still no call from Devyn. I frowned and looked back at the text exchange with my buddy Marcus. It had been more than two hours since he'd responded that they were done in court. I reread the first message I'd sent him at noon.

> **Owen:** Hey. Just checking in. Haven't heard from Devyn yet. Is the hearing over?
>
> **Marcus:** We were in and out in an hour. Pulled a few strings and managed to get her before a judge.
>
> **Owen:** Everything go okay?
>
> **Marcus:** I'll let her fill you in—attorney-client privilege and all. But it's safe to say, she left like most women who use my services—a very satisfied customer. ;)

I had the urge to punch him after that last comment—maybe even harder than I had the first time around. I took a deep breath and tried to ignore that it had been three hours since they'd finished in court, and Devyn still hadn't messaged me to let me know how it went. Maybe I was being ridiculous, but I'd expected her to text as soon as she got out.

Of course, my jealous ass couldn't help wondering whether she'd called *Robert* from the courthouse steps.

Whatever.

Between missing work to go to Boston on Friday, being distracted when I came into the office on Saturday afternoon, and now staring at my phone all morning—I really needed to pull my head out of my ass. I had clients to call back, staff to check in with, and buildings that weren't going to find buyers by themselves. So I forced myself back to work and didn't come up for air until the receptionist, Missy, popped her head into my office an hour or so later.

"You have a visitor." She smiled. "A very pretty lady."

My heart leaped.

Devyn.

She came to tell me the good news in person.

Maybe she wants to go celebrate.

I couldn't get out from behind my desk fast enough. But my racing heart screeched to an abrupt halt when I stepped out of my office and saw a beautiful woman, who was *not* Devyn.

Tarryn's face lit up with a smile. "Hey, you."

It felt like the wind had gotten knocked out of me. I had to mask my disappointment, pretending to be excited to see her. "Hey. What are you doing in New York?"

"I'm in town for the day."

The receptionist, as well as two of my newer agents, now watched the two of us like a ping-pong match. Considering Tarryn and I had done business a few times, and things hadn't exactly been professional, I thought it was best to catch up in private. I walked over and gave her a friendly hug.

"It's good to see you." I nodded toward the back. "Come into my office."

Tarryn's high heels clickity-clacked along the hardwood floors as she walked. I thought I might've caught a smirk on one of the agent's faces, so I cleared my throat and pointed to her laptop.

"Did you get everything set up for the Prince Street showing this weekend?"

"Uh, no. I'm working on it."

"Let's finish that up today, please."

She nodded and diverted her eyes to the screen.

Inside my office, I shut the door.

"Sorry to drop in on you like this," Tarryn said. "But I was in the area, so I thought I'd take a chance and see if you were here." She looked me up and down. "You look amazing, as always."

I didn't even have to check her out to know she looked incredible. Tarryn was gorgeous—a former Miss Kentucky who had moved to L.A. to do some modeling a decade ago and ended up becoming one of the most successful real estate agents on the West Coast. She'd opened her own brokerage two years ago, and I'd heard through the grapevine that she was killing it in the eight-figure-home-sales market in Malibu. We'd met when we were both starting out. She'd been working on a house sale out in California for a client who was buying a property from me in New York, and we'd been referring business to each other ever since. A few years back, we'd closed a giant deal, and I'd ended up licking celebratory champagne off her body at the end of the night. Since then, we hooked up once or twice a year, whenever one of us was in town.

I gestured to the couch in the corner of my office. "And you look like you eat those born-and-bred L.A. realtors for breakfast."

She grinned. "I did just steal two listings from an agent on that real estate reality show. I heard she bitches about me on an upcoming episode."

I chuckled. "So what brings you to town? I hope you're not setting up shop here. I don't think I want you as competition."

"I think it would be fun to go head-to-head with you." Tarryn's eyes sparkled. "But no, I'm not coming to the New York market. I have my hands full in California. I'm just here for the day. My friend is getting married, and I'm in the wedding party. We had fittings this morning on the Upper East Side. Her fiancé has a private plane, and he has businesses here and in L.A. She hasn't seen him in a week, so she went to his office wearing only a trench coat to surprise him. I thought I'd keep myself busy doing a little shopping before we head back later tonight."

"Nice. I've never flown private."

"Are you up for a drink? I was hoping maybe we could go to that little bar we went to last time I was in town."

My eyes immediately went to my cell phone. *Still no call.*

My gut reaction was to say no to drinks with Tarryn, make up an excuse. It felt wrong to spend time with a woman I'd slept with, but really, why shouldn't I? Devyn had made it clear that we were nothing more than friends. Hell, she hadn't even called me after the hearing this morning. So why not go enjoy myself? Maybe some time with Tarryn was exactly what I needed.

I checked my phone once more—maybe if a message came in, it would be a sign that I should decline. But I was disappointed once again. So I nodded. "You know what? Sure. Just give me five minutes to wrap things up here."

"Do you remember that overpriced pre-war we sold together up in Morningside Heights?" Tarryn lifted a toothpick with three olives and used her teeth to slip the first one off. "The woman who owned it, Mrs. Anderson, went into an assisted-living facility."

"Of course. How could I not? When we did the pre-closing walk through, the entire place was empty. At least we thought it was, until I opened the hall closet and a life-sized cutout of Nick Jonas scared the living shit out of me."

Tarryn laughed and pointed at me with the toothpick. "That's the one."

"Did you ever find out why that thing was there? Was the old lady a JoBro fan or something?"

"I'm glad you asked. Funny story...I keep in touch with the buyers. You know, check in once in a while and see how they like their new place to maintain the relationship and stuff. The new owner told me he found a shoebox in the attic, filled with unsent love letters to Nick from the old lady."

I laughed. "I was just telling Devyn stories the other day about the crazy shit we see. I need to tell her that one."

Tarryn sipped her martini and tilted her head. "Devyn? Is there a woman in your life these days, Mr. Dawson?"

My eyes slanted to my cell. *Still no call.* Sucking back the rest of my beer, I shook my head. "Nah. Devyn's just a friend."

Tarryn's eyes glinted. "Good to know."

Over the next hour and a half, Tarryn and I had too many drinks. She was always friendly, but the alcohol made her touchy feely. She'd laugh and hold on to my arm, or press her hand against my chest while she told a story. At one point, when there was a lull in the conversation, she scraped a fingernail along the top of my hand.

"I've missed spending time with you, Owen. It's easy between us, isn't it?"

It felt good to have someone flirt with me, to feel like *someone* wanted to touch me.

I smiled. "Yeah, it is, Tarryn."

She looked up at me from under thick lashes. "You want to go somewhere else for a drink? Maybe your place?"

Shit. The moment of truth. Tarryn was off-the-charts sexy— that wasn't even a question. And I knew we'd have a great time;

we had history that removed any doubt about that. There also wouldn't be any expectations after—it would be exactly what she said, *easy*. A good time. And part of me wanted to go. It had been a while. The physical urge was definitely there. Yet…I had so much emotional turmoil. *So, so much*. While I inwardly debated what the hell I should do, my cell phone started to vibrate on the bar. Devyn's name flashed on the screen. *Finally*.

You shouldn't answer it.

It's almost four o'clock in the afternoon. She's been out of court since ten this morning.

You're clearly not a priority to her.

Maybe you need to stop making her your *priority.*

But I really *wanted* to talk to her.

Tarryn glanced down at my vibrating phone, a curious smile on her face. "Need to answer that?"

I pursed my lips. *Fuck.* I couldn't ignore it. "Yeah, I do. I'm sorry. Will you excuse me for a second? It's a business call."

"Of course."

Stepping away from the bar, I swiped to answer.

"Hello?"

"Hey. I'm so glad I finally got you."

My brows drew together. "What do you mean *finally*? My call log doesn't show anything I missed."

"Oh, I called alright. And texted. Heath apparently thought it would be funny if he changed your name to Mia's and Mia's name to yours in my contacts. So I've been texting Mia, thinking it was you. I thought it was odd that when I asked what you were doing, you said you were running out to get tampons, but I figured you were just being funny."

"So you texted me today?"

"Of course. I wasn't even out of the courthouse before I texted you the good news."

"What happened in court?"

"Your friend was a godsend. I can't thank you enough for referring me to him. We got right in with a judge, and he granted me temporary, emergency custody. I have to jump through a million hoops, like a background check, home inspection, interviews with social workers, et cetera. But the kids can stay with me legally now. I'm so damn relieved, Owen."

It felt like a weight had lifted off my shoulders, which was fucked up because this wasn't my burden to carry. "That's great. Congratulations!"

"Anyhow, I'm sorry I didn't reach you earlier. It wasn't until I asked if you wanted to celebrate with me later that I finally figured out what was going on. Mia responded that she'd love to hop on a plane, but she had a new artist showing tonight. Mia manages an art gallery."

I'd stepped into the hallway that led to the bathrooms to talk on the phone. Two loud, drunk guys came out of the men's room laughing. Devyn heard the commotion.

"Are you still at work?"

"No. I, uh, stopped at a bar for a beer with a friend."

"Fun! Which one? Maybe I'll come meet you for a celebratory drink."

I hesitated, not sure how the hell to answer. "Umm…"

"*Oh*. Oh gosh," Devyn said. Apparently, she knew me better than I'd realized. "It's not a guy friend you're with, is it?"

"No, it's not. Tarryn is an old friend. She dropped by the office earlier."

Devyn was quiet for a few heartbeats. When she spoke again, all the happiness in her voice was gone. "Sorry to interrupt. Have a good time."

"Maybe we can have a drink a little later?"

"It's fine. I actually have a lot of stuff to do anyway. I need to go."

A minute ago she'd had time to come celebrate with me. Now she couldn't wait to get off the phone. "Devyn—"

"I'll talk to you later, Owen. I just wanted to tell you the good news. Thanks again for everything."

"Devyn, hang—"

"Bye, Owen."

She hung up before I could say anything more.

I stood in the dark hall, unsure what to do next, for almost a full five minutes. Did I take Tarryn home with me? Give myself the push I probably needed to move on from Devyn? Or did I go home and pine for a woman who had no interest in being with me? I knew what felt right in my heart, but where had listening to my heart gotten me? Nowhere fast. That's where. So maybe it was time I started listening to *other* organs.

Before I could finish deliberating, Tarryn came strutting down the bathroom hall.

I held up my cell. "Sorry about that. I just hung up."

"No problem." She pointed behind me. "I need to use the ladies' room."

"I'll meet you back at the bar."

When I returned to my seat, the bartender walked over. He motioned to my near-empty beer and the drained martini glass next to it. "You want another round?"

I nodded. "Yeah, sure. Why not?"

Tarryn came back a few minutes later. Rather than take her seat, she stood between my legs and grabbed the lapels of my suit jacket. "Are we getting out of here?"

"I just ordered us another round."

She pushed her big tits up against me and whispered in my ear. "I'd much rather have *you* than that drink."

I closed my eyes a moment. I wanted to...

I wanted to so fucking badly.

But...

I just couldn't.

Putting a hand on each of her shoulders, I looked Tarryn in the eyes. "I am one lucky son of a bitch to even have you join me for a drink, much less come home with me. But I can't, Tarryn."

Her smile wilted. "There's someone in your life?"

I nodded. There was no point in explaining all the complicated ins and outs. At its simplest, that was true. Devyn was someone in my life. Even if the *someone* in Devyn's life wasn't *me*.

She smiled sadly. "She's a lucky girl."

I kissed Tarryn's cheek. "Thank you for understanding. You're the best, Tarryn."

She wiggled her fingers, gesturing for me to run along. "Go. I'll even pick up the check. But if it doesn't work out, call me. You're worth the six-hour flight back for an afternoon."

I smiled. "Take care, Tarryn."

Twenty minutes later, I was sitting in my apartment, this time deliberating over whether I should go up to Devyn's apartment or not. It was one thing to leave Tarryn when my heart wasn't going to be in it—she deserved better than that. But did I have to go running to Devyn just because she called?

I kicked that thought around for a few more minutes, until the answer finally came to me.

Yes. Yes, I do.

Fuck it. I grabbed a bottle of wine and took the stairs two at a time without calling first.

When Devyn opened the door, I held it up. "I'm here to celebrate."

I'd expected her to be happy to see me. Unfortunately, she looked anything but.

She folded her hands across her chest. "What happened to your *date?*"

Was that...*jealousy?* I thought it might be. My smile widened. "I left. I wasn't into it."

"Why not?"

I caught her eyes. "I think you know why, Devyn."

She looked away. "Well, you shouldn't have done that."

I shrugged. "Welp, I'm here. So are you going to invite me in or not?"

"Fine."

She was definitely throwing me attitude, though I didn't mind at all. In fact, I found myself enjoying it.

Inside her apartment, I looked around. "Where are your new legal wards?"

"Heath is at work until seven, and Hannah is at her friend's house."

"Do they know about you getting custody?"

Devyn shook her head. "Not yet. I didn't even tell them I was going to court. I didn't want them to be disappointed if the judge said no for some reason. But I thought I might take them out for ice cream after dinner and surprise them with the news. They're going to be relieved."

I smiled and held up the wine. "That's great. You want to celebrate a little before they get home?"

"Sure."

Devyn was still acting a little distant, but not as icy as when she'd opened the door. I pretended nothing was wrong as I opened the bottle and poured us each a glass of merlot. Passing her one, I held my glass out to clink.

"Congratulations on gaining custody of the terrible twosome."

She smiled. "Thank you."

We both sipped. "So did the woman from CPS show up today?"

"Yeah. She's not too friendly. But when I showed her the signed order from the judge, she had no choice but to talk to me in place of Vera. She gave me a half-hour lecture on the importance of getting the kids to school and suggested I bring them down to social services for counseling. I'm hoping she's not the permanent case worker assigned to us. Marcus said they assign someone to do drop-in visits and stuff."

"Even if she is, she can't take the kids anymore, right?"

Devyn shook her head. "According to Marcus, she'd need to have a reason for removal and the court would need to agree."

"So those little shits can't skip school or get themselves in any more trouble then."

"Yeah. I have to do a better job of keeping them in line."

We talked about court for a while and all the things she had to do in order to maintain temporary custody. After, I decided to circle back to the attitude she'd had when I first walked in. "Can I ask you something?"

"What?"

"Were you jealous that I was out with another woman?"

Devyn looked away. "No."

My lip twitched. "No, huh?"

"I wasn't jealous."

It was difficult to keep a straight face, because she was so clearly full of shit. But…if she wasn't jealous, a few details wouldn't bother her, right?

I sipped my wine and watched Devyn's face. "Tarryn asked if I wanted to take her back to my place."

Her eyes narrowed. "That's nice."

"We've had sex before. So I don't think she wanted to sit on the couch and watch TV."

Devyn's face flushed red.

I couldn't help myself. I wanted to see her get pissed—admit she was damn jealous.

"Yeah, that Tarryn's a real wild woman in bed. Last time she visited, we broke a lamp. Knocked it right off the end table from the bed bouncing around so much."

I watched the muscle flex in her cheek, the same cheek that was turning a lovely shade of crimson. Yet she still wouldn't look at me.

"Devyn?"

Her lips pursed as she stared straight ahead.

"Devyn?" I said louder.

"What?"

"Look at me."

Her head whipped to face me, and she stared with daggers in her eyes.

I smiled. "It wouldn't bother you if I...fucked Tarryn?"

That did it.

She broke.

But she didn't yell at me like I expected.

Not at all.

Instead, she smashed her lips against mine.

It caught me so off guard that I took a few seconds to catch up. By the time I did, Devyn was hoisting herself over, climbing me like a freaking tree.

Fuck yeah.

This.

This was the chemistry we'd had from the very start.

I grabbed her ass with one hand, lifting her higher, and guided her legs around my waist, so lost in the moment that nothing existed in the world except this kiss.

Which was probably why I didn't hear the door open.

Or slam shut.

"Damn, sis. You're going to town on Rubber Ranger?"

Fuck.

My.

Life.

Heath.

♥CHAPTER 14

Devyn

The following morning, I sat at the desk alone, reliving the embarrassment—and amazingness—of last night.

That had been the best kiss of my life, but it wasn't too fun having to explain what'd been going on with Owen to my brother. Just when Heath and Hannah were officially in my care and I was supposed to be setting an example for them, too.

I needed to get a better handle on things, but at least it had been Heath, not Hannah, who'd walked in. Heath was a bit older, and I was pretty sure he had a good understanding of sex at this point. Although, it was probably time for me to have talks with both of them. I couldn't trust that Vera had done her due diligence.

Owen had gone home not long after Heath barged in yesterday, and Heath had spent the better part of the conversation we had after that teasing me, as I'd expected he would. I'd explained that Owen and I had been friends for a while, but that things had crossed the line a bit as of late. Of course, that wasn't entirely the truth, but it wasn't like I could explain how Owen and I had become acquainted. That might be a story for when we were all elderly.

In the end, Heath had seemed okay with things—likely because he genuinely liked Owen, and Owen had earned his trust. And he didn't make a big deal out of it when Hannah came home. To my knowledge, he hadn't mentioned anything to her. Nevertheless, I'd need to be more careful in the future.

For now, the kids were—hopefully—safely at school, and I could find my bearings again. I'd planned to get some work done, but all my mind wanted to do was replay that kiss. It had felt really good to have Owen's lips on mine and taste him again. I couldn't believe I'd willingly decided to walk away from that forever, to never see him again. I couldn't imagine that now.

My impulsive reaction when he'd asked if I was jealous *clearly* showed him where I stood. When I'd realized he was out with a woman, I hadn't been able to think straight. I'd been kidding myself when it came to Owen Dawson—in denial and trying to protect myself from getting hurt. That had been tolerable until the threat of losing my chance with him became very real.

My phone chimed, snapping me out of my thoughts.

Owen: I can't stop thinking about that fucking kiss.

Butterflies swarmed in my stomach. I closed my eyes for a moment.

Devyn: How did you know I was thinking about you?

Owen: I'm sorry Heath walked in on us, but I'm NOT sorry for WHAT he walked in on.

Devyn: He wants to kick your ass.

Owen: Seriously?

Devyn: No. He's good now.

Owen: I guess I should count my lucky stars he's not fully grown yet.

Devyn: He's more likely to frame you and put it on the Internet than cause physical harm.

Owen: That's very true.

Devyn: LOL

Owen: I need to get you jealous more often.

Devyn: Oh, so you think that's the secret, huh?

Owen: I do. And I have to tell you another secret.

Devyn: What is it?

Owen: I'm very fucking jealous of the actor who shall not be named.

Devyn: You are?

Owen: Of course. I feel like he still owns a piece of your heart, or maybe it's more like he's taking up real estate in your head. But I'd like to erase him from both places.

Devyn: Do you have a plan for that?

Owen: I have a Magic Eraser.

Devyn: LOL Do you now?

Owen: Yes. ;-) If I were there, I could show it to you.

Devyn: I guess I'm safe because you're at work.

Owen: Are you sure about that?

My heartbeat accelerated.

Devyn: What do you mean?

Owen: Are you sure I'm at work?

Devyn: Aren't you?

Owen: Let me ask you this... If I were there right now, what would you do?

The safety of hiding behind my phone made me bold.

Devyn: I'd try to pick up where we left off.

Owen: Then you should open the door and let me in.

I ran to the door to find Owen with his arms crossed and a gorgeously smug grin on his face. I wasn't even going to ask how long he'd been there... It didn't matter. He looked so hot in his crisp shirt and dress pants and that sexy, chunky watch around his wrist. It was mid-morning, so I wasn't sure if he'd gone to work at all or had come back home.

"Hey," he said, stepping inside.

"Hi," I breathed, barely able to speak before leaping into his arms. Our lips collided as I sighed, breathing him in like oxygen.

Owen spoke over my lips as the door slammed shut behind him. "Promise you're not gonna push me away again, because I don't think I can take it, Devyn."

"Pretty sure I'm gonna be begging for it this time."

With a fire in his eyes, he lifted me up as my legs wrapped around him. "I've been longing for you from the moment you left the hotel room that night. It's like my head...my fucking body— no part of me has been the same since."

"We should do something about that." I smiled down at him.

We kissed hungrily, our tongues colliding as we bumped into lots of things on the way to my bedroom, knocking some stuff over.

He laid me on the bed and stood over me as he slipped off his shirt. The sight of his gorgeous, sculpted torso and hard-on stretching through his dark trousers made my mouth water. His chest rose and fell as he stared down at me.

"I just want to look at you first. Everything went so fast our first night. I didn't get a chance to take it all in. Can I have a minute?"

I nodded as I slowly removed my top and tossed it aside, followed by my bra and eventually my panties.

Owen's eyes remained fixed on my naked body as goose bumps prickled my skin. There were few things more arousing than being desired like this.

"You are exquisite, Devyn. No one compares. No one."

Starving for his touch, my heart rate sped up.

He slid his tongue along his lip as the hunger in his eyes intensified. "Open your legs."

My clit throbbed as I spread my thighs. I'd never bared myself in such a way before. This was the first man I'd felt comfortable enough with to be so vulnerable.

"The last time we were together was frenzied. I want to take my time with you, Devyn. Okay?"

I nodded and breathed out, "Yes."

Owen hovered over me, and my legs trembled as he lowered his body and gently kissed my neck, licking a line downward. He stopped short of my groin and just breathed.

"Is something the matter?" I asked.

"Trying to figure out whether to savor you or eat you alive." His eyes met mine as he smiled.

I threaded my fingers in his hair. "Do what you see fit," I whispered.

He flashed a mischievous grin as he spread my knees wider and lowered his mouth to me. My breath hitched as I felt the wetness of his tongue circling my clit voraciously, his groans of pleasure vibrating against my sensitive skin.

"I could eat you all damn day," he rasped. "You taste better than anything."

Using his silky hair, I worked to direct his movements, very close to coming against his face. I tensed to stop it from happening.

He looked up at me with alarm. "Are you okay? Did I hurt you?"

"No. I just…almost came. That felt too good."

"Are you trying to say you're ready for me?"

"I am, Owen," I begged. "Please."

"Since you're being so polite…" He winked as he grabbed a condom from his pants and slid them down, revealing his swollen cock, glistening with pre-cum. Last time, I'd neglected to really appreciate how big and beautiful it was. I watched as he slid the condom over his shaft and squeezed the tip.

I loved feeling the weight of his body as he lowered himself over me, his hot breath against my skin. He cupped my cheek and looked into my eyes.

"Let yourself get lost in me today, Devyn. Don't overthink it, okay?"

"Okay." I smiled.

That was the last word I managed to utter before our lips smashed together. As his tongue searched for mine, I opened wider. Owen wrapped his hand around the base of my neck as he looked me in the eyes, sliding his slick cock along my clit. Back and forth. Back and forth. My nipples turned to steel as I grew wetter by the second. He then stuck his fingers inside me.

"You're so fucking wet, Devyn. Trembling for me. It's taking every ounce of strength not to fuck you so hard right now, even though *I* wanted to take it slow."

"You don't have to take it slow." I panted.

"Devyn…"

"Yeah?"

"I want you to be mine this time. I want to fuck you and know you're mine. Even if it can't be permanent. I need you to be fully mine right now, okay?"

"Okay…" I kept my eyes on his so he knew I wasn't just saying it for the sake of my neediness. "I'm yours."

I felt the burn of his thick cock entering me in one intense thrust. If a movement could speak, that one sure as hell said, *Mine.*

Opening my legs wider to receive all he had to give, I listened to the slick sounds of our arousal. This man had owned my heart for some time, but today, in this moment, he owned my body in a way he hadn't the first time. The trust that had built between us in the last month allowed me to fully surrender myself without any mental blocks, guilt, or hesitation.

My nails dug into his back as he continued moving in and out of me, harder and more intensely with each thrust until he bottomed out.

I lowered my hands, grabbing his ass as an anchor before sliding them up again to explore the contours of his back.

When I began to buck my hips to match his rhythm, Owen's eyes locked on mine. "That's it, Devyn. Give it to me. Give it all to me." He slowed for a moment, rolling his eyes back. "I almost fucking lost it. Don't you know owning you is my kryptonite?" He pushed in again with greater intensity, impaling me.

The bed shook as I surrendered to the ecstasy, my vision hazy and my mind in another dimension. Then the muscles between my legs couldn't take it anymore, and I began to lose it.

So in tune to my body, Owen knew. "Look at me, baby. Look in my eyes while you come around my cock." He let out an unintelligible sound as he rocked into me one final time before I could feel the warmth of his cum through the rubber. I fully let go, releasing the rest of my climax, my body so relaxed it felt weightless. That orgasm was more powerful than any that had come before, a testament to the man responsible for it.

Owen stayed inside of me for a while, whispering sweet words that were barely audible. He finally pulled out and briefly left to discard the condom. When he returned, he did something I'd been too scared to allow last time: he held me, wrapping my entire body in his warmth. We lay there entangled, my legs locked in his.

He spoke against my back. "I can hear the wheels turning in your head. Talk to me."

"There's nothing wrong, Owen. Nothing. Truly. That was amazing. I don't even want to think. I just want to keep enjoying this."

He kissed my back. "That sounds good, beautiful."

"Do you have to go to work?"

"No, I already canceled my appointments for the rest of the day."

I turned to face him. "You knew that this was gonna happen when you came to my apartment?"

"Yeah, somehow I did." He grinned. "Is that cocky of me?" He gripped my side. "Actually, no matter what happened, I knew I wanted to spend the day with you. I've learned not to get my hopes up, but I was pleasantly surprised with the way I was received."

We smiled at each other. I felt a little in awe of this moment.

"What are you thinking right now?" I asked.

He leaned his forehead against mine. "I want to say something to you, but I really don't wanna freak you out."

"Tell me…"

"I feel like you're everything that's been missing in my life, Devyn." I could feel his words against the side of my face. "I've told you I often feel like the odd man out around my friends, unable to figure out why I can't achieve the kind of happiness they have. And I know now it's because I'd never found the right person. I didn't understand what was wrong until I found exactly the connection I've been missing—with you."

My eyes started to water. "Why do you like me so much, Owen?"

Concern crossed his face. "Why do you even have to ask that?"

"I don't know… I just feel like you could have any woman in the world, because you're so damn good-looking and so gosh-darn sweet."

He kissed my nose. "I'm trying to get the one woman in the world I want."

"My situation is so messed up, though. It's chaos."

"Maybe a little chaos is what I need." He smiled. "Devyn, before we met, I felt dead inside. Sometimes you can't explain why someone is right for you. It just fits. When we're together, I feel alive—chaotic in a good way. I don't feel like I'm missing anything or need to be anywhere else. You're the realest woman I've ever met. You've opened up to me about your perceived flaws, but I think you're perfect. Even if your *life* isn't perfect, *you're* perfect. Perfect for me, at least. And even if you tell me I've totally freaked you out right now and you're done after today… I *still* wouldn't regret the time we spent together. You don't owe me anything, understand? All we ever have is today and right now. I am enjoying this day more than any other day in my entire life, and that's what matters. Don't think about tomorrow for a second. Just be with me now."

I caressed his stubble. "You're making it difficult to imagine going back to California, you know."

"Good. Mission accomplished." He kissed me. "In all seriousness, though, don't think about that right now."

I nodded and heeded his advice.

Owen and I had sex two more times that day, and when the clock struck three, I knew we had to make this place look like it hadn't been a sex den before the kids came home.

"Heath and Hannah will be back soon," I announced.

"If we told them we were just casually hanging out in the middle of the day, do you think they'd buy it?"

"Well, unfortunately, Heath knows better now, but I don't think it's going to be a problem if they see you here."

"So you don't mind if I hang out?" he asked.

"No, in fact, I'd love it if you did."

"Because I'm not ready for this day to end yet."

"Me neither," I said.

Owen and I showered together before we got dressed and made the bed.

When my brother and sister walked in around 3:45, you'd have thought Owen and I had been having a church service in here all day. Owen sat casually on the couch reading a magazine while I was across the apartment in the kitchen, preparing afternoon snacks.

That didn't stop my brother from busting our balls anyway.

"Oh look! It's Rubber Ranger Romeo."

Owen tossed his magazine aside. "Give your sister a break, Heath. She works hard for you. She doesn't need you teasing her."

"You're lucky I don't hate your guts," Heath told him. "I might be her little brother, but that doesn't mean I wouldn't kick your butt."

"Heath!" I scolded.

Owen grinned. "No, it's okay. I respect that. And I will heed your warning, sir."

"Are you guys dating or something?" Hannah asked.

Shit.

Owen looked at me for guidance.

"We're very good friends…" I turned to him and smiled. "In quotation marks."

Owen winked at me.

We ended up ordering sandwiches for dinner and eating at the table with the kids. I glanced at Owen over and over and wondered what the hell I'd been holding back for. This guy was the man of my dreams. I wished more than anything that he could spend the night, but it was way too soon for that, especially since my siblings were now on to us. There would be no easy way to sneak him in without their prying eyes catching it. They'd be watching us like hawks. I needed to set a good example, especially for Hannah. I needed to show her that you don't rush into anything with a man, even if he's an Adonis with a heart of gold.

Owen left after dinner, and the kids went to their rooms. Considering I'd gotten zero work done today, I decided to set up my laptop by the window, and at the very least, catch up on emails. I looked down at the calendar on my desk to get organized, and my heart nearly skipped a beat when I noticed a symbol in red placed more than two weeks ago. It should have been the start date of my monthly cycle. But I'd been so preoccupied with everything having to do with CPS, I'd missed that the date had come and gone with no period.

But relief replaced panic as I reminded myself that I'd used protection with Owen from that first time we were together, and it had been a while since Robert. The skipped period must've been stress-related.

A text from Owen interrupted my thoughts.

Owen: After I left your place, I went down to Billie's and caught her just before she closed the shop. I decided to get my first tat—something I could remember today by. Do you like it?

It was a photo of his wrist.

My jaw dropped.

A set of tiny quotation marks.

CHAPTER 15

Devyn

Three days later, I still hadn't gotten my period. I was starting to freak out, so I went to the drugstore and picked up an at-home pregnancy test. But I couldn't bring myself to do it. As I stared at the box sitting three feet away on the kitchen counter, I picked up the phone and called Mia.

"Hey!" she answered. "I was just thinking about you."

"Because you miss me so much?"

"Actually, an intern just walked into my office and said, 'You're never going to believe who has a giant dick.' Oliver and I switched offices last week. He's always warm, and his office AC sucks. I'm always cold, and my AC is freezing. Anyway, the poor intern didn't realize we'd moved, and he started talking before he looked up and saw me sitting at my new desk. The kid looked like he was going to shit his pants."

"What did you say?"

"I demanded he tell me who has a big dick, of course. It's some arrogant new artist we're showing at the gallery. Apparently the intern couldn't miss seeing it in the men's room. The dude is five foot nothing with a beer belly and a bad toupee. At least now I know where the arrogance comes from."

I laughed. "I'm almost afraid to ask, but why on Earth does that story remind you of me?"

"Oh. Remember when we first met and you were still living with your mother in that third-floor walk-up? She didn't pay the rent, so they kicked her out. But she managed to find a sucker to let her move into the building right next door. It was a third-floor walk-up, too."

I groaned. "Let me guess, you're remembering the cereal incident?"

Mia snorted. "You took your jeans off and sat in your damn underwear on someone else's couch, eating a giant bowl of their cereal. The couch wasn't even the same color as your mom's."

I sighed. "That poor eighty-year-old man definitely changed the locks after he came home to that. But in my defense, we moved *a lot*, so it was hard to keep track of where we lived, and I hadn't taken the old key off my keyring yet."

"Anyway…what are you up to today?" she asked.

I'd called her for support, yet suddenly I wasn't so sure I was ready to share what was going on. I was too freaked out to say the words.

"Not much. I should be working. But I don't feel like it."

"Who are you and what have you done with my best friend, Devyn? You *never* feel like not working. You're the only person I know who loves their job."

I was so busy staring at the stupid pregnancy test on the counter that I only half heard what Mia said. My focus had been nonexistent the last few days. I needed to know, one way or the other. So I forced myself to blurt out the reason for my mid-day call and lackluster work motivation. "My period is late."

"Oh shit," Mia said. "How late?"

I groaned. "Three weeks."

"You're not usually irregular, right?"

"Nooooo…" I sighed. "I'm pretty much like clockwork."

"But you have an IUD, like me, right?"

"I do. But I've had it for almost seven years now—that's the end of its effectiveness. I was scheduled to have it removed and get a new one, but then I had to cancel my gyno appointment to come to New York."

"Almost seven years? It's effective for a full seven, right?"

"The new ones say they're good for eight, but mine was only seven, and I've read that at the end it can be less effective. I've done nothing but google for three days. But Owen and I used a condom, too."

"A lot of people don't even get their period with an IUD. Maybe you just skipped a month. Or maybe you're stressed. That can throw your period off."

I'd thought of both those things, of course. But I had this really unsettled feeling in my gut. "Maybe…"

"Go get a test. Let's rip the Band-Aid off. There's no easy way around it."

I frowned. "I already have one."

"But you didn't take it yet?"

"No. I've been trying to work up the courage. That's why I called you. I need you to hold my hand through this."

"You got it, girl. Let's go pee-pee on the stick. You want to switch to Zoom so I can watch you do it?"

"I don't think that's necessary. But thanks." I bit my fingernail. "What if it's positive, Mia?"

"Then we'll talk about the choices you have. Until then, there's no use wasting energy. I made myself sick that time I thought I was pregnant in college. Then I wasn't, but I'd stressed so much, I ran myself down and caught the flu. Then I had to cancel my date with Troy Everett, and he wound up going out with Ainsley Quinn that night instead of me. A few years later, Troy created some dumb diet app that he sold for like a bazillion dollars, and now Ainsley has twins with mini Birkin bags, and you know what I have?"

"What?"

"Two vibrators. No freakin' Birkin. So take the damn test. *Be Ainsley Quinn*, not Mia Archer."

I chuckled, now glad I'd called. Mia's insanity was just what I needed to get through this. "Okay. I'm going to put the phone down so I can pee on the stick. I'll be back in a minute."

"And I'm going to go get a bottle of the wine we had at the showing last night and crack it open. Just in case."

"Isn't it eight thirty in the morning there?"

"I'm *that good* of a friend. Now go pee."

I went into the bathroom and opened the box. The test itself was wrapped in foil, so after I tore into that, I took a deep breath, sat down, and stuck the stick between my legs.

Tinkle. Tinkle. Tinkle.

My heart pounded as I set the test on the counter and peeked at the white control panel. Color was beginning to seep across already. I started the stopwatch on my cell and pressed the button for speakerphone while I washed my hands.

"You there?" I asked.

"I am. You know, wine for breakfast isn't really that weird. People eat grapes in the morning, don't they?"

I dried my hands and flipped the now-empty pregnancy test box over. My eyes widened. *Results in as little as three minutes.* "Holy crap. This thing only takes three minutes."

"How long did you want it to take?"

"I don't know. A year or two might be nice." I glanced over at the stick, but I couldn't look. In fact, I needed to get the hell out of this bathroom. "Can you tell me when three minutes is up? I can't sit waiting."

"You got it."

"Thanks." I walked back into the kitchen and leaned a hip against the counter. "Tell me about the last date you had. I need a distraction."

"Oh…it was a doozy. His name was Alan. First red flag was he asked me if I could drive. I don't mind meeting people at a restaurant, but this dude wanted me to pick him up. He said his car was in the shop. So I did it. I picked his ass up. As soon as he gets in the passenger seat, he tells me he needs to make two quick stops. I agree, even though I think it's a little weird. The first stop was a *nursing home*. He made me go in with him to visit his grandmother. The poor woman was sleeping when we walked in, but he woke her up to introduce me. We stayed about fifteen minutes. He then asked if we could do the second stop after we went to dinner. I said fine. He'd picked the restaurant—some cheap, hole-in-the-wall place. Dinner was boring—*he* was boring, so I couldn't wait for the evening to end. I'd forgotten all about the second stop until he reminded me when we got back in the car. He said it was only a few blocks away and gave me directions…*to the fucking supermarket*. I wasn't about to walk up and down the aisles in my heels, plus I was annoyed, so I told him I'd wait in the car. *A half hour later*, the guy strolls out with *five bags of groceries*. My date spent less on the cheap restaurant dinner than an Uber would have cost him to run all his errands. In hindsight, I don't even think the weirdo had a car in the shop!"

I laughed. "Only you, Mia."

"Well, we can't all be like you with a gorgeous real-estate tycoon chasing us around."

"Owen isn't chasing me around anymore."

"Really? How come?"

"Because you don't need to chase when a woman practically jumps your bones."

"*What?* You two are together? Why didn't you tell me?"

"It's only been a few days and, honestly, we're taking it one day at a time."

Beep. Beep. Beep.

"Oh my God." I covered my heart with my hand. "Is that the alarm? It's been three minutes already?"

"Yeparoo. So get your heinie in that bathroom. Because I'm already pouring my second glass of wine."

I took a deep breath and exhaled before walking back down the hall to the bathroom. Stepping inside, I closed my eyes for ten seconds and said a little prayer before looking down. Then…

Holy shit.

The room started to sway. I had to grab the towel bar because I felt that lightheaded.

"Mia…" My voice trembled. "Please tell me two pink lines means negative."

"*Two*, not one?"

There wasn't even one dark one and one faint one. They were both bright pink.

"There are two dark lines, Mia."

"Oh shit. Well, I guess taking it one day at a time with Owen just got fast tracked. You're about to plan nine months out."

My phone chimed with a new text from Owen. He was starting to grow impatient.

It had been six days since I saw him, three since I found out I was pregnant. But I couldn't bring myself to face him, because I knew I wouldn't be able to hide how much I was freaking out. I needed to see a doctor first. You know, to confirm that the *four* tests I'd now taken were all wrong. It was possible, right?

Owen: Hey, beautiful. How are you feeling today?

I felt awful about lying to him. The sweet guy had left chicken soup at my door yesterday when I said I wasn't feeling well. But my *busy with work* excuse had worn thin. It's difficult to say you can't carve a half hour out of your day when you're the boss, especially since Owen and I lived in the same building and he could be at my door with two minutes' notice.

Devyn: Not so great. Going to the doctor today.

At least that wasn't a lie. I really wasn't feeling so hot, and I was going to the doctor. She was just a gynecologist, not the sore-throat kind.

Owen: What time? I'll drive you.

Devyn: Oh, no. I don't want to get you sick. It's only two stops on the C train.

Owen: I'd rather risk it than have you take the subway when you're not feeling well.

Did he have to be so damn sweet? I already felt like shit.

Devyn: I'll be fine. Maybe I'll take an Uber.

Owen: I really don't mind driving you. I'll wear a mask, if that'll make you feel better.

Devyn: Thank you. I appreciate the offer. I really do. But I'm good.

Owen: Alright. But call me after to let me know what they say. Okay?

I was pretty sure I'd be telling more lies then. Yet I typed back.

Devyn: Sure. ☺

An hour later I was sitting in a paper gown, sweating as I waited for the doctor to come into the exam room. My leg bopped up and down, and I jumped at every noise I heard from the hallway. I was especially nervous since I'd had to pick a doctor from the Internet and wasn't seeing my usual gynecologist from back home whom I knew and trusted.

After a few more minutes, the door opened and a woman who looked younger than her picture on the practice's website walked in with a nurse in tow. She smiled warmly and extended her hand. "Hello. I'm Dr. Talbot. It's nice to meet you."

"Hi. I'm…" I extended my hand, but at the last second pulled it back and wiped it on my gown. Embarrassed, my face heated as I reached out a second time. "Sorry. I'm nervous. My name is Devyn Marks."

"Hi, Devyn. Is there something particular you're nervous about today?" She looked down at my chart. "I noticed you didn't write the reason for your visit on your information sheet. Are you here for a checkup?"

I hadn't been able to write the words. Saying them aloud was even harder. "I, umm…missed my period."

"Okay. Are you sexually active and there's a possibility you might be pregnant?"

I nodded.

"Are you on any form of birth control?"

"I have an IUD."

"And how long ago did you get that?"

I frowned. "Just about seven years now. It's due to come out. I had scheduled an appointment with my doctor in California to replace it, but then I unexpectedly had to come to New York, so I hadn't gotten around to it yet. I know the timeline is up to seven years, but I always use condoms too."

She scribbled some notes. "And when was your last period?"

"April first. So I'm a few weeks late now. I don't get much of a period since I had the IUD put in. Just some spotting, but I get that every month like clockwork."

"Any other pregnancy symptoms? Nausea, breast tenderness, fatigue?"

I shook my head. "No. But I did take a home pregnancy test."

"Oh. And that was positive?"

I frowned. "Four times. And actually, now that I think about it, I was sick once a few weeks back. But I thought it was something I ate."

The doctor smiled and closed my chart. "Why don't we do a quick examination and see what's going on? Early pregnancy isn't always detectable with a cervical exam. So after, we'll do a sonogram and some bloodwork to be certain."

"Okay."

The nurse pulled out the dreaded stirrups while the doctor washed her hands and put on gloves. It was difficult enough to relax during any internal exam, but particularly when you're a bundle of nerves wondering if you're pregnant. Dr. Talbot did her thing and then wheeled over the portable sonogram machine without saying much for a long time.

"I can confirm that you are indeed pregnant, Devyn."

Oh, God.

"I'm able to see the strings attached to your IUD, so I recommend removing it. Keeping it in has some increased risks for a pregnancy. I can do that now, if you want."

My head was spinning, but there was no point in keeping it in. So I nodded. "Sure. Thank you."

Removing it was quick and not nearly as painful as placing it had been. After, the doctor went back to scanning my belly.

"Would you like me to show you the pregnancy on the screen and perhaps try to hear the heartbeat? Or would you prefer I didn't do that?"

I swallowed. The moment felt surreal, like I was watching it happen to someone else. So I thought it might make it more real if I saw it, maybe even heard it. Taking a deep breath, I nodded. "I think so."

Over the next five minutes, Dr. Talbot pointed to various things on the screen—my anatomy, the gestational sac, a tiny flashing dot that she said was the heartbeat, but just looked like a black oval with some fuzz on the screen. It still didn't feel real.

Not until she reached for a dial on the machine and some crackling sounds came through the speaker. Dr. Talbot moved the wand some more, pushing a little deeper, and a *swoosh swoosh* sound echoed through the room.

Swoosh swoosh swoosh swoosh. The sound was rapid, but consistent.

My eyes widened. "Is that the heartbeat?"

She smiled. "It is. And it's a good strong one for this early in the pregnancy. Though, you said your last period was April first, correct?"

"Yes."

"That would date you at almost seven-and-a-half weeks right now. Gestational age is two weeks longer than when conception actually occurred. So according to your last period, you would have conceived approximately five-and-a-half weeks ago."

Today was May 23rd, and I'd slept with Owen on April 15th— I remembered because I'd filed my taxes on the last day this year, and I'd done that right after I arrived in the City. The timing was accurate.

"However," Dr. Talbot continued, "the embryo's size and appearance looks like it could be a bit older than that."

"Older? What do you mean? I definitely had my period on April first. I checked my calendar."

"Well, it's not unusual to spot during pregnancy, especially during the early stages. You said your menstrual cycle was not much of a period, which is common for women with a hormonal IUD. Perhaps what you thought was your period last month was a bit of spotting?"

"I don't understand."

"I could be wrong. But I would've guessed from the appearance and size that you're more like nine, maybe ten weeks pregnant."

I stopped breathing. "Nine or ten weeks? So conception would've been…seven or eight weeks ago?"

The doctor nodded. "That's right."

Robert had been away the two weeks before I left for New York. Which would mean, we'd last slept together…

Oh.

My.

God.

"Are you sure?" It felt like my throat was closing. "Nine or ten and not seven and a half?"

Dr. Talbot shook her head. "Dating a pregnancy is not an exact science. Embryos can be slightly larger or smaller than the norm, and not every woman ovulates exactly two weeks after their period. Some ovulate as early as six days after their cycle, others as late as the twenty-second day. For now, based on your period and the images, perhaps we'll date you somewhere in the middle. Your period puts you seven and a half. The size indicates more like two weeks farther along—about nine and a half." She picked up my chart and scribbled something. "So let's call it eight-and-a-half weeks, shall we?"

"No! It can't be eight-and-a-half weeks. I wasn't with anyone six-and-a-half weeks ago."

"Like I said, it's not an exact science. One week in either direction should be pretty accurate."

But one week in either direction changed everything. Seven-and-a-half weeks ago, I'd slept with Robert. Five-and-a-half weeks ago I'd been with Owen.

Oh fuck. I can't even be sure who the father is.

CHAPTER 16

Owen

It had been hours since Devyn's doctor visit, and she hadn't let me know how it went. Given the way she'd been acting all week, that wasn't exactly a surprise. But I was still worried something bad had happened, so I finally gave in and texted her.

Owen: Hey. Everything okay? How was the doctor?

It took about five minutes before she replied.

Devyn: I'm okay, yes. It wasn't anything like I'd thought.

What does that mean?

Owen: The doctor couldn't figure out what was wrong?

Devyn: She said I'm healthy, yeah.

Owen: Clearly that doesn't explain why you're sick. Are you feeling any better?

Devyn: A little. Just tired.

Owen: Okay. Will you let me know if you need anything?

Devyn: I will. Thank you.

Owen: K. Get some rest.

"What's going on, man? You haven't answered any of my texts."

I looked up. I'd been staring at my phone and hadn't even seen Brayden enter my apartment.

"Sorry. I've been busy," I said, my eyes returning to the screen.

"Bullshit. You're always busy. What's going on?"

Putting the phone aside, I let out a long breath. "Something's not right with Devyn. She's been avoiding me. It came out of the blue almost a week ago now. She says she's been sick, but I can't help but wonder if there's something more to it."

"You think she's playing games with you?"

"Nothing malicious." I stood and began to pace. "I think she might have freaked out a little after we slept together again. She started to back away right after that."

"Whoa. Again?" He grabbed two beers from my fridge and handed me one. "Back up. When did this happen?"

I cracked open my Sam Adams. "Last week."

"Why the hell didn't you tell me?"

I took a drink. "Sorry, I didn't realize I had to report to you. Do you tell me every time you have sex?" I glared. "Lately? I *know* that's not true. Because you've been secretive."

Brayden narrowed his eyes. "This is sort of like déjà vu, isn't it? You sleep with her, and she ghosts you? Apparently, you have a magical dick. It makes women disappear."

Magic Eraser.

I'd made that joke to Devyn once—though, not in this context. Sadly, Brayden did have a point. Devyn had literally disappeared the first time we had sex. This time, it was more of a figurative disappearance.

I looked away. "We had the most amazing time, and then everything just went to shit. I'm convinced something happened— but I don't know what. I'm wondering if it has to do with the actor she was seeing before she came out here."

"Actor?" His eyes went wide. "Which actor?"

"I don't want to say, because he's pretty damn famous and you'll know who he is. I don't feel like dealing with your ridicule. Plus, she wouldn't want me telling you her business."

"Well, that's no fun. I'm gonna get it out of you." He chuckled. "Anyway, if she's dicking around with Tom Cruise, why even bother with her?"

"I didn't say she was still fooling around with the guy. But he's been in her life for a while. He definitely still messes with her head, and I can't think of any other reason she'd do a one-eighty after we had a great day together." I put my head in my hands as I leaned my elbows against the kitchen counter.

"You're really fucked up over her. This isn't like you."

With no way to refute that, I reached for my beer. "I think I might be falling for her."

Brayden lifted his phone out and voice texted someone. "Dude, I can't handle this alone. Get down here. Owen thinks he's in love."

"What the hell are you doing?" I spewed.

He looked at the screen. "Holden's coming down."

"Is that really necessary?"

Brayden tucked his phone in his pocket. "This is a big deal."

No less than three minutes later, Holden barged in. "What's this now? Owen's in love with Devyn?"

I rolled my eyes. "You didn't need to come over just because this idiot couldn't keep things to himself."

Brayden crossed his arms. "The last time I checked, you've *never* been in love. This is pretty damn important, if you ask me."

I raised my voice. "I didn't *say* I was in love. I said I was *falling* for her."

"Falling in love, yeah." Brayden grinned. "We need to strategize and take out Chris Hemsworth before he ruins everything."

Holden looked understandably confused. "Chris Hemsworth?"

169

"It's not Chris Hemsworth." I shot daggers at Brayden. "He's married anyway."

"How do you know that?" Brayden laughed. "I thought you were too busy to keep up on entertainment news."

A few seconds later, the door opened and Colby entered.

"Are you freaking kidding me?" I groaned.

"What's going on?" Colby snickered. "Holden texted me that we have a *love* emergency."

I shook my head. "There's no emergency."

"We need to assess whether this is legit, and if not, knock some sense into you, Owen," Brayden said. "And if it is legit, we need to bust your balls anyway."

"My first question is…how do you know it's not infatuation?" Holden asked.

"I don't have an answer for you except to say it feels different. I know I've never been in love. And my feelings for Devyn are stronger than anything I've felt before. But it's too soon to call it love."

"Would you jump in front of a train to save her?" Colby asked.

I stopped for a second to ponder that.

Shit.

I would.

I nodded. "Yeah."

"I'm sorry to tell you, but you're in love," Colby said matter-of-factly.

Brayden nudged Colby. "She's dating Leonardo DiCaprio."

I glared at him. "Will you stop with that shit?"

Brayden shrugged. "You said I might know who the actor is. Since you won't tell me, the only way I'm gonna figure it out is through your reactions and process of elimination."

Colby raised a brow. "Actor? What's this all about?"

"Don't ask, please. Just someone she was seeing before she came out here. I'm not saying anything else about it."

"Okay…" Colby crossed his arms. "Well, are you going to tell her how you feel?"

"She knows how I feel, although I don't think she realizes how strong my feelings are. Anyway, now is not the right time to express anything more. She's been avoiding me for almost a week, and I have to figure out what's wrong before I do anything else to fuck it up."

"You think you did something to upset her?" Holden asked.

"It was his dick. It makes her disappear," Brayden cracked.

Holden lit up. "Wait… You had sex again?"

I reluctantly nodded.

Colby rubbed his chin. "Seriously, you think it had something to do with that?"

"I'm wondering if she's having regrets after it sank in." I stared into my beer bottle. "This last time was much different than the first. Everything felt more…serious. Might have been too much for her right now." I exhaled. "Because of her past, Devyn doesn't let people in very easily. I think she might've had second thoughts about taking things that far with me, given everything she has going on."

"She hasn't said anything specific to make you believe that, though?" Holden asked.

"She hasn't said shit. This is just my theory. As of right now, she claims she's not feeling well, but I have a strong feeling that's just an excuse. The last thing I want to do is force anything, so I won't be going over there. It just sucks…because I really care about her. But I don't think she's ready for anything with me."

"Either way, you need to be up front and tell her how you feel," Colby said.

"Not sure about that, man. Coming on too strong causes her to pull away. As hard as it is, I think I need to step back right now." I sighed. "You don't know her. She's very complex."

Holden laughed. "Well, so are *you*, dude. I mean, it's been how many years since you've even mentioned a woman? You're the pickiest prick I know, and for you to be saying you might be falling in love with someone…that's huge."

"Except I didn't actually *say* that. Brayden did. But thank you for your insight." I sighed.

"In my experience…" Holden paused. "Well, before Lala, of course… It's usually *after* you sleep with a woman that she becomes clingy. This is the opposite situation."

"That's what I mean. Devyn is unlike any other woman I've been with. The more she runs away, the more I want her. Real healthy dynamic."

"Any news on her mom?" Colby asked.

"No, Vera's pretty much totally MIA at this point."

"Those kids deserve better." Holden frowned. "Speaking of which…any reason why the girl would've been snapping a photo of me the other day?"

I laughed. "Hannah might have a little crush on you—like half the world. My guess is, she's gonna blow it up to poster size and stick it on her wall."

"Oh, really?" He seemed genuinely surprised. "That's cute."

"It's cute now, sure, but it wasn't when we were growing up and every girl we liked had a crush on you," Brayden noted.

Holden cleared his throat. "Not to interrupt all this love talk, but have you guys gone and gotten measured for your tuxes? We don't have all that much time."

Shit. Holden and Lala's wedding was coming up, and I certainly hadn't been thinking about my usher duties as of late.

"I'll get on that soon, Groomzilla," Colby said. "Lala told me you've been taking the reins on everything when it comes to the wedding planning. What's gotten into you?"

"Somebody has to do it." He shrugged. "My wife is the least-girly girl I know. She's given me full control of all the details, which, as you know, can be quite dangerous in terms of what we might end up with."

"Yeah, there'll be strippers or some shit." Brayden laughed.

"I'm glad you reminded me about getting fitted," I said. "Because honestly my head's been in my ass lately."

"All of you suck," Holden teased. "This is why Ryan would've been my best man if he were here. He was the only one of us on the ball with anything."

I smiled sadly. "Ryan would've definitely had his tux measurements by now."

"Oh, so you're saying I was actually *second* best?" Colby joked. "That's the only reason you asked me? This is news to me." Then he turned my way. "Oh, by the way, lover boy, what's the deal with the quotation-mark tattoo my wife inked on your wrist the other day?"

Crap. I was hoping to get away with not having to talk about that. "It's a personal thing between Devyn and me. I did it as a statement."

"Oh yeah. You're not in love," Brayden taunted.

Colby chuckled. "For a guy who said he would never get a tattoo, that's very interesting."

"It's hardly a tattoo." I rolled up my sleeve and displayed it. "It looks like four little moles."

Holden held out his full sleeve. "That's how it starts, man. Look at me now."

Brayden leaned in to see my tattoo. "So, tell us what it means."

I sighed. "For so long, she and I referred to each other as 'just friends,' but the 'friends' was in quotation marks. The quotation marks represent everything *else* going on with us that's beyond friendship. Sort of our denial, I guess."

The three of them were quiet until Holden finally said, "That's clever...but corny."

"Thanks for your opinion, jackass."

Colby clapped his hands. "Okay, have we decided what the official advisory is on this love dilemma? I have to get back to my kids."

I pointed my bottle toward him. "We're not deciding anything, and Brayden should've never opened his big trap. You guys can go back to minding your business. That's the official decision."

"My one piece of advice before I get out of your hair..." Colby said, eyeing me. "Don't pretend too hard not to care, because at some point she may believe you—especially if there's another guy in the picture. I get that she seems to scare easily, but you need to let her know where you stand before she books it out of town and you lose the one girl who matters to you."

My stomach felt unsettled at the prospect of Devyn leaving New York, though it seemed inevitable.

"For the record..." Holden said. "You and Brayden each have a plus-one option for the wedding, so maybe you should ask Devyn to be your date. It's gonna be a fun time."

I hadn't thought about that, but I would love to take Devyn to Holden and Lala's wedding, if only to have a fun night out.

I scratched my chin. "Yeah, that's an idea."

"If she's not engaged to Paul Rudd by then." Brayden winked.

After the guys left, I was no closer to understanding what was happening between Devyn and me, but I stopped myself from calling her. She'd indirectly made it clear she was looking for a breather.

I'd barely eaten today, so I decided to get some takeout from the Chinese restaurant down the street. I headed out, but froze when I got to the window of the place and saw her inside. Devyn stood at the busy counter, waiting for her order. She wiped her eyes as if she'd been crying. I stopped to watch her for a moment, while she didn't know I was there. But with each second that passed, I became more confused.

I had two choices: turn around and give her space, abandoning the spare ribs and fried rice I'd ordered—or face her, which would force her to admit what was going on.

Ultimately, I couldn't walk away. "Devyn," I called as I stepped inside the takeout joint.

She jumped, placing her hand over her heart, seeming shocked to see me. "Owen..."

"I'm sorry if I startled you."

"What are you doing here?"

"Likely the same thing you're doing. Getting Chinese?"

"Yeah, um…" She swallowed. "The kids were invited for pizza over at Heath's friend's house. Didn't feel like cooking dinner for just me, so…"

"Devyn, what's going on?" I shook my head. "I don't know what happened after I left your place that night, but you can't tell me you haven't been avoiding me. Was it the tattoo? Did it freak you out?"

She shook her head. "No, of course not. That was so sweet. I loved it."

"Are you sick? Because sickness doesn't make you cry like you are right now."

Her voice was barely audible. "I'm not sick, Owen."

My blood was pumping. "Are you gonna tell me what's going on?"

She looked into my eyes. "I can't. At least not right now. But please know it's *nothing* you did, nothing you said. I'm just going through something I need to work out on my own." She sniffled. "That's all."

I glanced over at the counter, where a paper bag with my name on it was ready. "My order is right there on the counter. I'm taking it back to my apartment. Clearly you had no intention of running into me tonight, and since you've made it clear that you want to be alone, I'm not gonna disturb you any further." I grabbed the bag. "You can call me when you're ready to be honest. But I won't accept anything less." I nodded once. "Have a good dinner, and I truly hope you feel better, Devyn. Because it hurts me to see you sad." As painful as it was, I turned around and didn't look back.

Walking out of there went against everything that felt natural. But I couldn't push her. I had to trust that she'd open up to me when she was ready.

A passing shower pummeled me during the walk home, and by the time I got back to my apartment, I had no appetite. I changed into some dry clothes and opened the ribs and rice. I took a couple bites, then just stared at the food.

The rain was coming down harder now. I wondered if Devyn had made it home safely. I kept seeing her crying in my head. *Fuck it.* I didn't care if it made her mad. I needed to make sure she was okay.

I opened the door to head up to her apartment, but stopped short at the sight of her standing in the hallway. Devyn was completely drenched.

"How long have you been outside my door?"

"A few minutes."

I looked down at her empty hands. "Where's your food?"

"My bag was so wet that the container broke through. Lo mein went everywhere—all over the sidewalk." Her voice trembled.

I pulled her close for a moment, my heart racing. Then I stepped back to let her in. "Come inside. I have plenty of food and currently no appetite for it."

I went to my room and grabbed a T-shirt from the closet. "Here's a dry shirt if you want to get changed," I said. "It's long enough to cover your legs."

"Thank you." She forced a smile before disappearing into the bathroom.

When she emerged, she carried her wet clothes out and placed them on the floor by the door. I loved seeing her in my shirt, but I could tell something was still very wrong.

"I know I upset you," she said. "And I'm sorry for not being honest."

"Well, I'm not gonna lie and say I'm having a great night—or a great week, for that matter—but I can take it, Devyn. I just wish you'd tell me whatever's going on, whether it has to do with Robert or otherwise." Expelling a long breath, I looked up at the ceiling. "Something happened after we slept together. I just don't know what." I examined her face—it looked sunken. "Have you eaten at all today?"

Devyn shook her head.

"Come share that food with me. We don't have to talk about anything until after you've eaten. Try to relax for a little bit, okay?"

She breathed a sigh of relief.

I plated the ribs and rice and popped open a bottle of wine.

Devyn held her palm out. "No wine for me."

"Are you sure?"

She nodded. "Yes."

"Want water?"

"That would be great."

Devyn certainly *looked* like she could use a glass of wine to relax. I knew I needed one right now. I poured myself some red and mostly watched her eat, taking a few bites of my food here and there.

"Thank you for this," she finally said. "You were right. I did need food and to calm down." She took a deep breath, still seeming on edge, but not as bad as before. She got up off the stool. "Can we go over to the couch?"

"Of course," I said, following her to the living room.

As we sat across from each other on my sofa, Devyn locked her hands together. Despite that, they were still shaking.

"Owen, you take such good care of me. You're the most amazing man. And you've been right to wonder what the hell has been wrong with me for the past week." She swallowed. "Something is *very* wrong. But it has nothing to do with how I feel about you or how amazing that afternoon we spent together in my apartment was."

Adrenaline coursed through me. "Does it have to do with *him*?"

She shook her head and started to cry.

What the fuck is happening? My stomach was in knots. "Did something happen with Vera…the kids?"

She shook her head again.

I moved over to her side of the couch and placed my hands on her shoulders. "Look at me, Devyn. Whatever it is, it's going to be okay. I just need you to tell me so I can help."

"I wasn't sick," she blurted. "But I *did* go to a medical appointment."

I gulped, the anticipation nearly killing me. "Okay…"

After a period of silence that felt endless, she hit me with it.

"I'm pregnant, Owen. The doctor confirmed it."

It took a few seconds to register.

She's pregnant?

And then the room started to spin.

"You're pregnant?"

She nodded.

Rubbing my palms on my thighs, I started to sweat, unable to find words. "This is… I don't even…"

"I know." She nodded rapidly. "I know it's a shock."

"You're sure?"

"Yes. I took many home tests, and like I said, the doctor confirmed."

I took her hand. "You were afraid to tell me because you thought it would upset me?"

"I wasn't sure how you'd feel. And I didn't know *how* to tell you. It's such a shock."

Trying to make sense of this, I just kept blinking. "How far along?"

"The doctor put it down as eight-and-a-half weeks. They go by the day of your last period. Which means conception is approximately two weeks earlier."

I tilted my head. "So it happened that night in the hotel? Our first night?" I rubbed my temples, wracking my brain to remember whether I'd used a condom *both times* that night. I was sure I had. But it didn't matter. It obviously happened anyway.

I knelt in front of her and laid my head on her belly. "I know you probably felt like this would be difficult news for me, but honestly, Devyn...it's not." I looked up into her eyes. "I'm not ready for this, and I'm sure you're not either, but...if an accident was gonna happen, I'm *so happy* it happened with you." I whispered, "Only you."

I stared up at the ceiling, overcome with emotion as the magnitude of this started to set in. "Wow." Not only was having a kid something I wasn't expecting now, it was something I'd doubted would *ever* happen for me.

"Owen..." She interrupted my thoughts.

I looked back at her, and she was crying again. An urgency grew inside of me. I needed to prove I was okay with this, that everything was going to be okay.

Still on my knees and grabbing both of her hands in mine, I started rambling. "I've fallen for you so hard. I'm not saying that because of what you just told me. I want you in my life. I want this baby. You're not gonna have to go through this alone. We can do this, Devyn. I'll do whatever it takes to make it work. Get you whatever you need and learn everything there is to learn about being a father. I'll buy every book, and heck, I'll even babysit for Holden and Colby. I—"

"Owen..." She shouted louder this time.

My heart nearly stopped when it finally hit me.

Six-and-a-half weeks?

I did the math as fast as my brain could possibly compute.

We'd met on April 15th—that was... *five-and-a-half* weeks ago.

Right? Or was it six-and-a-half weeks now?

Fuck.

My stomach dropped.

I *needed* reassurance.

My eyes found hers again. "It's mine, right?"

A teardrop fell down her cheek, followed by words that gutted me.

"I don't know."

❤CHAPTER 17

Devyn

It felt wrong to tell someone such monumental news over FaceTime. But what choice did I have? Two days later, my laptop was open on the coffee table, and my knee bopped up and down from nerves. I felt like I might throw up. Robert had just arrived in Italy and was going to be there filming for the next four months. At least I had some good news to lead with on the call, so I wouldn't have to jump into things too fast.

"So, I got a call from Stephen Solomon yesterday."

"Oh yeah? Rumor is he's a shoo-in for best director for that Vietnam movie he has coming out in October. Guy's on a roll the last few years."

"I'm glad you've noticed. Because a few months back, he and I had lunch. He told me about a new drama he was hoping to make. It's a book to film, and the novel was an Oprah Book Club pick. I pitched you for the lead role, but he wasn't ready to discuss casting quite yet. Yesterday he called and said he'd just finished reading the final screenplay." I paused for effect. "He agrees that you'd be perfect for it."

"Holy shit, really?"

"Yep. He wanted to know if you'd be interested in reading the script."

"Hell yeah."

I smiled. "I'll let him know and give him your address in Italy."

"Text me the name of the book after we hang up. I want to read that, too. I'll order it to my hotel from Amazon."

"You got it."

We talked about work for a while—how things were going there, an upcoming project he'd start once the current one wrapped, and his interest in going to one of this year's award ceremonies. I'd already requested tickets to all of them for him, so he'd just have to wait and see. When we came to a lull in the conversation, Robert smiled at me funny.

"What?" I asked.

"We make a good team, don't we?"

I'd had no clue how I was going to segue into telling him about the pregnancy, yet somehow he'd just rolled out the red carpet for me. My palms felt sweaty as I tried to formulate the right words to use.

"So…I, uh, have some other news I need to talk to you about."

"Yeah? Is it good news? Because I'm not sure I want to ruin the high I'm feeling right now with anything crappy."

I gnawed on my bottom lip. "I honestly don't know how you'll feel…"

Robert's face fell. "Shit. I was joking. But you look nervous, so now you're scaring me. What's going on, babe? Is there a problem with one of my upcoming jobs?"

"No, everything is fine workwise."

"Then what is it?"

I held my breath before spitting it out. "I…I…I'm pregnant, Robert."

He said nothing. I waited, but after a solid minute I couldn't take the silence anymore.

"Say something, please."

He swallowed. "Well, I didn't have that on my bingo card for this year."

"I'm sorry to tell you this way, on a video call. But I wasn't sure when we would see each other again."

He raked a hand through his hair and went quiet. Eventually, though, he nodded.

"You know what, Dev?"

"What?"

"You caught me off guard, but I can't say I'm upset about it."

"You're not?"

He shook his head. "I always imagined I'd have kids someday. I just assumed that day was still far in the future. But I'm thirty-four now, not exactly a spring chicken. And like I said, we make a good team."

Wow. Definitely not the reaction I'd expected. I covered my heart with my hand, feeling enough relief to make my eyes water. "Oh my God. It's like a giant weight has been lifted off my shoulders."

Robert smiled. "My girl's having my baby."

My.

Baby.

Oh shit.

No wonder that had gone so well. I hadn't dropped both shoes at once.

"Robert, I…"

"Did you pick out an obstetrician yet? Would it be weird if you went to my sister's husband? Andrew's practice is over in Calabasas. He's delivering their third early next year." His smile widened. "Holy shit. Our baby is going to have a cousin born the same year. That's pretty cool. I grew up with a ton of cousins, and the holidays were always so much fun."

"Robert, hang on…"

"When are you back in L.A.? I'll call Andrew and set up an appointment. I have to look at the filming schedule, but I can probably fly home for a day to go with you if we do it on a weekend. I'm sure Andrew will come in to see you, even if he doesn't have office hours. And we could—"

"Robert!"

He stopped abruptly. "What? If you don't want to see Andrew, if that makes you uncomfortable, I can ask him for some names. I'm sure he has plenty of qualified colleagues he can refer us to."

"Robert, I need to tell you something else."

He smiled. "Are you having twins? Because you already told me a soon-to-be two-time Academy Award-winning director wants me to read his script and that I'm going to be a dad. I don't think anything else is going to top that."

"Robert…" I closed my eyes. "I'm not sure you're going to be a dad. I'm not certain you're the baby's father."

The smile vanished from his face. "What?"

I explained the mathematics of the conception-date possibilities to him. "And the last time we were together was exactly seven-and-a-half weeks ago."

"Okay…but are you saying you've been with someone else since then?"

I nodded. "A little less than six weeks ago."

Robert's face twisted with anger. "Are you serious right now? Who the hell did you fuck?"

I felt awful having to tell him this, especially after he'd seemed genuinely excited about the prospect of becoming a father, but I wasn't going to let him talk to me that way.

"Who I've been with is none of your business."

"Like hell it isn't. I'd say it's definitely my business when you can't even tell me if you're pregnant with my damn kid. What did you do, hop into bed with the first guy you met in New York? Was it at the airport, for Christ's sake? Or maybe you joined the mile-high club and didn't even make it to New York before banging someone else."

Robert and I never spoke about who either of us slept with, not that there had been any men before Owen for me. But there certainly had been women for him over the years. Plenty. And we worked in a very small industry that thrived on gossip. I'd heard the rumors about his affairs.

"What did *you* do, hop into bed with the first extra you met on your last movie set? Who's in *your* bed at night while you're in Italy? Some twenty-one-year-old makeup artist from what I've heard…"

"This isn't about me," Robert snapped.

"That's right. It's not. It's about *us* and who we are to each other. We were *never* in a committed relationship. You've proven that with your actions, time and time again."

"So you're saying this isn't the first guy you fucked behind my back?"

My eyes widened. "I'm not having this conversation."

"Good. Neither am I."

I reached up to the edge of my laptop. "Goodbye, Robert. We can discuss this when you're able to be civil." Slamming it shut, I collapsed into the couch.

I wasn't sure which had been worse, pissing off Robert or breaking Owen's heart.

Later that morning, I spent a few hours walking around Central Park, trying to clear my head. It didn't work. Not in the slightest. Which was probably why I didn't even notice a woman waving at me from the window of the tattoo parlor until the door swung open.

"Hey, Devyn!" Billie yelled. "Hang on a second."

I stopped and forced a smile. "Hey, Billie."

"Do you think you can give me a hand for a minute?" She pointed to the shop window and a crooked poster hanging there. "I've been trying to get this sign straight for ten minutes. Every time I think it looks good, I come out to the street to double check, and the damn thing is lopsided. I'm beginning to think the window tilts when I'm not looking."

"Sure. What can I do to help?"

"Just stand there at the curb and direct me if it needs to go up or down while I'm inside."

"No problem."

Billie went back into the tattoo parlor. She peeled the poster from the glass, stepped back, and hung it...completely lopsided. I smiled and thumbed up on the right side. She adjusted it until I gave her two thumbs up, then affixed it to the window before coming out to the street to join me again.

"Oh my God." She chuckled. "That took two seconds, and it looks perfect. Thank you."

"It's definitely one of those things you need distance to see."

She nodded. "What are you up to? My one o'clock just canceled, and I have a few hours before the kids come home, so I was going to go grab some lunch. Want to join me?"

I guess my face answered before I did. Billie smiled and held up two hands.

"No biggie if you're busy. I forget not everyone has a schedule like I do, with random hours to kill during the day."

I liked Billie, at least what little I knew about her, and what was I rushing back to the apartment for? To beat myself up over the mess I'd gotten into?

"Actually, I'd love to have lunch."

Billie's eyes sparkled. "Maybe a glass of wine, too. Let me just grab my purse."

Fifteen minutes later, we were seated at a pub table in the bar area of a small Italian restaurant. The waiter came to take our drink order while handing us menus.

"I'll have a glass of sauvignon blanc," Billie said, then turned to me. "Unless you want to go wild and split a bottle. I'm not opposed to day drinking."

"I'd love to, but I can't." Realizing how that sounded, I quickly covered. "I have an important meeting later."

She turned back to the waiter. "Just a glass then. I'm woman enough to drink alone."

I smiled. "I'll have a water, please."

"No problem. I'll give you a few minutes to look at the menu."

After he walked away, I stared down at the lunch specials, but my brain was so unfocused, I couldn't read the printed words. I saw the letters, but it was like they were all blurry and jumbled. Luckily, Billie helped me out.

"The lasagna is really good here," she said. "So is the eggplant rollatini. I don't know what you're in the mood for, but if you want, we can split two things."

I shrugged. "Sure. The lasagna and eggplant sounds good."

The waiter came back with our drinks. Billie sipped her wine with a smirk on her face. It made me wonder if Owen had told his crew. I hadn't thought of that.

"So…I can't help myself. I have to say something."

Oh shit. "Okay…"

"I did Owen's tattoo. He told me the meaning behind it. I've always found men getting tattoos in honor of their women to be so romantic, but I didn't think I'd ever see the day."

"That Owen got a tattoo?"

"No, that the boy would be lovesick enough for such a romantic gesture."

Lovesick.

That made my heart hurt.

I tried with all my might to force a smile, but I just couldn't muster it. It was like an invisible heaviness weighed everything inside me down, and my lips followed. The mention of Owen's name resurfaced the image of his smiling face when I'd told him I was pregnant...and then how I'd destroyed that happiness when I'd had to tell him the baby might not be his. Tears welled in my eyes.

"Oh my God." Billie covered her mouth. "I'm so sorry. Did something happen between the two of you? I didn't mean to upset you."

The last thing I'd planned was to tell anyone else I was pregnant, but my insides felt like a volcano rumbling before the big eruption. Before I could stop myself, I started spewing all over the place.

"I'm pregnant, and when I told Owen, he was happy—not upset or angry—and then I had to tell him it might not be his because I'm a horrible person and slept with two men a few weeks apart, and my IUD needed to be changed, but my mother is useless, and how can I have a baby when I can't even get Heath to stop cutting school? Oh my God. What if I turn out like Vera, never paying my rent, taking off with a new boyfriend named Bo, and my baby winds up in foster care?" I started to hyperventilate. "My baby can't go into foster care."

Poor Billie's eyes widened. Though she quickly reached over and took my hand. "Close your eyes and take a breath, sweetie."

Hot tears streamed down my face. "Oh my God, Billie. What am I going to do?"

"You're going to listen to me for starters. Now close your eyes."

I squeezed them shut as tight as I could.

"Good. Now, give me three deep breaths. I'm going to count, and you're going to inhale until I get to five and then let it out. Keep your eyes shut and focus on nothing but breathing. Are you ready?"

"Not really."

"Let's do it anyway. Inhale and…one, two, three, four, five." She paused. "Now exhale and push out all the air in your lungs."

I did as instructed.

"Good, now let's do it again."

After a couple more rounds, my tears actually started to slow. I opened my eyes and looked across at Billie. She smiled warmly.

"Congratulations."

I wiped my cheeks. "Thank you."

"How far along are you?"

"Somewhere between seven-and-a-half and nine-and-a-half weeks. Which is the problem. I stupidly slept with Robert a couple of weeks before I left to come to New York. I'd been distancing myself from him, but I fell off the bandwagon."

"Robert is someone you had a relationship with?"

I nodded. "Off and on for three years."

"Okay. Will he make a good dad?"

I thought about it. Robert was self-absorbed and selfish in so many ways, but I'd seen him interact with his nieces and nephews. He was the kind of uncle who sat on the floor and played with them, and he kneeled down to their level to tell them they'd be okay when they scraped a knee. He was a good person. He'd just gotten caught up in the Hollywood life the last few years—too much being catered to and living extravagantly.

I blew out a jagged breath. "I think he would be a good dad, yeah."

"What about Owen? Do you think he'd make a good dad?"

I didn't have to think about that answer. "He'd make a great dad."

"Do you want a family?"

"I didn't think I did, but that somehow changed the moment I found out I was pregnant."

Billie smiled. "I know that feeling. Not only did I not want to have a baby, but I had a rule to never date a man with a child. What did I wind up doing? Dating a single dad with a baby momma who has a whole lot of baggage, raising his daughter as my own, and then getting pregnant myself. But you know what?"

"What?"

She squeezed my hand. "Sometimes the best things in life are the ones we don't see coming."

We talked for a long time—about pregnancy, Owen, and even Robert. Usually, I kept my relationship with him private, but I knew in my heart Billie was a person I could confide in. It was funny how sometimes you could barely know someone and yet know they could be trusted, yet the people we thought we knew so well were usually the ones who ended up burning us.

When the check came, Billie insisted on paying. She took the leather padfolio off the table, stuck her credit card inside, and held it up to the waiter. "There's a method to my madness," she said to me. "If I don't like you, I split the bill. If I do, I won't take no for an answer picking up the tab. Because then you'll feel obligated to buy me lunch—which means we'll become better friends."

I smiled. "I'd like that."

"I have to tell you, I'm the type of person who generally doesn't listen to advice on relationships or how to manage my family. I feel like what works for one person doesn't necessarily work for another, and that often leads to a feeling of failure. So I go with my gut." Billie held up a finger. "But I'm going to offer you a piece of advice anyway."

I laughed. "Okay…"

"Your relationship decisions need to be independent of your paternity results. Don't be with a man because he's the father of your baby. Be with a man you love with your whole heart. Life's too short to be stuck with the wrong guy."

I nodded. "That's good advice. Only I'm not even sure how to know who the right guy is."

Billie smiled. "It's easy. He's the one who makes you wonder if he can read your mind. Because he cares about what you need and makes that his priority."

❤CHAPTER 18

Owen

It was a nice day in the City, so in between showings, I did something unusual. Rather than go back to my office and catch up on work emails or return client phone calls, I grabbed a coffee and sat on a bench in Central Park—an attempt to sort out my very cluttered head. I'd vowed to be of clearer mind the next time I saw Devyn.

It had been two days since she'd dropped the bomb that she was pregnant. I certainly could've handled it better when she told me the baby might not be mine. I imagined few men in my predicament would have reacted calmly to that news, but I'd let my fear show when I should've been more cognizant of how tough the situation was for her. I had no desire to make already difficult circumstances worse. She had a lot on her plate—even before any of this happened. So, I needed to be strong on the outside, even if I felt like I was about to break on the inside.

There were just so many questions. Was I ready to be a father or kidding myself because of my feelings for Devyn? How would I be involved in her life if this baby wasn't mine and this Robert fucker was in the picture? Could I accept that…or would that mean the end of us? How would having a baby impact Devyn's ability to look after Heath and Hannah? How could she handle all that? My chest felt heavy just thinking about it all. I had to remind myself to breathe.

I'd never needed to talk to one of my friends so badly, but I couldn't betray Devyn's trust and tell any of the guys what was going on. It was too early for anyone to know. Anything could happen at this point. So, I'd keep the news inside and do my best to figure out how I was going to handle it on my own. So far I was doing a pretty shitty job, though.

Before this curveball, I'd been pondering what role I'd have in Heath and Hannah's life if Devyn and I were to end up together— how that might inadvertently turn me into a father figure. How ironic that this whole time I was possibly *already* a father.

The reality of it hit in waves.

I could be a father right now.

My kid would be fairly close to Hope and Maverick's ages. Colby, Holden, and I would be raising our kids together.

Then the other side of the coin always snapped me back to reality: *Devyn could be carrying Robert Valentino's baby.*

Sitting on this park bench had, in fact, done nothing to clear my head. Instead, my mind was working overtime.

My eyes wandered over to a little boy chasing some pigeons. His dad was only a few steps behind, smiling from ear to ear as his giggling son had the time of his life.

Would that be me in four years?

The hardest part was not knowing. I couldn't acclimate to the idea of becoming a father because I was afraid when I managed to get used to it, the truth would rip the rug out from under me. I had to prepare for both the best and worst-case scenarios at the same time.

The little boy I'd been watching suddenly tripped and fell. My stomach dropped. He'd been running so fast and not paying attention to where he was going. I stood up instinctively, wanting to help him, but his dad seemed to have everything covered. Sitting back down, I watched as his father bent to comfort him, checking the kid's legs for cuts and bruises, kissing his knee. Life for that little boy had gone from joyous to painful in a millisecond. But his tears eventually stopped, and the next thing I knew, he had a smile on his face again as he and his dad walked away hand in hand. I decided maybe the guy had offered to take his son for ice cream to make everything better. At least, that might've been what I would've done. Would I spoil my kid? *He? She?*

It might not be yours, Owen.

Snap out of it.

Man, could I relate to that little kid who fell. In two minutes, he'd gone from laughing to crying to smiling again. That felt like me lately. But ups and downs were a part of life; all you could control was whether you stayed down or got up and brushed yourself off. I guess I was at the same point now as that little kid when he fell flat on his face. It was up to me what to do next.

My phone rang, interrupting my thoughts.

It was Billie.

That's odd. She normally doesn't call me.

"Hey, Billie. Everything okay?"

"Yeah, yeah…just, um…calling to see how you're doing." She paused. "I had lunch with Devyn yesterday, and she ended up telling me about the pregnancy."

My mouth fell open. "Exactly *how much* do you know?"

"I know it might not be yours."

"Wow. Okay. I'm surprised she said anything. I didn't think—"

"She wasn't planning to, but she got pretty emotional, and it sort of came out." She paused. "Don't worry. I haven't told Colby or anyone else and don't plan to."

Phew. Because if Colby knew, the other guys would inevitably find out.

"How are you holding up?" she asked.

Billie wasn't someone to beat around the bush.

"Not good." I sighed. "I'm like an oscillating fan. My brain keeps moving from side to side—one second I'm angry and jealous that she could be carrying some other guy's baby, and the next, I'm hoping it could be mine." I stared over at an old woman peeling an orange on the bench across from me. "But I'm also scared, Billie. Because I don't know shit about babies, and I'm not ready for this. On the other hand, I'm also not ready to lose Devyn." I stared up at the sky. "It's just…a lot."

"You have every right to be confused and scared, Owen. It's not an easy situation. I mainly called because I wanted to let you know I'm here if you want to talk. Like I said, I won't say anything to Colby until you and Devyn tell me to. It's not my news to share. I assume you might want to wait until you know whether it's yours."

The idea of having to tell the guys Devyn was pregnant with someone else's baby made me nauseous. Fucking Brayden would continue to try to guess who "the actor" was. And I'd want to punch him.

"Thank you, Billie. I appreciate your discretion, and I have no idea when I plan to tell anyone. I haven't thought it through. I'm trying to grasp the magnitude of this myself before I begin letting other people's opinions in on the matter."

"I hear you." She sighed. "Life is funny, Owen. We don't always know why certain things happen. Sometimes you have to go along for the ride and see where it leads."

I shut my eyes for a moment. "How was she—Devyn—at lunch? You said she was emotional?"

"She's stressed to the max. She feels terrible for putting you in this position."

I shook my head. "She shouldn't. It takes two to tango. This is as much my responsibility as it is hers." An urgency to see her grew in my chest. "I'm glad you called. I've been trying to give her space, but now that I know she opened up to you, I feel better."

"I don't get the impression that space is what she needs right now."

My chest hurt. "Thank you." I nodded. "I needed to hear that."

After I hung up with Billie, I shot off the bench and went back to the building instead of back to work. In my rush to leave, I disrupted a group of pigeons, who flew away from me in unison. I laughed for the first time in days, thinking about the giggling little boy.

And about my little boy—or girl.
My child—or not.

When Devyn opened the door forty-five minutes later, I held up a Key lime pie I'd picked up on the way home.

"I thought maybe you could use this."

Her mouth spread into a smile. "It's not gonna solve all of my problems, but it sure as heck won't hurt, Dawson. You know I never turn down Key lime pie." She stepped aside. "Come in."

"I heard the way to your heart is through your stomach." I placed my free hand on her belly. *That sort of has double meaning now.* A jolt of electricity shot through me as I felt the heat of her abdomen. *My baby could be in there. Holy shit.* I shook the thought from my head. Devyn covered my hand with hers. Our eyes locked for a few moments, and even though I wanted to kiss her, I refrained. It didn't seem like the right moment.

Instead, I set the pie on her coffee table and said, "You know what I realized today?"

"What a clusterfuck my life is?" she answered.

"Well, that, too." I winked. "But no. I thought back to when you vomited that morning at the hotel in Boston."

"Yup." She nodded. "It all makes sense now, doesn't it?"

"It does." I sighed, rubbing my palms together. "So...Billie called me today."

Devyn crossed her arms. "Oh."

"I'm surprised you told her, but I'm glad you did."

She shrugged. "I hadn't planned to. She caught me in the middle of a breakdown, and it all came barreling out. Billie makes it easy to open up."

"She emphasized that she's not going to say anything until you give her the okay."

"Yeah, she mentioned that to me, too. I appreciate it. The less people that know right now the better," she said.

"I agree. And I won't say anything either, obviously, until you feel comfortable. It's no one's business but ours."

"Thank you." Devyn nodded. "I haven't said anything to Heath and Hannah, and I would hate for them to accidentally find out from anyone other than me. Right now, the only person who knows besides Billie is Mia." She hesitated. "Well, and Robert..."

My stomach sank. "You told him."

"Yeah, I had to."

"Of course." I exhaled, trying my best to remain neutral. "How did he react?"

"It started out pretty positive, until I had to tell him it might not be his." Her face turned pink. "Then he kind of shamed me for having slept with you so soon after he and I were last together. He seems to forget that we were never in an exclusive relationship and that he's the furthest thing from monogamous and has been with multiple people himself."

I fucking hated this guy. My jaw stiffened. "Double standards, anyone?"

"I really wish he had nothing to do with this situation." She shook her head. "I thought I did everything right, Owen. I always made sure he used protection as a backup to my IUD. And you know you and I used protection. The fact that I'm pregnant truly blows my mind."

"Nothing is foolproof, I guess. Sometimes, for reasons unbeknownst to us, fate has other plans. This was clearly meant to be." I looked down at her belly again. "This little one beat the odds."

She rubbed her stomach. "Whether I wanted this in my life right now or not, I think you're right. It *was* meant to be. I hope someday I can see that." She tilted her head to examine my face. "How are *you*? I left you in kind of a tizzy the other night."

I reached out to cup her cheek. "I'm okay, Devyn. I've been doing a lot of thinking, as you might expect—probably more thinking in a twenty-four-hour period than ever before in my life."

"Did you come to any conclusions?"

"Yeah, one." I smiled.

"What?"

"I'm still crazy about you." I caressed her skin with my thumb. "None of this changes that."

She closed her eyes briefly, seeming to relish my touch. "How is that even possible?"

"How is that *not* possible? You're still you—just with a little human growing inside you now."

"But it might not be yours…" she whispered.

Her words cut like a knife, a stark reminder that I needed to tread lightly, even if my emotions were getting the best of me. The cold reality of this situation meant I couldn't let my heart hijack my head.

"I'm not gonna lie, Devyn. I'm scared as fuck—of each scenario. If I'm about to be a father, I have a hell of a lot to learn and prepare for. And if the baby's not mine, I have to deal with the risk that Robert could complicate things between us. So, yeah, I'm terrified. But not in a way that makes me feel differently about you." I reached for her hand. "The only reason I'm scared is because *so much* is at stake."

She squeezed my hand and looked into my eyes. "I want it to be yours, Owen. Very badly."

Me, too. "I think the biggest challenge for me is trying to stop myself from falling in love with the idea of this baby being my kid. Every time I start envisioning him or her—my baby—with your beautiful eyes, I have to stop myself from going there." *I can't breathe.*

Her lashes fluttered. "You said you weren't sure if you wanted kids…"

"I know what I said. And I also know from watching my friends that even the most unlikely people can become great fathers. Both Colby and Holden have said becoming a dad is the best thing that ever happened to them." I smiled. "I might not be ready, but there's no way I won't fall in love with my kid."

Devyn's eyes glistened. "What do we do, Owen? It's going to be a while before we can find out the paternity. I left the doctor's office in a fog the other day, so I didn't even get a chance to speak to her about the risks of having an amniocentesis to find out about paternity. I may not know who the father is for a long time."

There was only one choice.

"Then I say…we live life. Continue getting to know each other. Share an occasional pie." I paused. "And generally try not to freak out. We'll need to help each other with that." I leaned in to kiss the top of her head. "We keep figuring out how to keep your brother and sister safe, too. And with each week, we'll be closer to the answer." I wiped a tear from the corner of her eye. "But make no mistake, the whole time, while pretending to be calm, I'll be wishing this baby is mine. And if it is, I'll figure out a way to become the dad this baby deserves."

Devyn sniffled. "What if it's *not* yours?"

That was the burning question. More than anything, I wanted to give her a clear answer. But I couldn't.

"Is it okay to admit I'm not ready to go there right now? That I don't want to think about that?"

She nodded. "Yeah, it's okay."

"We have some time, Devyn. This is not something we have to figure out this minute." I paused. "You know…when Ryan died, it hit us all hard. But his death taught me not to take life for granted anymore. I'm alive. I'm healthy. You're healthy. This baby is hopefully healthy. We're all gonna be okay. Life is a privilege, even when times are tough. It's a privilege to experience it all—the good and the bad."

"Losing someone so close to you puts things in perspective, huh?"

"It does. The ability to be here with you right now, to share a pie, and to ponder the fact that I *could be* having a child is a blessing, even if it's not the perfect situation."

Devyn let out a long breath. "Thank you for putting my mind at ease, even if just for today." She wrapped her arms around my neck. "What can I do for you? What do you need from me to get through this?"

"You sure you want to ask a question like that?" I asked seductively.

She raised a brow. "Loaded question?"

"Actually, I know *exactly* what I want."

"What?"

"I'd love for you to be my date to Holden and Lala's wedding next week."

Her eyes widened. "Seriously?"

"Yes."

She beamed. "I would love to go."

"Cool." I grinned. "Then that's what we focus on next. Let's not worry about anything else until after the wedding."

Devyn smiled, and I could feel her shoulders relax. "I can deal with that."

"I get to bring a plus-one, but shhh… I won't tell anyone it's actually plus two."

🖤CHAPTER 19

Devyn

"**H**oly shit!" Two days later, Heath busted into my room while I was getting dressed. Getting an eyeful of me standing in my underwear, he turned around as quickly as he'd rushed in and groaned, "Is there a pain-free way to poke your own eyeballs out?"

I'd been about to put on a bra, but instead grabbed my bathrobe from the bed and wrapped it around me. "You don't barge into a room with a closed door without knocking, Heath!"

"I'm sorry." He kept his back to me while he spoke. "But there's someone here."

I pulled the tie of my robe snug. "Well, they'd better be important. And besides barging in, you need to stop with the language."

"But this is *holy shit* worthy."

I rolled my eyes. "I'm decent. You can turn around."

"I'd rather not look at you. Maybe forever."

"Who is here, Heath? Is it CPS?"

"No. The dude from *The Last Man Down* is here, that movie about the fighter pilot. The freaking pilot is in our living room."

My eyes bulged. "Robert? Robert's here?"

"I didn't ask his name. But he's looking for you."

Shit. I walked over to my brother and nudged his back. "Go put your shoes on. You need to leave for school."

"But the actor is in our living room—"

"Get your shoes on and grab your backpack, or you're going to be late."

He groaned again but went across the hall to his bedroom while I walked out to the living room.

The sight of Robert standing there took my breath away. He had a giant bouquet of white roses in his arms—there had to be five dozen. When he saw me, he smiled, and I swear, his teeth gleamed like in a cartoon.

"There she is…" he said.

"Robert, what are you doing here?"

"Coming to see my girl." His eyes dropped to my stomach. "Or girls."

"*Shhh…*" I looked behind me and lowered my voice. "My brother and sister are here. I haven't told them yet."

Robert hooked an arm around my waist and hauled me against him. "You look sexy as shit. Maybe you're glowing."

From behind me, a door slammed shut. I tried to disentangle myself from Robert's hold before my siblings walked in, but Robert didn't let go. He gripped my waist tighter and held on. Of course, Heath's eyes zoned right in on that hand. Hannah took one look at the man standing next to me and her mouth dropped open.

"Oh my God. You're…that guy."

Robert grinned. "Which guy?"

"The one from the movies."

"You mean *Top Gun?*"

She shook her head. "No, the one that didn't suck."

Robert chuckled and pointed to Hannah. "Yep. That's your sister alright."

"What are you doing here?" Heath asked. "Are you Devyn's client or something? She never mentioned she knew anyone *this* famous."

"I am her client. But Dev's also my girlfriend."

Heath and Hannah's eyes grew wide as saucers. I shook my head and peeled Robert's fingers from my waist. "You guys are going to be late for school. You better get going."

"But…"

I prodded Heath forward. "CPS is already up my butt. You guys need to be on time. Now skedaddle."

Neither of them looked very happy, but they moseyed to the door.

"Have a good day, guys!" Robert yelled. "Nice to finally meet you, Helen and Heath."

I shot him a dirty look. "It's *Hannah*."

Once my siblings were out the door, I took a deep breath. "Why did you do that?"

"Do what?" He looked clueless.

"Tell my brother and sister I was your girlfriend."

Robert shrugged. "Because it's the truth."

I shook my head. "What are you doing here, Robert?"

He held up the flowers. "I came to bring you these. And those…" He gestured toward the living room couch and a giant pile of gifts I hadn't noticed.

"How…how could you have carried all of that?"

"My assistant carried half."

I frowned. "The gorgeous little twenty-two-year-old, starry-eyed blonde you hired recently?"

Robert flashed a cocky grin. "Sounds like someone's jealous."

"Seriously, Robert, you should be in Italy. What are you doing here?"

He cupped my cheeks. "I came to apologize. You caught me off guard on the phone, and I acted like an asshole."

In all the years Robert and I had been seeing each other, I didn't think he'd ever apologized. I wasn't sure what to do with it.

"Can you forgive me?" he pouted.

I sighed. "Of course."

"I was just lashing out because I was hurt. So I wanted to make you hurt, too."

"I know."

"Can we talk? I can only stay for a few hours. I have to be on set tomorrow morning, so I have an afternoon return flight to Rome."

"Sure. Let me put some clothes on."

Robert tugged at my robe tie. "Or...you can take some off, and we can kiss and make up and talk later?"

I shook my head. "I'm going to go change."

"Shame." He winked. "You want to put these in water first?"

"I doubt Vera has a vase, and if she does, it's probably not big enough to fit that rose bush you bought." I pointed to the kitchen. "Why don't you see if you can find one while I get dressed?"

"Sure."

Inside the bedroom, I locked the door and leaned against it. I couldn't believe Robert was here, that he'd come to apologize and talk. Any other time in the last three years, I would've been excited. But now...I wasn't sure how I felt. I cared about him. That wasn't a question. And I was relieved to know he wasn't going to be a jerk about this pregnancy. That was a stress I didn't need. But was I excited to see Robert the way I would've been a year ago? The type of excitement a woman gets when she hasn't seen her man for a while?

A knock at the bedroom door startled me from my thoughts.

"Dev?"

"Yes?"

"The only thing I can find that will hold the flowers is a blender."

"Oh. Okay."

"Do you want me to use that?"

"Ummm... Give me a minute to finish getting dressed, and I'll look around the rest of the apartment."

"Sounds good."

After I heard Robert's footsteps retreat, I forced myself to get dressed. I wasn't going to be able to figure out how I was feeling right now anyway. And it was probably best that Robert and I talked first. That might make things clearer. After I threw on shorts and a T-shirt, I dug through the hall and bathroom closets for something to put flowers in. The only thing I could find was a wastepaper basket, but that was a better choice than a blender people ate out of.

Robert was leaning against the kitchen counter when I returned. I'd been too shocked earlier to notice how good he looked. The man was movie-star handsome, with blindingly perfect bone structure, sandy blond hair that always needed a cut, a deep year-round tan, and Paul Newman-esque blue eyes. Irresistible charm tied up the package with a big, beautiful bow.

I smiled. "Looks like you've had some time in the sun between takes."

"There are a lot of outdoor scenes."

The flowers were laying on the counter. I picked them up and plopped them into the garbage can without removing the cellophane wrapping.

Robert raised a brow. "Are you throwing my roses out?"

I turned on the faucet and added water. "It's the closest thing I could find to a vase." When I was done, I opened the refrigerator door. "You want something to drink?"

"I'll have whatever you're having."

"I'm having water."

"Water? You drink coffee until it's late enough to switch to wine."

I frowned. "Not anymore. Caffeine. And wine is out, too."

"Oh. Shit. Yeah, right. I didn't even think of that."

"But I can make you a cup, if you want?"

"You sure you don't mind?"

"I might take a few sniffs, but I think I'll live."

Robert smiled. "Okay. Thanks."

After I brewed a cup in the Keurig, I motioned toward the living room. "Why don't we go sit."

"Lead the way…"

I had to move *thirteen* gifts from the couch to make room for us. "What's in all these boxes?"

"Baby gifts. I went a little crazy. I don't like the color yellow, so some of the boxes have two of the same outfit, one in pink and one in blue."

I was *definitely* not ready for baby clothes. "Do you mind if I don't open them right now?"

Robert shrugged. "Whatever you want."

The room got quiet, and Robert watched me over the brim of his mug as he drank. "How are you feeling?"

"Pretty good. I'm tired, but I think that has a lot to do with stress. No morning sickness or anything."

"Stress isn't good for you or the baby. I read it in my new copy of *A Dumb Man's Guide to a Pregnant Woman.*"

"That's actually a thing?"

"Yep. I started it on the plane on the way over. I'm about forty-percent done."

"Then you might know more than me."

Robert lifted his chin to the pile of presents now on the floor. "*What to Expect When You're Expecting* is in one of those boxes. You'll catch up."

I smiled. "Thank you."

He looked down into his coffee mug for a long time before meeting my eyes again. "You know what I've realized over the last few days, now that I've had a chance for the news to sink in?"

"What?"

"There's no one else in the world I would want to have a baby with."

My heart sank. And here I'd been hoping this child belonged to another man. I took a deep breath and blew it out audibly. "You've apologized. But I also owe you an apology. I'm mortified that I can't tell you for sure if you're the father or not."

"I'm not gonna lie, that part is not easy to swallow. I let myself stew over it for a day or so, but then I realized you were right. We weren't exclusive. I saw other people occasionally, so it wasn't fair to expect you to be monogamous when I wasn't."

Wow. The shocks just kept coming. I smiled sadly. "You sound so…enlightened."

"I spent three grand on therapy over Zoom the last few days."

Now *that* sounded more like the Robert I knew. "Well, seems like it worked at least."

Robert took my hand. "I want this, Dev. I want this baby to be mine and for you to be my baby's mother."

"You do?"

He nodded. "You're going to be a great mom. You have your priorities straight. Like all those times I selfishly tried to get you to fly out to L.A. recently? You made your siblings your priority because they need you. That was the right thing to do. You *always* do the right thing. It's not even something you have to think about like I do. It's just who you are. And I'm hoping I can learn from you, because I want to make our baby my priority, no matter what. I'm not going to be as good at it as you are, but if you have a little patience with me, I promise to try really hard to get it right."

My eyes filled with tears. "Thank you for saying that."

Over the next few hours, Robert and I talked. *Really talked.* I was certain we'd never had a more mature conversation, or as deep. We spoke about his absentee father, my nonexistent parents, and how we both planned to learn from their mistakes, not repeat history. Before I knew it, it was almost lunch time, and I hadn't looked at my phone or opened my laptop. So when Robert went to use the bathroom, I grabbed my cell.

I had a dozen texts, but the third one from the top made my heart stop.

> **Owen: I'll come up at 11:30 to grab you for lunch. The little Italian place you went with Billie recently okay?**

Shit! My lunch date with Owen had completely slipped my mind. I looked up at the corner of my phone for the time. *11:10*. The last thing I needed was Owen showing up with Robert here. So I quickly texted back.

> **Devyn: I'm so sorry for the last-minute notice. I need to cancel.**

> **Owen responded almost immediately.**

> **Owen: Everything okay? Are you feeling alright?**

I didn't want to lie. He'd been so honest with me, even when it wasn't easy. But I hated to make him feel bad, too. I chewed my fingernail, feeling like a horrible person as I tried to figure out what to say. Eventually, I decided he would be more upset with a lie than a truth that hurt.

> **Devyn: Robert is here. He showed up at my door this morning—to apologize for how he acted and talk things through.**

I stared down at my phone, anxiously waiting for a response. After a long couple of minutes, the dots started to jump around, but then they stopped again. Robert returned from the bathroom, but I kept my phone in my hand for the next hour. Sadly, it never buzzed with an incoming text. I even checked my messages twice, to make sure I hadn't missed anything.

"Are you hungry?" Robert asked. "I have a couple of hours until I have to leave for my flight. You want to grab something to eat?"

The thought of running into Owen, or even one of his buddies, while out and about with Robert took away any appetite I might've had. "I'm not really too hungry. But why don't I order us something? I'll Uber Eats it."

"Good with me." Robert smiled. "With so little time, I'd prefer not to share you with anyone anyway."

Share me with anyone. I forced a smile and checked my phone once more.

Still nothing...from the man he was sharing me with.

♥

I'd just climbed into bed when my phone buzzed from the nightstand. *Owen* flashed on my screen. My pulse sped up, and I flicked the bedside lamp back on.

Owen: Is he staying the night?

My heart ached. That's what he'd been thinking all day? That Robert was still here and going to spend the night? God, I sucked. I hadn't texted him again because I was trying to give him space. But I'd made things worse.

Devyn: No, he's gone. He went back to Rome. He had to get back to the set.

I waited on pins and needles while Owen typed back. It seemed to take forever, or at least it felt that way.

Owen: Can we talk? I can come up, or you can come down here. But I know the kids are probably sleeping.

I pulled back the blanket, already climbing out of bed.

Devyn: It's fine. Come up.

Owen: I'll be there in five.

I'd taken a hot shower earlier, trying to unknot the ball of tension in my neck. But I'd been too lazy to wash my hair, even though it had gotten wet. One glance at the mirror and I regretted not even brushing it out. If my complicated life didn't scare Owen away, this look might seal the deal. I spent five minutes trying to clean myself up, but I needed more like five hours. Or maybe five days.

Owen knocked lightly. I swung the door open before he had a chance to lower his arm.

"Hey." I smiled.

Owen's face was grim. He nodded. "I'm sorry to bother you so late."

"It's fine." I stepped aside. "I'm glad you did. Come in."

Two steps in the door, he stopped short. I had to follow his line of sight to figure out what was wrong.

The gifts.

Shit. They were piled up on the floor, higher than the coffee table. I still hadn't opened a single one.

"Sorry," I said. "Robert brought them. I didn't feel up to opening any."

Owen took a deep breath and gestured in the other direction. "Kitchen?"

I forced a smile. "Sure."

Unfortunately, I'd forgotten about the flowers, too—the dozens that were impossible to miss. Owen's eyes snagged on them immediately. The face he made could only be described as defeated.

"I'm sorry," I said. Picking up the wastebasket, I looked around, then opened the cabinet under the sink and tucked them inside.

Owen smiled sadly. "You didn't have to do that. But thanks."

"Do you want something to drink? A glass of wine, maybe?"

"No, thank you."

We sat down at the kitchen table across from each other.

"How are you feeling?" he asked.

"Physically? Fine. Emotionally? A wreck."

He nodded. "I guess your talk didn't go well?"

"No, it was fine. But you didn't text me back, and I've been worried you were upset."

"I'm sorry. I didn't mean to make you worry."

"There's no need for you to apologize. I'm sorry Robert showed up unannounced, and that I had to cancel our lunch."

Owen raked a hand through his hair. "I couldn't stop thinking that this is how it might be. If Robert is the father, you'll be spending lots of time with him. It would be inevitable." He shook his head. "I know it was my idea to live in the moment, but I couldn't stop myself from picturing it. I just needed some time."

"Of course. I don't blame you. Who wouldn't need some processing time?"

Owen went quiet for a minute. I could see the wheels turning in his head.

"What did you feel when you saw him?" he finally asked.

"Surprised."

"No, I mean your feelings." He tapped his chest. "In here."

I thought about it. "Honestly, I think I was more worried about what you would think than anything."

"Do you love him?"

"I care about him. And maybe I do love him in some form. We have a lot of history together. But I don't know that I love him like you're asking me, like a woman loves a man she wants to be with."

Owen swallowed. He looked across to the living room to the pile of wrapped gifts. "I can't compete with that guy. He's famous and rich. I do pretty well, but he'd be able to give you a very different life."

"I don't need you to compete. And I don't need anyone to give me any certain type of life. I can take care of myself."

He looked up into my eyes. "Then what do you need from me, Devyn?"

"I just need *you* to be *you*."

Owen closed his eyes. When he opened them, he extended his hand. "Then come here. Because me being me really needs to kiss the shit out of you. I've been jealous all day, and I want to feel like you're only mine for a little while."

♥CHAPTER 20

Owen

That weekend, Holden and Lala's wedding was just the escape Devyn and I needed. With our attention focused on the happy couple, we were able to forget about our worries, for one day, at least.

The ceremony at St. Sebastian's church was the perfect length, not too long, and the reception followed at Club Noir downtown. Holden knew the owner and was able to rent the entire space. It felt more like a night out than a formal affair. There were candles everywhere in the dimly lit space and a giant disco ball hanging from the ceiling. The dance floor was the centerpiece, and Holden's band was scheduled to play a couple of sets later, although there was a DJ to start the evening. The vibe was all *very Holden*.

He'd done a damn good job planning all the details—even the flowers, which he swore Lala had nothing to do with. I'd have to tease him more about that sometime. Lala looked beautiful in a lace, strapless gown with a black sash around her waist. Her curly hair was pulled back into a loose bun with some pieces framing her face.

One traditional thing, perhaps, was a long head table draped in a black tablecloth and adorned with candles and roses in different shades of red. When I spotted the empty chair next to Holden's, I nearly lost it. That's where Ryan would've been sitting, and I knew in my heart he was with us in spirit.

I'd been tough on Holden when he started pursuing Lala, skeptical of his intentions. Lala was like a little sister to me, and I'd felt like I had to protect her the way Ryan would've. Holden had a reputation, and I'd had a hard time separating that from his genuine feelings for her. But I could see now that my worry wasn't necessary. The more times I saw how much Holden cared for Lala, the more I learned to trust his intentions. And now, I couldn't imagine any other outcome than this one.

Ryan's chair wasn't the only thing making me emotional today. Having Devyn by my side as I watched one of my best friends get married meant a lot. More than anything, though, I couldn't stop thinking about the fact that she could be carrying my child. Every few minutes, that thought would cross my mind. And then Robert and his fucking gifts and flowers would infiltrate my brain and ruin it.

Devyn was in a particularly good mood tonight, with a light in her eyes that was rare lately. It felt like she'd let go of all of the uncertainties, even if only for a day. She looked gorgeous in a sleeveless black dress and red heels, her hair done half-up, half-down. She wore a thin string of pearls, understated but incredibly sexy.

Colby cleared his throat and tapped the mic, pulling everyone's attention to the stage, where he was readying to give his best-man speech.

"Is this thing turned on?" He smirked. "Of course, it's turned on, like everyone else in Holden's vicinity." He laughed. "It has a boner for the sexy drummer boy."

Holden rolled his eyes as Lala playfully shook him.

"As you all know, one of my best friends in the world, Holden Catalano, got married today. Which means hell has officially frozen over."

I chuckled, glancing over at Devyn, who had a huge smile on her face. Once again, it made me happy to see her so relaxed.

"Holden was kind enough to roast me on my own wedding day, so it's only fair that I get to do the same. But Holden specifically requested that I not share any salacious stories about him." Colby looked over at Holden. "Which is why I had so much trouble coming up with this speech—blank page for days."

Holden shrugged as everyone laughed.

"Seriously, though, in our tight-knit group of five, he was the last one we expected to get married. Holden always had women falling at his feet. And I do believe he'd still be single if he hadn't fallen in love with Lala. She is the only woman on Earth who could possibly get him to settle down. And in case anyone has been living under a rock, I should point out that Lala happens to be our good friend's sister." Colby sighed and looked up at the ceiling, appearing as though he might break down. "Ryan is no longer with us, and we miss him so much," he continued after a moment, his voice shaky. "But we know he's looking down on this day and saying, 'What the hell is my sister thinking?'"

Colby winked at Holden. "Holden's affinity for Lala over the years was probably the worst-kept secret ever. We all knew he had feelings for her as far back as when we were teenagers. I once caught him and Lala on the roof of Lala and Ryan's house together. He tried to give me a bogus excuse about why he was up there with her—something about watching the stars. But I knew the only thing he wanted to watch was her."

A few *awwws* moved through the crowd.

"It took years for them to actually find their way to each other," Colby continued. "And if you knew Holden during those in-between years, you know that all of us being here today is a bigger miracle than Jesus turning water into wine."

The crowd roared.

"I mean, Holden wasn't the *biggest* playboy on the planet or anything." He paused. "But if that guy had died, well…" He grinned. "Holden would've taken the crown."

My shoulders shook in laughter.

"But along came Lala." He looked over at her. "Unfortunately, she was engaged. But thankfully, when God made Holden, he forgot to add a morality chip." Colby shook his head as he looked over at them. "Sweet Lala, the beautiful brainiac. I used to think you were the smartest girl on the planet. But then you had to go and ruin it by marrying this guy."

Colby flashed a wicked grin as he looked out at the audience. After the laughter dissipated, he said, "All kidding aside, it's clear to us now that you two are perfect for one another. You balance each other like yin and yang. Holden used that analogy to describe my wife, Billie, and me, so I'm stealing it because, well, I'm not that creative. But I have to say, it probably applies even more accurately to Lala and Holden. There is no smarter woman or dumber man alive."

Devyn's jaw dropped as she looked over at me in amusement. I just shrugged.

"I'm happy that the guys and I decided not to kill you, Holden, when we found out about you and Lala," Colby said. "Because then none of us would be here celebrating today. And where would Holden be without you, Lala?" Colby checked his watch. "He would be just waking up around this time with a hangover." He smiled. "Now the only girl keeping him up all night is baby Hope."

"Truth," I muttered.

"I'm gonna wrap up this speech now," Colby announced. "I know you all want to get to the food, but that's not the reason I'm ending here. It's because I'm running out of good things to say without having to delve into Holden's X-rated past."

The crowd laughed.

"I'll just say this. I don't know of two people who love each other more. And if Ryan were here—after we calmed him down and convinced him not to beat the crap out of Holden—I know he'd see things as we do. Holden loves Lala more than life itself. And no two people in the world deserve each other more. That's not another hidden insult, either. No punch line on that one. It's the truth." Colby lifted his glass. "To our honorary sister, Lala, and our crazy but lovable friend, Holden. May you have a long and prosperous marriage, filled with the same joy bestowed upon me and Billie." He paused. "And may you eventually settle the debate about which of you is prettier."

The sound of clapping rang out. It brought me immense relief that Colby was the one who'd had to get up there and give that speech. I couldn't have done it half as well. Public speaking was never my thing.

I reached for Devyn's hand. With our fingers threaded together, I brought her hand to my mouth and said, "Thank you for being my date today."

"It's my pleasure. Happiness is contagious, you know?"

"If this were before I met you, I'd be thrilled for Holden, of course, but probably a bit lonely. Weddings have a way of making you reflect on your own situation. It's hard not to compare someone else's joy with what might be lacking in your own life."

She nodded. "I know *exactly* what you mean."

I squeezed her hand. "Comparison is the thief of joy, right?"

"That saying is definitely true."

"It's why I plan to go out and buy a hundred baby gifts this week." I exhaled.

"Don't you dare. I told you, all I need is for you to keep being you. You give me your time and attention. That's something Robert knows he could never give me. He tried to make up for a lot by bringing those gifts. But they mean nothing."

I looked down at our hands. "As much as everything is up in the air right now, I feel fulfilled whenever I'm with you—in the moment. It's why today is much better with you by my side. I'm enjoying just hanging out with you."

Even if these days are all we have before reality crashes down on us.

"There's nowhere I'd rather be than here with you right now, Owen. Weddings are normally tough for me, too. They used to remind me of what my life was missing. And that would lead to memories of my mom and the lack of love there. I think everyone just wants to be loved, you know?" She looked out toward the head table. "But I don't need to compare my life to anyone else's today. Because *you* make me happy. And that's a good feeling."

"I'm glad, beautiful." I smiled. "Do you have to be home by a certain time tonight?"

"Heath and Hannah are spending the night at Heath's friend Lucas's house. He's the one friend whose parents I know. I spoke to them and everything."

"That's great. I'm so glad we don't have to rush back."

"Hey, I'm headed to the bar," Brayden interrupted. "What do you guys want?"

I looked over at Devyn, feeling badly that he'd put her on the spot.

"Just a seltzer with lime would be great," she said.

"A seltzer with lime *and tequila* coming up." He winked.

"No, really." Devyn held out her palm. "Alcohol hasn't been agreeing with me lately. So I'm taking a break."

He laughed. "Seriously?"

"Yeah."

"Well, that blows. Weddings are much more fun when you're drunk." He turned to me. "Seltzer for her. Beer for you?"

"Yeah. Any kind is fine. Thanks, man."

Brayden patted me on the shoulder and headed for the bar.

Devyn sighed and spoke in a low voice, "How long can I get away with that excuse?"

"Don't worry about it." I rubbed her leg. "It doesn't matter what anyone thinks."

"I guess it will come out soon enough." She rubbed her tummy. "I can only hide it for so long."

"We can say you had too much Key lime pie…"

She chuckled.

The thought of Devyn's belly swelling over the months to come gave me chills. I wondered how soon we'd be able to do a paternity test. She'd said she planned to discuss it with her doctor at her next appointment. I shook that thought from my head, because there was nothing to be done about it now.

After Brayden returned with our drinks, they served dinner. Devyn and I had both chosen steak, which was cooked to perfection.

Later, after watching Holden smash cake into Lala's face during the cake cutting, I turned to my gorgeous date and held out my arm. "Shall we dance, Miss Marks?"

"I would love to, Mr. Dawson." She flashed a huge smile. "Thank you for asking."

Devyn followed me to the dance floor as "Love Shack" by the B-52s began. Her laugh was infectious as she bounced to the music. I'd never seen her so carefree. I didn't know what was going on tonight, but I wanted to bottle it up. I clapped my hands as she shook her hips, and I couldn't resist bringing her in for a kiss. I was crazy about this woman and didn't care who witnessed that.

We danced to three more songs before she suddenly stopped and stumbled over to the edge of the dance floor.

My heart sank as I followed. "What's wrong, Devyn?"

"I don't know. My stomach started to hurt just now. A lot of cramping all of a sudden." She held on to her abdomen. "I think I need to go to the restroom."

"Yeah." I looked around frantically. "Let's find it."

Weaving through people, I took her hand and rushed her over to the corner of the venue where the bathrooms were.

My pulse raced as I waited outside the ladies' room. After three minutes, I couldn't take it anymore. I cracked the door open. "Everything okay in there, Devyn?"

"I'll be right out," she hollered, her voice echoing.

She hadn't exactly assured me that things were okay.

The door opened, and Billie emerged with a sullen look on her face.

"What the hell is going on?" I asked.

"I happened to be in there when she walked in." Billie frowned as she whispered, "She's bleeding a little, Owen."

"Fuck," I muttered, staring at the bathroom door.

"It doesn't necessarily mean anything, but I think you should take her to the emergency room."

"Yeah." I nodded. "Of course." I looked beyond her shoulders, hoping the door would open.

A few seconds later, Devyn finally came out.

Billie rubbed her back.

"Billie told me," I said. "Let's get you to the hospital."

Seeming in a daze, she nodded and took my hand.

The music faded into the distance as we made our way out of the club. I was certain I'd have some explaining to do—particularly to Holden—but I couldn't worry about that now. Devyn was the only thing that mattered.

We got in my car, and I raced to the nearest hospital. I had to remind myself to slow down, because the only thing that could make this worse was an accident.

By some miracle, when we got there, they took us right in after I explained that she was pregnant and bleeding.

Devyn was given a bed with a partition separating her from the next person.

We were alone for a moment, and she turned to me.

"I'm scared." Her eyes glistened.

I took her hand in mine. "I know."

I wanted to say something encouraging, but I refused to give her false hope when I didn't know shit. I was scared, too, but admitting that also wouldn't help.

A tear rolled down her cheek, and I reached out to swipe it. Holding her hand, I bounced my legs nervously, waiting for a nurse or doctor to enter.

Finally, someone came in, took her vitals, and drew some blood. Someone then wheeled in a machine.

And everything after that happened pretty fast. Before I knew it, they had turned on the ultrasound screen. The doctor was silent for a long while as she moved the wand over Devyn's stomach. Then she pointed to the screen. "You can see the heartbeat right here. Everything looks stable."

"Oh, thank God," Devyn breathed.

My breath left me, not only because I was relieved, but because I couldn't believe my eyes. *There he is.* Or she. There was a little head. It was moving. And I could *see* its little heart beating.

That could be my kid.

Holy shit.

I hadn't been prepared for this. But I felt so much love inside me that it was scary. I wasn't even sure if this baby was mine, yet I still felt it. Love. Fear. So many emotions pummeled me.

"Do you see him, Owen?" Devyn whispered.

"I do," I muttered, still staring at the screen.

"Everything's checking out fine," the doctor said, interrupting my trance. "It's not unusual to experience some bleeding and cramping during the first trimester. Sometimes, of course, it can mean miscarriage. Other times, it's perfectly normal. But you should take extra care to reduce stress and get good sleep." She turned to me. "You can breathe now, Daddy. Everything looks okay."

Daddy.

If only I could truly breathe. But that wouldn't be happening for a while.

CHAPTER 21

Devyn

"Ta-da!"

My mouth dropped open. Mia stood on the other side of my door with her arms up in the air.

"Oh my God. What are you doing here?"

"I was able to finish everything I needed to do a few days early, so I jumped on the redeye last night."

"Why didn't you tell me?"

"I thought it would be more fun to surprise you."

"Well, why are you standing out there? Get over here. I need a hug!"

Mia squeezed me tight, and I felt my shoulders loosen and drift down a few inches. I hadn't realized how much I needed my best friend here. "God, I missed you." I sighed.

"I'm glad to hear that. Because I've been a little jealous with all the Billie and Lala talk lately. I was starting to feel like I was being replaced."

"Never!" I smiled and waved her inside. "Come in. Come in."

Mia wheeled her pink luggage into the apartment. "Are Heath and Hannah here? I can't believe I'm finally going to get to meet them."

I shook my head. "They're already off to school. They left ten minutes ago."

"Damn. It's just as well, I guess. Because I have an appointment in less than an hour."

"You have to work already? I thought you said you'd get a few days off before you had to jump into stuff at the new gallery?"

"I do. My appointment isn't work related. It's personal."

"Oh?"

Mia grinned and clapped her hands. "I'm getting a tattoo!"

"What? Are you joking?"

"Nope. I had the tattoo dream again."

She didn't have a single one, but Mia had been having recurring dreams about getting tattoos for longer than I'd known her. They happened once or twice a year, and each time, the dream started with a tattoo and ended with her meeting some random hot guy. In one dream, she got a tattoo of a crescent moon, and later that day she met a neurosurgeon. In another, she had the outline of a butterfly tattooed on her thigh, and when she went back a few weeks later to have it colored in, there was a famous rock star getting inked in the chair next to her. She left the tattoo parlor and went on tour with him. Sometimes she had the same dream more than once.

"What was the dream this time?"

"It was a new one. I was in a foreign country getting a tattoo. I'm not sure which one, but it was really pretty with high cliffs. After the tattoo was finished, I went for a walk along the waterfront, and some gorgeous guy yelled to me from his yacht. He pointed to the bandage covering my wrist and asked if I was okay. We wound up having espresso on his yacht, and when I took off the bandage to show him what I'd gotten, he had the same *exact* tattoo. We sailed around the Mediterranean all summer."

I chuckled. "But I thought you were against *actually* getting a tattoo? I believe your exact words were, '*You don't put a bumper sticker on a Bentley.*'"

"I borrowed that quote from Kim Kardashian during my reality-TV phase when I thought she was my guru. Now I'm into motivation and mindset podcasts, and I've changed my tune. I need to work on manifestation. If I'm ever going to meet Prince Charming, I need to put it out there to the world that I'm here for it. Getting the tattoo from my dream is my way of doing that."

"I wish you would've told me. I could've asked Billie for an appointment. Her work is amazing."

"Girl, who do you think is doing my ink? I stalked her the day after you told me you'd made a new friend." Mia winked. "I was sizing up the competition, but you were right. Her work is incredible. When I found out yesterday that I could switch to an earlier flight, I called her shop. The woman who answered said there was a six-month wait to get a tattoo from Billie and asked if I wanted to be put on the cancelation list in case of a last-minute opening. I told her I'd love to, but I was only in town for a few days. We got to talking, and I said I was visiting my friend who lived in the same building as the tattoo parlor. A minute later, Billie herself was on the phone and offering to come in early to pop my cherry. Apparently your name has some big pull around here."

"Oh, I'm so glad! You're going to love her."

"Where can I open my suitcase?" Mia looked around. "I need to wash my face and put some makeup and a cute outfit on. I want to look good for the pics you'll be taking of me getting my first tattoo."

I smiled. "Come on. I'll make space in my bedroom."

Mia lifted a brow as she grabbed her suitcase. "*Your* bedroom. Not Vera's?"

I sighed. "I flipped the mattress and bought new sheets, so I think I can call it mine for now."

Mia followed me down the hall. "No news about her, I take it?"

"Nope. Not a peep. It's like she vanished. This is the longest she's ever been gone."

"I can't believe the bitch hasn't even called to check on—" Mia suddenly paused. "Umm, what the heck is all this?"

I'd forgotten about the now-five-foot-tall pile of gifts stacked in the corner of the bedroom. All of which were still wrapped. I frowned, looking at them. "Oh. That's Robert. I told you he showed up with a bunch of gifts. I've also been getting deliveries—international from Italy and local from department stores. Sometimes two or three a day show up. I had to tell the kids Robert and I had an argument, and that's why I'm getting all the deliveries. I haven't told them about the pregnancy."

"Why haven't you opened any of it?"

I shook my head. "I don't know. I can't bring myself to do it. I know at least some of them are baby clothes, because Robert mentioned that. I think seeing it would make it all too real."

"How about I open them? I love presents."

I shrugged. "Maybe after Billie's."

A little while later, Mia and I headed down to the tattoo parlor. My best friend was filled with a nervous energy, and I wasn't sure if it was because she was gun-shy about the needle, or excited about the prospect of manifesting her future. Either way, Billie's energy when she opened the door was a match.

"Eeep!" She held open her arms. "I get to tattoo a virgin and meet your best friend! I'm so excited."

Mia swamped Billie in a hug. "So am I! I've heard so much about you. Thank you for taking care of my girl."

Billie laughed. "It's been my pleasure. Not that there's been much for me to do, other than lend an ear." She locked the front door behind us. "We don't open until ten, but people tend to wander in off the street if I leave it open. Come on back. I picked us up some coffees on my way in." She winked at me. "Decaffeinated for you, of course."

Mia and I followed Billie from the reception area to the studio. Two steps in, Mia gawked wide-eyed at the walls. "Oh my God. This artwork is *ah-mazing*. Who painted these?"

Billie bit down on her bottom lip. "I did."

Mia's eyes bulged. She wandered over for a closer look. "Holy shit. Have you ever shown your work?"

"Only when my mother harasses me. She runs a gallery here in the city."

"Which one?"

"It's called The Holland Gallery."

Mia's mouth dropped open. "The one owned by Renee Holland?"

"That's the one."

"Wow. That's a prestigious gallery. Though I hear the owner's a real bitch to work for."

Billie grinned. "She is. Even more of a bitch to be a daughter for."

Mia covered her mouth. "Oh my God. Renee Holland is your mother? I'm so sorry. You said she runs the gallery, and I just thought…"

Billie was completely unfazed. She waved Mia off with a chuckle. "Don't be sorry. You're not wrong. My mother is a raging bitch."

"She's discovered so many up-and-coming artists. She's legendary in the art world. Artists do one little show with her, and they can add an extra zero to their price tag."

"She has a good eye. I'll give her that," Billie said. "People and parenting skills…not so much."

Mia shook her head as she stared at the walls. "Well, I'm no Renee Holland, but if you ever want to do a show with me, I'd love to host you. I'm opening a new gallery for The Renshaw Group. Maybe you've heard of them?"

"Yeah, of course. They're big on the West Coast."

"Hopefully big on the East Coast soon, too. Thanks to me."

Billie smiled. "So how are you feeling about your first tattoo? Do you want me to get started right away, or do you prefer to have your coffee first? I know some people are anxious and would rather jump right into things."

"I'd rather hang for a bit. Enjoy the coffee and company, if you have time."

"Not a problem. There's no rush. I don't have my first appointment until noon." Billie looked at me. "How are you feeling, momma?"

"Pretty good. Thanks."

"No more issues since the night of the wedding?"

I shook my head and peeled back the plastic tab on my decaf. "No, thank God. It's been three days now and no cramping or bleeding. I know the doctor said it's normal to have some light spotting, but it definitely doesn't feel normal when it happens."

Billie nodded. "I've been keeping in touch with Owen to see how you are. I didn't want to bug you."

"I know. He told me. Thank you for checking in. We both really appreciate it."

"I hope you don't mind me asking, but did you talk to the doctor yet about paternity tests?"

I shook my head. "My next appointment is a week from tomorrow. I figured I'd do it then."

"Mav's sleep schedule has been off lately. He's been waking up in the middle of the night. I give him a binky to suck on, and he usually falls back asleep right away, but then it takes me hours. Which means I've been watching random TV shows in the middle of the night. One of them was a talk show about a woman who was sleeping with twin brothers and wasn't sure which was her baby daddy to be."

"Oh my," I said. "And I thought my predicament was bad..."

"I know, right? Anyway, I got sucked into the show last night because I needed to know if Brandon or Landon was the daddy. When the host announced the paternity results, he said they were ninety-nine-point-nine-percent accurate, so I assumed the woman had an amnio. But at the end of the show, they did a commercial for their sponsor—the one who had done the paternity test. It said the test was noninvasive. Obviously an amnio is pretty invasive, so I was curious and looked it up. Apparently they can now test for paternity with a blood test and a cotton swab of the inside of the mouth. And it can be done as early as seven weeks."

My eyes widened. "Really?"

Billie nodded. "I wrote down the name of the test. The commercial said it only takes two days to get results, and they're even approved for use by courts to prove paternity."

"Holy crap. I had no idea."

"Neither did I. I saved the link to the website. If you want, I'll text it to you."

"Yeah, definitely."

After that, Billie took out the drawings she'd done last night based on what Mia had told her. Mia *ooh*ed and *ahh*ed and let out a few squeals, but I had to force a smile on my face. I was too busy thinking about the fact that I might not have to wait seven months to find out the father of my baby. It should've made me ecstatic, yet I felt nothing but anxiety. Luckily, Billie started Mia's tattoo, and I got to sit and try to sort out my feelings to the peaceful sound of the needle humming.

Two hours later, Mia's wrist had some artwork. Neither Mia nor I had wanted to see the tattoo until it was finished.

Billie peeled the rubber gloves from her hands. "All done. Are you ready to view your ink?"

Mia nodded and squeezed her eyes shut. She'd been facing the other direction the entire time Billie was working, but now she turned and opened her eyes. "Oh my God! It's gorgeous!"

I peered over for a look. "Wow. It really is. It pops off her arm."

Mia had gotten a tattoo of a tiny bumblebee with a flower on the inside of her right wrist. The colors were so vibrant, and the bee looked almost 3D. Her eyes welled up. "Granny Bea would've loved it. It's perfect, Billie."

Mia had lost her parents in a car accident when she was only five, so her grandmother Beatrice raised her. They'd been super close until she died two years ago. Mia tended to work long hours, and Bea always used to remind her to slow down, to *stop and smell the flowers once in a while*. Mia even had the saying engraved on her grandmother's headstone. So the tattoo of a bee smelling a flower was perfect for her.

"It's really amazing, Billie," I said. "It makes me want to get one."

"When you're ready, I'd be honored."

Billie gave Mia a bunch of after-care instructions, then rubbed some ointment onto her wrist and wrapped it with clear cellophane. The shop had come alive as she was finishing up. Justine, the receptionist, was now at the front desk, and Deek, one of the tattoo artists who worked here and also lived in the building upstairs, was busy setting up his station. Pretty soon, Billie's first appointment showed up, too.

"Thank you so much for coming in early to do this for me," Mia said. "It's everything I'd hoped for and more."

"No problem. I'm glad you like it."

"Maybe the three of us can go out for a drink while I'm in town?"

Billie nodded. "I'd like that. I'll invite Lala too, if you don't mind. We've been trying to get each other out once in a while, so we aren't talking baby talk twenty-four-seven."

"That would be great," Mia said. "I'd love to meet her."

We all hugged goodbye. Out in the reception area, Mia approached the counter. Justine stood in front of the register.

"What do I owe you?"

"The boss said this one's on the house."

"What?" Mia shook her head. "I can't do that. She just drew a work of art on my body. Whatever her fee is, I'm sure it's not enough. But I need to pay her."

"Billie said Devyn is family, so that makes you extended family. She has a *family doesn't pay* policy. Trust me, I've worked here for years. There's no point in arguing with the woman when she's made up her mind."

"Gosh, that's so incredibly generous." Mia looked at me. "That drink is going to have to be at least a dinner now, with dessert and expensive wine, too."

I smiled. "That sounds like a good plan to me."

Two more customers walked in, so we thanked Justine and moved out of the way. Mia was busy shoving her credit card back into her wallet as we walked to the door, so she didn't see a third person coming in until she smashed right into them. Mia wobbled, almost losing her footing, but the guy gripped her elbows, steadying her.

"*Whoa*. Mi dispiace tantissimo!" he said. "Are you okay? I'm so sorry, signorina!"

Mia's jaw dropped open. "Oh my God."

I seconded that sentiment, only I didn't say it out loud. *Damn.* This guy was gorgeous. Olive skin, bright green eyes, and the bone structure of a Greek god—or actually, an Italian god. He had longish hair, which wasn't usually my thing, but totally worked for him. Not to mention, the dreamy Italian accent elevated him from an easy ten to at least a twenty.

"Sei ferita?" he said. "You are hurt?"

Mia just kept staring.

The man's face grew concerned when she didn't answer. "Miss?"

I nudged my friend. "Mia, answer. Use your words."

She closed her mouth and shook her head, blinking. "Oh… yes. I'm fine."

230

He smiled. "Yes, you are. *Very fine*, signorina."

Billie must've heard the commotion. She walked out from the back room. "What happened? Is everything okay?"

"Everything's fine," I said. "Mia just bumped into this man on our way out."

"Are you okay, Mia?" Billie asked.

But Mia's eyes were still glued to the guy. "He thinks I'm fine."

Billie chuckled. "Mia, this is Marcello. He's a guest tattoo artist here for the next few months. Marcello, this is Mia and Devyn."

Marcello lifted Mia's hand to his lips for a kiss. "Sei bella."

"No hitting on my friends, Marcello," Billie warned. "Or I'll send your ass back to that little village you call home in Italy."

I wasn't sure Marcello had even heard his boss. He and Mia were locked in one hell of a serious gaze. Apparently, I wasn't the only one who noticed.

"Earth to Marcello," Billie said. When he didn't budge, she stuck two fingers from each hand in her mouth and let out an ear-piercing whistle.

That did the trick. Marcello let go of Mia's hand and waved goodbye.

Billie rolled her eyes playfully. "Bye, guys. I'll text you soon about drinks, Dev."

"Okay, great."

Mia made it to the door, but abruptly stopped. "Wait! Marcello!"

He turned.

"Are there any cliffs in your village in Italy?"

"Yes. Of course. Many. I live in Positano. Very, how you say… mountainous?"

"Any chance you own a giant yacht?"

Marcello smiled. "A yacht? No."

I chuckled and pushed the door open. "Let's go, crazy lady…"

CHAPTER 22

Devyn

To think it started out as a normal Sunday. Heath and Hannah were at the Y, and I was having some alone time, grateful for the quiet.

Everything changed when the phone rang, interrupting my peaceful window-watching and coffee.

"Hello?" I answered.

An automated voice came on the line, asking if I wanted to accept a collect call from a correctional facility.

My heart sank. I just knew.

After I accepted it, I heard her voice, which sounded strained. "Devyn…"

I blinked. "Mom?"

"I'm in big trouble. I need your help."

"Where the hell are you?"

"I'm in jail—in Boston."

It should've surprised me, but it didn't.

"What happened?"

"I can't talk long. But I need you to come bail me out."

It felt like steam was coming out of my ears. "Why should I do that?"

"I know I shouldn't have left."

I blew out a frustrated breath. "You're gonna have to act a bit more regretful than that."

"I'll explain more when you come."

"What's the name of the jail?"

"South Bay Correctional Facility."

"I can't believe this," I muttered.

"Please, just come. I promise I'll explain everything. It's very unsafe here."

Without even answering, I hung up and took a moment to breathe. As much as she didn't deserve me running to her rescue, I couldn't leave her there. I needed to get her back here—even if it was just to give her hell.

Owen had a bunch of showings today. The last thing I wanted to do was bother him or ask to borrow his car, which he was using to get from location to location. My next thought was to call Mia, but she had an important event at the new gallery today.

Billie didn't work on Sundays… While I hated to interrupt her day off, she'd repeatedly offered to watch the kids whenever I needed. I'd told myself I wasn't going to take her up on it unless I absolutely had to. But this qualified as an emergency.

I rang her.

"Hey, Devyn," she answered. "What's up?"

"Billie, I need to ask a favor." I swallowed. "Can I have Heath and Hannah hang out at your place today? I've got to go out of town until probably tonight."

"Of course, but what's going on? You sound upset."

"My mother's in jail in Boston. I have to go bail her out."

"Oh my God. What did she do?"

"I don't know yet. And I'm not sure I care."

"How are you getting there?"

"I'm gonna rent a car."

"Are you sure? You can borrow ours. Or what about Owen?"

"I don't want to leave you and the kids without a car. And I don't want to interrupt Owen while he's working. I don't know how long I'll be gone exactly. So I'll feel more comfortable renting one."

"Okay... Well, tell the kids to come on over whenever. They can hang out for as long as you need. They can spend the night, too."

"Thank you so much, Billie. I appreciate it. They're at the Y now, but I'm gonna have them head straight to your place when they get back. I'm not telling them what's going on yet."

"No worries. I won't say anything."

So grateful for her generosity, I sighed. "Thanks again. I appreciate your help."

Thankfully, there was a rental car place not too far from the building, and forty-five minutes later, I was able to get a small sedan.

I hit the highway, but grew more anxious with every mile.

At one point, as I continued to drive north on I-95, I got a buzzing sensation in my fingers, like pins and needles from the base of my hand to my fingertips. I gripped the steering wheel, and a rush of heat overtook my body. Then my vision got a little blurry as adrenaline rushed through me.

It was an old, familiar but most unwelcome friend. *Panic.* I hadn't had a panic attack in years—until now. And there was no safe place to pull over. That only made the panic worse. I felt trapped.

After several excruciating minutes, I finally got off at an exit somewhere in Connecticut.

Pulling into a church parking lot, I put the car in park and tried to breathe. Afraid I wasn't going to be able to get back on the road, I needed to talk to someone to calm myself down. I immediately dialed Owen, who picked up on the second ring.

"Hey, Devyn. What's—"

"I need you to stay on the phone with me."

"What's wrong?"

"I just had a panic attack on the highway."

"Are you hurt?" His voice shook.

"No, no, no. I'm fine. I got off the freeway and am sitting in a church parking lot."

"You left the city? What were you doing on the highway?"

"I'm headed to Boston."

"What? Why?"

Resting my head back on the seat, I sighed. "It's Vera. She called me from jail there. She wants me to bail her out."

"Why didn't you call me?"

"You have back-to-back showings all day. I didn't want to bother you. But when I panicked, you were the only voice I needed to hear."

"Where are you right now?"

"Connecticut."

"I need you to be more specific."

I squinted to see the sign. "St. Andrew's Church? White with a big steeple. Probably about thirty miles outside the City."

"Let me look it up." He paused. "Okay. That's in Greenwich." I heard some things moving around as he said, "I'm headed over there now."

I sat up suddenly. "Owen, you can't leave your commitments. I only called to talk so I can calm down enough to get back on the road."

"Already in my car, Devyn." The fasten-seatbelt warning beeped. "The last couple of showings can wait."

"I really didn't call so you'd come. I feel bad."

"Don't. I'd much rather see you than work anyway. Besides, you shouldn't be driving if you're anxious. Not only that, you shouldn't have to do this alone."

His words made my heart want to burst. "I've handled everything alone most of my life, Owen."

"That doesn't mean it's right." He paused. "You don't need to anymore. Okay?"

"Okay," I whispered.

"Not to mention, now's not a good time for you to be stressed. Especially after what happened the night of Holden's wedding."

He has a point. "I thought I could handle this alone. But the panic caught up to me at the most inopportune time."

"Are you okay waiting in that spot until I get there?"

"Yeah, but what are we gonna do with my rental?"

"We'll leave it parked. I'll drop you off there on the way back from Boston."

I blew out a shaky breath. "Thank you, Owen."

"Let's stay on the phone," he said.

Relaxing my shoulders, I shut my eyes. I felt like crap for interrupting his day, but I was so damn happy that I wouldn't have to go to Boston alone.

♥

It cost two-thousand dollars to get Vera out of jail until her first court hearing in a month.

My head spun as we exited the courthouse, Owen on one side of me and Vera on the other. We walked back toward the lot where Owen's car was parked.

It turned out my mother had been arrested because she'd freaking stabbed her boyfriend. While I knew Vera was nuts, I also knew she wasn't a violent person.

"What the hell really happened?" I asked her.

"Bo came at me with a broken wine bottle, so I grabbed a kitchen knife and swung it to try to protect myself. Didn't mean to actually stab him. He called the police and told them I'd attacked him unprovoked. But it was self-defense."

"What condition is he in?"

"He's fine—in good enough condition to try to take me down and call the cops when he knows damn well why it happened." She sighed. "I should've killed the bastard when I had the chance."

"There were no witnesses?"

"No. It was just the two of us at his house—besides his German shepherd."

Owen, who'd looked like he wanted to ream her a new asshole from the moment he saw her, had been holding back, probably for my sake. But he finally lost it. "What the hell have you been doing in Boston while your kids have been fending for themselves?" he spewed.

"Who is this guy, Devyn?" Vera asked, as if he hadn't been with us the entire time.

"He's…" I hesitated.

"I'm her boyfriend," Owen answered matter-of-factly. "I'm also your landlord, although we never formally met."

Boyfriend. Okay then.

"Ah. I thought you looked familiar. It's nice to formally meet you."

"I wish I could say the same, Vera."

Owen disarmed his car, and the three of us got in. Owen and I sat in the front and my mother in the back.

"So, I suppose we're not gonna get any logical explanation for your disappearing act?" I said.

"I needed help with the rent. I thought Bo was a good guy for a while. Told me he'd take care of me if I came to live with him up in Somerville for a while."

"Doesn't he know you have kids?" I seethed.

"He does."

"He didn't care that you left them?" Owen asked, glaring at her through the rearview mirror.

"I thought Heath could fend for himself and his sister for a while. I know maybe that sounds crazy to you, but he's a responsible kid."

"He's fifteen!" I yelled.

Owen shook his head.

"I was alone a lot at fifteen," my mother said.

I whipped around to face her. "That's probably why you're so fucked up."

Vera's eyes widened. "That's how you speak to your mother?"

I turned back around and closed my eyes, so spent from this day.

Owen responded in my place. "Vera, I think you lost the right to any respect the day you walked out on your kids—actually, the first day you walked out on Devyn many years ago."

"How much have you told this guy, Devyn?"

"He knows everything," I murmured.

"Well, no wonder you don't like me, Owen. But trust me, you don't know me or my motivations. I think my kids are better off without me sometimes, so I leave them be occasionally. Heath and Hannah are smart kids. Trust me."

I straightened in my seat. "That makes no sense. No kids are better off left to fend for themselves without their parents. As much as you hurt me growing up, I always wanted you around. That's the messed-up part."

She reached out to touch my shoulder. "I'm sorry, Dev."

I winced from the contact. "How many times have I heard that, Mom? Really…"

After a long moment of silence, Owen spoke again. "You can't possibly know how lucky you are that Devyn cares as much as she does, how lucky you are that despite everything, she'd come to bail you out. Do you have any idea how much she's sacrificed to be here for her siblings?"

"No one asked her to," Vera had the nerve to say.

I turned to look at Owen. His expression was just…sad. I knew he felt bad for me. Which I hated. But at the same time, I felt validated that he was finally witnessing it with his own eyes. He could see what I'd had to endure for so long, how unreasonable and narcissistic Vera was. How hopeless it was to try to get through to someone whose perception of reality was so warped.

"That's exactly why what she's done is remarkable," he responded. "No one asked her to come help. She just did. That's what you do for love, Vera. For family." He reached for my hand and brushed his thumb along mine.

I couldn't imagine how different this ride would have been if I'd come to get her alone. It would've sucked. Life felt much different when someone had your back.

"Well, now that I'm coming home, you can return to your life in California," she said.

I turned around to face her again. "You're joking, right?"

"No, of course not."

I raised a brow. "You think I actually trust you not to bolt on them again?"

She shrugged. "I don't plan on going anywhere."

"Right." I huffed, crossing my arms. "And what about your pending court dates in Boston? What a mess. God knows how many times you're gonna have to go back there."

"The case will be thrown out once they look into his background. He's been violent before."

"Then why the hell would you have left your family to be with this man?"

"I don't know." She sighed. "You can't always choose who floats your boat. Kind of like you and that actor, right? Certainly he's not the best person on the inside, but I'll bet he's good in the sack."

"Why would you even say something like that right now?" I scolded.

"Well, why should I respect your boyfriend's feelings when he doesn't respect me?"

Owen raised his voice. "You don't have to respect me, Vera. But you need to start respecting your daughter."

"You know what?" she huffed. "You're right. I'm sorry. I'm sorry for all of this. I just want to get home and go to sleep."

"Oh, you poor thing." I rolled my eyes. "So tired."

"Well, I am. Have you ever been to jail? You don't know what it's like."

"I haven't," I snapped back. "Which is kind of a miracle given my childhood."

When we arrived, Owen refused to drop me off at the rental car, which was still parked in that church parking lot. He said he'd handle getting the car back to the City in the morning. I was profoundly grateful for that, since I was exhausted and just wanted to get home.

I'd filled Billie in on what was happening, and she'd offered to keep the kids overnight so we didn't have to make a scene. I'd asked her to continue not saying anything to them about Vera. I'd go over there in the morning before they had to go to school to explain things. The kids were under the impression I'd gone to meet a potential client.

When we arrived back at the apartment, Vera finally mentioned Heath and Hannah for the first time all day.

"Where are my kids?"

"Nice of you to ask about them," I said sarcastically. "They're at a friend's for the night. They have no idea what a mess you've gotten yourself into, and I don't want to scare them this late."

She kicked off her shoes. "Okay, then. I'll take advantage of the peace. Gonna take a shower and head to bed."

"Yeah, you do that," I said bitterly. I turned to Owen and muttered, "She's enjoying the peace. How nice, right?"

Owen didn't say anything, just wrapped his arms around me. "I'm so sorry."

I spoke into his chest. "It's not your fault."

"Well, I feel like *someone* needs to apologize for that woman. You deserve much better."

"In some ways, I wish she'd never come back. Now I have to figure out how to manage *her* as well." I looked up at him, noticing my reflection in his gorgeous blue eyes.

"Why don't you stay at my place tonight? I promise I won't try anything. Just wanna sleep next to you."

Normally, I would've taken Hannah's bed, but I wasn't ready to leave Owen. Tomorrow was going to be a shitshow. All I wanted tonight was to fall asleep in Owen's arms.

"Yeah." I nodded. "Let's get out of here."

Back at Owen's, he drew a bath for me and left me alone to soak.

When I emerged from the bathroom, he'd sliced up an apple and topped it with peanut butter. He served it to me on a plate with some chocolates.

"It's not much. But it's the best I could put together with a near-empty fridge. If it weren't so late, I would've gotten you some pie."

"This is perfect," I said as I bit into an apple slice. *It really is.*

Owen rubbed my feet while I ate my apple and peanut butter. I held out a slice for him, and he took a bite. A little of the panic from earlier returned for a fleeting moment, though not because of Vera. I'd suddenly remembered what Billie had texted me the other day: the website for a noninvasive paternity test that could be done as early as seven weeks. I almost wished I'd never found out about that. I wasn't ready.

If there was a chance I could lose Owen after finding out? I might not *ever* be ready.

❤CHAPTER 23

Owen

Devyn had been quiet most of the night. Who wouldn't be after the day she'd had? Though she seemed especially lost in thought once we got into bed. She lay on her side, facing the other direction. I wanted to give her space, but then I heard her breath hitch.

"Dev?"

"Yeah?"

"Turn over."

"I can't." She sniffled.

"Why not?"

"Because you'll be sweet to me, and then I'll completely lose it."

I put my hand on her shoulder and gently guided her onto her back. "Maybe you need to lose it in order to feel better."

She groaned. "God, why can't you be mean? There you go..." Devyn flailed her arms around. "Are you happy now? I'm crying. I'm *freaking crying*."

I sat up, scooped her from the bed, and cradled her in my arms. "No, I'm not happy you're crying. I'm really fucking pissed at Vera about it. But *you* need to let it out, sweetheart."

Devyn burrowed her head into my chest. Her shoulders began to shake, and I felt warm tears trickle down my skin. I stroked her hair and whispered, "I got you. I know it feels like everything is a mess right now, but I promise it's going to get better."

She sobbed. "How? How can you promise that?"

"Because I'm going to stay right next to you and hold your hand. The weight is lighter when you aren't carrying it alone."

Devyn let out a wail. "God, you're so good. I don't even deserve you."

"Don't do that. Don't put yourself down. Your mother's actions are not a reflection of you."

She wiped her cheeks and shook her head. "How am I supposed to leave the kids with her? She's going to pull this again. It's only a matter of time."

"Would you consider fighting her for custody? I mean, you're already their temporary guardian, and she's just been arrested for assault after taking off on her kids. I can't imagine her actions wouldn't be taken into consideration if you wanted to get permanent custody."

"I don't even know how I'm going to run my business and have a baby, much less have *three* kids."

"It's a lot. I get it."

She took a deep breath and let out a shaky exhale. "But on the other hand, how can I leave them with her? I feel like Heath and Hannah have just started to trust me. The last thing they need is another person who ditches them. If I left, the next time Vera took off they wouldn't even call me. I'd just be another person they can't depend on, and they'd fend for themselves."

"What if you stay close, so they always feel like you're around? You can keep an eye on Vera and step in as needed. That way they don't feel abandoned, yet you also get a little room to live your own life with the baby."

"That would be ideal. Except I live in California."

My heart sank. Of course, I'd always known her permanent home wasn't here. I guess I'd ignored it lately, hoping she'd magically start thinking New York was where she belonged. I wasn't sure I wanted to know the answer, but I couldn't *not* ask now…

"Would you ever consider moving here?"

"It would be really difficult with my job. Most of my clients live out in California, plus all of the connections I need to maintain."

"There's always Zoom…"

"I know." She sighed. "It's just hard to think about moving or making any major changes in my life when…you know, there's so much unknown."

And there it was. The ever-present elephant in the room: paternity. Would living here be a choice if Robert turned out to be the baby's father? I'd imagine she'd have to share custody with him, and flying a baby back and forth for weekend visitation wasn't practical. That got me thinking… Would I uproot my life to be with her? Assuming she wanted to be with me, even if the baby turned out to be his, would I consider leaving New York and following her back to California? It would be like starting my career over, since all of my contacts and connections were here in the City. Hell, I wasn't even sure if my broker's license was transferable out there. And would I be breaking up a family if I did all that? Maybe she and Robert would reunite if I wasn't in the picture—raise their child together. That thought made me feel sick.

"There's…something I should probably tell you," Devyn said.

I froze. That didn't sound good. "What?"

"I think I'm going to be able to find out the paternity of the baby soon—sooner than I thought."

"Oh?"

She swallowed and nodded. "I had assumed the only way was to get an amniocentesis, which isn't usually done until fifteen to twenty weeks. And I wasn't even certain that was the right thing to do, since having the test carries some risks to the baby."

"Okay…"

"But it turns out there's a noninvasive test now. It's as simple as a blood test and a swab to the inside of your mouth, and a few days later we'll know if the baby is yours or not."

"And when can you get that done?"

"I did some research online, and it seems like it can be done anytime now."

"Wow."

Devyn's shoulders slumped. "Yeah."

Finding out we wouldn't have to wait should've felt like good news, yet it didn't. One look at Devyn's face told me she wasn't excited either. I knew why I felt glum—because what if the test confirmed I wasn't the baby's father? Not knowing had made it easy to hold on to hope…

My eyes locked with Devyn's. After a few long moments, I squeezed her hand. "Do you want me to go with you to get the test?"

She tried to smile, but couldn't quite pull it off. Her eyes filled with tears. "What if the baby is Robert's?"

I wished I had an answer that could make her feel better. I hated to see her upset. But I also couldn't lie to her. "I don't know."

The following morning, Devyn left my apartment early to get the kids from Billie and Colby's. They were both off school this morning but had to go in for Regents Exams in the afternoon. She planned to take them out to breakfast and break the news that Vera was back. When I'd cleared my calendar yesterday afternoon to drive to Boston, I'd also rescheduled everything I had for this morning—just in case. So for a change, I wasn't rushing to get to the office. I felt like I needed to talk to someone, but not many people knew about Devyn's pregnancy. Though as I passed the tattoo parlor, I realized there was one person who knew just about everything going on with me. Billie was the perfect person to speak with, too, because of her own situation.

Justine, the receptionist, wasn't at the front desk when I walked in, but the bells jangled above the door, prompting Billie to pop her head out from the back. Seeing me, she stepped the rest of the way out from behind the door.

"Hey, stranger." She smiled. "How's it going?"

I shrugged, attempting to turn the corners of my lips upward, but I suspected it might've looked more like a grimace. "It's been an interesting few days."

"I bet. Devyn filled me in a bit about Vera's arrest when she came down to pick up the kids. That woman has a lot of balls calling for a bailout after the crap she's pulled."

When I didn't respond, Billie squinted. "You doing okay, Owen?"

"My head's pretty screwed up, to be honest."

She nodded and gestured toward the front door. "You want to take a walk and grab some coffee?"

"Sure. If you have time."

"I do. Just give me a second. Justine's in the back taking a quick ink inventory. I need to tell her I'm going out for a bit."

She disappeared for a few minutes and came back with a fringed purse slung across one shoulder. I opened the front door for her.

"Are you in a rush?" she asked. "There's a new café a few blocks over that has a sign for pistachio coffee. I've been dying to try it."

"Sounds good. Lead the way."

Billie and I made small talk while we walked. At the café, we argued over who was going to pay for the coffees, and I forced my card on the cashier. Then we strolled to the small park across the street and sat down on a bench.

"So talk to me." She peeled back the plastic tab on the top of her coffee. "What's got you freaked out?"

I smiled. "And here I thought I was playing it so cool."

"Is it because Vera is back? You're worried Devyn is going to go back to California?"

"Of course that's a worry, but oddly, I think we could figure out the long-distance thing if we had to. I'd be willing to try anyway."

"Wow. Okay. Then what's bothering you?"

I raked a hand through my hair. "I found out last night that there's a simple test for paternity, and we can find out in just a few days."

Billie smiled sadly. "I actually knew that. I'm the one who told Devyn about the test. Isn't that a good thing, though? You'll know definitively if you're going to be a dad or not."

My chest felt heavy. "But what happens if it's not me? Do I bow out and let them try to be a family?"

"Oh gosh. Is that what has you freaked out? Owen, a family isn't the sperm and egg donor and the kid they produce. What makes a family is love and commitment, showing up every day when someone needs you. Do you think I'm not Saylor's mother because we don't share blood?"

I shook my head. "I don't even remember the days before you came into Colby and Saylor's life. You're the best thing to happen to both of them."

"And they're the best thing that's ever happened to me. Anyone can be a mother, but it's something special when a child *chooses* to accept you as their parent, and you *choose* to accept them as your child."

I nodded. "I get that. And what you and Saylor have is amazing. I guess my issue is less about the baby and where I would fit in, and more that I'm terrified Devyn still has feelings for Robert. What if he's the father and she wants to give things another shot with him?"

"Well, I'm not going to sugarcoat it. I guess that's a realistic concern."

I frowned. "Thanks."

"But what are you doing about it?"

"What do you mean? What can I do about it? I can't make her not have feelings for some guy."

"No, but she obviously has feelings for you, too. Fight for what you want."

"How do I do that?"

"Put your heart out there. You've been really supportive, going with her places, helping out with the kids—your actions show you're committed. But a woman also likes to hear it. Have you told Devyn you're in love with her and you want to be with her no matter the outcome of the paternity test?"

My heart started to race. "No."

Billie shrugged. "I'm no love expert, but maybe you should start there. The worst thing that could happen is you go for it and it doesn't work out. But I have to imagine that's a heck of a lot easier to move on from than *not going for it* and always wondering if things might've turned out differently if you had."

She had a point. I'd kick myself in the ass for a long time if I didn't give it all I had. I took a deep breath and nodded. "You're a wise woman, Billie. Even if you did pick my dumbass friend Colby."

She grinned. "Damn straight I am. Now get off your ass and go get your girl."

♥

I wiped my palms on my jeans for the third time in ten minutes and reached for the door handle. Not to sound like a total cheeseball, but the sight of Devyn standing on the other side of the threshold took my breath away.

"Hey." She smiled. "I can only stay about fifteen minutes. Heath gets off of work at the pizza place at eight, and I'm going to walk over and pick him up. I think he said about ten words when he saw Vera after school, so I thought maybe he'd want to vent in private."

I nodded and stepped aside. "Probably a good idea."

Devyn's eyes widened when she stepped into the kitchen. "Oh my God. What is all this?"

"I told you I picked us up some dessert."

"You said dessert, not an entire bakery."

I guess I had gone a little overboard. The kitchen table had four white bakery boxes, one filled with various mini pastries, one with a half-dozen cupcakes, one with a pound of cookies, and of course, a Key lime pie.

Devyn licked her lips as she perused the contents of each. "Oh gosh. If you're dumping me, can you please not do it until after I've stuffed my face?"

"Dumping you?"

"You said you bought dessert and wanted to talk to me about something. This looks like a consolation feast. You know, '*I'm sorry I don't want you in my life anymore, but here, stuff your face with this napoleon. You'll feel better.*'"

I chuckled. "Sit. I'll get you a plate and something to drink."

Devyn had a cannoli in her mouth by the time I got the milk out of the fridge. It made me smile to see her eat.

"How was Hannah tonight? Any better than when you told her Vera was back this morning?" I asked.

"Quiet. It's going to take her a while to get over being pissed at Vera. If she's anything like me, it will probably happen the day before Mother Dearest takes off again. I swear, the woman has impeccable timing."

"How are you holding up?"

"Better now with this cannoli. Aren't you going to have anything?"

I hadn't even eaten dinner. I'd been a nervous wreck all day, and it felt like I might vomit if I put food in my stomach.

"What is it you wanted to tell me?" Devyn shoveled the rest of the cannoli into her mouth.

I'd spent the day thinking about the right way to tell Devyn how I felt about her, even rehearsing in the damn mirror. But now that she was sitting across from me, I drew a blank. "Uhh…"

Devyn's face fell. Her hand covered her heart. "Oh my God. You look so serious. What's wrong? Oh no. You *are* dumping me, aren't you?"

"No…no, no…"

"Then what is it? Are you okay?"

God, I was really blowing this. I shook my head. "I'm fine. I… I guess our talk last night about the paternity testing got me thinking."

"Okay…" She looked wary. "Are you nervous about it?"

"No. Well, yes, but that's not what I wanted to talk to you about."

"Then what is it?"

I took a deep breath. This was not how I'd envisioned telling Devyn I was in love with her. I didn't have much experience since I'd never told anyone else. Yet somehow, I'd imagined it would be…I don't know…less conversational and more from the heart. Maybe there was too much space between us. I pushed my chair back from the table and held out my hand. "Come here."

"On your lap?"

I nodded. "Please."

She smiled. "Okay."

Once we were touching, I felt a heck of a lot calmer. I pushed a lock of her hair behind her ear. "I've been doing a lot of thinking, and I want you to know that I want to be with you, regardless of what the paternity test says. Because…" I looked into her eyes, swallowed the lump of nerves in my throat, and took the biggest leap of faith I'd ever taken in my life. "Because I'm in love with you, Devyn."

She covered her heart with her hand. "Oh gosh. I wasn't expecting that."

"I'm sorry. I know it's not the most romantic moment to tell you. But your doctor's appointment is in two days, and with everything going on, I don't know how much romance we're going to have time for. But I thought it was important for you to know I'm in for the long haul. I want to be with you, Devyn. I have no clue what that looks like—where you're going to be living, if the child you're carrying is mine, or if you're going to have a baby and two teenagers to raise—but I need you to know that however things turn out, I want to be there."

Devyn glanced around the room at anything but me. "I...I don't know what to say."

"You don't have to say anything. I just wanted you to know."

She nodded, averting her eyes. "Okay...um, thank you."

After thirty awkward seconds, she stood. "I should get going so Heath doesn't start home without me." She practically ran to the door. "Thank you for the desserts and, um, talk."

CHAPTER 24

Devyn

The following morning, more gift-wrapped boxes arrived. Today even looking at them left me overwhelmed. Opening them wasn't an option anymore, since I had nowhere to hide everything. How the hell would I explain it to the kids if they found baby things? It was bad enough that I'd asked Mia to keep the other stuff Robert had sent so no one suspected anything. But Mia didn't have room for more. And it wasn't like I could ask Owen to hang onto Robert's gifts. So, I piled these newest shipments into the small closet off the living room and prayed no one would notice.

Then I picked up the phone and dialed Robert in Italy.

"Hey, babe," he answered.

"You *really* need to stop sending stuff."

"I don't want to. I have no other way to show you I'm thinking of you. Besides, this could be my child, which means I'd have *every* right to spoil him."

"You know my family doesn't know yet! I've had to hide everything. It's stressing me out."

"Ah. Shit. Okay...I hadn't been thinking of that." He sighed. "I'll have to find another way to spoil you, I guess." Robert paused. "Speaking of which..."

I squinted. "What?"

"We're gonna need a bigger place."

"*We?*"

"Yes, *we*. Or at least me...until I can convince you to move in."

"You live in a mansion. It's big enough."

"There's not enough land, though. I'm thinking of putting my place on the market and getting something with a bigger yard and a massive pool."

My stomach was in knots. He was moving *way* too fast here.

"You don't need that much more space for one child."

"It wouldn't be just one. Your brother and sister can live with us, too, because I know you don't want to leave them."

The room felt like it was tilting around me. "You don't know what you're saying." I rubbed my temple. "You don't want to live with two teenagers. You're practically a teenager yourself—at least the way you act."

"Well, it's time I grew up, isn't it?"

I paced. "How exactly do you plan to conduct your normal *shenanigans* in a house full of people—people you'd need to be setting an example for, mind you?"

"I'd be done with all that. Once you move in, once I'm a father, that's it."

People didn't change that easily—another thing Vera had taught me. I rolled my eyes. "Yeah, right."

"I mean it," he insisted. "I've got to grow up sometime, Devyn. And there's no person worth making that change for more than you." He exhaled. "I love you."

I shut my eyes.

Robert had told me he loved me countless times before, and this time felt just as empty as all the others. *Owen's* proclamation the other night, however? *That* felt real. Too real. It had caught me off guard, and I still hadn't figured out how to process it. All I knew was it meant something. It had meant *a lot*. And I'd totally screwed up my reaction.

"I do think you believe everything you're saying right now. But I feel like I know you better than you know yourself. Once this pregnancy is over and reality comes crashing down, you're going to be overwhelmed. And you'll run—right back to your old ways."

"I want a life with you. I want a family. Why can't you believe me?"

"What if this baby isn't yours?"

Several seconds went by before he finally said, "Well, then I'll still want you. And I'll take care of you and the baby."

"Why would you do that?"

He raised his voice. "Why do you always question my feelings for you, Dev? I've told you time and time again, you're the one person who sees me for me, the one woman in this world I can trust. You're the person I want to settle down with." He paused. "What can I do to prove I'm serious?"

When I remained silent, he hit me with another question.

"What does this other guy have on me?"

"I trust him," I said immediately.

"That fucking hurts," he murmured.

"Well, you asked." I shook my head. "I guess the truth *does* hurt."

"Is it *just* that? He's trustworthy…or do you *truly* care about him?"

"I care about him."

"Are you in love with him?"

I hadn't fully opened my heart to Owen, hadn't let myself feel all the things naturally happening between us, because I'd been so scared. But I wasn't going to analyze my feelings for him on the phone with Robert, that was for damn sure. And I certainly wasn't going to admit to Robert that I loved Owen before I'd said those words to Owen himself.

"I'd prefer not to discuss my feelings for Owen with you," I explained.

"Why? They affect me. I need to know what I'm dealing with, Devyn. I need to know whether you have genuine feelings for another man while you could be carrying *my* baby inside of you. Because if that's the case, it's fucked up."

I pulled my hair. "Well, welcome to my life."

"You've got to give me some assurance here, Dev."

"I can't give you anything right now, Robert. I'm sorry. I've never been more confused in my life, and I have nothing to give anyone at the moment."

"How soon can we find out the paternity?"

I felt nauseous. "I have a doctor's appointment coming up. I'm gonna broach the subject with my OB. There's a test I recently heard about that can be done sooner, but I'm only gonna do it if it's accurate. I don't want to risk a false result or put the baby in any kind of harm. So I need to figure out my options."

"What day is the appointment?"

"Tomorrow."

"Will you promise to keep me posted?"

"Yes, of course."

I could hear someone talking to him in the background.

"They're calling me," he said. "I have to go."

"Okay," I told him, relieved that this conversation was coming to an end. "Good luck on set today."

"Thanks."

Vera crept up behind me after I hung up. "You talking to the golden boy?"

I hoped she hadn't heard anything I'd said to Robert. She'd slept through the kids leaving for school and had now rolled out of bed close to noon. Feeling anxious, I ignored her question and grabbed my purse to head out the door. "I'm leaving. I'll be home before the kids get back."

"Where are you going?" she asked.

"Out for some air." I slammed the door behind me.

As I headed outside, I pulled out my phone to call Mia.

She picked up on the second ring. "Hey, Dev."

"Are you busy for lunch?"

"I'm showing a client around the gallery but should be free soon."

Weaving through people, I asked, "Can you meet me? I'll come to you. Headed that direction now."

"Sure. You sound frazzled. Are you okay?"

"I just need to talk."

Mia met me at a restaurant down the street from her gallery. She strolled in about ten minutes after I'd grabbed a table. Her ass hadn't even hit the seat before I blurted it out.

"Owen told me he loved me."

Her eyes widened. "Wow…really?"

"He also said he wants to be with me, even if the baby isn't his."

She leaned her elbows against the table and smiled. "That's a big move on his part."

"I know." I shook my head. "Robert said the same thing, but honestly, coming from him, it's not the same. I feel like he'd say anything at this point to keep from losing me. He has this…strange attachment to me. Because I'm the one woman who cared about him before he was famous. I think he wants to keep me around because it makes him feel good. But he's not capable of being true to me."

She arched a brow. "And Owen? What are his intentions in telling you he loves you?"

I took a deep breath. "Owen thinks he's in love with me."

"You don't think he's *actually* in love with you?"

As much as I didn't want to think about Vera right now, she was the first thing that came to mind when Mia asked that question.

"You know my mother has never once asked how I'm doing since she's been back?"

Mia narrowed her eyes. "Why did you do that?"

"Do what?"

"Switch the conversation from Owen to your mother."

"Because she's the reason I'm afraid to lose people. Someone like Owen could destroy me, Mia. If I let myself fall in love with him, and this baby ends up *not* being his... I don't know that he can handle that. He'll end up leaving. Or maybe I'll sabotage things because I'll feel like he'd be better off in a different situation. But loving Owen and letting him love me back is about the scariest thing I can imagine." I rubbed my stomach. "Scarier than this life growing inside of me." I exhaled. "So yeah, my mind went to Vera. Because she was my first experience with how much it hurts when love goes bad."

"I get it, Devyn." Mia reached her hand out for mine. "But you have one life. You have to find a way not to let what your mother's done ruin it. You're dating a man who seems to love you. You could be carrying his child, and he says he wants to be with you no matter what. You have no reason to believe he's going to hurt you. Look at the facts."

Despite the logic of her words, I felt panic surging inside of me. "I need to know who the father is. That's what it comes down to."

"Why the rush? Because if Owen's not the dad, you're gonna walk away?"

"Wouldn't that be the right thing for his sake?" I cried.

"Not if he loves you, no. The fact that he wants to be with you regardless says a lot. Through his actions, the man's given you every reason to believe what he says. That's what you need to go on."

The waitress came by to ask if we wanted to start off with drinks. I'd never wished I could have a cocktail more than today. But alas, it would be plain seltzer for me.

After we were alone again, Mia smacked her hand on the table. "You know what I think you need?"

"What?"

"A break from all this analyzing. Try to put it out of your mind until the doctor's appointment. Enjoy some time with Owen. Let him love on you. Try to accept it instead of pushing it away. Because you know what happens if you push hard enough?"

"What?"

"Eventually it works."

I shut my eyes. "Thank you for taking time out of your day to meet me, Mia. I owe you for all of the times you've had to listen to my shit."

"Someday I'm gonna meet the one, and you're not gonna be able to stop me from rambling on about him. So you'll get to make up for it."

I smiled. "I can't wait."

"Although, with my track record, I might be rambling about it to your daughter." She laughed.

I'd taken what Mia said earlier today to heart. So even though this was the eve of my doctor's appointment, I vowed not to let that ruin the night Owen and I could have together. It was high time I gave him the response he deserved to his love proclamation the other night—an honest one. When he'd said the words, I'd freaked out. He deserved better.

I knocked on his door, praying he was home.

He opened, looking amazing as always with his dress shirt unbuttoned at the top and rolled up at the sleeves.

"Hey." He smiled. "This is a nice surprise."

"I freaked out after you told me you loved me," I announced.

He chuckled. "I know you did."

I shrugged. "I guess it was obvious."

"Yeah. That's not news, Devyn." He stepped aside. "Come in."

I paced. "Do you hate me?"

"Of course not."

"Do you wish you could take back those words?"

"No, because I meant them."

I stopped pacing. "I don't want you to take them back."

He placed his hands on my shoulders. "Breathe. I'm not going anywhere. Take your time."

"Part of me is afraid to let these feelings in—not just yours, but my feelings for you. I keep using my mother as an excuse for my behavior, but...she really did fuck me up, Owen."

"Seeing her in person, in action?" He shook his head slowly. "It brought home why you're so guarded. I really dislike her, for the way she treats you and your siblings. And I especially dislike her for making you believe you're somehow unlovable. I get why you are the way you are, Devyn. You don't have to explain a damn thing to me."

"I'm sorry I've been such an idiot."

He pinched my cheek. "Hey, don't talk that way about my girlfriend."

A chill ran down my spine. "You introduced yourself to my mother as my boyfriend, but is that real? *Am* I your girlfriend?"

"Do you want to be?"

For once, I allowed myself to answer honestly, without overthinking. "More than anything."

"It's a little backwards that I told you I loved you before I officially asked you to be my girlfriend."

"Or that I potentially got pregnant during our first night together?" I smiled.

"Or that we had sex before we *truly* met?" He laughed, wrapping his hand around my waist. "I guess we've been backwards this whole time, huh?" He brushed his finger along my neck. "How long can you stay tonight?"

"Vera's babysitting. So…" I sighed. "The one good thing about her being back."

"That's all she's good for."

I gripped his shirt. "I'm staying as long as you want me to. I don't want to think about the appointment tomorrow, if I can avoid it."

"That's been our problem all along—too much thinking and not enough *everything else*."

"What do you have in mind?" I asked suggestively.

"You on top of my face," he said. "Would you be interested in that?"

"I would," I whispered.

Desire filled Owen's eyes as he led me to his bedroom. After he undressed me, he lifted off his shirt. Goose bumps formed on my skin as he ran his hands up and down my body.

"You're cold. I'll warm you up. Lie down."

My back hit the mattress as I bounced on it. Owen hovered over me and traced his finger along my skin, sliding it all the way down to my groin. He took a moment to look at me. I could feel myself getting wetter by the second, unable to predict what he was going to do.

Then he lowered his face between my legs, and his hot tongue caused me to flinch from the sudden pleasure. I bent my head back, allowing myself to enjoy every moment. I gripped the sheets as my restless legs moved to keep up with the intensity of his tongue, which was now circling my clit.

"I love to taste how wet you are," he muttered over my skin, his stubble tickling.

As his tongue continued to lap at me, I could hear the sound of my own wetness.

Owen suddenly moved back. "That was just a warmup." He repositioned himself on the bed before waving his finger at me. "Come over here."

My nipples hardened as I crawled toward his rock-hard body.

"Don't think about anything right now except riding my face."

With my legs on each side of him, I lowered myself onto his eager mouth. Owen placed a hand on each of my ass cheeks, guiding my movements over him.

I didn't know if it was the hormones or what, but I'd never been so damn aroused by a man going down on me before. My clit throbbed over his mouth as the low sounds of his pleasure vibrated through my core.

He reached down and unfastened his pants before starting to jerk himself off. That turned me on, prompting me to move faster over him. Pulling on his hair, I bucked my hips as my eyes rolled back, my orgasm threatening to burst through me at any moment.

"This is so fucking hot, you riding my face like this, Devyn," he rasped. "I want to do this every damn night with you."

I let out an unintelligible sound as I bit my bottom lip, willing my climax to hold off a bit longer.

"You taste so fucking good. I can't wait for you to come all over my mouth."

Oh, God.

I'm close.

My mind felt like it had left my body. *This.* This was exactly what I needed. In this moment, I hadn't a care in the world. I pressed my clit harder against him.

"That's it, baby," he mumbled.

His breathing accelerated as he pumped himself faster. Knowing he was about to explode was all it took to push me over the edge. A rush of adrenaline tore through me as I came in multiple bursts of pleasure.

"Come all over my mouth, Devyn. Give it to me." He groaned.

Owen's breaths eventually slowed as his chest rose and fell.

I rolled over, limp and more relaxed than I'd been in a long while.

"Thank you," I barely had the energy to whisper.

"Believe me, the pleasure was all mine."

Owen and I lay facing each other, blissfully sated, for several minutes. I was about to offer to get up and make us breakfast for dinner when my phone rang. It was on the nightstand closest to Owen.

Unfortunately, he looked down and saw the name on the screen before I did.

"It's Robert." He rolled his eyes. "You'd better take it."

My heart raced as I cleared my throat. "Hello?"

"Where are you?" he asked.

"Why?"

"I'm at your apartment. Your mother said you're not here."

Oh no.

My pulse quickened. "You're in New York?"

Owen's eyes widened.

"I flew here for tomorrow's appointment."

CHAPTER 25

Devyn

"**O**wen, this is Robert. Robert, this is Owen."

I couldn't believe I was doing this—taking two men to the doctor with me. But Robert had stopped film production and flown in all the way from Italy, and Owen... Well, if I was going to allow Robert to go, the other prospective father certainly had every right to be there. Plus, Robert had really put a damper on things last night when he'd shown up. I'd left Owen's apartment with my undies still damp from fooling around to go downstairs and deal with another man. Who, of course, tried to convince me to spend the night with him at his hotel. By the time I got back up to Owen's place, his face was so sullen, it looked like someone had run over his dog.

Robert stood taller, squared his shoulders, and extended a hand. "I hope you'll understand if I don't say it's nice to meet you."

Owen eyed the waiting hand, then promptly shoved both of his into his pants pockets. "The feeling's mutual."

Oh Lord. This was going to be loads of fun.

Owen pulled out his phone. "I'll order us an Uber uptown to the doctor."

Robert waved him off. "My limo is already pulling around."

"Of course it is," Owen mumbled.

"I hope you don't mind, babe." Robert put a hand on my shoulder. "But I have a tight schedule this morning. As soon as we're done at the doctor, I need to hightail it back to the airport. My driver will drop me at JFK and then take you home."

Owen's jaw tightened. "That's not necessary. I'll get a car for us to go back to the apartment building." He looked at me. "Is that okay, *babe*?"

I rubbed my temples. "Whatever."

Luckily the limo pulled to the curb. I hoped things would improve once we were on our way. But no such luck. The only thing that changed was that I was now sandwiched between the two men, shoulder to shoulder.

"So, Aiden," Robert said. "What is it you do for a living?"

"It's Owen. And I work in real estate."

"Really? I'm thinking about buying a place here in the City."

I craned my neck to look at Robert. "You are?"

He nodded. "Your mom is here and your sister and brother. I figured we'd be visiting often once you're back home in California. Plus, I loved the script you sent me from Stephen Solomon, and it's going to shoot here." Robert leaned forward to speak to Owen. "Maybe you can look for a place for us? I was thinking a three- or four-bedroom brownstone on the Upper West Side?"

Owen gritted his teeth. "I'll refer you to someone."

Robert shrugged. "Suit yourself. But if you pass up opportunities to earn a good commission, you're going to be living in that shitty building with Vera forever."

Owen's cheeks heated. "I *own* that building, and it's not shitty."

"Well, it's not exactly the type of place you'd want to raise a family."

"Two of my buddies live in the building and are raising their families there. It's *exactly* the type of place I'd want to raise my kid."

"Then you obviously haven't spent enough time on the Upper West Side—"

"*Alright, enough!*" I held my hands up. "Why don't we just keep quiet for the rest of the ride?"

"Fine with me." Owen shrugged.

"Whatever." Robert looked out the window.

I was never so grateful to pull up in front of a gynecologist's office. The three of us remained quiet while we rode the elevator up to the thirty-first floor. When we arrived at suite 3160, both men reached for the door handle at the same time.

I sighed. "I'll open it."

The first time I'd been to Dr. Talbot's office, there were two other women in the waiting room. This time, it was wall-to-wall people. My shoulders slumped as I walked up to the reception desk.

"Hi. Devyn Marks. I have a nine o'clock appointment with Dr. Talbot."

"Sign in on the sheet, please. But just to let you know, Dr. Talbot had an emergency this morning, so she's running a little late."

"How late?"

The woman frowned. "She hasn't arrived yet. So at least an hour."

Oh, God. The thought of sitting with these two for that long made me want to run back out of the office—and into traffic. Robert leaned over, speaking to the woman through the small cutout circle in the glass. "I'm sorry to bother you, but I flew in for the appointment and have to catch a plane early this afternoon. Would there be any way we might be able to get in first when the good doctor arrives?"

The woman's lips twisted. "Everyone here is busy. You'll just have to wait your—" She looked up for the first time, and her jaw dropped. "Oh my God. You're Robert Valentino, aren't you?"

Robert flashed his signature movie-star smile. "I am."

The woman looked like she was going to piss her pants. "God, I loved you in *Last Tango*. I'm such a big fan. I've seen all of your movies."

"So you're the one…"

The woman threw her head back, laughing as if he'd just told the funniest joke. Meanwhile, I rolled my eyes. I'd heard him use that '*So you're the one*' line a thousand times.

But Robert knew how to lay on the charm when he needed to. It might not work on me anymore, but most women were putty in his hands.

He lowered his voice. "I know what I do makes me no more important than anyone else waiting. In fact, I'd venture to guess I have the most trivial job here. But I'm filming in Rome, and me being here today means we had to shut down production. If I miss my flight this afternoon, all of the crew is going to have to stay an extra few days. It doesn't sound like a lot, but so many of them have families they've been away from a long time and schedules they need to adhere to. So if there's anything at all you can do to get us in quickly when the doctor arrives, I'd appreciate it."

The receptionist batted her eyelashes and leaned forward. "I'll see what I can do."

He winked. "Thank you."

We stepped back from the reception desk and looked around the packed waiting room. There weren't three seats together, but there were two on one side of the room and one on the other.

Robert put his hand on the small of my back and lifted his chin to the two seats. "Why don't we go sit there?"

"Actually," I said, "you two go sit there. I'm going to sit over here."

Before either of them could object, I stalked over to the lone seat and parked my butt. Robert and Owen glanced around again, as if some seats might've magically opened up since the last time they checked. Neither of them looked happy, but they sat side by side. Owen folded his arms across his chest and stared straight ahead while Robert leaned his elbows on his knees and scrolled on his phone.

Over the next hour, I did my best to avoid eye contact with either of them. Only one woman had been called back so far, but at least they'd started taking patients. Ten minutes later, the receptionist Robert had schmoozed called my name. Turned out he was good for something today...

The starry-eyed woman smiled as she showed us to an exam room in the back. She took a gown from the drawer and held it out to me, but her eyes never left Robert as she spoke. "Everything from the waist down comes off."

I took the gown from her hands. "Thank you."

"The doctor should be in in just a few minutes."

Robert checked the woman's nametag and smiled. "Thanks, Laura. You're the best."

Once she stepped outside, the two men looked at me.

"Uh, I'm not changing with both of you in here. Can you wait outside, please?"

"Of course," Owen said. "Sorry."

He opened the door and stepped into the hall, but Robert didn't follow. I looked at him expectantly.

"What?" He shrugged. "You said you didn't want to change with both of us in here. I figured you'd be fine with me. It's not like I haven't seen you naked plenty of times before."

I put my hands on Robert's back and shoved him. "Get out."

I took my time getting changed, then decided to take an extra minute or two to close my eyes and try to calm down. I didn't want my blood pressure to be sky high when the doctor came in. But halfway through my third cleansing breath, there was a knock at the door and it started to open.

"Can't you just give me one—*oh*, Dr. Talbot. I'm sorry. I didn't realize it was you."

She smiled and looked at the two men standing eagerly behind her. "Looks like we have a full house today."

I sighed. "Yeah."

"Is everyone coming in for your exam?"

"Actually, if you're doing an internal, can we do that alone and then bring them in after?"

"Absolutely."

I blew out a heavy breath and nodded. "Great, thank you."

Dr. Talbot turned and pointed down the hall. "Why don't you both go back to the waiting room, and I'll have the nurse grab you in a few minutes?"

Once the door closed, Dr. Talbot pushed her glasses to the end of her nose. "You doing okay?"

I shook my head. "Can we lock the door and stay in here for a few months?"

She smiled, set the chart in her hands on the counter, and pulled over a stool. "Talk to me. The last time I had two handsome men like that flanking me, I didn't look half as stressed as you. Oh wait, that never actually happened to me…"

I chuckled. "I don't know if you remember my first appointment, but I was a little freaked out when you told me the baby's measurements weren't exactly aligned with how far along I would be according to my last period, so we couldn't nail down a date of conception."

"I suspected perhaps it wasn't a planned pregnancy…"

"No, it definitely wasn't."

"Are the two men with you today potential fathers?"

I nodded and covered my face with my hands. "God, I'm mortified."

"Don't be. Things happen. And it takes two to make a baby, so you shouldn't be carrying this all on your shoulders alone."

"I'd prefer to be carrying it on *two* sets of shoulders, rather than three. I was planning to talk to you about paternity-testing options today. I read there's a noninvasive test? I'd been under the impression that an amnio was the only way to find out who the father was."

"Not anymore, thankfully. A mother's blood contains free-floating cells from the fetus. So a DNA profile of your baby can be made as early as seven weeks. We take a blood sample from you, the same as any other type of routine bloodwork you'd get done. Then we collect a DNA sample from the potential father using a mouth swab. The lab can use a fingernail clipping or hair sample if a mouth swab isn't available."

"Wow. I had no idea."

Dr. Talbot nodded. "It's been a godsend—not just for paternity testing, but we can do most genetic testing that way these days, too. In the past, if something came up on the sonogram or in lab work that made us suspect a chromosomal disorder, we'd have to perform invasive procedures that were risky to the mother and baby. Now it's quick and simple."

"How accurate is the testing?"

"Ninety-nine-point-nine percent. Really the biggest risk is human error that can occur during the processing."

"And how fast do results come back?"

"The lab we use quotes three to five days. But I've gotten results back as soon as two, depending on how busy they are."

I took a deep breath. "Do you think we can do it today?"

"Absolutely. I can see how stressed this is making you, and stress is not good for you or your baby. Aside from causing elevated blood pressure, prolonged stress suppresses your immune system and affects sleep, both of which make you more susceptible to illness and infection. Taking care of you is taking care of your baby now, so your focus needs to be on reducing stress and eating and sleeping well. Those are the best things you can do to contribute to a healthy pregnancy."

I nodded. "Okay. Let's do the test today."

"I'll have the nurse get the samples as soon as we finish up here." Dr. Talbot stood and walked to the sink. She washed her hands before pulling a pair of gloves from a box on the counter. "I'd like to do a quick sonogram after I examine you. Would you like the men to come back in for that?"

"I guess I should."

She snapped on one glove then the other. "Any other questions for me?"

"I do have one. Is the potential father's name listed on the sample or anything? Confidentiality is an issue for one of the men."

"No, samples sent to the lab are identified by number only."

"Okay, great."

Dr. Talbot smiled. "So I take it the gentleman who was in here wasn't just a Robert Valentino lookalike?"

"No, it wasn't. It's him."

She nodded. "Would you like me to explain the DNA testing to them after we're done, or do you prefer to handle that yourself?"

"It would be great if you could."

"No problem."

"Thank you."

Dr. Talbot did a quick internal exam and then told the nurse to bring Robert and Owen back in. The exam room was small, but it felt claustrophobic once the two of them were in here.

Owen took my hand. "How did everything go?"

"Good."

Not to be outdone, Robert walked around to the other side of the exam table and took my other hand. "How are you holding up?" he asked.

I glanced back and forth between them—one holding each hand—and swallowed. "I'm fine. Everything is fine."

Dr. Talbot flicked off the lights. "Why don't we get started?"

Everyone's eyes were glued to the sonogram screen. We got to hear the baby's heartbeat, and the doctor gave us a quick anatomy tour. It was surreal, but we could actually see the baby sucking its thumb.

Robert stood tall when the lights came back on. "I sucked my thumb until I was three."

Through my peripheral vision, I saw Owen's face fall.

Dr. Talbot must've noticed, too. "Eighty percent of babies suck on their fingers at some point." She smiled politely. "Why don't we let Devyn get dressed, and she can meet the three of us down the hall in my office to talk. Second door on the right."

"Thank you."

The office had three guest chairs. Not surprisingly, the men had left the one between them open for me. I took the seat, anxious as hell for this appointment to be over. Dr. Talbot explained the DNA testing to the three of us. She was thorough, going over the accuracy and minimal risk we'd already discussed. When she was done, she looked at me.

"So we'll draw your blood down the hall on your way out. Would you like us to swab one cheek as a process of elimination or both? The lab charges per DNA profile, so doing two would be extra."

Robert raised his hand. "You can just swab mine."

Owen frowned. "I live locally, so it makes more sense to do mine—just in case there's an issue. Plus..." He reached over and took my hand. "I'll be with Devyn when she gets the results, not halfway around the world."

Robert shook his head. "It makes more sense to use mine."

"Why?" Owen said.

Dr. Talbot held up her hands. "Okay, so *two mouth swabs* it is."

Ten minutes later, we walked out of the building, all three of us having left our DNA behind.

"The limo should be here any minute," Robert said. "I texted the driver before we left the office, and he was around the corner waiting. That went quicker than I thought, so we can drop you before I head to the airport. Aiden probably needs to get back to work anyway."

The man on my other side piped in. "No, *Owen* doesn't need to get back to work. I'll take Devyn home. Wouldn't want you to miss your flight and be stuck here any longer than necessary."

"I'll drop her," Robert said.

"I'll do it," Owen countered.

I put my hands out, keeping the two of them separated. "Stop it! No one is dropping me. I'm taking a cab. Alone."

"But…"

I looked to my right. "Goodbye, Robert. Have a safe flight back to Rome." I looked to my left. "Go to work, Owen. Have a good day."

Neither man looked very happy, but I didn't care. I started walking and never turned back. It was definitely going to be a *very long* three to five days.

❤️CHAPTER 26

Devyn

The following day, I paced as I spoke to Mia over the phone. "Now that it's done, I'm freaking out. As much as I need to know, I'm *not* ready."

"I get it. This isn't the kind of thing you'll ever be ready for."

"I feel like I can't breathe until the results come in."

"I can only imagine." She paused. "How's Owen handling things?"

I peeked out the window, noticing the raindrops gathering on the glass. "He's busy with a bunch of showings today. But I feel bad for the way I handled things. He and Robert kept trying to show each other up. When I left them both standing there after the appointment yesterday, I'd had enough. But I shouldn't have taken it out on Owen. It wasn't his fault. Robert had egged him on."

"Give yourself grace. You've been so stressed. I don't know how anyone could've handled Robert showing up like that. I can't blame you or Owen for behaving badly. The situation is tough on everyone."

"When the results come in, I need to let my family know. It's been hard keeping this from them. Although, I'm truly dreading it—not so much telling Vera, but when my brother and sister find out I'm pregnant, they're gonna freak."

"You're pregnant?" came a voice behind me.

I turned suddenly.

Hannah.

My heart dropped when I saw her standing there. She was supposed to have gone to the store with Vera and Heath.

My heart pounded. "I have to go, Mia. I'll explain later." I hung up. "I didn't know you were there."

"It started raining, so I came back to get an umbrella," Hannah said, eyes wide.

Placing my hand on my chest, I asked, "Where are Mom and Heath?"

"They're outside waiting for me." She looked at me carefully. "You're pregnant?"

"Yeah," I whispered. "I was going to wait to tell you."

"Because you don't want to tell us you're leaving?"

"No." I stepped toward her. "This doesn't change anything. I won't leave you guys, although I don't yet know where *we* should all be living."

"Owen's the father?"

How could I lie to her? "That's why I didn't want to tell you yet. I'm…actually not sure."

Her shoulders slumped. "Oh."

I rambled nervously. "This is very embarrassing for me to admit. But as you know, I'm an adult. And I do have…sex. I've always been responsible. But something went wrong. Let that be a lesson to you."

As she stood there looking shell-shocked, I continued. "The baby is either Owen's or Robert's. We had a DNA test and are waiting for the results. We should get them in a few days."

Vera burst through the door. "What's taking you so long, Hannah?"

Heath was right behind her.

"Devyn's pregnant," Hannah blurted.

My brother's face went white.

Vera's mouth curved into an amused smile. "Well, I'll be damned. I guess you're more like me than I thought."

My cheeks burned. That was a huge insult, in my book.

I spent several excruciating minutes sitting down with my brother and mother and regurgitating what I'd explained to Hannah. This wasn't the way I'd envisioned telling them. Not in the least. The mood wasn't congratulatory. That's for sure.

Heath echoed Hannah's fears. "There's no way you're gonna have time for us anymore."

"That's not true." I reached for his hand. "While I wasn't expecting this, it doesn't change *anything*. I will do everything it takes to make sure you're both taken care of."

"Not necessary," Vera interrupted. "I don't plan on going anywhere again, Devyn."

I glared at her. "And how many times have I heard that?"

"This is a wakeup call. I'm gonna be a grandmother, for Christ's sake. You don't need to worry about Heath and Hannah. I'll be here. You take care of yourself, baby girl."

I didn't want to get into an argument right now for the kids' sake, so I refrained from repeating all the reasons she couldn't be trusted. Not to mention, I'd reminded her several times since she'd been back that I had legal custody of the kids now, so her being here was of little relevance anymore.

I turned to Heath. "Once the paternity results come back, I'll know a lot more about my plans. But those plans will always include you guys. I promise."

Much to my relief, Heath and Hannah each came around to give me a hug. Vera refrained from joining in, which was smart, because I wouldn't have reciprocated.

After my brother and sister sat back down, Vera reached out toward me. "You're gonna be just fine, Devyn. You're a naturally maternal person."

"Well, that's what happens when you have to raise yourself, I suppose," I quipped.

"If you let me move in with you, I can babysit," Hannah suggested.

It broke my heart that she felt the need to say that, as if she needed to earn her way into my life. But before I could respond, Vera chimed in.

"Well, I for one hope the baby is Robert Valentino's."

I gritted my teeth. "Why would you say that?"

"Isn't it obvious?" She shrugged. "Cha-ching."

"I do just fine on my own. I don't need his money."

"Well, *I* could sure use it." She chuckled.

I felt sick to my stomach. Not only because of her attitude, but because her comment reminded me of Owen's need to compete with Robert. Since Robert showed up, Owen hadn't been in a good place. He hadn't come to see me since the appointment. And I didn't like the way I'd left things. I also had to wonder if seeing Robert in person was just the thing to make Owen doubt everything. No doubt that had been Robert's intention.

After the rain stopped, Vera and the kids headed out shopping again. Left alone, I turned things over in my mind until my phone rang around 6 PM.

It was Owen.

My heart leapt as I picked up. "Hey, I'm glad you called. I miss you."

"Are you busy right now?" he asked.

"Not really."

"Can you come down to Holden's for a minute?"

"Holden's? Why? What's going on?"

"Just something I want to show you."

"Okay. I'll be right there."

The door to Holden's and Lala's apartment was open a crack when I arrived. As I entered, I nearly melted at the sight before me.

"What's going on here?" I asked.

Owen turned to look at me and flashed a gorgeous smile. In his arms was baby Hope. He rocked her gently, still wearing his work clothes, his sleeves rolled up. Holden and Lala didn't seem to be home.

"Look at you." I took a few steps forward. "Pretty sure if I wasn't already pregnant, this sight alone might've done it." I rubbed my thumb along Hope's hairline. She looked so comfortable in his arms. I couldn't blame her. "Are you babysitting, Dawson?"

"Well, I stopped in to say hello, and Holden and Lala happened to be talking about how they hadn't been out to eat—just the two of them—in a while. So I offered to stay. Hope pooped before they left, so I should be good. They said they'd be back in an hour. They only went to the Indian place right around the corner—you know, just in case I needed them to come back." He laughed.

"Is this your first time ever watching a baby?"

"It is, actually." He shrugged. "But maybe I need to get used to it?"

Maybe.

I hated his choice of words. I'd planted that seed of insecurity.

"Can I hold her?" I asked.

"Of course." Owen placed baby Hope in my arms. While I'd held babies before, I wasn't entirely comfortable. Looking down at her sleepy eyes, reality began to set in.

"It's hard to believe this is gonna be my life soon."

"You're gonna be such a good mother, Devyn."

Rocking the baby, I looked up at him. "Because I had such a great example?"

"Well, because you had such a great example of what *not* to do." He paused. "And because you're a genuinely good person with a huge heart. Your brother and sister are lucky to have you." He kissed me softly on the side of my forehead. "And this baby inside of you? She's really lucky you're her mom."

"Her?" I arched my brow. "A girl, huh?"

"Yeah." He smiled. "That was weird, right? It just sort of came out." He winked. "Maybe I know something you don't."

A shiver ran down my spine. "You think it's a girl?"

"I kind of do." He smiled.

"Well, I guess we'll have to decide whether to find out."

"One big reveal at a time, though, right?" Owen sighed.

"Yeah." I exhaled, looking down at Hope.

"As cocky as Robert is, he does care about you."

My eyes shifted up, wide with surprise. "What makes you say that?"

"After you left us standing there yesterday, he and I had a talk. He gave me a ride home, and we chatted on the way."

I squinted. "That sounds dangerous."

"Don't get me wrong. It's not a bromance or anything. Far from it. But after you were out of sight, he dropped the act a little. Gradually the smug expression on his face changed. I could see real fear in his eyes. He admitted that he's scared. And I told him I was, too. He might not know how to be a good partner, but I could tell he cares about you."

"Wow, I'm surprised you guys didn't continue the pissing match. That's impressive."

"In the end, hating one another doesn't serve us. He knows that. We both want what's best for you. We both think we're the one who's best for you. The difference is, I *know* I'm the best for you." He ran his hand along my back. "But none of that matters unless *you* feel that way."

I stared down at Hope for a while. "I told my mom and the kids tonight, Owen."

"What?" His eyes widened. "I thought you were going to wait until—"

"I know. I wasn't going to say anything until after the test results came in. But unfortunately, Hannah walked in during my phone call with Mia. She heard me talking about being pregnant. Then I was forced to tell Vera and Heath, including the paternity-test part."

"Well, shit." He cringed. "What was their reaction?"

"The kids were relatively unfazed about the DNA test. They're mainly paranoid that this means I'll be too busy for them."

"I can't blame them for worrying, but we both know that's never going to happen."

Owen and I moved over to the couch with the baby. We sat together for a while until she was almost out cold.

I watched as Hope's eyes finally closed. "She's asleep."

"She's so relaxed in your arms. You have the magic touch with her."

"Watch me have a baby who never sleeps." I chuckled. "That would be my luck."

Owen leaned over and placed his cheek on my belly. My heart fluttered as he spoke to the baby. "You're gonna sleep for your mama, right? You have no idea how lucky you are, little one. And I can't wait to meet you."

"What's going on? Why are you talking to her stomach?"

Owen jumped back. Holden had appeared in the doorway, with Lala right behind him.

We hadn't noticed them walk in from their date, and I must've not fully closed the door behind me when I entered the apartment, because there was no warning.

Shit!

Owen stood to greet them.

Holden smacked Owen's shoulder. "Something you're not telling me, man?"

I'd never seen Owen turn so red. I didn't want him to have to lie to his friend. And I suspected he was about to—for my sake. So I intervened.

I got up off the couch. "I'm pregnant, actually..."

Lala gasped.

Holden's jaw dropped. "What? I was only kidding." He turned to Owen. "Holy crap."

I handed a sleeping Hope to Lala. "Before you say anything else, I need to explain that the reason we haven't said anything is because there's a chance Owen's not the father."

Owen shut his eyes momentarily, then wrapped his arm around me in solidarity.

"We're awaiting DNA test results," I added, "and we're going to tell everyone once we know for sure."

"It hasn't been easy keeping it from you guys, but that was the best decision, given the circumstances," Owen said.

"I need to put her down for this. Hang on." Lala disappeared into the nursery while the three of us stood in awkward silence.

Holden's mouth was hanging open.

Lala returned and patted my arm. "Are you okay?"

"Not really." I smiled slightly. "But I will be."

"May I ask who the other potential father is?" Holden asked.

"Robert Valentino."

His eyes widened. "The actor?"

Lala gaped.

I nodded. "He and I have dated on and off for years. It started before he was famous. He's never been my boyfriend. But we slept together shortly before I came to New York."

"And then she met me..." Owen shrugged.

I nodded. "Thus, the situation we're in. This wasn't something I wanted. I don't understand how it happened because I was careful. But nothing is foolproof."

"I get it." Holden held out his palms. "You don't owe me any explanations. It was only by the grace of God that I got lucky over the years and never had an accident myself. You can only be so careful, and shit happens." He shook his head. "Not that the *pregnancy* is shit. It's…wonderful. I mean, congratulations."

"Thanks." I chuckled. "I think."

Holden turned to Owen. "I can't believe you've been holding on to this."

"I was hoping I'd be able to give you guys good news. You know, joining your ranks and all. But I don't know if it's gonna turn out that way." He pulled me closer. "I've made it clear to Devyn that I'm all in regardless."

After a moment, I tried to make light of the situation. "Well, you and Lala certainly got more than you bargained for tonight."

Lala sighed. "I can't believe this."

"You're telling me." Holden laughed. "Owen is the last of the guys I ever thought would have a kid."

Owen chuckled. "Believe me, no one is more surprised about this than me, man."

"I won't say anything to the guys," Holden promised.

"Thanks. We'll be getting the results in a few days. So it won't be a secret for much longer."

"Billie knows, though," I said.

Holden raised his forehead. "No shit?"

"Billie's the best secret keeper." Lala elbowed her husband. "Unlike *some* people."

"Not true," Holden said. "I hid the fact very well that you and I were messing around back in the day." He looked over at Owen, and his eyes began to water. Then he sniffled. "Fuck…"

I looked at Holden in shock.

"Are you crying?" Lala laughed a little.

"I'm getting emotional." He wiped his eyes. "I never thought

Owen would be a father. I know we don't know for sure, but damn, I'm about to lose it anyway."

Owen smacked him on the back. "You and me both, dude."

♥

The following day Owen and I were supposed to go out to dinner after he got off work, but he took a detour.

He parked in front of a beautiful brownstone downtown in Gramercy Park. We got out and stood in front.

I looked around at the upscale neighborhood. "What are we doing here?"

He gestured toward the stairs. "I thought you might want to take a look. It's coming on the market and hasn't been formally posted yet. A friend of mine is the listing agent. Four bedrooms."

"Why would I be interested in looking at this?"

"Isn't it obvious?" He nudged his head. "Come on. He let me borrow the key."

The house was beautiful inside: high ceilings, gorgeous crown molding, a dark wood staircase, and beautiful architecture. I followed Owen through the space in a daze.

We stopped in the kitchen, and I had to ask, "Are you doing this because of what Robert pulled? Saying he was looking for a place here?"

"Of course not." Owen crossed his arms. "This has nothing to do with him, Devyn. This is about *us*. We need more space. And even if you decide you want to move back to California, we could be bicoastal. We'll need a bigger place here no matter what."

I looked out the window at the small garden in back. I couldn't, in good conscience, let Owen buy a property when I didn't know how he'd feel if Robert ended up being the father.

"It's beautiful. But wouldn't you want to wait until..." My words trailed off.

Owen stared into my eyes. "I've told you the paternity results don't change anything for me. You're the one who seems to be holding back. At first I thought your hesitation was because you refused to believe my word, but I'm not sure if that's it anymore."

My heart raced. "What are you saying?"

"If you can't decide to be with me, you must still have feelings for *him*."

Fear stabbed through me. "That's not it, Owen. I just don't want you getting in over your head."

"I've given you my word that you have my heart regardless of the outcome of that test. But you haven't done the same. You haven't given me any assurance. I'm not sure what more I can do, but maybe there's nothing. The ball is in your court, Dev. You either want me in your life or you don't." His face reddened. "But if you're gonna choose him, please let me know sooner rather than later."

❤️CHAPTER 27

Devyn

"**M**iss Marks, do you have a moment?"

I looked up. "Umm…sure."

Hannah stepped out of her court-appointed counselor's office and walked over to where I sat in the waiting room. I stood and whispered to her, "Anything you need to tell me?"

My sister rolled her eyes. "No."

"Okay. Wait for me here."

Dr. Friedman couldn't have been much older than me. This was the second time we'd come for my sister's new Saturday-morning appointment, but the first time she'd asked to speak to me.

She closed her office door behind us and extended a hand to the couch. "Please, make yourself comfortable."

I sat hesitantly. "Is everything okay?"

"Yes, I'm sorry. I didn't mean to scare you. Everything is fine. Hannah is a wonderful girl."

"Oh." I blew out a worried breath. "Thank God."

She took the seat across from me with a warm smile. "Hannah gave me permission to speak to you. I generally do a few individual counseling sessions and then start family therapy. When a minor is removed from the custody of a parent, we use the group sessions to open up lines of communication between the child and parent. But Hannah has expressed that she doesn't want her mother to participate in the family-counseling sessions."

I frowned. "She's very mad at her."

Dr. Friedman nodded. "Hannah would like to have you come instead."

"Is that allowed?"

"There are no set rules for counseling. Our goal is to rebuild trust with the custodial parent. When children are removed from a parent's custody, they usually have feelings of abandonment, even after the parent returns. Our sessions are an outlet for the child to acknowledge how they feel, validate that their concerns are real, and to begin to work through what can be done to rebuild the broken trust. If we don't repair damaged bonds, childhood abandonment issues can develop into serious mental-health conditions later in life. Studies show that youths who learned to fear abandonment struggle more with anxiety, depression, and self-esteem issues. It also can affect adult relationships—leading to a persistent fear or rejection with a mate. It's not uncommon for adults with unresolved issues to have difficulty committing to relationships."

"I see…"

"I think some family therapy will help Hannah. Hopefully she will be open to her mother coming at some point, but for now she talks mostly about you."

I wasn't sure if that was a good thing or a bad thing, but I supposed getting her talking was half the battle. "Okay. Whatever I can do to help."

"Great. Thank you." She folded her hands on her lap. "Before we all meet together, it would be helpful for me to know your status."

"My status?"

She nodded. "Hannah seems to think you're leaving soon. She mentioned you're going to have your own family to deal with."

I closed my eyes. God, as if these kids didn't have it bad enough with Vera for a mother—now they start to trust me, and I'm being noncommittal, too. My eyes welled up.

Dr. Friedman grabbed the tissue box next to her and leaned forward.

"Thank you." I plucked two out and blotted my eyes. "I'm pregnant. I feel terrible that I haven't been able to assure my sister and brother that I'm sticking around. My life is out in California, or at least it was when I came to New York to stay with them. My work is there, my apartment, my friends… But now I'm not sure what I'm doing. And I'm afraid I may be making things worse with Hannah and Heath. If I leave them, they're going to feel like they can't depend on me, either."

"It sounds like you have a lot on your plate."

"I do, but I don't want the stuff going on in my life to hurt my siblings."

She nodded. "I think some sessions to discuss how you're both feeling would be good for you and your sister. I sense that Hannah might be pulling away from you, preparing herself for your departure."

"She has been more distant lately, quieter and keeping to herself. I thought it was because her mother is back."

"Children with abandonment issues expect everyone in their life to disappear. So they're often afraid to love."

I felt that statement deep in my chest. "I'll do whatever I can to help Hannah."

Dr. Friedman smiled. "Great. Why don't you plan to join us for next week's session, then?"

"Okay."

Hannah was quiet on the walk home from the therapist's office. I wasn't sure if I should push after she'd spent an hour opening up to someone. Once we got back to the apartment, she went straight to her room and blasted music with the door shut. Vera was watching some soap opera on the couch. I decided it was time she and I had a little heart to heart, so I picked up the remote and flicked off the TV.

"I was watching that."

"I'm sure it won't be difficult to pick up tomorrow without seeing today's ending. Those shows are just the same thing over and over anyway."

"What's so important?"

It was difficult not to roll my eyes. "Your children."

"What about 'em?"

"You're screwing them up."

"I'm doing the best I can. It's not easy being a single mother—something you're about to find out unless you can hook one of those men and get them to stick around a while."

"You're not doing the best you can. Far from it. How was taking off with some guy you barely know the best for your kids?"

"I told you I was going to stick around from now on. Stop harping on the past."

"Do you know how many times I've heard you say you weren't going anywhere and then you took off again? More times than I can count. So I apologize if I don't find your promises reliable. Now you're hurting Hannah and Heath. They need reliability and structure in their life. Your disappearing acts are going to make them afraid to rely on anyone as grown-ups."

"Good! Then I'm doing them a favor. Any man I've ever trusted takes off at some point. It'll make it easier if they learn that now. They don't need to grow up thinking the world is rosy."

I stared at her, and Dr. Friedman's words replayed in my head. "*It's not uncommon for adults with unresolved issues to have difficulty committing to relationships.*" I'd never known my grandparents—

anytime I'd asked about them or any other member of Vera's family, she'd blown me off. "What happened to you as a child?" I asked.

"What are you talking about?"

"Were you and your mom close?"

She scoffed. "What are you, Dr. Phil now?"

"Just answer the question."

"My mother was busy. She cleaned houses and tended bar to put food on our table."

"How come you don't keep in touch with her?"

"Why should I? She told me to get out when I got pregnant with you at seventeen. I called her once when you were born, after your useless father took off and left me. She told me if I was calling for money to lose her number."

Jesus. Talk about history repeating itself. I suppose Vera was just giving what she'd gotten in life. While it helped to understand why my mother was the way she was, it made me more determined than ever to *stop* the vicious cycle. Hannah and Heath needed therapy, and to believe not everyone was like their mother. I had no idea what was going on in my own life, but I vowed right then that I would make sure they didn't wind up like Vera.

After all, I wasn't like her...*was I?*

Vera picked up the remote and flicked the TV back on. If I'd thought there was any chance of getting through to her, I would've tried harder. But she needed more than me lecturing her.

I sighed and stood. "I'm going to go out for a little while."

She didn't look away from the television. "Whatever."

Heath was working at the pizza place, but I stopped at Hannah's room to let her know I was going to run some errands. Her response was almost as enthusiastic as her mother's.

Outside, the sun was shining so I decided to take a walk. I hoped the fresh air and change of scenery would clear my head, but I couldn't stop thinking about what the therapist had said about the long-term effects of abandonment. "*It's not uncommon for adults with unresolved issues to have difficulty committing to relationships.*" It was easy to see Vera could never settle down, but did I have issues, too?

I'd always joked that my mother had screwed me up, but I'd never looked inward too deeply. What committed relationships had I been a part of? I'd dated, but most of the men I had been with weren't commitment types.

Right?

I thought back to when Robert and I had started seeing each other. Had he ever actually said he didn't want an exclusive relationship? His career had started to take off, and I just always assumed he'd want to be free to play the field.

In hindsight, was it him who didn't want to commit, or…had I been the one afraid of a relationship?

If I didn't let myself get attached, it wouldn't hurt so much when he walked away…

Oh, God.

Was I already Vera? Had I been the one failing to commit all along, even though I'd blamed it on him?

The only other man I'd been in an adult relationship with was Owen. But there were so many good reasons I hadn't committed to him, right?

We haven't known each other that long.

I might be carrying another man's baby.

He lives in New York, and I live in California.

I'm taking care of two teenagers.

My life is chaotic.

Though…he'd told me he loved me. None of those barriers seemed to stop him from committing.

Oh, God.

I am Vera!

I had a bag full of excuses, ready to pull one out at all times—reasons things could never work. Why didn't I ever just *try*? Forget all the obstacles and see what happened—give love a chance. Because I was afraid I'd come to depend on someone and then they'd leave, just like my mother did.

I walked and walked, lost in my head for the better part of an hour. When I finally stopped and looked around, I realized I was in Gramercy Park, the neighborhood Owen had taken me to the other day to look at that brownstone. After a few more blocks, I found myself standing in front of it.

Could I picture myself living here? Pushing a stroller in that beautiful tree-lined park at the corner? Picking herbs from the little garden out back, cooking in the kitchen when my sister and brother came over after school? Or maybe they would live with us.

I closed my eyes and visualized it.

Playing Christmas music while we put up a tree in the big front bay window.

Our baby sleeping in her crib while Owen and I drank a glass of wine on the couch. His arm wrapped around my shoulder, my head snuggled into his chest while we talked about our days.

Window boxes filled with petunias in the spring and mums in the fall.

A picture of our toddler stuck to the stainless-steel refrigerator with a magnet from South Carolina—one of the places we stopped on our road trip last summer. I melt looking at it. Our little girl is all smiles, sitting atop Owen's shoulders as we walk along the beach.

Me falling asleep in Owen's arms every night.

I wanted it. *I really, really* wanted it.

And it was so close for the taking, dangling right in front of my nose.

Yet…

I was terrified to reach out and grab it.

When I finally opened my eyes, I found an older woman standing in front of the brownstone on the top step. From her curious face, it seemed she might've been there watching me for a while.

"Sorry." I blinked myself back to reality and shook my head. "I, uh, was just admiring your beautiful house."

The woman smiled and pointed to the real estate sign hanging from a post. "It's for sale, you know."

"I came to see it the other day. It's lovely."

"It's also a good spot for people watching. I've been coming out here almost every evening for forty some-odd years." She sat down on the steps and patted the spot next to her. "Join me, if you're not in a hurry."

"Sure. Why not?" I took a seat next to the woman.

"Name's Francine Meyers, but my friends call me Fanny."

"I'm Devyn. It's nice to meet you."

"So, Devyn, is it just you or were you looking at the house as a place to raise your family?"

"I came with my boyfriend."

She smiled. "I'd hoped a nice couple would buy this place. Me and my Arthur had so many good years here. We had a lot of love and laughter inside these walls. Raised four kids *and* a husband here."

I chuckled. "Can I ask why you're moving? Are you retiring somewhere warmer or something?"

Fanny nodded. "It's too big for me these days, so I'm headed down to Florida to live near my sister. A condo. No maintenance. It's just me now. My Arthur passed last year."

"I'm sorry for your loss."

"Thank you. We had forty-nine good years together."

"Wow. Forty-nine years of marriage. That's a long time."

She smiled. "It is. Yet the only thing I regret about my time with Arthur is that we didn't meet sooner."

I covered my heart with my hand. "That's so sweet."

Fanny and I grew quiet, watching a woman walk by with two little girls. They were probably about six or seven, both wearing blue and gray plaid Catholic-school uniforms with matching bows in their pigtails.

"Can I ask you something, Fanny?"

"What's that, dear?"

"Did you know in your heart that you and Arthur would be married for almost a half century when you got together?"

"I was only twenty-two. I don't know that I looked that far ahead, but the one thing I knew for sure was that I'd regret it if I didn't take the chance with that man."

I smiled and looked over my shoulder at the brownstone one more time. The thought of missing out on putting up a tree or not having magnets on the fridge made my heart squeeze.

"Thanks, Fanny. I have to run. There's something I just realized I need to do."

She winked at me. "Go get 'em, girl."

I practically ran all the way back to the apartment. I had no idea what I was going to say or do, but I was done letting my fears control me. Even if it didn't work out, Owen was worth taking the risk. I wanted it all.

The baby.

Two teenage siblings.

Owen to come home to every night.

Maybe even a dog or cat.

And screw it—I wanted the brownstone, too.

Oh my God. I'd definitely lost it! *I'm not even an animal person.*

But I didn't care. After my epiphany, the only thing that mattered was getting to Owen.

At the apartment, the elevator didn't come in three seconds, so I bolted for the stairs. Thank God he only lived on the second floor, because I was completely out of breath by the time I ran up.

Owen opened the door, took one look at my red face and huffing and puffing, and freaked out. "What happened? What's wrong?"

"Nothing." I bent over and put my hands on my knees.

"Are you sure? Why are you out of breath?"

I held up a finger as I gulped air. Once I was able to speak, I stood. "Sorry."

"What's going on, Dev? You're scaring me."

"Well, that makes two of us. Because I'm scared to death."

"What am I missing here? What are you scared of?"

"You, Owen! I'm scared of you!"

"Why are you scared of me?"

"Because what happens if you leave me?"

Owen's face fell. "You got the results? I'm not the father?"

"Oh my God! No! The results didn't come back yet."

"Then what is it? Why would I leave you?"

"I don't know. But I'm afraid…"

Poor Owen had been totally lost, but suddenly he seemed to catch on. His face softened, and he stepped closer and cupped my cheek. "I'm not going anywhere, Dev."

"Good. Because…because I love you."

His eyes widened. "You do?"

Tears welled in my eyes as I nodded. "And I want it all with you. Even the dumb dog."

"What dumb dog?"

"Just shut up and kiss me."

He slipped an arm around my waist and hauled me against him. "Yes, ma'am."

It was like the Earth shifted as our mouths collided. All of my fears seemed to melt away.

At least until my cell phone rang…

CHAPTER 28

Owen

A call from Devyn's doctor had interrupted our moment, and we'd both thought the results were ready. But Dr. Talbot was only calling to give Devyn the results of some other bloodwork. It had taken a while to come down from the adrenaline rush of thinking we were about to answer the paternity question.

And now, two days later, we were still waiting. I remained on cloud nine after Devyn told me she loved me, but also on the edge of my seat. We were now on day five of what was supposed to be three to five days before we got results. The wait was pretty much killing us at this point.

Today Devyn had accompanied her siblings to the indoor pool at the Y for the afternoon. Since my showings were over for the day, I was jumping out of my skin waiting for her to get back. I decided to visit Holden in one of the empty apartments I knew he was fixing up for new renters.

The door was open, so I let myself in. Holden was under the sink.

"Knock. Knock." I announced myself.

He slid out from under the cabinet. "Hey! How you holding up?"

I was thankful at least one of the guys knew so I could vent.

"Still no results." I blew out a breath. "Pretty much a nervous wreck, but not as bad as I was before."

"What changed?"

"Devyn said she wants to make this work regardless of the results. That was huge. She told me she loved me, which she hadn't done before. So that takes some of the pressure off when it comes to the DNA test."

"Nice." He smiled. "I'm glad to hear that."

"Robert might try to interfere if the baby is his, but knowing she made the decision to be with me *before* the results came in means a lot."

"Yeah. No shit. You'd always have wondered otherwise."

"Right. I'd never want to feel like she was only choosing to be with me for the baby's sake."

"Totally. I get it." He stood and smacked me on the shoulder. "Looks like you're gonna be raising a kid no matter what." Holden held out his hand. "Welcome to the no-sleep club, man."

I shook with him. "Crazy, right? *Me*, of all people."

"Never thought I'd see the day." He looked up at the ceiling. "Ryan's been playing some crazy games up there, sending us all babies." Holden got back down on the ground and slid into the cabinet. "I gotta get this going, but keep talking."

"What's wrong with the sink?"

"Pipe has a leaky joint," he answered.

A few minutes later, a deluge of water sprayed out everywhere.

"Fuck!" he yelled. "Pipe burst."

As Holden ran to go shut off the water, I rummaged for a pot to collect some of it. I ended up totally soaked from my head to my crotch before the water stopped.

Holden returned. "I'm a fucking idiot for not turning off the water before working on the pipe."

"Well, you didn't expect it to burst."

I hung out for a few more minutes, but then figured I'd let him be. "Well, I just wanted to say hello. You need anything before I go?"

"Nah. I'm good." He came out from under the sink for a moment. "Keep me posted, okay? Lala and I are waiting with bated breath, too."

"You know I will."

Totally drenched, I headed down the hall. As I entered the elevator, I got a text.

Devyn: Where are you? I'm in front of your apartment.

Owen: Heading over there now. I was hanging out with Holden upstairs. Stay there. Coming to you.

When I got to my floor, I saw her standing at my door. She ran toward me, wrapped in a towel with her hair soaking wet. We each looked like we'd escaped a monsoon.

"What happened, Devyn? Why are you still in your bathing suit?"

Had something gone wrong at the pool? Was there an accident?

She gasped for air. "The doctor called." The few seconds it took her to catch her breath were the longest of my life. "I ran here to tell you…"

My heart was beating out of my chest. "Okay?"

"It's yours, Owen." Her voice trembled. "You're the father."

A cloud of euphoria enveloped me. "Oh my God."

Tears filled her eyes. "I know."

My hands shook. "Oh my God."

"We're so lucky." A tear fell down her cheek.

I repeated again, "Oh my God!" My voice echoed in the hallway as I lifted Devyn up and swung her around. I shut my eyes. "I feel like I can breathe for the first time since you told me you were pregnant."

"Me, too, Owen."

I put her down and knelt, placing my head against her belly, which was just starting to pop. "This is *my* baby inside of you. Holy shit."

She threaded her fingers through my hair. "Yes."

"*My* baby," I muttered.

"Yes!" she cried out.

I jumped up, lifting her again and squeezing her tightly.

"What the hell happened? Did we have a flood?"

We turned to find Colby standing there, holding two coffees. He looked understandably confused.

I put Devyn down.

"What happened is…I'm having a baby, Colby." I beamed.

"What?" His eyes went wide. "First off, why are you all wet?" He shook his head. "But what?"

"Burst pipe," I said.

"Ran from the pool to tell him the news," Devyn added.

"Okay, secondly…what?" He laughed. "You guys are having a baby?"

"Devyn and I have known she was pregnant for some time, but… It's a long story. We needed to keep it under wraps for a while, but now we can shout it to the world."

Colby's mouth was practically hanging open. "Well… congratulations! Does anyone else know?"

"Holden," I reluctantly answered.

His eyes narrowed. "You told *Holden* before me?"

"He overheard Devyn and me talking one day—he and Lala, actually. They found out by accident."

"He kept it a secret?"

I shrugged. "Miracles do happen."

"Your wife also knows," Devyn added.

"Really?" He shook his head. "Damn, she didn't let on at all."

Devyn nodded. "I know. She's a good friend. I'm sorry I made her keep it from you."

"Brayden doesn't know?" he asked.

"No. He'll be the last to find out."

"He's not gonna be happy about that." Colby chuckled. "Let's go to my apartment and call him now."

The three of us walked together to Colby's, and I dialed Brayden as soon as we got there.

"What's up?" he answered.

"We're all at Colby's. Get down here. I need to tell you something. Big news." Then I hung up.

Billie entered the room from the kitchen, holding baby Maverick. She looked surprised to see Devyn and me. "Hey, guys. What's up? Were you swimming?"

"You knew about the pregnancy, huh?" Colby said, walking over and smacking her ass.

Billie shrugged. "I did."

"It's mine, Billie," I announced.

Her eyes widened. "Yes!" She jumped for joy. "Hell, yes!"

Colby squinted and turned to me. "Who else's would it have been?"

"Again, long story for another day."

He opened his mouth but then nodded, opting not to push further.

Brayden entered the apartment. "Why are you both wet?"

I wrapped my arm around Devyn and pulled her close. "We're having a baby."

"Remind me to stay out of the water, then." Brayden laughed, but his face turned serious when it hit. "Wait, really? She's pregnant?"

"Yeah, dude."

He looked between us. "How long have you known about this?"

"Fully? Just the past ten minutes or so," I said.

"Is this good news?" he asked.

"Yes. We're happy." Devyn smiled.

"So happy." I kissed her on the forehead. "The best accident ever."

"Congratulations, then." He hugged us both. "You sure know how to shock the shit out of someone."

"You'd better get to work, Brayden." I patted him on the back. "You're gonna be the only one of us without kids soon."

He held his palms out. "I'm good. Happy to be the odd man out for a *long* while."

Holden skidded into the open doorway. "Billie just texted me. I heard it's yours!"

Brayden squinted. "What are you talking about...yours?"

"Don't worry about it," Holden said, flashing me an apologetic look.

Then Lala walked in carrying Hope. She ran right over to Devyn. "I'm so happy for you guys!"

Colby's daughter, Saylor, came out of her room. "Why is everyone yelling?"

"Devyn and Owen are having a baby," Colby told her.

Saylor looked up at us. "Are you guys boyfriend and girlfriend?"

"We are." I rustled her hair.

"I didn't know that." She shrugged.

Devyn and I looked at each other and laughed.

Devyn moved away from me for a moment and raised her voice over the commotion of everyone's conversation. "I just want to say something, please."

"Shhh..." Holden waved his hand. "Let her talk."

"Hi," she said awkwardly once she had everyone's attention. She fiddled with her fingers. "I just wanted to say, from the moment I came here and met all of you, I admired the close friendships you have—the family you've formed. Because of my background, I felt undeserving of that kind of bond. I envied you all. For the longest time, for reasons I won't get into now, the status of Owen's and my future together was up in the air." She reached for my hand. "I'm so happy that I can finally see that future. And I'm even happier that it includes all of you. You've been nothing but kind to me from day one. I hope you have room for one more member of your crew."

I placed my hand over her stomach. "Technically, two more members."

"That's true." She laughed.

Billie blew a kiss at us. "We love you, Devyn."

"And *I* just want to say," Brayden interrupted, "from almost the moment I was attempting to steal you from Owen, Devyn, it was clear you only had eyes for him. I couldn't be happier that my best friend finally found the woman of his dreams. He's waited a long time for you."

"Thank you, Brayden." She smiled, then shivered.

We needed to get out of these wet clothes.

I grabbed her hand. "If you'll excuse us, we both need to dry off. We'll celebrate more later."

As we walked out the door, Brayden called after us, "Will you tell me the name of the actor she was dating now?"

I gave him the finger—lovingly—as Devyn and I headed down the hall.

I'd given Devyn one of my T-shirts to wear after we took a hot shower together. She'd asked me to be there when she called Robert to tell him the news, so we sat next to each other on my couch as she dialed him.

She rubbed her palm along her thigh as she waited for him to pick up.

"Hey, Robert," she finally said, taking a deep breath. "We got the results." She paused. "The baby is Owen's." She exhaled and licked her lips.

I watched as Devyn blinked and nodded as she listened to whatever he was saying.

"I know," she said. "I'm sorry to tell you over the phone like this, but there was no choice." A few seconds went by. "He and I are going to raise the baby together. *Be* together. I love him, Robert." She reached for my hand. "I really do." She turned to me. "He wants me to put him on speaker so you can hear him."

"Sure." I inhaled slowly, gearing up for an uncomfortable discussion.

She placed the phone between us.

"Hey, Owen," Robert said.

"Hey."

"Congratulations."

"Thank you. I appreciate that. I know this hasn't been easy for you."

"It hasn't, but it is what it is. I respect you for being by her side all this time when I couldn't." After a moment, he said, "I haven't always treated Devyn the way she deserved. But I love her more than anything in this world. I'll *always* love her. I hope you know that, Devyn. I wish I'd known our time together before you moved to New York was our last. I would've appreciated it more, cherished every second. I really did think I could change for you, for this baby. And I'm not gonna lie, this hurts like hell. But I have to trust that everything is meant to be. I'm happy you've found someone who loves you, someone I know will make a great father."

"Thank you, Robert," I said. When I looked over at Devyn, her eyes were watery.

I understood why she was crying. She'd had a long history with this man, even if it was rocky. She cared deeply for him. I'd give him that.

"I have to film a sad scene today," Robert said. "I doubt I'll have any problem delivering." He chuckled, though I could hear the melancholy in his voice.

"Yeah..." she whispered.

"I want to say one more thing, Devyn, before I let you go."

"Okay," she said.

"You've been there with me from the beginning. The one thing I won't accept is losing you as a friend. I hope you're okay with that, Owen. Because I'm not going anywhere in that regard."

"As long as you don't touch her, we're good." I winked at her. "Kidding—sort of."

"And if you ever hurt her," he said, "I'll use the karate training I got for that martial arts film on you."

I chuckled. "Noted."

After he hung up, an incredible feeling of peace engulfed me.

I rubbed her leg. "I don't know about you, but I feel more relaxed right now than I have in ages."

"Me, too." She placed her hand over mine. "It's making me horny, actually."

I arched a brow. "Really?"

"Yeah. Stress hampers my libido, but when I truly feel carefree...all I want to do is have sex."

"Well, remind me to book you a membership at a massage place." I stood and held out my hand. "Come, let me take care of that."

Devyn followed me into my bedroom, but that was the last moment I took the lead.

"Lie down, Owen," she demanded, taking charge of the situation.

I did as she said and happily sat back and watched as she slipped my shirt over her head and moved to sit on top of me. My dick swelled.

I gently squeezed her nipple, her breasts more supple than ever. I made a guttural sound. "Your body is changing by the day. And I'm totally here for it."

She rubbed her tits together. "I figured you might like the way these are looking."

"Fuck, yes. You keep getting more beautiful."

She reached into my boxers and took out my swollen cock before lowering her mouth to suck me. Her relaxation-induced horniness must have been contagious, because I nearly came from the sensation of her hot mouth wrapped around my cock.

I bent my head back. "Can we just freeze time right fucking now?"

Devyn twirled her tongue around the head, lapping up every bit of pre-cum that had formed at the tip.

"What did I do to deserve this?" I hissed.

"You're my baby daddy."

I smiled, too much in the zone to conjure a clever response to that. I dug my fingers into her hair and relished every second. "That feels so good, but I want to come inside *you*, not your mouth."

"Stay lying back then," she said. "My turn to ride you."

Fuck yes. "You will *not* hear me complain about that."

Devyn removed her panties before sinking down onto my cock. Unprecedented pleasure swept through me as she moved her beautiful, wet pussy up and down over my shaft.

With my hands at her hips, I pushed her down over me until I was balls deep.

"I love you so fucking much, Devyn," I said, looking into her eyes.

"I love you, too," she mouthed before her eyes rolled back.

After only a couple of minutes, Devyn's sounds of pleasure rang through my bedroom—my cue to let myself go. As her pussy clamped around me, I came so hard my legs trembled beneath her.

Devyn bucked her hips until her orgasm came to a gradual halt. She collapsed on me and met my eager mouth as we fell into a deep kiss.

After we came down from that high, we faced each other, our naked bodies tangled in the sheets.

I rubbed the side of her face with the back of my fingers. "I've never been happier than this moment."

"Me, too. I mean that."

"We finally told everyone and had the conversation with Robert, which is obviously a huge load off, but you know, that's not the most important talk of the day."

"Did we forget someone?" Her eyes went wide. "Actually, you're right. I still need to tell Mia and the kids you're the father."

"That isn't what I meant." I slid down, lowering my head to her stomach. "I haven't spoken to *my baby* yet."

"Ah…" She grinned.

"Hey, little one. I can finally say it out loud. It's me, your daddy. And I can't wait to meet you. I don't know what I'm doing when it comes to being a dad, so I hope you cut me some slack. But I promise to learn. And I promise to love you and do everything I possibly can to keep you safe." I looked up into Devyn's eyes. "Me and your mom."

She looked down at her stomach. "This is my chance to prove I'm nothing like Vera—or her mother."

I reached up to cup her cheek. "You're gonna break the chain, beautiful. And I'll be there every second to witness it."

❤CHAPTER 29

Owen

A month later, I met Holden in Gramercy Park. He whistled a catcall when we arrived at the brownstone. I smiled, thinking how much things had changed in the last year or two. Holden Catalano whistled at good-looking real estate these days, instead of women.

"Damn." He shook his head. "You got the cash for a place like this in this swanky neighborhood?"

"I have half. I figured I could mortgage the rest and the payment would be manageable."

"Especially with two incomes. Devyn must be psyched."

"I wanted to talk to you about that. You can't mention that we came here today. Devyn has no idea I'm hoping to put an offer on the house. I want to surprise her."

Holden's brows shot up. "Are you sure that's a good idea? What if she doesn't like it?"

"I brought her to see it last month, right before it came on the market. She loved it. Plus, it's a great investment property. If it turns out she doesn't want to live here, I could always rent it out. The price is right, and this area gets top dollar for rent. I've been saving for a few years with the intention of buying some sort of property for passive income."

I knew the brownstone was a good financial investment because I knew the New York City real estate market. But Holden knew plumbing and heating, so I'd asked him to come check out the place before I put an offer in to see if anything glaring was wrong with the mechanics. I planned to have an engineer do a top-to-bottom inspection if my offer was accepted, but I was about to drain my bank account and felt like I needed a second opinion before that.

The owner wasn't home this morning, so the listing agent had given me the combo to the lock box hanging on the front door. I gave Holden a quick tour before we got into the nitty gritty of the HVAC system and plumbing. We were there more than an hour as he tested out various mechanics.

"I should tell you the pipes are lead and dangerous, the heating system is on its last leg, and the walls are lined with asbestos." Holden smacked dust from his hands as he climbed up from the floor after looking under the sink. "But none of that's true. It's just going to suck not having you in the building anymore."

"I know. I've gotten used to having you clowns close by. But Devyn really wants to have space for Hannah and Heath. Right now she still has temporary legal guardianship. Vera has to take some parenting classes and go to counseling before the court will even consider restoring her custody after the shit she pulled. And Dev wants to make sure the kids know there's always room for them with us regardless. My gut says they'll wind up living with us for the long haul."

"That's a big undertaking, my friend. A new baby, two teens, and a big fat mortgage."

"It is. But I've never been happier."

Holden smiled. "The HVAC system is less than five years old, pipes are all corrosion-resistant copper and PVC, and I don't see any stress cracks or structural issues."

I blew out a relieved breath. "Thanks, man. I appreciate you coming with me."

"No problem. But you know it wasn't a freebie. Your ass is babysitting next weekend so I can take my hot wife out to dinner."

I chuckled. "You got it."

I locked the house behind us, and as Holden and I walked down the front steps, a woman approached. I hadn't met the homeowner, but I'd spoken to her on the phone... "Are you Mrs. Meyers?"

"Sure am."

I extended a hand. "Owen Dawson. Thank you for letting me see the house this morning. I appreciate it."

"No problem. But I'm afraid you've wasted a trip. I just got an offer a half hour ago."

My face fell. "Really?"

She nodded. "Sorry to have you come for nothing."

Panic washed over me. I'd seen my family living here—actually dreamed about it the other night. I'd pictured Devyn and me wallpapering the baby's room, pushing a stroller through the park at the corner, and making dinner side by side in the kitchen while music played.

"Have you accepted the offer already? I'll make a better one if you haven't signed the paperwork yet."

The woman smiled. "I accepted. The paperwork isn't signed, but this house means a lot to me. I met the buyer, and I'm happy it's going to good people who want to raise their family here. I got a fair price, so I'm afraid it's a done deal."

Dejected, I didn't bother to tell her I had wanted to raise my family here, too. I forced a smile. "Okay, thank you. I'll talk to the listing agent and put in a backup offer anyway. Just in case something falls through."

"Good luck in your search."

"Thanks."

I walked away with a hollow feeling in my gut. Holden put a hand on my shoulder. "Sorry, man. I could tell you really had your hopes up."

I shook my head. "I can't believe someone just bought the place out from under me."

"I know. It sucks. It's a great house. But over the last few years I've come to believe everything happens for a reason, in its own time. There's something bigger and better waiting for you."

He meant well, but I didn't *want* something bigger and better. I'd had my heart set on that place. It felt right. I looked back one more time and felt a pang of loss in my chest.

The rest of the afternoon, I couldn't shake this melancholy feeling. I went back to the office and trolled the new sales listings to see if anything interesting popped up. But everything was either way out of my price range, in a crappy neighborhood, or too small for what Dev and I needed. I was kicking myself in the ass for taking too long to make an offer. If I'd done it an hour earlier, that house might've been mine. The only time my mood perked up was when Devyn called.

"Hey, babe," I answered.

"I think I just felt the baby move!"

"Holy shit. Really?"

"Yep. I was sitting on the couch after a two-hour work conference call, eating some Oreos. I ate two and really wanted to break out the milk and dunk the rest of the package. But my pants are already tight, so I stopped myself. I got up to put the cookies in the cabinet, to get rid of the temptation, and the minute I shut the cabinet door, I felt a kick."

"Holy shit."

"I know! This baby kicked me because she wanted Oreos, and I wasn't going to give her any more."

I smiled. "You realize you just used *she*."

"I did?"

"Yep."

"Well, I guess you're rubbing off on me. Why are you convinced this baby is a girl, anyway?"

"I don't know. But I'm more convinced than ever now that she wants something sweet."

"Aww...is that because her mother is so sweet?"

"That, and maybe also because I watched her mother shovel half a Key lime pie into her mouth last night."

"Watch it, buddy, or I'll have my little girl kick you."

My smile widened. "I can't wait."

"We're going out to dinner tonight, right?"

I'd almost forgotten that I'd made a reservation at a romantic little place. I'd hoped to be surprising her with news about an accepted offer on the brownstone.

"Yep. Seven-thirty."

"Okay! But do you think you can stop on the way home and pick something up for me?"

"Sure. What do you need?"

"More Oreos. The baby made me finish the entire package after all."

I chuckled. "You got it. I'll see you in a little while."

I was still bummed about losing the brownstone, but my spirits had lifted. I couldn't wait to get home and feel those kicks myself.

Devyn was waiting in my apartment when I walked in an hour later. We hadn't officially moved in together, but I'd given her a key so she could work in peace during the day, and she'd stayed over most nights since Vera got back. Walking in to find her made even the shittiest of days feel a hell of a lot better.

I set the box in my arms on the kitchen counter and pulled her in for a kiss. "You look beautiful."

"Did you forget the Oreos?"

"Boy, someone's anxious. Are you having a craving?"

She shook her head. "No, but I haven't felt the baby kick again, so I was hoping if I ate one, she might kick for you."

I motioned to the box. "They're in there."

Devyn's eyes widened as she took the top off. "This *whole box* is Oreos? How many did you buy?"

I shrugged. "Whatever they had on the shelf at the mini mart down the block. I think there were thirteen packages."

"Thirteen packages? Are you insane?"

I smiled. "I *really* want to feel the baby move."

Devyn laughed and took my hand. "Come on. Let's go sit and see what happens."

We sat on the couch for a half hour, but the baby didn't move. Though we did manage to eat a half-dozen cookies. At this rate, we were *both* going to have a big belly.

"We better get going," I said. "The restaurant is downtown."

I'd picked a place in Gramercy so I could walk her by the house after dinner and tell her the news. Now it was just an inconvenient half hour Uber ride downtown in traffic. But whatever. I'd be sitting next to my girl. Nothing else was as important.

At the restaurant, we shared two dishes—fettuccini carbonara and caprese-stuffed balsamic chicken. Neither of us had room for another bite, but when we saw Oreo cheesecake on the menu, I had to try.

Devyn leaned back in her chair with her hands on her belly. "I can't eat another morsel."

"Well, you're going to have to eat one more spoonful. Then I'll tell our little pipsqueak she can't have any more. Hopefully she'll kick you."

Dev rubbed her tummy. "I'm starting to wonder if what I felt was gas, not the baby kicking."

"Oh great," I teased. "Now you tell me? *After* I've stuffed a pregnant lady with food. I'm using a different blanket tonight so I'm not stuck under your smelly one."

Devyn tossed her napkin at me with a laugh. "Jerk."

A few minutes later, the waitress brought out a huge hunk of Oreo cheesecake. I'd been joking around when I ordered it, but I did really want to feel the baby move. So I scooped a heaping mound onto the spoon and held it out to Devyn. "Open up."

She opened her mouth wide, and I pulled back the spoon. "Hang on. That's all it takes for you to open like that? I think I'll save the dessert and use it at home later…"

Devyn squinted. "Give me that now."

"Oh, happily…"

Unfortunately, the baby didn't care that Devyn only got one bite of Oreo cheesecake. She didn't bust a move. We left the restaurant full, but happy anyway. Outside, I pulled out my phone to call an Uber.

But Devyn reached over and stopped me. "Let's take a walk. I need to burn off some of that dinner, and this neighborhood is so pretty."

"Okay." I nodded in the opposite direction of the brownstone. "The park is around the corner."

"Actually, could we walk that way?" She pointed. "The houses are so nice."

I was still sour over losing the property, but there wasn't much I wouldn't do to make Devyn happy. So I shrugged. "Sure. Of course."

We walked down East 19th Street side by side, talking about taking a trip to California now that the kids were out of school for the summer. Devyn needed to have some meetings, and she wanted to get a few things from her apartment. We still hadn't figured out how things would work long term, with her having to go back and forth for business.

"I was thinking," she said. "I'm friendly with a woman who owns a competing casting agency. Her name is Suzie. She got married last year, and I know she wants to have a family someday.

Maybe I'll reach out and see if she might be interested in joining forces. She lives in L.A., so she could probably handle a lot of the in-person stuff, and I could take on more of the Zoom meetings and admin work. I don't think it would totally alleviate my need to travel to the West Coast, but it would help. Plus, we could cover each other when we had kids and stuff."

"That sounds great, if you're okay with it. But if you aren't, I can work my schedule so I can take care of the baby whenever you have to be out there. I'll do whatever you need. You're giving up a lot to make New York your primary home."

Speaking of which, the home I'd hoped we'd call ours was only two houses away. I wondered if Devyn would notice.

She shook her head. "I think I'll reach out. Suzie might not be interested, but I'd like to settle in here, and to do that, I need to know my business is covered. Also, I need a place to live. There's no room for me with Vera back."

"You can stay with me."

"Actually..." Devyn stopped. "I was hoping *you'd* stay with *me*."

"Where?"

She pointed to the brownstone. "Here. I loved this house when you took me to see it. But I was too afraid to make a commitment back then."

Shit. I hated to tell her it was too late. I closed my eyes. "I'm sorry, babe. It's sold already."

Devyn grinned. "I know. I bought it."

My eyes popped open. "You what?"

She bit her lip through a big smile. "I bought it for us."

"What are you talking about? When?"

"Today. I made an offer, and Fanny accepted it."

"Fanny?"

"Francine Meyers. The lady who owns it. She's really sweet."

I looked over at the brownstone and back to Devyn. "Are you serious?"

She nodded. "When I found out I was pregnant, rather than run away or wait until we knew who the father was, you committed to me. You've been committed to me since the day we met. It's time I showed you I'm in it for the long haul, too. My home is wherever you are, Owen."

"Devyn." I shook my head in disbelief. "I came to this house *today*—with Holden. I asked him to look at the structure because I was planning on making an offer myself. I wanted to surprise you. But on our way out, the owner told us she'd just sold it—to good people who wanted to raise their family here."

"Wow."

"I can't believe this. I've been bummed all day because I thought someone else bought it."

"Nope. It's all ours. Well, ours and the bank's. I only have half the money to put down."

"Jesus Christ, Dev. I was going to put down half too! I guess together we can buy it outright. Our two halves make a whole."

Devyn's mouth dropped open as she reached for her belly. "Oh my God. The baby moved. Owen, hurry. Give me your hand."

I reached out to hold Devyn's belly. After a few seconds, I felt a distinct movement. It wasn't so much a kick, but more like a small ball rolling from left to right. My eyes widened. "Holy shit! I feel it."

"I think she's pissed again."

"Because of the Oreos?"

"No, because you said our two halves make a whole. Our two halves make three!"

❤EPILOGUE

Owen

Six months later

"**D**id you see that?" Devyn asked.

We'd just left the apartment building after a quick visit with Colby and Billie. Devyn, Heath, Hannah, and I were packed into my car, and I'd spotted Brayden while we were stopped at the last light. He wasn't alone.

"I sure did," I said as the traffic started moving again. "*He* obviously didn't see *us*."

Brayden had a woman pinned against the wall of a building at the end of the block. They were kissing, oblivious to the world around them. I'd gotten a quick look at her when he pulled back. She looked a little older than him, although I couldn't be sure. Maybe that was my imagination, based on the comment he'd made once about women his own age not being mature enough.

"He hasn't mentioned that he's been seeing anyone," I said. "But with him, that's no surprise."

"We should've honked." Devyn laughed.

"I doubt he would've noticed. He seemed pretty into her."

"I got them kissing on camera," Heath called from the backseat.

"Don't post anything online!" Devyn scolded.

"I won't. But I can use it as leverage the next time I need some cash. Brayden is good for that, right?"

"Too bad it wasn't Holden," Hannah chimed in. "I wouldn't have minded watching *him* kiss like that!"

Devyn chuckled and rolled her eyes. "You're a lost cause, sis."

Life had been good these past months. Devyn and I had kept busy decorating our new home and getting it ready for the baby, though we'd opted not to find out the gender. Somehow we both knew we were having a girl.

Our relationship with her siblings had only grown stronger, despite the fact that they weren't living with us. After completing her required classes and months of family counseling, Vera had been granted custody of Heath and Hannah again, but Devyn and I never let them out of our sight for too long. Half the time, they were hanging out at our house anyway.

Things had been smooth overall. Maybe a little *too* smooth. And if I'd thought spotting Brayden making out against the wall outside the building was the most interesting thing that happened today, I was sorely mistaken.

It was getting dark out. The four of us were supposed to be going straight to a dinner at the home of one of my work colleagues in Connecticut tonight. But twenty minutes into our drive on the highway, we hit bumper-to-bumper traffic.

In the midst of the standstill, Devyn turned to me. "Uh-oh."

My eyes widened. "What's wrong?"

She looked down. "I think my water just broke."

"Are you sure you didn't pee a little? You said that's been happening lately."

"Ew…" Heath grunted from the backseat.

"I'm positive it's not that," Devyn said, holding her stomach. "This is different. It's a lot more."

Devyn was past her due date, already scheduled to be induced in a couple of days.

This isn't good.

"We need to turn back toward the City and go straight to the hospital," she urged.

A rush of adrenaline shot through me. "Traffic isn't budging even a little." I started to sweat as we remained stuck in a sea of cars.

A few minutes later, Devyn leaned her head against the back of her seat. Her breathing became labored.

I grabbed her hand. "What's happening?"

"This doesn't feel right." She panted.

My heart raced. "What do you mean?"

"I'm feeling a lot of pressure. It came on all of a sudden."

"What *kind* of pressure?"

"Like I have to push."

Hannah gasped as Heath said, "Oh crap!"

I reached for my phone. "I'm calling an ambulance."

The dispatcher picked up. "Nine-one-one, what's your—"

"My fiancée is in labor! We're stuck in traffic on ninety-five north just past the Darien exit. I need you to send help right away."

The woman got some information from us and assured me that an ambulance would be headed our way. She offered to stay on the line just in case we needed her, so I kept the phone in speaker mode.

"I'm scared," Devyn breathed.

As much as I was shitting a brick right now, I *needed* to be calm for her. "Don't worry, baby. We're going to get you out of here."

"Is she gonna have the baby in the car?" Hannah asked.

"Ow!" Devyn screamed as if answering her.

"What's happening? Tell me what you're feeling now," I asked, starting to panic despite my vow.

"I don't think we have much time," she answered between breaths.

Think, Owen. Think! "Okay. Here's what we're gonna do. There's more room in the backseat." I removed my seatbelt. "Devyn, let's get you back there. Heath, get out. You take the wheel. If traffic starts moving, just drive to the next exit."

Devyn and I made our way to the back, switching places with Heath and Hannah.

Heath flashed a goofy smile. "I can't believe you're letting me drive!"

"Yeah, well, desperate times call for desperate measures— sometimes illegal ones." I sighed. "Sadly, you proved yourself the day you took my car for a spin without me knowing and came back unscathed."

"Ow. Ow!" Devyn moaned. "It's getting worse!"

"Where the fuck are they?" I yelled, rubbing her leg. I looked behind me, unable to see anything besides rows upon rows of car lights.

Forcing myself to feign calmness once again, I tried to reassure her. "We got this, Devyn. Everything is going to be okay, baby. I promise." *Where the hell is the ambulance?*

"I'm not gonna make it until they get here!" She screamed.

Oh my God.

"Sir, do you need my help?" the dispatcher asked.

I'd nearly forgotten she was still on the line.

"I need you to get the ambulance here!" I shouted. "That's what I need!"

"I'm not sure what's causing the delay, sir. But let's get you prepared in case you need to deliver the baby."

Me?

Before I could process her statement, the dispatcher asked, "How far along is she?"

"She's full-term, past her due date, scheduled to be induced this week," I shouted into the phone.

"Okay."

"It's coming out!" Devyn announced. "I can feel it!"

Oh no.

She and I worked to pull her pants and underwear down as I started to sweat profusely.

"Help!" I yelled. "It's coming!"

"Do you have spare clothes you could place around her?" the woman asked.

I immediately took off my jacket and turned to Heath and Hannah. "Give me your coats."

"Aw, man. I just got this jacket," Heath muttered.

"Hurry up!" I ordered.

After they handed me their coats, I placed one under Devyn.

"You're gonna need something to wrap the baby in as well."

"I can't do this," I muttered.

"Yes, you can. Just breathe and do as I say."

I took a long, deep breath in and let it out slowly.

When Devyn screamed in pain again, I felt it in every fiber of my being. There was no more *"I can't do this"* after that. I *had* to do this.

Our baby was coming, whether I was ready or not.

A few seconds later, when I looked down between her legs, I saw it.

"Oh my God. There's something there. I think it's the baby's head! I see hair!"

"Okay. Make sure there's a towel near you, and place your hand down by the head to keep it from coming out too fast."

Devyn let out the loudest scream I'd ever heard as I reached down and guided *our baby* out of her. Then came the crying—the most beautiful sound.

The baby was in my arms, wiggling. Time seemed to stand still for the most surreal moment of my life. My mouth fell open as I froze, in complete awe, staring into my child's eyes. Then I snapped myself out of it long enough to wrap the baby in my coat and place her on Devyn's chest.

The sound of sirens registered in the distance. The ambulance was finally making its way toward us through the traffic nightmare.

I'd been so in shock that I hadn't checked to confirm whether we'd in fact had a baby girl. Or was it a boy?

Devyn finally looked up from the baby on her chest and whispered, "It's a boy."

What? "A boy?" A tear fell from my eyes. *I have a son.*

It was radio silence from the front seat. I think the kids were just as shell-shocked as I was.

The paramedics finally converged upon our car and cleared a way for us to pull over. They assisted with the delivery of the placenta—which I had no freaking idea was even a thing. (Probably good that I hadn't a clue, or I might've fainted after all.) Then they brought Devyn and the baby into the ambulance. Since Heath couldn't legally drive, I wasn't able to ride with Devyn to the hospital. Letting her and my son go ahead while I figured out the quickest way to get to them was excruciating. It felt like my entire life was in that ambulance as I watched it speed away.

The following day, Devyn and I were alone in her Connecticut hospital room while she cradled our son. Mia had just left, so we were in between visitors.

I rubbed his delicate caramel brown hair with the back of my finger. "I can't believe how wrong I was."

"About having a girl?"

"About everything." I shook my head. "I thought being a father would feel unnatural to me, but from the second I held him in my arms, it felt right. I nearly forgot to give him to you when he came out. I know it's only been a day, but I feel like I've known him forever. Like, I can't imagine a time when he wasn't here. Like I was born to be his dad."

She smiled up at me, her eyes glistening. "You know, we should probably come up with a name at some point."

"You mean we can't call him Baby Dawson forever?"

We'd been so sure our baby would be a girl that we hadn't thought about boy names.

"What about Devin?" I suggested. "Spelled D-E-V-I-N. But pronounced like Devyn."

Devyn nodded as she looked down at our son. "Devin Dawson. That has a nice ring to it." She lifted him and placed a soft kiss on his forehead. "It would be an honor to share a name with him."

"We have a deal, then." I hesitated a moment. "I'd like his middle name to be Ryan, if that's okay. It's sort of a tradition the guys already started."

Not a day went by when I didn't feel Ryan's spirit, and it had seemed stronger since my son was born.

"Of course," Devyn said. "I expected that. Whether it was a boy or a girl, that's one thing I was sure of, that we would honor Ryan in some way."

"Thank you."

There was a knock at the door.

"Come in!" I said.

Holden and Lala entered the room, followed by Billie and Colby.

"Where are the babies?" I asked. No one seemed to have brought any children.

"Colby's mom is watching everyone so we can meet our new nephew in peace," Billie said.

They surrounded us and took turns meeting baby Devin one by one.

"He's so precious!" Lala whispered.

"Dude, you're the GOAT," Holden said as he smacked me on the back. "Delivering your own baby? I thought I was the most handy of the bunch. But that shit is a whole different level of talent. You take the prize, man."

"Ryan is certainly orchestrating some crazy shit from up there." I chuckled. "You'd be surprised what you can do when you have no choice, though."

"I'm so pumped for us to be raising our kids together," Billie said.

"Brayden better get on that," Colby added. "He's the only one left."

"Speaking of Brayden, I have an interesting story for you…" I said.

Holden's eyes lit up. "What?"

But this didn't seem like the right time. "I'll tell you guys later," I promised.

"Where are Heath and Hannah?" Billie asked.

"Owen took them home last night, but Vera's borrowing her friend's car and dropping them off in a bit," Devyn said.

"She's not coming up to meet her grandchild?" Lala asked.

Devyn looked over at me, then explained, "I told her I preferred she meet the baby after we leave the hospital."

I was proud of Devyn for setting boundaries and putting her mental health first. Vera always managed to upset her, and we needed to enjoy this in peace, without any unwanted distractions.

After our friends left, Devyn and I had a few-minute window before her brother and sister were set to arrive.

"I have a surprise for you," I said.

"Oh?" She smiled.

I reached over to a bag I'd brought back with me after I'd gone to our house to grab some of Devyn's things earlier. Inside was a box that had been on ice.

"I got you a pie on my way back this afternoon."

"Yum!" She beamed. "I could definitely go for a piece."

"I couldn't mark our son's birth without his mama's favorite dessert."

The last Key lime pie I'd given Devyn had happened to have a ring box hidden inside. I'd proposed to her one night when she was about six months pregnant. It might not have been the most elaborate proposal, but it was very *us*—a little messy, but still perfect in the end. We couldn't wait to plan our wedding once things settled down.

Devyn took a plastic fork from me and reached over to her bedside table to dig into the pie, being careful not to get any on our sleeping baby.

After a bite, she looked at me and said, "Is it just me or does this taste especially good?"

"Everything tastes better when you're happy," I told her with my mouth full.

"I really am—happier than I've been in my life, Owen. And surprisingly calm about all of this. I don't doubt myself as a mother anymore."

"I love hearing that." I smiled. "But what changed?"

She licked whipped cream from the corner of her mouth. "You believe in me. And that helped me believe in myself."

I bent to kiss her lips before leaning down and placing another on my son's cheek.

The door opened, and in walked Heath and Hannah.

"Hey, guys." I grinned.

"How's my baby nephew doing?" Heath asked.

Devyn looked down at the baby. "He's sleeping, actually." She turned to Hannah. "Why is your face all red?"

Heath chuckled. "We ran into Holden on the way in."

"Ah..." I laughed.

After a few moments, Heath announced, "So...I have a feeling you're gonna be mad about something."

Devyn turned to him. "What did Vera pull now?"

"Nothing. Ma is being good. Still nuts. But it's not like that."

I arched a brow. "What's going on, then?"

Heath cringed. "I had a video go viral today."

"Why is that a bad thing?" I asked.

He hesitated. "Because it's sort of…a video of Devyn giving birth in the car."

Devyn's eyes were like saucers. "What?"

"Don't worry," Heath said. "I blurred out all of the gross stuff. You can't see anything."

"Why would you do that, Heath?" I scolded.

"Blur it out? Because it's nasty."

"That's not what I meant," I raised my voice. "Why the hell would you have filmed it?"

He shrugged. "Figured you'd want to document it."

"Sure, but not for half the world!" I ran my hand through my hair and started to pace.

"Give me the phone." Devyn held her hand out. "Let me see it."

I walked over to the other side of the bed to look at it, too.

He was right. You couldn't see anything aside from Devyn's face and the back of my head. *Thank God.*

"Turn up the volume," I said. He did, but I still couldn't hear anything because Heath had added music: "Push it" by Salt N Pepa.

We all watched the video several times.

On the final replay, my eyes wandered over to the numbers at the right side of the screen. "Five-million views?"

"That's insane!" Devyn laughed, seeming to have calmed down.

Then I noticed something. Among the hundreds of comments on the post, one caught my eye. I pointed to bring it to Devyn's attention. "Look at that comment right there." A chill ran down my spine.

Of course, I knew it wasn't *really* him.

It was some guy with the Philadelphia Eagles logo as his profile picture. The Eagles were Ryan's favorite team. But it was the profile *name* that really stood out.

RyanEaglesFan: Way to go, man. Proud of you.

GUESS WHAT'S COMING!
BRAYDEN'S BOOK

Dear Readers,

Since we first introduced these four best friends in *The Rules of Dating*, we have adored this world so much that we knew we needed to continue telling all the guys' stories. And you don't have to wait long to find out what fate has in store for Brayden!

Brayden's story is coming in July, 2024
and is available for pre-order now
(https://bit.ly/RulesOfDating)!

ACKNOWLEDGEMENTS

Thank you to all of the amazing bloggers, bookstagrammers and BookTokers who helped get everyone excited about *The Rules of Dating My One-Night Stand*. Your enthusiasm keeps us going, and we are so grateful for all of your support.

To our rocks: Julie, Luna and Cheri – Thank you for your tireless support of our work and always being there to brighten our day.

To Jessica –Thank you for making Owen and Devyn shine!

To Elaine – An amazing editor, proofer, and formatter. You do so much for us, and we are grateful to also call you a dear friend!

To Julia – Thank you for your amazing attention to details. Your eagle eyes make our manuscripts squeaky clean.

To our agent, Kimberly Brower – Thank you for helping to get our books into the hands of readers internationally. We look forward to seeing where Owen and Devyn land around the world!

To Kylie and Jo at Give Me Books Promotions – We appreciate all that you do to promote our books and create excitement!

To Sommer – Thank you for bringing Owen to life on the cover!

To Brooke – Thank you everything you do for us in the background!

Last but not least, to our readers – Simply put, without you, there would be no us. Thank you for always showing up. We love and appreciate you!

Much love,
Penelope and Vi

OTHER BOOKS BY
Penelope Ward & Vi Keeland

The Rules of Dating
The Rules of Dating My Best Friend's Sister
Well Played
Not Pretending Anymore
Happily Letter After
My Favorite Souvenir
Dirty Letters
Hate Notes
Rebel Heir
Rebel Heart
Cocky Bastard
Stuck-Up Suit
Playboy Pilot
Mister Moneybags
British Bedmate
Park Avenue Player

OTHER BOOKS FROM PENELOPE WARD

I Could Never
Toe the Line
Moody
The Assignment
The Aristocrat
The Crush

The Anti-Boyfriend
Just One Year
The Day He Came Back
When August Ends
Love Online
Gentleman Nine
Drunk Dial
Mack Daddy
Stepbrother Dearest
Neighbor Dearest
RoomHate
Sins of Sevin
Jake Undone (Jake #1)
My Skylar (Jake #2)
Jake Understood (Jake #3)
Gemini

OTHER BOOKS FROM VI KEELAND

Something Unexpected
The Game
The Boss Project
The Summer Proposal
The Spark
The Invitation
The Rivals
Inappropriate
All Grown Up
We Shouldn't
The Naked Truth
Sex, Not Love

Penelope Ward is a *New York Times, USA Today*, and #1 *Wall Street Journal* Bestselling author. With over two-million books sold, she's a 21-time New York Times bestseller. Her novels are published in over a dozen languages and can be found in bookstores around the world. Having grown up in Boston with five older brothers, she spent most of her twenties as a television news anchor, before switching to a more family-friendly career. She is the proud mother of a beautiful 17-year-old girl with autism and a 16-year-old boy. Penelope and her family reside in Rhode Island.

Connect with Penelope Ward
Facebook Private Fan Group:
https://www.facebook.com/groups/PenelopesPeeps/
Facebook: https://www.facebook.com/penelopewardauthor
TikTok: https://www.tiktok.com/@penelopewardofficial
Website: http://www.penelopewardauthor.com
Twitter: https://twitter.com/PenelopeAuthor
Instagram: http://instagram.com/PenelopeWardAuthor/

Vi Keeland is a #1 *New York Times*, #1 *Wall Street Journal*, and *USA Today* Bestselling author. With millions of books sold, her titles are currently translated in twenty-seven languages and have appeared on bestseller lists in the US, Germany, Brazil, Bulgaria, and Hungary. Three of her short stories have been turned into films by Passionflix, and two of her books are currently optioned for movies. She resides in New York with her husband and their three children where she is living out her own happily ever after with the boy she met at age six.

Connect with Vi Keeland
Facebook Fan Group:
https://www.facebook.com/groups/ViKeelandFanGroup/)
Facebook: https://www.facebook.com/pages/Author-Vi-Keeland/435952616513958
TikTok: https://www.tiktok.com/@vikeeland
Website: http://www.vikeeland.com
Twitter: https://twitter.com/ViKeeland
Instagram: http://instagram.com/Vi_Keeland/

Made in the USA
Las Vegas, NV
15 January 2024

84394545R10196